AMISH

Hawaiian

ADVENTURES

New York Times BESTSELLING AUTHOR

WANDA &
BRUNSTETTER
& JEAN BRUNSTETTER

SHILOH RUN PRESS

An Imprint of Barbour Publishing, Inc.

The Hawaiian Quilt © 2016 by Wanda E. Brunstetter
and Jean Brunstetter
The Hawaiian Discovery © 2018 by Wanda E. Brunstetter
and Jean Brunstetter

Print ISBN 978-1-64352-204-3

eBook Editions:
Adobe Digital Edition (.epub) 978-1-64352-206-7
Kindle and MobiPocket Edition (.prc) 978-1-64352-205-0

All scripture quotations are taken from the King James Version of the Bible.

Cover design: Buffy Cooper
Cover photography: Richard Brunstetter III, RBIII Studios

Published by Shiloh Run Press, an imprint of Barbour Publishing, Inc., 1810 Barbour Drive, Uhrichsville, OH 44683, www.shilohrunpress.com

Our mission is to inspire the world with the life-changing message of the Bible.

ecpa Member of the
Evangelical Christian
Publishers Association

Printed in the United States of America.

THE
Hawaiian
QUILT

To LeAnna Lehman,
a special Amish friend who has visited the Hawaiian Islands.
And to our friends, Bob and Sue Miller, who have a
heart for the Amish people.

Be not forgetful to entertain strangers:
for thereby some have entertained angels unawares.
Hebrews 13:2

Prologue

Middlebury, Indiana

Mandy Frey gazed at the travel brochures lying on the kitchen table. The pictures were so vibrant and enticing she could almost smell the soothing scents of the tropical flowers and hear the gentle lapping of ocean waves. Ever since her Mennonite cousin Ruth went to the Hawaiian islands for missionary training two years ago, Mandy had yearned to visit. For a little over a year, she had saved toward the trip. She'd invited three of her closest friends—Barbara Hilty, Ellen Lambright, and Sadie Kuhns—to go on the cruise with her. They'd kept their plans secret until they had enough money and had made arrangements for time off from their jobs. They would leave in one month, traveling by train to Los Angeles. From there, they'd be on a cruise ship for four-and-a-half days until they reached their first Hawaiian island.

Paging through another brochure, dazzling pictures of cascading waterfalls and scenic mountains heavy with vegetation gave her goosebumps. Everything seemed so colorful in Hawaii—even the exotic birds. She wished she was there right now.

Excitement bubbled in Mandy's soul as she envisioned herself sitting on the beach with her toes in the warm grains of sand, inhaling the salty air. "This is a trip of a lifetime," she murmured. It was one she would probably never make again, so Mandy wasn't about to let anything or anyone dampen her spirits.

But the hope of nothing spoiling her enthusiasm didn't last long. When she'd told her parents this morning about her plans, Mom wasn't happy and tried to talk her out of going, saying Hawaii was too far away.

She'd also mentioned if Mandy had a problem while she was there, her family wouldn't be readily available to help.

Dad hadn't said much, other than telling Mom their only daughter was a grown woman and had the right to make her own decisions. Mandy could have hugged him right then and there, but held back, not wanting Mom to feel hurt or left out. Mandy's younger brother, Milo, had sided with Mom, but Mandy ignored his concerns. She and her friends had booked their trip to Hawaii through a local travel agency, and she would not change her plans. The only person left to tell was her boyfriend, Gideon. She hoped he would take the news well.

Chapter 1

*A*s Mandy sat with her friends, waiting to board the cruise ship that would take them to Hawaii, her thoughts went to Gideon. It had been difficult saying goodbye to him before their driver took them to the train station in Elkhart. She felt bad about his negative reaction when she'd told him she planned to make this trip with her friends. She should have said something sooner, so he would have been more prepared for her departure.

Diverting her thoughts, Mandy watched the young boy sitting across from her, bouncing in his chair while drinking a can of orange soda. He spilled it down the front of his shirt and started howling and kicking his feet.

Patiently, the child's mother got up and took him by the hand to the restroom.

Mandy leaned close to Barbara and whispered, "That little guy is sure a handful."

"*Jah.* I don't envy his mother. He'll probably keep her plenty busy on this trip."

Mandy listened to the steady hum of voices around her. The terminal was filled with an air of excitement, but her thoughts returned to Gideon, remembering his hurt expression as he held her hand. "I don't want you to go, Mandy, but if this is what you want, then you have my blessing and ought to follow your heart. I'll be here when you get back, and then we can talk about our future."

Mandy didn't know if her future was with Gideon. They'd been

11

courting over a year, and she'd suspected for some time he wanted to propose marriage. He'd no doubt held back because she hadn't committed to joining the church. Since every couple planning to get married in an Amish community must first join the church, there was no point in him proposing until they both had been baptized and become church members.

I may feel ready when we return from this trip, she mused. *If I do, then I'll take classes to prepare for church membership.*

Ellen snapped her fingers, causing Mandy to jump. "Our number's been called. It's time to board the ship."

On the Cruise Ship

"*Ach,* this room is much smaller than I thought it would be, even if it is nicely decorated. It's not much bigger than the two tiny rooms we had on the train that brought us to California." Barbara's eyebrows rose as she made a sweeping gesture of the room they'd been assigned. "And how are the four of us supposed to sleep when there are only two beds?"

Mandy shrugged. "Maybe someone made a mistake and gave us the wrong room." She couldn't imagine how these arrangements would work. Their travel agent had told them the room they'd booked would sleep four, and it included two bunk beds. They'd either been misinformed or someone made an error. Perhaps two other people on the ship had been shown a room with four beds. They needed to get to the bottom of this before they unpacked their suitcases.

"Look, there's one of the Pullman beds! The other one is up there too." Sadie pointed to the ceiling above one of the small beds on the floor, and then to the other. "Remember, our agent said it would be similar to a top bunk bed, except instead of being held up by posts extending from a bottom bunk, it's supported by brackets attached to a wall. It can be folded up into the ceiling when not in use to create more space in the room."

"It's certainly folded up right now." Ellen raised her head, squinting her blue eyes. "How are we supposed to get the beds down from the ceiling?"

"We won't have to worry about putting them up or down, because one of the ship's attendants will pull the beds down for us at night and raise them again each morning when our room is serviced." Sadie's tone was typical—so matter of fact.

Mandy couldn't help grinning. *Leave it to Sadie to know all the details.* Even at home, whenever the four young women planned to do something together, Sadie made sure of the details. She was usually responsible for making all the arrangements too. Last month when the girls got together to do some sewing at Sadie's house, she'd made certain everything was laid out before they arrived. She had even provided them with needles, thread, and scissors. All Mandy, Ellen, and Barbara had to bring was the material they planned to cut and sew. Sadie prepared a casserole for their lunch that day. The smell of it warming in the oven had greeted them as soon as they'd entered the house.

Barbara cleared her throat, bringing Mandy's thoughts to a halt. "I hope I don't have to sleep in one of those upper bunks. I'd feel claustrophobic being so close to the ceiling."

"Me too," Ellen agreed. "And I'd be worried about falling out."

Mandy folded her arms. She didn't want to sleep on a top bunk, either, but this problem would be resolved sooner if she volunteered. "I'll give it a try. How about you, Sadie?"

Heaving a sigh, Sadie gave a nod. "Since we've settled the sleeping arrangements now, why don't we unpack?"

"It can wait awhile. Right now, I want to take a tour of the ship." Smiling, Barbara pointed to the door.

"I'm all for that!" Ellen pushed a strand of golden-blond hair back under her white head covering and moved toward the door, no doubt as eager as Barbara to check things out.

"Let's go for a walk and look at what's available for us on a few of the outside decks. I'd like to see if there are any good books in the library too," Sadie suggested. "Afterward, we can head up to the room where lunch will be served buffet style."

Feeling a gurgle in her midsection, Mandy placed both hands on her stomach. "Thinking about all the food that'll be available to us on this cruise makes me *hungerich*."

"I hope we don't run into bad weather or rough waters during our trip." Barbara placed both hands on her stomach. "It wouldn't be fun if any of us got seasick."

Mandy wrinkled her nose. "I don't even want to think about getting *grank*."

"How about this." Sadie lifted her hands above her head, yawning nosily. "The first person who gets sick has to buy the rest of us lunch when we get to Maui."

All heads turned to look at her with furrowed brows.

"Okay, guess it's a bad idea. Let's just relax and have fun."

It took awhile to find their way up to the room where they would be served dinner each evening, but with the help of one of the ship's attendants, they finally made it. Mandy was glad when she and her friends were seated at their table a few minutes before 6:00 p.m., which was when the meal was supposed to be served. They would sit at this same table for all their evening meals during the cruise. They'd also have the same waiters.

"I don't know about anyone else, but I'm not used to having a four-course meal for supper." Ellen placed a linen napkin across her lap.

"Me neither." Mandy glanced at the fancy dishes, noticing the blue vine pattern on the rim, and several pieces of silverware beside each plate. She hoped she wouldn't mess up and eat with the wrong utensil or accidentally drink from her neighbor's glass. That would be so embarrassing.

"I'm still full from all the food we had for lunch." Barbara groaned. "Not sure I'll be able to eat all my dinner."

Sadie tapped Barbara's arm in a motherly fashion. "Eat what you can."

"I don't like to waste food. *Sis en sin un e schand.*"

Ellen rolled her eyes. "Wasting food is a shame, but I don't think it's a sin."

"Probably not." Barbara raised her slim shoulders in a brief shrug. "I can only imagine what my *mamm* might say if she were here right now and I didn't eat everything on my plate."

"Well, none of our mothers are here, so we should relax and enjoy ourselves." Sadie reached for the salt and pepper and sprinkled some on her salad.

After they prayed silently and began to eat, introductions were made among those sitting closest to them. Since the same people would be seated at their table every evening, Mandy thought it was a good idea to get acquainted.

"Are the four of you nuns?" the young Asian woman sitting on one side of Mandy asked.

"No, we are not." Sadie spoke up. "We're Amish."

Blinking rapidly, the woman tilted her head to one side. "Amish? But I thought by the way you prayed and the plain clothes you wear. . ."

Mandy stifled a giggle as Sadie shared a brief history of the Amish and their way of dress. "Nuns dress different than we do," she added.

As the meal progressed, Mandy and her friends discussed what an adventure it was being on the ship and how eager they were to get to Hawaii. From what Mandy's cousin told her about the Big Island, which would be the last island they visited, each day would be filled with many things to see and do. Of course, with only one day spent on each of the islands, they'd have to pick and choose what sights to see. They could either sign up to go with one of the tour groups or strike out on their own. It was logical to go with a group. But since they had to be back at the ship by a certain time each day, they'd have to make every minute count and see as much as possible.

If we ventured out on our own and didn't make it back in time, we could become stranded, Mandy thought, while cracking the crab shell on her plate. *We'll need to make sure it never happens.*

The first three courses of their meal were delicious, but filling. When it came time for the last course—a scrumptious-looking strawberry cheesecake—Mandy was too full to eat it. Their waiter came by the table and offered to box it up so she could take it back to her room. Mandy declined, saying she wouldn't be able to eat anything more tonight. Between breakfast in the morning, a buffet lunch around noon, plus tomorrow's evening meal, she didn't think she'd have room to eat much else. *Maybe I won't have a big lunch every day,* she thought. *Tomorrow, I may try some pizza or a hot dog at one of the snack areas I saw earlier today.*

"For a while I thought we weren't going to find our room," Ellen said as the four of them prepared for bed. "This ship is so big, and with several dining rooms on board, it's easy to get lost."

"I know." Mandy sighed contently as she brushed her long hair. "But it's worth getting lost to be able to say we were on this enormous boat."

"The dining room looked so nice. It's amazing how many details were put into the design of the ship's interior." Barbara sat on one of the twin beds, removed her hairpins, and placed her head covering on the nightstand next to her bed.

"Shall we play a game or sit and talk awhile?" Ellen asked.

Sadie yawned. "I don't know about the rest of you, but I'm *mied* and more than ready for bed." She glanced at one of the bunks overhead, which had been dropped down from the ceiling while they were out of their room. Two ladders had also been set in place, making it possible to climb up to the beds.

Mandy wasn't eager to sleep in either bunk. She'd had a terrible experience sleeping on one when she was younger and had ended up on the floor with a bruised tailbone. But at least the attached side rails on these bunks should keep her from falling out. "Which bed do you want, Sadie?" she asked.

"It doesn't matter to me. Why don't you choose?"

Mandy picked the bunk above Ellen's bed, and after telling her friends good night, she climbed the ladder and settled in. She didn't get up in the middle of the night most of the time anyway, so other than feeling cramped, she would manage. The mattress wasn't too bad—a littler firmer than she'd like, but it would have to do. As tired as she was, she didn't even care.

Curling up against her pillow, she closed her eyes and prayed for her family back home. She also prayed for Gideon and asked God to give her a sense of direction about whether she should join the Amish church or not. Before drifting off to sleep, Mandy prayed, *Heavenly Father, please keep us safe on this journey, and may we return home with many wonderful memories to cherish for the rest of our lives.*

Chapter 2

*W*hen Mandy awoke the following morning, she felt strange—almost as though someone had rolled her around while she was sleeping. She could sense the ship swaying and knew the sea must be rough. *What a contrast from the calm of last night.* She pushed her sheets aside and climbed carefully down from her bunk. Once her feet hit the floor, she rubbed her eyes, trying to clear her vision.

"*Sis mer iwwel.*" Ellen groaned from her lower bunk.

"If you're sick to your stomach, it's probably from the rocking of the ship." Mandy looked at Sadie and Barbara who were already up, but not dressed. "Do either of you feel seasick?"

"So far, I'm okay, but we should probably put some of those motion-sickness drops behind our ears, in case the rest of us do start to feel grank. It's a good thing I brought this along." Sadie took the bottle out of her traveling case and dabbed some behind both ears, then passed it to Ellen, who did the same. When Ellen was done, she gave the bottle to Mandy. After she'd put drops behind her ears, she handed it to Barbara.

"If I'd have known last night this would happen to me, I would have put some of the drops on before going to bed." Ellen sat up, clutching her stomach. "I won't be able to eat anything, feeling like this, but you three should get dressed and enjoy the breakfast buffet." Moaning, she continued holding her stomach.

"I wouldn't feel right about leaving you here alone." Barbara looked out the window and grimaced. "The rain is coming down hard. What a way to begin our day."

"I wouldn't feel right about leaving Ellen, either." Mandy opened the satchel containing her personal items and removed a homeopathic medicine she'd brought along. "This is for nausea and dizziness." She handed it to Ellen with a fresh bottle of water. "If it doesn't help, let me know, and I'll see what's available from the ship's infirmary."

Ellen took the remedy and reclined on her bed. "I'll be fine by myself while you're eating breakfast." She reached for the sheet and blanket, pulling them up to her shoulders. "I need to lie here awhile. I only wish the ship would stop moving so much."

Mandy looked at Sadie and Barbara, and when they both nodded, she hurried to get dressed. By the time they were ready to leave the room, Ellen was sleeping.

"Hopefully, she'll be okay," Sadie whispered. "One of us can check on her as soon as we're done eating."

As they headed out the door, Mandy turned to look at Ellen again. She wanted to stay with her childhood friend, but since Ellen had insisted everyone go to breakfast and couldn't be helped while she was sleeping, Mandy quietly stepped into the corridor and shut the door. She'd make sure to eat quickly and not be gone too long.

Ellen woke up with her stomach churning. She sat up for a moment, but the feeling didn't go away. All at once, her throat constricted, and she covered her mouth. Jumping out of bed, she dashed to the bathroom, barely making it in time. When the vomiting subsided, her ribs felt sore, and she was exhausted. With her stomach empty, and a feeling of shakiness, all she wanted to do was climb back in bed. *Will this ever go away? How long am I going to be seasick? Sure hope I don't feel like this the whole cruise.*

Tears welled in Ellen's eyes as she lay staring at the ceiling, still fighting waves of nausea. *So much for those anti-nausea drops and homeopathic medicine. Maybe they would have helped if I'd taken them sooner.*

Hearing a knock on the door, Ellen pulled herself off the bed. Since she was still in her nightgown and knew she looked a mess, she hoped it wasn't one of the ship's attendants. When she opened the door a crack, she was surprised to see Mandy.

"Sorry if I woke you. I forgot my room key," Mandy apologized.

"It's okay. I was awake."

"I ate a quick breakfast and brought these back for you." When Mandy stepped into the room and closed the door, she placed several packets of saltine crackers and a can of ginger ale on the small table between the beds. "How are you feeling? Did the homeopathic remedy help at all?"

"Not really. I threw up while you were gone, and I still feel a bit woozy and nauseous." Ellen sighed deeply. "Sure hope I don't feel like this the rest of the way. We still have three more days before we get to our first stop on Maui."

Mandy took a seat. "I hope this storm passes soon and the ship moves into calmer waters. Even though I'm not sick to my stomach, the rocking affects my equilibrium. Maybe it would help if we went out on our balcony for a while and breathed in some fresh air. For now, at least, the rain has stopped."

"I doubt it'll help me, but I guess I could try." Ellen slipped into her robe, and they stepped onto the small veranda. The blowing wind and choppy waters were reason enough for her stomach to be upset all morning. Grasping the railing, she drew in several deep breaths, which helped a little, but those lingering gray clouds above didn't remove her dismal outlook.

Mandy placed her hand gently on Ellen's shoulder. "I'm sorry you're not feeling well. This is supposed to be a fun trip for all of us."

"It will be once we're on dry land." Ellen groaned. "I must be a land lover."

"Same here. Since I can't swim, it makes me *naerfich* looking out at nothing but water and seeing no escape except the ship we're on."

"Then why'd you want to take this trip so badly?"

"Because I wanted to see Hawaii. And even though I haven't joined the church, I knew my folks would disapprove of me flying."

"Same here."

"We'll keep praying this will go away for you, and you'll soon be back on your feet." Mandy stared out at the rough waters. "I'm excited to see

Maui, but I wish we could spend more time there. There's only so much we can see in a day."

"Guess we should be happy for what we get. At least we'll have a taste of Hawaii and should have a lot to tell our families when we go home."

"I'm glad I purchased a digital camera before we left. I plan to keep a journal and put together a scrapbook with pictures from our trip. Then whenever I miss Hawaii, I'll take it out and relive all our precious memories."

Ellen snickered, despite her fluttering tummy. "How do you know you're going to miss Hawaii? You haven't been there yet. Maybe it's not as special as you think."

"Of course it's special." Mandy gave a playful grin. "I've seen the pictures my cousin took from her time on the Big Island. Looking at them made me want to see all the beautiful flowers, palm trees, and colorful birds for myself." Mandy tried tucking the blowing stray hairs back under her head covering, but it was no use. The wind had a mind of its own.

"Don't forget about the coconuts, pineapple, and papaya we'll get to taste. Didn't you say Ruth brought back a pineapple for you to sample?"

"She did, and I loved it." Mandy smacked her lips. "I ate some at breakfast this morning, as well as slices of mango. They were *appeditlich.*"

"Nothing sounds delicious to me right now." Ellen shivered, rubbing her arms. "It's chilly out here. Think I'd better go back inside."

When they stepped into the room, Barbara was lying on her twin bed, reading a Hawaiian magazine. Sadie sat on a chair nearby, mending one of her dresses that had somehow gotten torn.

"I didn't realize you were back," Mandy said.

"We've been here about five minutes." Sadie held up her turquoise dress. "I brought this one along because it's kind of a tropical color."

Mandy smiled, then pointed to the crackers and ginger ale. "Why don't you try those now, Ellen? A little something in your *bauch* might help, and you do need to keep hydrated."

"I like saltines anytime," Barbara commented, before sticking her nose back in the magazine.

"Guess I will try a little." Ellen opened one pack of crackers and took a seat on her bed. Nothing appealed, but maybe the saltines would help settle her stomach. Her mother always gave them to Ellen and her siblings whenever they got stomach flu and couldn't keep anything else down. Maybe tomorrow she would feel better and could explore more of the ship.

Middlebury

Gideon stood at the entrance of the barn, sipping hot chocolate and admiring the snowflakes glistening in the sunlight like crystals. As a young boy, he had loved to take his sled up the small hill behind their place and slide down at unimaginable speeds. Back then, he'd thought it was pretty exciting. When Gideon and his siblings came inside afterward, Mom always had a cup of hot chocolate waiting for them. Now he was in his early twenties, and this kind of weather seemed like an inconvenience, not to mention downright cold. Gideon still thought the snow was pretty, but it gave him more things to worry about.

"It's too early for *schnee*," he muttered. "Sure hope the roads don't get bad." Most horse and buggies did well in the snow, but the cars on the roads were what he worried about. Some drivers went too fast, while others crept along at a snail's pace.

As Gideon turned toward the stalls needing to be cleaned, his thoughts went to Mandy. No doubt she and her friends were on the boat by now, enjoying better weather than this. He disliked having her so far away. Gideon still didn't understand why she wanted to go to Hawaii so bad. He was eager for Mandy to come home and make a decision about whether she would join the church or not.

He paused and closed his eyes, as an image of Mandy's pretty face came to mind. Her eyes, matching the color of her silky brown hair, seemed so expressive when she talked. Gideon had never seen eyes as beautiful as hers. They were a rich coffee color, but what made them so unique was how they almost turned green, depending on the color of dress she wore.

Mandy smiled a lot too, and got along well with others. *It's no wonder she enjoys being a waitress,* Gideon thought.

He wondered what she was seeing and doing on the cruise ship. Gideon supposed it was a fun adventure, but being here was all he needed to be content. *I wonder if she's nervous about traveling so far from home, especially on a ship floating in a big body of water like the Pacific. Since Mandy's never learned to swim, I would think she'd be scared being surrounded by all that water. Sure hope she gets this trip out of her system and will be content when she comes home.*

He gave himself a mental shake. *I probably shouldn't be worried. Mandy will be back in a few weeks, and everything will be fine. If we are truly meant to be together, she'll be ready to take classes preparing her to join the church soon after she arrives.*

Chapter 3

On the Cruise Ship

*R*eady to leave their cabin, Mandy took a moment to write in her journal:

*Today is Sunday, our third day at sea. Before we went for
breakfast this morning, we sat in our cabin and had our devotions.
It was nice to set a time aside to read God's Word and reflect on
His promises.*

*The weather's improved, and Ellen's feeling better. I'm glad things
are looking up for her now that the ship isn't swaying like it was
before. The storm was a bit unnerving to our group, and probably for
a lot of other people on board as well.*

*It was nice all four of us could sit together and share the morning
meal. A few minutes ago, we got back from breakfast. I ate too much
again. It's hard to pass up all the delicious food; especially the fruit and
seafood. It would be easy for a person to put on extra pounds, taking
in all the tantalizing food and lounging on the deck or in our room.
Maybe I'll visit the exercise room later today and use the treadmill. I
need to burn off the extra calories.*

*No matter how many times I look out the door of our balcony, it
seems strange to see nothing but water, with no land at all in sight.
It's kind of eerie and makes me feel somewhat isolated, even though
we're on a ship with over two thousand passengers. I'd love to see some
dolphins, like some of the folks at our dinner table said they had earlier
today. Maybe we'll still get the chance.*

"Are you ready to do some exploring?" Ellen placed her hands on the desk where Mandy sat.

"Give me a moment." Mandy set her pen and journal aside. "I want to put on some sunscreen, since it's so bright out today."

"Good idea." Ellen picked up her tube of sunscreen and put it in her tote bag, along with a pair of sunglasses. "Since Barbara and Sadie have already gone out to sit by the pool and read, I'd better take this along. I don't think they took theirs."

"They did seem in a hurry to get going."

"No more than I am. After feeling so sick and staying in the room yesterday, I'm anxious to get out for some fresh air and sunshine."

Mandy slathered some sunscreen on her face and arms, then put the camera in her tote. "Let's go!"

After sitting in one of the lounge chairs by the pool awhile, Mandy saw an elderly couple walk by and pick out two empty chairs. Based on their conversation, they seemed eager to get some fresh air by the pool. The woman took her seat carefully and waited for her husband to do the same. He, though, sat rather abruptly, sending the lounge chair crashing as it flattened like a pancake.

"Oh, dear! Robert, are you all right?" With a worried expression, his wife turned toward him.

"Only my pride is hurt," he panted, struggling to get up.

Before Mandy could react, Sadie jumped up and went to help him. Once he was on his feet, she stood his chair up and made sure it was locked in place.

"Thanks for coming to my rescue." His face was bright red. "Bet I looked pretty foolish."

"I'm glad you weren't hurt." Sadie smiled and returned to her seat beside Ellen. "I can't believe how many people sat there watching and didn't even try to help."

Ellen nodded. "A lot of them had their phones out. Sure hope they weren't taking pictures of the poor fellow."

Some people don't seem to care about others, Mandy thought. *I'm glad Sadie helped the elderly man. He could have been seriously hurt.*

After lounging awhile, Sadie said she was craving some ice cream. "Why don't we all head for the sundae shop?" she suggested.

Mandy glanced at her cell phone, noting the time. "It won't be long till it's time to eat lunch. If we have ice cream now, it'll ruin our appetites."

"Not mine." Sadie shook her head. "If anything, an ice-cream cone will whet my appetite."

Mandy fought the urge to roll her eyes. One thing she and Sadie disagreed on was the kind of food they ate. Mandy treated herself to ice cream once in a while, but she didn't go overboard on sweets—especially not before eating a big meal. "You can go to the sundae shop if you want to." She licked her lips, trying not to think how good an ice-cream sundae would taste. "I'm gonna stay here and enjoy the sunshine. When I talked to Mom last night, she mentioned they were getting snow in Middlebury."

Barbara clicked her tongue. "I can't believe they're getting schnee so early in November. I hope it's all gone by the time we go home."

"They could have more by then, which is why we'd better enjoy the sun while we can." Sadie stood. "Who's going with me to get ice cream?"

"Guess I'll come along." Barbara gathered up her things and left her chair.

"I'm going to stay here with Mandy. It's fun to watch the children play in the pool." Ellen lifted her arm up and grinned. "Think I'm getting a little color too."

"Okay, then, we'll see you two at the lunch buffet." Sadie waved and headed off, with Barbara at her side.

Mandy glanced over at Ellen and grimaced. "I bet those two won't be able to eat much lunch."

Ellen gave her stomach a few thumps. "I will. After only crackers and ginger ale for the past twenty-four hours, I'm more than *eiferich* to eat."

"I'm eager too, but I won't overdo it. I want to save room for our supper this evening." Mandy glanced at the cute little blond-haired girl sitting on the side of the pool. Despite her mother's coaxing, the child refused to get in the water.

She might be afraid because she can't swim. Mandy brushed a strand of hair away from her face. Since she had never learned to swim, she could relate to the young girl. Mandy feared going into the pond on her parents' property, which her four brothers enjoyed. Mandy's dread of water kept her from learning to swim or even float. She remembered how, on hot summer days, she would hold her long dress up so it wouldn't get wet and wade into the shallow part of the pond near the shoreline. The cool water felt good on her bare legs and feet, and she'd been satisfied with that. When Mandy was eight years old, her brother Michael, who was ten at the time, pulled her into the water where it was over her head. Certain she would drown, Mandy flailed her arms and screamed so loud their father came running. Within seconds, he dove into the water and rescued her. Sobbing and clinging to Dad's neck, she vowed never to go in the pond again. Of course, she had, but only knee deep. On several occasions, Dad had offered to teach her to swim, but Mandy flatly refused. Even with her fear of the water, she found it fascinating and looked forward to watching the waves hit the shore when they were on dry land.

Mandy's brother Mark had kidded her about making a trip to Hawaii by boat, since the ship would be surrounded by water. Mandy's response was, "I'm not worried about it, because I won't go anywhere on the ship where I could fall overboard."

Then her youngest brother, Melvin, piped up. "What if the ship sinks, like the *Titanic*?"

Mandy squeezed the arms on her deck chair. *Leave it up to my* bruder *to give me a hard time.* She could only imagine how horrible it must have been on the *Titanic*, with nowhere to go but the cold ocean water. Even so, she couldn't let these feelings get the best of her. Thinking happier thoughts, she reflected on how her parents had given each of their five children a name beginning with the letter *M*. Michael, almost twenty-three, had recently married Sarah Yoder. Milo was eighteen; Mark, fifteen; and Melvin, twelve. Mandy would celebrate her twenty-first birthday on January 28. She would be home from her trip way before then and figured her parents would do something special for her. Maybe Mom would cook a big meal and invite Mandy's closest friends to join them. Or perhaps they'd all go out to one of her favorite restaurants in the area.

Growing up with teasing brothers hadn't been easy, but she'd survived her childhood—although she had always longed for a sister.

Of course, she reasoned, *I have my three best friends, and they're almost like sisters.*

"Are you daydreaming?" Ellen nudged Mandy's arm. "I've been talking to you, but I don't think you heard a word I said."

"Oh, sorry. I was deep in thought." Mandy turned to face her friend. "What did you say?"

"It's getting windy, and I've had enough sun." Ellen unrolled her sleeves.

"You're right, the wind has picked up. Why don't we go check out one of the gift shops? Or would you rather go back to the room and rest awhile before lunch?"

"I've been in our room too much already. Let's go shopping." Ellen stood and smoothed the wrinkles in her dress. "Maybe I can pick up a few trinkets to give to family members back home."

The two friends gathered up their things, but before they left the pool area, Mandy paused and took a picture of the little girl she'd been watching earlier. *I hope someday I'll have a daughter as cute as her.*

Middlebury

"Miriam, it's good to see you." Peggy Eash smiled when Mandy's mother entered her quilt-and-fabric store on Monday morning. "Is there anything

I can help you with?"

"I need some thread."

"Well, you know where the notions are kept." Peggy pointed to the notions aisle.

Miriam nodded, picked up a shopping basket, and headed down the aisle. She had almost reached the thread display when she noticed Peggy's son Gideon. "I'm surprised to see you here this afternoon. Aren't you still working at the upholstery shop?"

"Things are a little slow there right now, so I have the day off. I'm helping unload a shipment of fabric and some other things that came in this morning." He brushed his dark hair off his forehead.

"I'm sure she appreciates your help, especially with Barbara gone." Miriam picked out two spools of thread then stepped aside so Gideon could set down the box he held.

"Have you heard anything from Mandy?" he asked, kneeling beside the box.

"We talked for a while last night." She dropped the thread into her basket.

"Are she and her friends still on the boat?"

"Jah. They should be almost to Hawaii by now. They're scheduled to reach land tomorrow."

"How's Mandy doing?" He looked up at her with a curious expression.

"She's fine, but Ellen got seasick on Saturday."

Gideon's forehead wrinkled. "You'd never get me on a boat for all those days. I'd probably be grank as soon as I got on board."

"From what Mandy said, the ship is quite large, so unless the waters get really rough, I wouldn't think the boat would sway too much." Miriam picked out a few more spools of thread. "I hope she's enjoying herself and will return with lots of good memories."

"Aren't you worried about your *dochder* being so far from home?"

"I'm not fond of the idea, but as you know, Mandy is twenty years old. I certainly couldn't forbid her to go. She's old enough to make her own decisions." Miriam pursed her lips. *Although if I had my way, Mandy would be here right now—not off on a cruise to see what Hawaii is all about.*

"I didn't want her to go," Gideon admitted, "but I gave her my blessing."

"If you'd asked her not to go, maybe she would have stayed. As long as you two have been courting, I would think she'd want to please you and not go gallivanting off to see what a tropical island looks like."

"If I'd asked Mandy to stay, she might have resented me, and it could have affected our relationship." Gideon began pulling new skeins of yarn from the box.

"You may be right." Miriam hoped Mandy appreciated her boyfriend and would make a commitment to join the church soon. Maybe after this trip, she would settle down and take life more seriously.

Chapter 4

The Island of Maui

Since Mandy and her friends had stayed up late Monday night, visiting and looking at the stars and the full moon, it was hard to get up the next morning. However, the excitement of arriving at the port in Maui and the sounds of people in the hallway talking got them all out of bed.

Mandy and Barbara had signed up to go with a tour group to the visitors' center at the Haleakalā volcanic crater, as well as the Ali'i Kula Lavender Farm. Sadie and Ellen would tour the huge aquarium at Maui Ocean Center and explore the town of Lahaina, where many shops and restaurants were located.

Watching from one of the decks as the ship entered the harbor with a smaller boat guiding it into place, Mandy's enthusiasm mounted. After seeing nothing but water for the last four days, it was a thrill to finally spot some green. She could hardly wait to step on dry land and view the beautiful sights awaiting them.

Lahaina

"Wish we could have gone on a tour watching for humpback whales," Sadie commented as she and Ellen, along with the others in their tour group, started their walk through what appeared to be quite an old town. "Unfortunately from what I read in the brochure, the whales won't migrate here from Alaska until December."

"I agree it's a disappointment, but it'll be fun to do some shopping." Ellen gestured to an enormous tree with a twisted trunk, growing across the street. "That tree is certainly unusual. I wonder what it's called."

"It's a banyan," their tour guide explained. "A lot of them grow here on Maui." Everyone stopped walking as she told about this particular tree, and how it covered over two-thirds of an acre, with a dozen main trunks. "The Banyan tree was originally brought to Maui from India and planted over 140 years ago. Back then it was only eight feet tall, but now it's grown to a height of sixty feet."

Sadie tipped her head back, shielding her eyes from the bright glare of the sun as she studied the monstrous tree. It was nothing like any of the trees they had back home.

With her camera ready, Sadie suggested she and Ellen take their picture by the Banyan tree. Since neither of them had joined the church yet and they wouldn't put their photos on display, it should be okay. Handing her camera to an older woman who was on the tour, they posed for a picture.

After the photo was taken, they continued the tour, pausing along the waterfront to watch some of the boats going in and out of the harbor. It was a clear, sunny day, and Sadie was glad she'd remembered her sunglasses.

Everyone went their own way for a while, visiting shops. They would regroup at a set time to board the bus that would take them to the Maui Ocean Center. Sadie looked forward to going because she'd read a beautiful pamphlet describing the center's unique attractions.

"Let's get one of those." Ellen pointed to a Hawaiian Shave Ice stand. "It looks similar to an ice-cream cone, only I've heard it's more refreshing."

"Jah, let's do." As Sadie and Ellen started walking, Sadie bumped her toe against the sidewalk and lost her footing. She regained her balance in time to right herself, and kept going.

"Are you okay?" Ellen clasped Sadie's arm.

"I'm fine. Jarred my back a bit, but at least I didn't fall. It was embarrassing, but it could have been worse." Taking a deep breath and exhaling, Sadie moved on.

When they stepped up to the stand, Sadie studied all the different flavors they offered. "Now I don't know which one to choose."

"Think I'll try a coconut-flavored shave ice." Ellen reached into her purse for the money. "As soon as you decide, we can order, and it'll be my treat."

"*Danki*." Sadie continued to study the list of flavors and finally decided on a *li hing mui*, which meant "salted plum." In case she didn't care for the taste, she added a bit of cherry flavor to it, as well.

They sat on a bench to eat the delightful, cooling treats and watched the people from all walks of life passing by. Sadie had thought people might stare, wondering about their plain clothes, but with so many others representing different parts of the world, their way of dressing seemed to go unnoticed.

When they were almost finished with their shave ice, Sadie noticed some syrup from the bottom of the paper cone had dripped out. "Oh, no!" She pointed to the front of her blue dress. "I hope it won't leave a stain." She threw the remainder of the treat in a nearby garbage can.

"I packed some stain applicator for the trip," Ellen said. "When we get back to the ship you can put some on your dress. Good thing we brought extra clothes with us."

"It's also good we had our picture taken before this happened."

"Let's look for a restroom so you can try to get some of the mess out now," Ellen suggested.

Sadie picked up her tote bag and held it in front of her dress. "If I can't get the syrup out with soap and water, I'll carry my bag in front of me the rest of the day."

Ellen snickered.

After they located the public restrooms, Sadie took care of the stain as best as she could. Following that, they went into a few of the shops. In one, she spotted some petrified shark's teeth.

"Were those found here on Maui?" Ellen asked the woman behind the counter.

"No, they were actually discovered off the shores of Florida, along the Gulf of Mexico."

Sadie thought it would be strange to buy something found in Florida when they were here on Maui, but then she'd also seen souvenirs and clothing in some of the shops that had been made in other countries.

"I'm looking for something inexpensive to take home to my family," Ellen said after they left the store selling shark teeth. "And I'd like it to be useful."

"I saw some Hawaiian-made purses at one of the shops. Those might be nice for the women in your family. There are some wooden items in this shop right here that might be useful." Sadie stepped up to the window for a closer look. "What do you think? Should we go inside and look around?"

Ellen drew in her lower lip and squinted. "Maybe I'll wait till we visit some of the other islands before I buy any gifts. I'm sure we'll have plenty of opportunities to shop."

Sadie shrugged. "Okay, but if we see something along the way that catches our eye, we ought to get it because you never know if you'll see anything like it again."

Haleakalā Crater

"Did you ever see anything so strange?" Barbara asked as she and Mandy stood with several others at one of the observation areas, looking at the lava formations.

"Seems like we've landed on the moon." Mandy giggled. "Course, I've never been to the moon, so I really can't say."

Barbara tipped her head back and looked up. "Did you hear that *gedumor?*"

"What noise?"

"It sounded like geese honking."

"Oh, those are the nēnē geese," their guide explained. "They're an endangered species and live on the wooded slopes of Haleakalā."

Mandy took out her camera and snapped several photos of the

surrounding area. She could see for miles, clear out into the ocean. There was no way she could ever describe this unusual place without showing her family and friends a few pictures. She felt thankful she'd come to Hawaii, and what they were seeing today was only the beginning.

On the Cruise Ship

After Sadie and Ellen boarded the ship again, they headed for their room to get ready for the evening meal. They found Barbara and Mandy there.

"We had a good time today." Ellen yawned. "I'm tired, but no worse for wear."

"I don't know about the rest of you, but I can't wait to eat." Mandy gave a sheepish smile when her stomach growled. "I've snacked on a few roasted macadamia nuts. It's hard not to get carried away because they're so good."

"I tried a couple of them, but they're not as appealing to me, so I've been snacking on chips." Barbara sat in a chair with a bag of Hawaiian-style chips in her lap. "You're all welcome to try some if you want."

"Those sound tempting." Ellen walked over and reached into the bag. "They even smell good."

"What's on the front of your dress?" Mandy pointed.

"Ellen and I had some shave ice today. Mine ended up leaking on me." Sadie helped herself to a few macadamia nuts. "These are so good." She glanced at the clock. "There's still a little time before we head up for dinner, so I'm going to change out of this dress, put some stain remover on the spot, and soak it in the sink."

"Hopefully it'll come clean." Mandy moved to the window with her camera to take a few pictures of the beautiful sunset. "Would you look at that? We're seeing the hand of God again, jah?"

During dinner, the girls talked about the things they'd seen that day.

"The best part for me," Barbara said, "was visiting the Ali'i Kula

Lavender Farm. It was beautiful, and I bought a few lavender gifts at the Gallery Gift Shop to take home for family."

"It was a nice place to visit," Mandy agreed, while reaching for her glass of water.

"What was it like?" Ellen asked.

Eyes sparkling like fireflies on a hot summer night, Barbara told about the breathtaking views and walking paths. "It was interesting to hear the history of how the farm came to be, and we got to see and smell the pretty lavender plants."

"We were thankful for our tour guide, who explained everything," Mandy interjected. "It was so peaceful. We wished we could have stayed longer."

"That's how I felt when the group Sadie and I were with visited the Maui Ocean Center." Ellen blotted her lips with a cloth napkin. "My favorite part was the outdoor turtle lagoon. It was fun to see the turtles playing in the water and basking in the sandy area provided for them."

Sadie took a bite of roast beef, then set her fork down. "Watching the turtles was enjoyable, but the best part for me at the ocean center was the indoor part of the aquarium, where we saw many species of native Hawaiian fish."

Ellen smiled. "After our tour we ate lunch at the Aquarium Reef Café and browsed the gift shop, where they had all kinds of treasures."

"Did you buy anything?" Mandy asked.

"No, I'm waiting until we get to the next island in the morning."

"Speaking of which. . ." Mandy tilted her head. "I hear the ship's motor running below, which means we're getting ready to leave port." *I can hardly wait to see what adventures await on Oahu tomorrow.*

Chapter 5

The Island of Oahu

$\mathcal{M}$andy shivered in anticipation as she waited to leave the ship. She and Sadie would tour Pearl Harbor while Barbara and Ellen explored the Polynesian Cultural Center. There wasn't time to go on both tours, so the four friends had decided to split up and then share their experiences during dinner. Later on, they'd also exchange pictures.

Mandy chose Pearl Harbor because she'd studied the World War II attack and was saddened to think how many people lost their lives because of it. Sadie was also interested in history, and especially wanted to visit the USS *Arizona* Memorial, which she'd heard was one of the most popular visitor attractions in Hawaii.

"I'm eager to see the cultural center. The brochure I have mentions it's a forty-two-acre lagoon park." Ellen placed the brochures in her tote bag. "We'll be able to see Polynesian dance, costumes, and songs, and learn how they used to live. From the pictures I've seen, it appears to be a special place with natural beauty, showcasing the culture of the Pacific. There will be so much to see and do, all in a single day."

"I'm excited too," Barbara agreed. "It will be interesting to learn about the various aspects of Polynesian culture."

"Oh, look, there's a beautiful *reggeboge*! It must be raining somewhere on the island."

Mandy looked in the direction Sadie pointed. Sure enough. A gorgeous rainbow spanned the sky. Its bright colors pierced the clouds, captivating her as she admired the rainbow's beauty. Looking closer, she noticed a double rainbow, but the colors were in reverse of the brighter one.

Mandy thought about the Bible passage where God placed a rainbow in the sky after the flood as a promise to never again destroy the earth by water. Whenever she saw a rainbow, she remembered God's promise, and it made her feel closer to Him. *Our heavenly Father created many wonderful things for our enjoyment,* she thought. *Too bad some people take them for granted or don't notice at all.*

Polynesian Cultural Center

"This is fun!" Ellen could hardly contain herself as she and Barbara sat in a canoe.

Their paddling guide led them through a lovely lagoon, slowly maneuvering from one end of the cultural center to the other. After spending most of the morning on their feet, looking at many of the exhibits, it felt good to sit and enjoy a more leisurely pace. She'd picked up a disposable camera at the first gift shop they'd visited and had already taken several pictures. Her camera wasn't fancy like the digital one Mandy purchased before leaving on their trip, but it would capture some of the special places Ellen was seeing today. Tomorrow, she'd also have more picture-taking opportunities when they visited the island of Kauai.

She leaned back, closing her eyes for a brief time, enjoying the perfumed fragrances in the air. "Can you smell the flowers?" Ellen tilted her head farther and sniffed deeply, to catch more of the pleasant aroma.

Turning to face her, their handsome young guide spoke up. "The fragrance you're enjoying is from the gardenia flower growing over there." He pointed toward the bank of the man-made freshwater lagoon. "They do smell wonderful."

Barbara smiled. "I agree. The scent of those flowers is so different than any we have back home."

"Where are you two from?" he asked.

"Middlebury, Indiana," Ellen replied.

"You're a long way from home. How do you like Hawaii so far?"

Ellen's cheeks felt hot as she murmured, "It's amazing."

"I couldn't agree more." Barbara dipped her hand into the water as they glided quietly along.

"Maybe you'll come back someday. We see a lot of returning guests here at our center." He winked at her.

Stifling a snicker, Ellen exchanged looks with her friend. Then to ease her embarrassment, Barbara leaned closer to Ellen and whispered, "What should we do after this?"

"I'm hungerich, so maybe we should eat lunch."

"Sounds good to me. There's a snack stand at the Marquesas Village inside the center."

"They have good food, and the prices aren't bad." Their guide smiled and winked at Barbara again.

Ellen wondered if he was flirting with her friend. If so, she was glad Barbara wasn't flirting back.

"Thank you for the information." Barbara turned to look at Ellen. "After we eat, maybe we should stop by the Polynesian Marketplace, which has many handcrafted items. I bet we can find some nice things to buy."

"They do have some interesting items," their guide interjected.

"I need to be careful not to spend all my money in one place," Ellen said. "We still have two islands to see, not to mention our stop in Ensenada, Mexico, before returning to Los Angeles."

"So you came by cruise ship?" the young man asked.

Before either Barbara or Ellen could respond, he added, "I've never been on a big boat like that." He paused, lifting his oar out of the water. "So, what's it like?"

"It's an interesting way of traveling," Barbara replied. "There are a variety of shows to see on board and incredible amounts of elaborate food to eat. It's like a small floating town, with shops, swimming pools, and many other things to see and do. So far, it's been quite enjoyable."

"Except for me getting seasick one day." Ellen leaned closer to Barbara. "I wonder how things are going with Mandy and Sadie."

Pearl Harbor

A lump lodged in Mandy's throat as she stood on the USS *Arizona* Memorial platform, looking into the water. She could see an outline of the submerged ship. A taped narration played close by, telling about the attack. This was the final resting place for the 1,177 crew members who lost their lives when the ship was sunk by the Japanese on December 7, 1941.

"This is so sad," she whispered.

Sadie nodded slowly, clutching her handkerchief.

Mandy could hardly fathom the horrible chaos that went on during the bombings. This wasn't the only ship that had been attacked in the harbor. The *Nevada, Tennessee, West Virginia, Maryland, Oklahoma*, and *California* were also hit. The battleship *Pennsylvania* was in dry dock that day for repairs.

Since the Japanese attack had been a surprise, many of the bombs and torpedoes hit their targets. The damage to the ships was severe, causing great loss of life and many ships to sink.

When Mandy closed her eyes, she could almost smell the pillars of smoke and hear the loud booms as the enemy aircraft swept in. She shuddered thinking about the shouts of anguish from those who'd been injured and the sorrow of family members who lost a loved one that fateful day. War was a terrible thing. She wished there could only be peace.

"It's time to go, Mandy." Sadie touched her arm. "They've announced the boat that brought us here is ready to transport us back to the visitor's center."

Glancing once more at the remains of the ship beneath them, Mandy turned away.

"What shall we see next?" she asked Sadie when they reached the visitor's center a short time later.

"I'd like to walk through the USS *Bowfin*. The submarine is docked outside the Bowfin Museum. The cost for museum admission and a tour of the sub is twelve dollars, which includes getting a digital audio player to narrate the tour."

"It does sound interesting. It's a good thing neither of us is claustrophobic, because from what I've read, submarine quarters are tight."

"When we're done touring the *Bowfin*, if there's still time, we could visit the USS *Missouri*," Sadie rushed on. "It's famous for being the site where Japan signed the formal surrender, ending World War II in 1945."

"You certainly know your history." Mandy moved in the direction of the submarine.

"I've often wished I could have lived in the past. Course, not through something as serious as a world war," Sadie quickly added.

On the Cruise Ship

When the girls sat down to dinner that evening, they shared their adventures of the day.

"The best part of visiting the Polynesian Culture Center was learning how to make a fire by rubbing two sticks together." Barbara's eyes gleamed. "It was hard work, but the Samoan villagers made starting a fire look effortless."

"I'll bet it was fascinating." Mandy cut into a piece of baked chicken. "Pearl Harbor was not only interesting, but quite emotional. Too bad we didn't have time to see the cultural center too."

"What was your favorite part of the day?" Sadie focused her gaze on Ellen.

"I enjoyed the canoe ride, but even though it was relaxing, our tour guide made me kind of naerfich. He seemed overly talkative and flirted with Barbara." Ellen's brows pinched together. "But watching several skilled artisans carve some beautiful pieces from various types of wood was also interesting."

"Oh, and don't forget the food," Barbara interjected. "We had a tasty lunch at one of the snack stands inside the center." She looked at Mandy.

"Where did you and Sadie eat?"

"Between the USS *Arizona* Museum and the USS *Bowfin* Museum there's an open-air café." Mandy paused for a sip of iced tea. "Of course, the food wasn't nearly as good as what we're being treated to tonight."

"We have had some delicious meals on this trip." Sadie lifted her fork and took a bite. "I wouldn't be surprised if I've gained a few pounds. When we get home, I'll most likely have to diet and exercise."

"Speaking of home, have any of you heard from your family lately?" Ellen asked.

"I got a call from my mamm this afternoon," Mandy replied. "She mentioned the weather there has warmed a bit. Instead of snow, they're now getting rain."

"We had some rain today too," Sadie reminded. "Although it was a warm rain, so I didn't really mind it."

Barbara's forehead wrinkled. "I almost feel guilty being here where the days and nights are so balmy, while our family and friends are dealing with pre-winter weather."

"We should enjoy it while we can." Mandy's enthusiasm slowly diminished as reality sank in. "Because all too soon our *wunderbaar* vacation will be over." She didn't tell the others, but part of her wished she never had to go home. Mandy didn't dislike her home in Middlebury—it was where she'd grown up and met her friends. But the sensation of being somewhere new made her feel like all her burdens had been removed. *Of course,* she reminded herself, *if I lived anywhere else, I'd miss my family and friends.*

Chapter 6

The Island of Kauai

*D*on't forget your cell phone, Barbara. I may want to borrow it to call my folks today," Sadie said as they prepared to leave the boat Thursday morning.

"No problem." Barbara held up her phone. "It's charged up and ready to go in my travel tote."

"Are you two sure you don't want to go with us to see the Waimea Canyon?" Sadie turned to face Mandy and Ellen.

Mandy shook her head. "I'm sure the canyon is beautiful, but I'd rather see a few things on my own this time, instead of going with a tour group." She looked at Ellen. "Do you still want to explore with me, or would you rather go with Sadie and Barbara?"

"I'd like to go with you and see Spouting Horn, or whatever else we have time for before the ship moves on this evening." Ellen smiled. "It'll be fun to be on our own."

"We'll be going to see the canyon on a bus with our tour group," Barbara stated. "But how will you two get to the places you want to see?"

"Guess we'll have to call a taxi, because only the town of Lihue is within walking distance of the port," Mandy replied.

Sadie squeezed Mandy's shoulder. "Be careful out there, and make sure you're back on time. The boat will probably head for the Big Island sometime during our evening meal."

"Don't worry. We'll be here in plenty of time." Mandy pulled her cell phone from her purse and held it up. "The clock on this device keeps me right on track."

Koloa Estate

When Ellen and Mandy stepped out of their taxi cab, Ellen paused and sniffed the air. "Can you smell it, Mandy?" Her excitement mounted. "The wunderbaar aroma of *kaffi* is all around us."

Mandy chuckled. "Of course it is—we're at a coffee farm."

"Jah, but I never thought it would smell like this." Eager to go inside the visitor's center, Ellen grabbed Mandy's hand. "Let's ask about taking the walking tour."

"Don't you want to try some kaffi first? The brochure I picked up says there are several kinds to sample inside the visitor's center."

"Good idea." Ellen started walking in that direction, and Mandy followed.

The aroma of coffee greeted them inside the building, even stronger than it had been outside. It didn't take Ellen long to find the room where the free samples were located. She and Mandy tasted all of them—chocolate, dark-roasted peaberry; coconut caramel; vanilla; chocolate macadamia nut; hazelnut; and Hawaiian-style Irish crème.

Ellen turned to Mandy and grinned. "After all those samples, we should have enough energy to keep going for the rest of the day."

Mandy nodded. "Maybe a little too much energy. I'm not used to drinking so much kaffi at one time."

"Let's go on the walking tour, and then we can check out the gift shop before our taxi picks us up." Ellen reached into her tote bag to get her camera. "Oh, oh."

"What's wrong?"

"I can't find my camera. I must have left it in our room on the ship."

"No problem. I have mine, and I'll share it with you. We can take all the pictures we want."

Since they had the option of meandering through the shade of the coffee trees on their own or waiting for a time when a tour would take them, Mandy suggested they start walking by themselves. "There are signs along the way identifying the different coffee varieties, as well as telling about the coffee process. We can learn what we want to know without a tour guide." She quirked an eyebrow. "After all, this day is supposed to be about branching out on our own."

Ellen stopped, pointing to a sign. "*Aloha e komo mai.*"

"I wonder what it means."

Ellen smiled. "It means 'Welcome.'" Before Mandy had a chance to ask, Ellen explained that she found the words in a little Hawaiian booklet she'd bought at the Polynesian Cultural Center the previous day. "I left it in our room on the ship, but wish now I had it with me."

"Guess we should both study your book so we can say a few Hawaiian words while we're here."

"Good idea. I'll take it out of my suitcase when we get back to the ship, because it won't do us any good unless we have it with us when we're touring the islands." Ellen's forehead wrinkled. "I'm surprised I even remembered what I'd read about how to say 'welcome.'"

As they moved on, they came to other signs identifying the different coffee varieties. Up ahead, they found even more informational markers explaining the process from initial blooming, through harvesting and processing, to the final roasting.

They ended the tour by sitting on the veranda to enjoy sweeping views of the plantation and coffee trees, leading down to the ocean. The palms moved in the gentle breeze as Ellen and Mandy sat together eating the ice-cream cones they'd purchased at the snack bar.

"I'm glad we came here." When Mandy finished her cone, she stood and tossed her napkin into the trash can. "It's time to check out the gift shop and call our taxi so we can move on. Also, maybe we should get a high-protein snack to take with us."

"You're right," Ellen agreed. "With nothing in my stomach but ice cream and coffee, I feel a bit shaky."

Mandy glanced at her cell phone. "The time is going quickly, and I do want to see Spouting Horn yet, don't you?"

"Of course. According to the brochures I have, it's a sight to behold." Ellen finished the rest of her cone and rose from her seat.

Waimea Canyon

"I wonder how things are going with Ellen and Mandy," Sadie said as she sat beside Barbara on the tour bus taking them up the long, curvy road to the viewpoint.

Barbara's brows lifted. "I still can't believe they went off by themselves. They're gonna miss seeing what some call the 'Grand Canyon of the Pacific.'"

"It was their choice, and I'm sure they'll get to see some things as awesome as what we'll be witnessing today. Besides, we'll take plenty of pictures."

"I suppose." Barbara looked away, staring out at the scenery as the bus traveled along.

"This has sure been a wonderful trip, getting to see so many unusual and beautiful things." Sadie sighed. "It's almost like stepping inside the pages of a book."

"It has been pretty amazing," Barbara agreed. "Too bad we can't spend more time on each of the islands. But then again, we should be glad for what we have been able to see. Our trip might be more expensive if the ship remained docked for more than a day on each island. We'd probably still be at home, working to save more money, instead of being here, enjoying ourselves." She pulled a package of mints from her purse and offered one to Sadie.

"Danki." Sadie smiled and put one in her mouth.

When the bus came to the viewpoint, it stopped and everyone got out. Sadie stood staring at the panoramic view of the colorful canyon, with its rugged, craggy surface and deep valley gorges. The rock formations of beige, red, and green seemed almost surreal. "How could anyone believe there is no God?" she whispered in awe.

"I understand what you're saying. Oh my, I wonder how it all came about." Slowly, Barbara shook her head.

"It was formed from the steady process of erosion, due to a catastrophic collapse of the volcano that created Kauai millions of years ago. At least, that's what it says here." Sadie lifted the brochure she held. "When Kauai was still continually erupting, a portion of the island collapsed. It then formed a deep depression, which became filled with lava flows."

Barbara sucked in her breath. "All I know is, what we are looking at is gorgeous. I see it as the handiwork of God."

Sadie nodded. "Well said."

Spouting Horn

"Watch now! Watch real close, 'cause it's gonna blow." Mandy lifted her camera in readiness to see water shoot upward through an opening of lava rock, as she'd read about.

Ellen stood beside her, holding tightly to the rail. "I don't see anything, Mandy. When is it supposed to happen?"

"I don't know the exact moment; that's why we need to watch."

A minute later, it happened. As a huge spray of water shot upward through an opening, it created a great moaning sound. "I got it!" Mandy shouted as she snapped a picture. "That was absolutely incredible!"

"And it never ceases to amaze me."

Mandy's head jerked at the sound of a deep voice close to her ear. Startled, she turned to see a young man with tousled sandy-blond hair hanging almost to his shoulders. He stood right beside her and wore a pair of dark blue cutoffs and a white T-shirt.

"You've seen it before?" she questioned.

"Oh yeah, many times." His cobalt-blue eyes twinkled as he gave her a dimpled smile. "I live on the island, so I can come here whenever I have time. The spray from Spouting Horn can shoot as high as fifty feet in the air. Oh, and you might also like to know that the original name for this natural wonder is '*puhi,*' which means, 'blowhole.'"

"It sounds like you know a lot about it." She tossed the ties on her head covering over her shoulder to keep them from blowing in her face.

"Sure do. According to Hawaiian folklore, a giant lizard protected this area, until a young man named Liko challenged it. Of course, this threatened the people who came here to fish or swim." He paused, his thick lashes brushing his cheeks as he blinked. "During the battle, Liko plunged a sharp stick into the lizard's mouth."

"What happened next?" Mandy felt drawn into his story.

"Well, Liko leaped into the water, luring the lizard in too. Then he swam into a small lava tube in the rocks, leading to the surface. The lizard followed and got stuck in the tube. So today, what you witnessed when the water shot up was the lizard's roar. And he does it every time Spouting Horn blasts into the air."

Mandy giggled. "What a great story. Thanks for sharing it with us."

"Us?" He tipped his head, looking at her curiously.

She glanced to her left, thinking Ellen was still there, but her friend had wandered off and was kneeling beside a mother hen and her baby chicks in the grassy area. Mandy had read about all the chickens roaming free on Kauai, but these were the first she had seen. "My friend is over there." She pointed over her shoulder with her thumb. "This is our first time to Kauai, and I'm impressed with what we've seen so far. There's so much colorful foliage and beautiful flowers—even more so than the other two islands we've already seen."

"It is beautiful here." His hands made a sweeping gesture of the landscape. "That's why it's known as 'The Garden Island.'"

"I'd heard that, and it makes sense to me now." Mandy took a picture of Ellen and the chickens. She would surprise her with it when they got home.

"Where are you from?" he asked.

"We live in northeastern Indiana."

"Amish country?" He slipped his sunglasses on.

She nodded.

"I figured you were Amish by the way you're dressed." He kept his focus mainly on Mandy, glancing briefly at Ellen as she watched the mama hen and her chicks.

"Have you ever been to Indiana or met any Amish people?" Mandy asked.

"Nope. I grew up in Portland, Oregon, but I've read about the Amish and seen some shows on TV about them."

Mandy frowned. "Don't believe everything you read and especially what you see on television. Not everything people say or think about us is true."

He rubbed the bridge of his nose. "Figured as much. Not everything people say about those who live on the Hawaiian Islands is true, either."

Ellen returned to Mandy's side and tugged her sleeve. "Should we go look at some of the souvenir booths now? I'd like to see if there's anything I might wanna buy to take home."

"You'll find some nice locally-made items," the young man said.

Mandy smiled. "It's been nice talking to you. Thanks again for the information about the blowhole—even the story you made up."

"Oh, I didn't make it up. The legend's been around a long time." He lifted his hand to wave. "Enjoy your time here on the island."

As the girls made their way toward the booths, Ellen leaned close to Mandy. "Do you always talk to strangers?"

"I do when I want to learn something." Mandy giggled. "I thought what he told us about the blowhole was interesting."

"Told *you*, don't you mean? I was looking at the chickens."

"You should have been looking at the water shooting up. It was much more interesting."

"I did see it blow, but when the stranger engaged you in conversation, I let someone else take my place at the railing."

"If you'd stayed, you would have heard an interesting folk story about a lizard and a man doing battle in the ocean."

Ellen rolled her eyes dramatically. "Really, Mandy, I'd never have believed something so *narrisch*."

"It wasn't foolish. It was fun." Mandy gave Ellen's arm a gentle tap. "You need to relax and be more outgoing. A person can learn a lot from talking to strangers."

Lihue

After stopping for a late lunch and doing a bit of shopping, Ellen suggested they start back to their ship.

"I'm sure we have plenty of time." Mandy reached into her purse to retrieve her cell phone and was surprised it wasn't there. "That's *fremm*."

"What's strange?"

"I thought I put my cell phone in my purse after we were done eating, but it's not there."

"Maybe you laid it down somewhere. Could you have left it in your seat or on the table at the restaurant?"

"I'm not sure. I suppose it's possible." Mandy started moving in that direction. "We need to go back and see."

When they entered the restaurant, Mandy told the hostess she'd lost her cell phone and thought it might be there, but she was told no cell phone had been found when their table was cleared.

"Okay, thank you." Mandy felt her heart beat faster. She needed her phone to keep in touch with her family, not to mention keep track of the time.

"Where else could you have left it?" Ellen's gaze flitted around the area.

"I have no idea." Mandy took several deep breaths to calm herself. "I need to find it, Ellen. Help me think where it could be."

"Let's retrace our steps."

"Okay." Fear clutched Mandy's heart. Losing her phone was much worse than if she'd lost her camera.

After looking in several places with no luck, Mandy finally gave up. "Guess we'll have to discontinue our search. We need to get back to the ship."

"You're right." Ellen rested her hand on Mandy's arm. "I'm sorry I wasn't paying closer attention. If I had, I may have seen where you laid the phone down."

"It's not your fault. I was careless." She turned away from Ellen and bit her lip.

They were several blocks from their cruise ship, so they had plenty of walking to do. The sun was beginning to set over the horizon, reflecting off the water's surface. Hot and cool colors swirled in the sky and waves. It looked like something one would see in a painting, but this was even better because it was real.

Mandy and Ellen walked at a fast pace, yet Mandy's heartbeat slowed while she gazed at the sunset. *I wonder if there are any legends about the sun in Hawaii,* she mused. *If there are, I'd love to listen.*

As they approached the dock, Mandy's eyes widened, and her stomach churned. She turned to Ellen. "Where's our cruise ship?"

With a trembling hand, Ellen pointed.

Mandy saw it then, some distance away. The boat had already headed out to sea. She gasped. "Oh, no! We missed it!"

Chapter 7

On the Cruise Ship

Sadie squeezed her purse handles so tight, the veins stood out on her hand. "Oh, dear. I'm getting nervous, Barbara. The ship's on its way to the Big Island, and we haven't seen any sign of Mandy or Ellen."

"I'm sure they're somewhere on the ship," Barbara said. "We must have missed them on our way to dinner. This boat is enormous, and a lot of passengers are milling around, so at this point, let's not worry."

"I realize that, but it's time for supper. Mandy and Ellen should be sitting here beside us at the table." Sadie looked around, hoping their friends were on their way and would join them any minute.

Barbara shrugged. "Maybe they couldn't find the dining room."

"It doesn't make sense. As many evenings as we've all come up to this deck, they surely would be able to find their way here by now."

Barbara drank some water. "Perhaps they ate too much for lunch and decided to skip the evening meal. I remember the time Mandy mentioned she'd like to visit the exercise room on the ship. Maybe she and Ellen are there, working out on one of the machines."

Sadie's brows lifted. "And miss dinner? I don't believe it."

"If they're too full to eat anything right now, I can understand them not wanting dinner." Barbara leaned forward. "Or maybe they went to the ship's library and became lost in a novel."

"They should have been in our room when we went there to change before coming up to dinner." Sadie pursed her lips. "I hope you're right about why they're not here, but I have a horrible feeling they didn't make it back to the ship before it pulled away from the dock."

Barbara coughed, nearly choking on her water. "Ach, that would be *baremlich*! If Mandy and Ellen didn't get to the ship on time, they're stranded on Kauai!"

Lihue

Ellen clutched Mandy's arm. "What are we going to do? The boat left without us, and now we're stuck here for who knows how long and without our luggage." For the first time since they'd begun their journey, she sounded desperate to go home.

"Calm down." Mandy spoke softly, hoping to ease her own fears. She had to admit, even with her friend standing right beside her, it was a lonely feeling being so far from home in an unfamiliar place. "It won't do us any good to get *umgerrent*."

"How can we not be upset?" Ellen's voice rose while she twisted her head covering ribbons around her fingers. "We're stuck here, with no place to even stay the night. And remember, you don't have your cell phone anymore. If you still had it, you could at least call Sadie and Barbara and tell them what's happened. Imagine how worried they are by now. I sure would be if our roles were reversed."

While Mandy and Ellen talked more about their situation, an elderly man and woman walked up to them.

"I don't mean to interrupt," the lady said, "but my husband and I couldn't help overhearing what you two were saying about missing your ship."

Mandy barely managed a nod.

"I'm sorry to hear it. If you're looking for overnight lodging, perhaps you'd be interested in staying at the lovely bed-and-breakfast where my husband and I have been staying in Kapaa for the past two nights. I heard the owner mention they have a vacancy, so I don't think getting a room would be a problem." She brushed her thin, gray bangs to the side of her forehead before looking at her husband who nodded.

Mandy's ears perked up when the elderly man mentioned the people who ran the B&B were Christians. "That's why my wife and I have come back to stay there again. The Palos are so kind and down to earth. Real nice, genuine folks. We'd be happy to give you girls a ride to their place." He held out his hand. "My name is Frank Anderson, and this is my wife, Dottie. We live in California, and this is our third time on Kauai."

Ellen and Mandy introduced themselves, then Ellen turned to Mandy. "What do you think we should do?"

"I don't believe we have much choice. We need a place to stay this evening."

As Mandy sat in the backseat of Mr. and Mrs. Anderson's rental car, her throat constricted. *This whole mess is my fault. If only I hadn't lost my phone. What's going to happen to us now? Surely the ship won't come back to get us. I remember what we were told when instructions were given to all passengers about not being late. Now we we'll need to find another way home.*

She glanced at Ellen, sitting behind the driver's seat, while fingering her head covering ties again. *What is she thinking?* Mandy rubbed her hand on her chest. *Is Ellen as upset with me as I am with myself?* She had told her friend to calm down a while ago, but now Mandy was upset. She needed to pray and ask God to help them.

Closing her eyes, she sent up a silent prayer. *Dear Lord, please help us find a way to get in touch with Sadie and Barbara. And show us what we need to do in order to get home.*

Kapaa

Sometime later, they pulled up in front of a large, two-story house. The sun was about to disappear below the horizon. Mandy didn't know if it was because they were in Hawaii, but the sky was breathtaking as it turned from a brilliant orange to a deep scarlet red. The porch light was on, and Mandy could read the sign by the front door: The Palms Bed-and-Breakfast. The name seemed appropriate, since two large palm trees, silhouetted by the sunset, stood in the yard.

Frank turned off the engine, and when he and Dottie got out, Mandy and Ellen did the same. Going up to the door without any luggage seemed strange. Since she and Ellen had not made reservations, she wondered if they would be allowed to stay.

Both of them held back until the Andersons entered the house. A pleasant-looking Hawaiian couple, who appeared to be in their late forties, greeted them.

"Luana and Makaio, these two young women missed their cruise ship and need a place to stay tonight," Dottie explained. "They're Amish, and their names are Mandy Frey and Ellen Lambright. Would you have a room for them?"

"I'm sorry to hear of your predicament." A look of concern was quickly replaced by Luana's pretty smile, revealing perfectly white teeth. "We have two rooms left, but one is reserved for some people who are expected to arrive later tonight. Would one room with twin beds work for you?" She directed her question to Mandy. "It's the Primrose Room."

"That would be fine." Mandy hesitated, biting her lip. "How much does the room cost?"

"For a single room with a shared bathroom, the cost is ninety-five dollars per night," Makaio spoke up.

"We'll take it." Ellen's cheeks turned pink when she looked at Mandy. "Is that okay with you?"

Mandy nodded. It wasn't like Ellen to speak up so boldly, but in this case, she was glad she had. Mandy was relieved they had enough money between them, even though it wouldn't last forever. They wouldn't be able to stay here too many nights, but for now, what other choice did they have? Mandy was dog-tired and stressed out from all the drama they'd gone through today. Ellen had to be feeling it too. *I wonder if Barbara and Sadie are exhausted from worrying about us.*

Mandy couldn't wait for her head to hit the pillow; although she wished she and Ellen were on board the cruise ship. *On a positive note,* she thought, *I'll have a nice bed to sleep in tonight rather than a tight upper bunk in our ship's cabin.*

She suddenly realized that they needed to get in touch with their folks as soon as possible to let them know what had happened. Hopefully, they could send them enough money for tickets on another cruise ship that would take them back to the mainland.

"Could we borrow your phone?" Mandy asked Luana after the Andersons headed down the hall to their room. "I'll pay you whatever it costs for the long-distance call."

"Certainly, but don't worry about paying us back. We have unlimited long-distance." Luana spoke in a bubbly tone as she pointed to the phone sitting on a desk where the guest book lay. "Please, help yourself, and don't forget to sign our guest book."

"Thank you so much." Mandy looked at Ellen. "I'll call my folks first, and then you can call yours."

"What about Sadie and Barbara? How are we supposed to let them know where we are?"

"That's a problem. I can't call Barbara's cell phone, because her number was programmed into my phone and I didn't write it down." Mandy released a frustrated groan.

"Maybe when you call your parents and explain what happened, you could ask them to get ahold of Barbara's parents, because they surely have her cell number," Ellen suggested.

"Good idea." Mandy picked up the receiver and punched in the number for home. After getting her parents' voice mail, she left a message explaining what happened. She also gave them the phone number for the B&B, reminding them of the five-hour difference in time between Indiana and Hawaii. Then she handed Ellen the phone. "Your turn."

"I'm bummed. The last thing I want to do is make this call to my folks. They'll be so worried when they get my message." The sound of dread in Ellen's voice was evident.

Hopefully by tomorrow, one of them would hear something from someone back home. Mandy prayed everything would work out.

On the Cruise Ship

"Did you get ahold of Mandy?" Sadie asked when she stepped out of the bathroom and saw Barbara with her cell phone.

Barbara lay back on her bed. "Unfortunately, no. I did leave a message, though."

"How many messages does that make now?" Sadie sipped a cup of tea she'd made for herself.

"Three." Barbara sighed. "If they did miss the boat, which I'm almost sure is what occurred, what's gonna happen to them?"

Sadie sat down on Ellen's bed. "I don't know, but they're both *schmaert*. I'm sure they'll figure something out. We'll pray they get help this evening and things will work out as smoothly as possible under the circumstances they're facing."

"It's hard to have faith sometimes—especially when something like this happens." Barbara's voice cracked. "This is horrible. It's sure put a damper on our vacation."

"I agree. It'll be hard to get off the ship in Hilo tomorrow morning and go with the others who signed up to see the volcano." Sadie looked down at the bed and brushed her hand over the blanket. "It's probably not the right time to say this, but. . ."

"What were you going to say?"

"I'm taking Ellen's bed and leaving the cramped upper bunk behind."

"I don't blame you for choosing to sleep there, and Ellen can't say anything if she's not here to talk you out of it." Barbara's eyes teared up. "Maybe we shouldn't go sightseeing tomorrow. We should probably stay here and keep trying to get in touch with Mandy and Ellen."

"What would that solve? You can keep calling her when we're on the Big Island."

"True." Barbara picked up her cell phone again. "Think I'd better give my folks a call and tell them what happened. I'll ask Mom to let Ellen and Mandy's parents know about them missing the boat. After that, you can call your parents." She grimaced. "Everyone—especially Mandy and Ellen's family—will be *umgerrent* when they hear the news."

Chapter 8

The Big Island

Sadie stretched her arms over her head and released a noisy yawn. She hadn't slept well last night, despite being in her friend's bed. Thoughts of Ellen and Mandy kept her awake. Now she and Barbara were scheduled to take a tour to see the volcano, but neither of them felt like going anywhere. How could they have fun while their friends were stranded on Kauai?

"Even if we're not in the mood for sightseeing, we need to leave the ship and join the tour." Barbara gathered her sunglasses, along with her phone, and put them in her purse.

"You're right. We may never visit Hawaii again, so we should try to make the best of this beautiful sunny morning. I hope we hear something from Mandy today."

"Jah." Barbara reached for her sweater and held it up. "You may want to bring yours too. I heard it can be a bit chilly near the volcano."

"I'll get mine." Sadie gathered up the rest of her things and put them in a tote. "Let's be off."

Kapaa

"This is a lovely room," Mandy commented as she and Ellen put their only dresses on Friday morning before joining the other guests for breakfast. "The Primrose Room—what an appropriate name. The entire space looks like a beautiful flower."

"And don't forget these." Ellen gestured to the twin beds, each covered with a lovely quilt. "Wouldn't it be nice to buy a Hawaiian quilt to take home when we go?" Ellen walked to the bed and ran her fingers over the material.

Mandy brought her hands to her chest. "I would love to own one, but I hear they're expensive." She moved over to the mirror and put her head covering on. "If we end up staying here awhile, maybe we could make one. I don't think they're much different than our Amish quilts."

"That may be, but we won't be here long enough to make a quilt." Ellen moved toward the door. "We'd better go downstairs. From the delicious aromas coming up the steps, breakfast must be ready."

Mandy was almost to the door when she dropped her handkerchief. She bent to pick it up and noticed a little wooden statue on the floor under the dresser. "I wonder what this is."

Ellen turned around. "What?"

Mandy reached for the small object and held it up. "Have you ever seen one of these before?"

"No, I have not." Ellen ran her finger over the dark-colored sculpture. "It's smiling face carved into the wood looks so peculiar. Let's ask Luana or Makaio about it."

When Mandy and Ellen entered the dining room a short time later, they were greeted by Mr. and Mrs. Anderson, already seated at the table.

"Did you two sleep well?" Dottie asked.

"I did." Mandy grinned and pulled out a chair at the table. "The bed was a lot more comfortable than the upper bunk I slept on during our time on the ship."

Ellen pulled out a chair and sat beside Mandy. "I had a good night's sleep too."

Two other couples entered the room and took seats at the table, and everyone introduced themselves. The middle-aged couple were from Washington State, and the newlyweds who'd arrived last evening lived in Canada.

Smiling cheerfully, Luana stepped into the room carrying a plate of scrambled eggs. Makaio, wearing a pale green shirt with palm trees on it, was right behind her, bringing a platter of sausages and a bowl of white rice. Already on the table were two bowls of fruit—one with pineapple and strawberries, the other with papaya and blueberries.

Mandy's mouth nearly watered, thinking how good everything looked. No doubt it would taste equally yummy.

"If anyone would like Spam instead of sausage, I'd be happy to bring some out." Makaio's prominent cheekbones rose. "I kinda like the stuff."

Luana poked her husband's arm and chuckled. "Don't let him fool you. My man is addicted to Spam."

"I especially like it with scrambled eggs and rice," he added. "My dad likes it too. He raised me on it."

"Thanks anyway, but I think I'll pass." Mandy averted her gaze. Although she wasn't a picky eater and was willing to try many things, she'd never gotten acquainted with Spam until she'd tried it on the cruise ship during breakfast their first morning. One glance and one sniff was all it took for her not to like it. She didn't understand how anyone could eat the stuff. *Then again,* she thought, *some people might question my taste for seafood.*

"Did you both sleep well?" Makaio asked.

"Oh yes," Ellen replied. "It was good to sleep in a bed that didn't feel like it was swaying back and forth."

"I have a question." Mandy held out the small statue she'd discovered. "I found this under the dresser in our room and wondered what it was."

"It's a tiki," Makaio explained. "One of our previous guests must have bought it from a gift shop and left it in the room. Guess we missed seeing it there when we cleaned."

"Do the little statues have a special purpose or meaning?" Ellen asked.

"Well, some who live on our island believe if a totem such as this has been carved with a scary expression, it will keep away evil spirits."

"Others with a friendlier appearance, like the one you're holding, are thought to bring good luck," Luana added. "Of course, as Christians we don't believe in such superstitions." She held out her hand. "Unless you want to keep the tiki, I'll dispose of it, because I don't feel comfortable keeping it around. I wouldn't want anyone to get the impression we worship idols or even believe in the fantasies surrounding the carvings."

Mandy was glad the Hawaiian couple didn't believe in such things, and she gladly handed the tiki to Luana.

"If everyone is ready, we can eat breakfast now." Makaio then asked if anyone objected to him saying a prayer before the meal.

The guests all shook their heads. Even though she was used to praying silently, Mandy had no objections to a prayer spoken aloud. She was glad the Hawaiian couple were Christians and remembered seeing a Bible lying on the coffee table while walking through the living room last night. It eased some of Mandy's inner tensions and gave her a sense of peace.

"Dear Lord," Makaio prayed. "We thank You for this food and the hands that prepared it. Bless the meal, and may it bring nourishment to our bodies. Thank You for the opportunity to make new friends and get reacquainted with those we have met before. In Jesus' name we pray, amen."

Mandy felt certain Makaio and Luana were devout Christians, not only because of the heartfelt prayer he'd given, but from the scripture verse on a plaque hanging above the buffet at the other end of the room. It quoted Hebrews 13:2: "Be not forgetful to entertain strangers: for thereby some have entertained angels unawares." She had a feeling every visitor who came to this bed-and-breakfast was treated special—as though they were an angel.

Middlebury

Stepping around mud puddles, Miriam headed down the driveway to the phone shack to check for messages. She'd meant to see if there were any this morning, but it had been raining so hard she'd waited. Even now, at one o'clock in the afternoon, the rain fell, although it had been reduced to a drizzle. She was glad there'd been no more snow, but they'd had rain for the last several days, leaving the yard a mess. She looked forward to spring when the weather warmed and she could be outside in her garden. Miriam longed to see budding trees and flowers opening their petals. She glanced at one of the maples in their yard and frowned. Like all the rest, it was barren of leaves. The birds sitting on its branches looked as miserable as she felt. None of them even chirped a tune.

Miriam moved on. When she approached the phone shack, she shook the rain from her umbrella and stepped inside. The blinking light on the answering machine signaled messages waiting. She took a seat in the folding chair and clicked the button. The first message was from Gideon's mother, asking if Miriam needed any more thread. They had an overstock of both black and white, which would be on sale for half price.

The next message was from Miriam's driver, saying she would be free to take her to the chiropractor's later in the week. *Good to hear. With the pain I've had in my neck the last few days, I need to go in as soon as possible.*

As Miriam listened to the beginning of the third message, she smiled. It was from Mandy.

"Hi, Mom and Dad. I wanted to let you know Ellen and I missed the ship last evening. We are staying at the Palms Bed-and-Breakfast, in the town of Kapaa, on the island of Kauai." Following a short pause, her message continued: "Barbara and Sadie are on the boat, heading for the Big Island, but I have no way of contacting them. Unfortunately, I lost my cell phone, which is why we were late and missed the ship's departure." Another pause. "Don't worry about me, okay? Ellen and I have a nice place to stay until we're able to book passage home. Ellen has called her parents too. If Barbara should call, please let her know we're okay. Oh, and if you could please call Barbara and Sadie's folks and tell them what's happened, I'd appreciate it. I'm going to give you the phone number for the B&B so you can contact me. When you call Barbara's mamm, would you please ask her for Barbara's cell number? It was programmed into my cell phone, but I didn't write it down. Oh, and don't forget about the time difference here when you call me back, because I'm five hours earlier than you are in Indiana. I need to let you go for now, so Ellen can call her folks. I hope to hear from you soon. I miss you all. Please give my love to everyone."

Miriam wrote down the phone number her daughter gave for the place they were staying, and then she listened to the message a second time to make sure she hadn't missed any information. Without listening to any of the other messages, she called and left messages for Barbara's and Sadie's parents. Immediately after, Miriam dialed the number for the B&B and brought her hand to her forehead. *It's no wonder I didn't want Mandy to go on that trip.*

Kapaa

"We've had many people at our B&B, but no one quite like Mandy and Ellen," Luana said after she and Makaio returned to the kitchen. "I've heard about Amish people but never imagined we'd have the chance to meet any. They're nice young women, don't you think?"

"Yes, they seem to be. They sure dress different than other people here on the island, though." Makaio opened the refrigerator and removed a pitcher of guava juice. "I put some pineapple juice on the table earlier, but maybe our guests would like some of this."

Luana smiled. Her husband thought of everything this morning. "I can't help but wonder if the Lord may have brought Mandy and Ellen to us for a reason." She lowered her voice, to be discreet.

He tipped his head while squinting his dark eyes and leaning in closer to her. "What reason?"

"I'm not sure, but I feel like they are supposed to be here. It's as though God brought them to us for a purpose."

"Maybe so. You've had feelings about certain other guests in the past."

"I've also been thinking, since the girls have only the clothes on their backs, after breakfast, I'll see if they'd like to go shopping to look for a few modest dresses, some sleeping attire, undergarments, and sandals."

"Good idea. They sure can't wear the same dress every day they're here." Makaio started for the dining room but turned back around. "How long do you think they will stay?"

Luana was about to respond when the telephone rang. "I'll get it. You can go ahead and take the juice in to our guests." She reached for the phone and picked up the receiver. "The Palms Bed-and-Breakfast."

"Hello. This is Miriam Frey. Is my daughter, Mandy, there?"

"Yes, she is. I'll go get her." Luana set the receiver on the counter and hurried to the dining room. "Mandy, your mother's on the phone. If you like, you can take the call on the extension in the kitchen."

Mandy jumped up, dashed into the kitchen, and eagerly grabbed the phone. "Hi, Mom."

"Ach, Mandy, it's so good to hear your *mundschtick.*"

Tears welled in Mandy's eyes, blurring her vision. "It's good to hear your voice too. I guess you got my message."

"Jah. I called as soon as I heard it." Mom sniffed. "Are you and Ellen all right?"

"We're both fine. Makaio and Luana Palu, the owners of the B&B where we are staying, are nice Christian people. They welcomed us with open arms."

"I'm glad to hear it. Being stranded in a place where everyone is a stranger has to be frightening."

"We were scared at first, but not anymore." Mandy switched the receiver to her other ear.

"How's the weather there, Mom?"

"Cold and rainy."

"I don't miss the colder weather. It's eighty degrees here on Kauai."

Mom sighed. "Must be nice. I'm anxious for spring to come and bring warmer weather."

"Did you get ahold of Barbara's parents?" Mandy asked.

"I left a message for the Hiltys, as well as the Kuhns, but it could be awhile before I hear anything back. When I do and they give me Barbara's cell phone number, I'll be sure and call you again so you can get ahold of her."

"Good. She and Sadie are probably worried about us."

"I imagine they would be. It's hard to believe they'll be coming to

Middlebury without you and Ellen." Mom paused. "What can your *daed* and I do on this end to get you home again?"

"Nothing yet. I'll need to find out when another cruise ship will be coming this way from Los Angeles and how much it will cost for Ellen and me to make the journey. It should be cheaper this time, Mom, because it will only be one way."

"It will be less, and if you need money for your ticket, we'll see what we can do."

"Danki, Mom. Tell Dad and the rest of the family I said hello. I'll call you again soon."

Mandy remained in the kitchen a few minutes after she hung up the phone, thinking things through. It took her a year to save enough money for this trip to Hawaii. Could her parents afford to pay for her ticket home?

Chapter 9

The Big Island

I'm glad we brought our sweaters along, because the breeze blowing here isn't helping things." Sadie pulled hers closer and fiddled with one of the buttons. "It's much cooler up here by the Kīlauea Volcano than in Hilo, where our ship docked."

"The cooler temperature feels kind of good." Barbara pointed to the lava tube up ahead. "I'm glad we were able to come. I mean, how often does a person get to see an erupting volcano, much less be so close to one?" She spoke excitedly.

"You're right." Shuffling her feet, Sadie pressed her lips slightly together. "It's too bad Ellen and Mandy couldn't be with us today. They're missing out on this experience, not to mention the unusual scenery. There is no way we can adequately tell them about this, except for the pictures and postcards we'll bring home." She paused. "Have you tried calling Mandy again?"

"I've called three times again this morning. All I ever get is her voice mail." Barbara frowned. "I can't figure out why she doesn't answer her cell phone. It's usually stuck to her like glue."

"Maybe the battery is dead. Or perhaps she has it muted or in vibration mode." Sadie stepped around a fallen branch on the path. "But with all the messages you've left, she really should have called you back by now."

"I agree, and my fear that something bad happened to them is increasing by the minute. I've been praying for their safety."

Sadie nodded. "I've been praying for them too, so let's try not to worry. Since there's nothing we can do, we ought to make the most of our day."

As they walked up the trail, Barbara's cell phone rang. "Maybe it's

Mandy." She reached into her tote bag and withdrew the phone. "Hello. Oh hi, Mom. How are things going? You did?" Barbara turned to face Sadie and gave her a thumbs-up.

"What's going on?" Sadie asked as she stepped aside from the path.

"I'll tell you as soon as I hang up."

While Barbara continued talking to her mother in Pennsylvania Dutch, Sadie studied one of the brochures their tour guide gave them during the bus ride. According to the brochure, two active volcanoes were on the Big Island— Kīlauea and Mauna Loa. Kīlauea was the more accessible of the two, which was why the tour guide had brought them here.

Since Sadie and Barbara had stopped walking while Barbara talked to her mother, the others in their tour had gone ahead and were probably making their way through the lava tube already. Sadie was eager to go, but equally anxious to hear what Mrs. Hilty had to say, so she waited patiently.

Barbara looked at her expectantly. "Sadie, would you write down this number for me?"

"Sure." Sadie took a notebook and pen from her purse and wrote down the number Barbara told her.

After a bit more conversation, Barbara finally clicked off the phone. "I'm so glad my mamm called. The good news is she heard from Mandy's mother. The bad news is Mandy called her to say she and Ellen missed the boat and are stranded on Kauai."

"Which is exactly what we suspected." Sadie clasped her tote tightly. "How in the world did they miss the boat? Why weren't they paying attention so they could get back to the ship on time?" She shifted her weight to the other foot.

"Apparently, Mandy lost her cell phone and, after spending too much time looking for it, when they arrived at the port where our ship had been docked, it had already left." Barbara rubbed the side of her face, where a mosquito had bitten her. "Now our two friends are staying at a bed-and-breakfast, and Mom got the phone number from Mandy's mamm."

Sadie was relieved Mandy and Ellen were okay, but she also felt a bit irritated. If they'd gone on the tour to see the beautiful canyon with them, this would never have happened. All four of them would be here right now, preparing to see the volcano's crater at the Kīlauea Visitor Center.

Kapaa

Luana smiled with anticipation as she entered one of the dress shops at the Coconut Marketplace with Mandy and Ellen. It felt nice to be able to help the girls out. The garments here were much brighter, with bold prints, than what the young Amish women normally wore. She hoped they wouldn't be offended by her suggestion to wear one of the dresses sold in this store.

"There's certainly a lot to choose from, isn't there?" Mandy reached up and touched a dark purple dress. "They're so beautiful."

Luana looked at Ellen, who stood off to one side, eyes wide. *She's probably never seen dresses like this before.*

"I'm going to try this one on." Mandy took down the purple dress. "Ellen, have you found one you like?"

Slowly, Ellen shook her head, looking back at her friend with a bewildered expression.

"How about this one?" Luana pointed to a pretty blue muumuu. Like the purple dress Mandy chose, this one was also long enough to cover most of her legs.

Ellen hesitated at first, but finally removed the dress from the rack. "I suppose I could try it on."

The store clerk showed the girls to the dressing rooms. While they tried on the dresses, Luana looked at her cell phone to check for any messages. Seeing none, she made a mental note of the other places she wanted to take Mandy and Ellen. Unfortunately, the marketplace didn't have shoe stores anymore, but Sole Mates on Kuhio Highway had plenty of sandals and flip-flops to choose from. Luana would stop there on the way back to the B&B. For underwear and sleeping attire, they would visit another clothing store near Kapaa.

When Mandy stepped out of the dressing room, Luana's breath caught in her throat. The deep purple offset by Mandy's chestnut hair and brown eyes was stunning. Of course, the stiff white cone-shaped bonnet on the young woman's head looked out of place with a muumuu. *I wonder how Mandy would look with her hair down and a hibiscus or plumeria flower behind her right ear. When we get back to my house, I'll look and see if I have some nice scarfs the girls can wear over their hair instead of their white bonnets.*

A few minutes later, Ellen exited the dressing room. Her cheeks were flushed pink, and she kept her gaze to the floor. The blue dress she wore was lovely, but Luana sensed the poor girl felt uncomfortable wearing a garment such as this.

"You both look so nice." She smiled. "Are your dresses comfortable, and are those the ones you would like?"

Mandy nodded enthusiastically, but Ellen barely moved her head up and down.

"All right then, if you want to change back into your Amish clothes, I'll pay for your dresses and we can be off. There are some other stops we need to make."

"Oh, no." Mandy shook her head. "You don't have to pay for our dresses. We both have money."

Luana held up her hand. "Save it toward your tickets home or anything else you may need. I want to buy the dresses—it'll be my treat."

Mandy took a seat at the desk in the room she and Ellen shared at the B&B and opened her journal. Before starting to write, she thought about their friends. *Sadie and Barbara are probably seeing something interesting today. I hope they take pictures. I can't wait to check out all the photos from our combined trip when we're all back home.*

Refocusing on her journal, she began to write:

It was fun shopping with Luana today, but the dress I bought feels a bit strange—almost like a nightgown. It's called a muumuu. Mine is a dark purple with pretty lavender flowers. Luana said they are called plumeria. The room Mr. and Mrs. Anderson are staying in here at the bed-and-breakfast is called the Plumeria Room. It has a king-sized bed and private bath. Ellen and I share our bathroom with guests in the Gardenia Room. After tomorrow, no one will be staying there for a while, so we will have the bathroom all to ourselves.

Mandy paused and lifted her pen. The dress she wore was actually quite comfortable, even if it felt odd to be wearing something with such a bold print. She and Ellen would probably need to wear clothes like this for as long they were visiting. Mandy felt like she was ready to step out of her comfort zone. Being here in Hawaii was a whole new experience for her and Ellen.

Looking in the mirror, she chuckled at the image staring back at her. *I do look funny, though.* She reached up and touched her white head covering. *It looks out of place with the Hawaiian dress. Think I'll wear the black scarf Luana gave us.*

Mandy removed her head covering, and was about to pin the black scarf in place, when Ellen entered the room. "What are you doing?" She stepped up to her.

"My traditional head covering doesn't go with my muumuu, and besides, I don't want it to get dirty. I've decided to wear the scarf instead." Smiling, Mandy picked up the scarf and pins. "We wear scarves when we're working in the yard or around the house at home, right?"

"Jah, but we're not working here." Ellen moved away from Mandy and flopped down on her bed. "I'm only going to wear the Hawaiian dress when my Amish dress is being washed, like it is now, and never out in public." She pointed to the bodice of her blue muumuu with white hibiscus flowers. "When I'm wearing this, I don't feel like myself. I feel as though I'm dressing up for one of those silly skits we sometimes put on during family get-togethers." Crossing her arms, she frowned. "It wouldn't feel right to wear this dress all the time. And if my parents were here, they'd agree with me."

Mandy moved over to the mirror to secure her scarf. "You can do whatever you want, but since neither of us has joined the Amish church yet, we're not breaking any rules by wearing these Hawaiian dresses."

"True."

"And they are quite cozy."

"I guess." Ellen slid off the bed and moved over to stand by the window, "Oh look, there's a nice *gaarde* at the back of the house. It looks like a vegetable garden."

Mandy joined her, leaning her elbows on the windowsill. "I'll bet Luana and Makaio raise all, or most, of their own produce. Should we take a walk outside and see what's growing?"

Ellen nodded but remained motionless. Then she lifted her hands and removed her own covering. "Maybe I will replace this with a scarf for now. I wouldn't want my white head covering to become soiled."

Mandy smiled. "I hope you're not doing this because of me."

"Well. . ." Ellen dropped her chin. "You do have a point. They don't go with what we're wearing."

After they both had secured their scarves, Mandy hurried to the door and opened it. She would finish writing in her journal later.

Chapter 10

Middlebury

Gideon didn't feel like going to church, but his folks would be upset if he stayed home. He yawned and stretched one arm over his head, holding tightly to the reins with the other hand as he guided his horse and buggy down the road in the direction of the Hiltys' place, where church would be held. Last night, he'd had a troubling dream about Mandy and hadn't slept well. In the dream, he and Mandy were riding in his buggy, chatting pleasantly as they headed down the road. Suddenly, she clasped his arm and said, "I've decided not to join the church. The Amish way of life isn't for me."

He'd pleaded with Mandy to change her mind, yet she stood firm, repeatedly saying the Amish life was not for her. The dream seemed so real. When Gideon woke up, he was drenched in sweat. He'd tried to calm himself by getting out of bed and opening the window for some fresh air, but it hadn't helped much. Even now, as he approached the Hiltys' home, Gideon felt apprehensive. *If Mandy hadn't gone to Hawaii, I wouldn't be having these fitful dreams and conflicting thoughts. If she was here right now, everything would be fine between us.* Even as the thought entered his head, Gideon wasn't sure it was true. He'd sensed an unrest in Mandy for some time and kept trying to convince himself she would eventually join the church. The dream he'd had last night only reaffirmed his fears.

"I need to stop thinking like this," he mumbled, guiding his horse, Dash, into the yard.

Soon after he stepped down from the buggy, he was greeted by his friend, Paul Miller. "Where's your Sunday *hut*?"

"My hat's right here." Gideon pointed to it.

Smirking, Paul reached up and snatched Gideon's hat off his head. "This isn't a Sunday hat. Looks more like something you'd wear to clean the barn."

Gideon jerked his head back and let out a yelp. "Ach! I was wearing my straw hat this morning while getting my horse. Guess I forgot it was on my head when I left home to come here." His cheeks felt like they were on fire. "This old hat will stay in my buggy, 'cause I don't want anyone else knowing I forgot to wear my black Sunday hat."

Just then, Mandy's dad, Isaac, stopped by. "Have you heard about Mandy?" he asked Gideon.

Quickly tossing his hat into the buggy, Gideon shook his head. "Heard what? Is she okay?" Fear rose in his chest.

"She's fine, physically." Deep lines formed at the corners of Isaac's brown eyes when he frowned. "She and Ellen are stranded on the island of Kauai."

Gideon opened his mouth. "How can they be stranded? I thought the cruise ship she and her friends were on was taking them from island to island."

"It has been, but they missed the boat when it was leaving Kauai to go to the Big Island."

"What about Sadie and Barbara?" Paul questioned. "Didn't they go on the trip to Hawaii too?"

"Jah." Isaac rubbed his forehead. "Unfortunately, my daughter and Ellen went off by themselves when the ship docked that morning. If they'd been with the tour group, they wouldn't have been left behind."

In an effort to calm himself, Gideon drew a deep breath. "How's Mandy going to get home?"

"They're working on it. I'm guessing they'll try to book passage on the next cruise ship coming to Kauai. Of course, it could be expensive."

"If she needs money for her ticket, I'd be willing to chip in."

Isaac gave Gideon's shoulder a squeeze. "We'll let you know."

"I tried calling her yesterday but only got her voice mail." Gideon groaned.

"Mandy had more troubles. She lost her cell phone on a sightseeing excursion. When they found a place to stay, she called us. Said she and Ellen are staying at a bed-and-breakfast run by some nice Christian folks."

Gideon felt a little better hearing Mandy had a place to stay. "Could I have the number there so I can give her a call?"

"Sorry, but I don't have it with me right now. If you drop by our place sometime tomorrow, I'll see you get it." Isaac pointed to the large shop, where the service would be held. "Right now, though, we'd better be going inside."

As Gideon turned his horse over to Barbara Hilty's brother Crist, he made a decision. As soon as he got the number of the place where Mandy and Ellen were staying, he'd call and let her know he'd be willing to pay part, or even all, of her fare.

Kapaa

A few minutes before 9:00 a.m., Mandy and Ellen entered a church building with Luana and Makaio. The Andersons were on their way home, having checked out after an early breakfast.

It was nice of the Palus to invite us to join them for church today, Mandy thought as they signed the guest book. Since she and Ellen had washed their Amish dresses the day before, they were able to wear them to services. Mandy was glad, because she would have felt funny wearing a muumuu to church, even though many other worshipers were dressed in Hawaiian-style clothing.

But if we had worn muumuus, we'd look less conspicuous, Mandy thought, observing the sanctuary as she followed Makaio and Luana to a seat. Several people had already greeted them, and one lady gave Mandy and Ellen each a shell lei, which looked a bit strange over their dresses; especially since the Amish didn't wear jewelry. A few others glanced their way with strange expressions. *Amish people have probably never visited this church before.*

It wasn't all that common for the Amish to visit Hawaii. The village of

Pinecraft in Sarasota, Florida, was more of a possibility, since they could travel there by bus or train. Mandy knew a few people from her community who had gone there for vacation during the winter months, but the only person she knew personally who'd visited any of the Hawaiian Islands was her cousin Ruth.

Her muscles relaxed a bit as she took in a few easy breaths. *Well, it's a new experience for us as well, because this is my first time in an English church.*

Mandy was about to sit down when she spotted a tall young man with thick, shoulder-length blond hair on the platform, holding a ukulele. Several other people also sat on the platform with musical instruments. This seemed strange to her, since no instruments were ever played during an Amish church service. Sometimes at home or for family gatherings, Mandy's dad would play his guitar, which added to the pleasure of singing songs for fun or private worship.

Returning her focus to the young man with the ukulele, she thought she'd seen him before—not from back home, but someone she'd met on their trip. As the music and singing started, it all came back to her. He was the same man she'd talked to when she and Ellen visited Spouting Horn on Friday. *What a coincidence. I wonder if I'll get the chance to speak to him after church. If so, will he remember me?*

Later in the afternoon as Mandy and Ellen sat in the Palus' living room, chatting, she thought about the young man again and wished she'd had the opportunity to at least say hello. But he'd been busy talking to several others after church, and she didn't want to interrupt.

"So how did you two young women like our service today?" Makaio's question drove Mandy's thoughts aside.

"It was certainly different." She reached for the glass of guava juice Luana had brought out earlier. "Nothing like our church services at home."

"What are they like?" Luana questioned.

Mandy glanced at Ellen, who sat quietly beside her on the sofa. When her friend remained quiet, Mandy answered. "Our services are held bi-weekly in the home, barn, or shop of church members who take turns hosting the service. We sit on backless, wooden benches for three hours, and there are no musical instruments."

"That's interesting." Luana tapped her lips with a finger. "Think I'd have a hard time sitting that long on any bench or chair."

"Another thing different from your church is the women and girls sit on one side of the building during our services, while the men and boys sit on the other," Ellen spoke up.

"And also," Mandy interjected, "our sermons are preached in German, not English."

Makaio's thick brows furrowed. "I wouldn't be able to understand the message, since I've never learned the German language. I can speak our native Hawaiian language fluently, though."

"Would you teach us a few words?" Mandy asked. She was interested in learning new things. And since the Hawaiian word book Ellen had bought was in her suitcase on the ship, they had no guide to teach them any of the words they may want to know.

He nodded. "You may already know the word *Aloha*. It's a familiar Hawaiian greeting and farewell."

Mandy and Ellen bobbed their heads.

"Our alphabet consists of only twelve letters," Luana explained. "There are five vowels—*a, e, i, o, u,* and seven consonants—*h, k, l, m, n, p,* and *w*."

"Here are a few common words," Makaio said: "*Hana,* which means work; *nani,* meaning beautiful; *kāne,* man; *wahini,* woman; and *keiki,* child."

"I'm a wahini." Mandy pointed to herself and chuckled. "When we get home I can't wait to tell my dad he's a kāne."

"If you're interested, I'll teach you some more Hawaiian words while you're here." Makaio picked up his ukulele. "Right now, why don't we sing a few songs? Afterward, maybe we can talk my dear wahini into serving some snacks."

"You won't have to talk me into it." Luana patted her husband's knee. "I'd planned all along to bring out some special treats."

As Makaio began to play the ukulele, Mandy became almost mesmerized. "I have a battery-operated keyboard at home, and my dad plays the guitar, but playing the ukulele would be even more fun." She clapped after he finished the first song.

"If you stay here long enough, I'd be happy to teach you." Makaio's grin stretched ear to ear.

On the Cruise Ship

"I should call Mandy," Barbara announced as she sat with Sadie in their cabin that evening. "Since I have the number of the place they are staying, I want to find out how she and Ellen are doing."

Sadie set her book aside and leaned forward. "Good idea. Let them know we've been praying for them too."

Barbara grabbed her purse and took out her cell phone, as well as the slip of paper with the number for the B&B. A few seconds later, a pleasant-sounding woman answered. "Aloha. This is the Palms Bed-and-Breakfast."

"Is Mandy Frey there? This is Barbara Hilty. I was one of her traveling companions on the cruise ship."

"Yes, she and Ellen are both here. I'll put Mandy on."

After a minute, an excited voice came on. "Barbara, is it really you?"

"*Jah*, and it's sure good to hear your voice. I got this number from my *mamm*, who got it from your *mamm*. How are you and Ellen doing?"

"Were both fine. Did your mother explain how we missed the boat and ended up staying here?"

"She sure did. I bet you were frightened when you realized you'd missed the ship."

"We were."

"Tell them we were frightened too," Sadie whispered.

Barbara repeated what her friend had said.

"Did you realize what had happened?" Mandy asked.

"Not at first, but as the evening progressed, it didn't take long for us to figure out you'd been left behind. Up until then, we thought you might be somewhere on the ship. It seemed strange you didn't show up at dinner, but we figured you may have had a late lunch and weren't hungry. So many thoughts ran through our heads it was hard not to *druwwle*."

"Sorry for causing you to worry. Ellen and I have no luggage, of course."

"It's here in the room. Sadie and I will make sure both your suitcases go with us on the train when we reach Los Angeles."

"*Danki*, we appreciate it."

"How are you managing with only one dress?" Barbara questioned.

"Luana, the lady who runs the B&B with her husband, bought us each a muumuu."

Barbara pursed her lips. "A what?"

"A muumuu. It's a Hawaiian dress. Mine is purple with pretty flowers on it."

Barbara pressed her palm against her mouth to keep from gasping. She couldn't imagine how her two friends would look wearing Hawaiian dresses.

"Remember when we talked about how we wished we could spend more time on each of the Hawaiian Islands?"

"*Jah.*"

"Well, now Ellen and I are able to do it."

Barbara grimaced. Being stranded on an island was not what she would have wanted for herself or her friends. "Have you talked to Gideon yet? I'm sure he'd like to know what happened."

"No, and I forgot to ask Mom to tell him. I'll say something the next time I call home."

Wow! Barbara cringed. *If Gideon were my boyfriend, he'd have been the first person I would have called to let him know what happened. What is Mandy thinking?*

Chapter 11

*M*onday morning as Barbara and Sadie reclined on chairs near the pool, they talked about how they would arrive at Ensenada, Mexico, within the next few days.

Sadie yawned. "The sun feels so warm. I'm feeling sleepy all of a sudden. Think I'll take a nap."

"Go right ahead. I may end up falling asleep too." Barbara watched some of the people by the pool. By the time she and Sadie had arrived, nearly every chair had been taken. They'd been fortunate to find two lounge chairs together. A young couple with a small child took the last three seats. The curly haired boy threw his towel down and bounced on his chair. He sat only a few minutes, then jumped into the pool, splashing a good amount of water onto the deck, sending a spray of water on Sadie.

Her eyes snapped open, and she leaped out of her chair like she'd been stung by an angry hornet. The boy's mother walked quickly over to Sadie. "I'm so sorry. My son gets pretty excited whenever he has a chance to be in a pool. I'll make sure he stops splashing."

"It's okay. No harm done. The warm sun will dry my dress in no time." Sadie sat back in her chair. "What a full trip this has been." She looked at Barbara. "We've been fortunate to visit four of the Hawaiian Islands, and now we'll get to see a bit of Mexico before returning to Los Angeles."

Barbara nodded. "I only wish Mandy and Ellen were with us. They're missing out on so much."

"When they book their tickets on another cruise ship, I'm sure they will go from there to the Big Island, like we did."

"Maybe so, but by then, we'll either be home or close to arriving."

Barbara slipped her sunglasses on. The frames felt warm from being in the direct sunlight. "I still can't believe Mandy didn't call Gideon right away. You would think she'd want him to know what happened."

"She was probably upset when they got stranded and wasn't thinking clearly." Sadie grabbed her glass of pineapple juice and took a sip. "Our friends are bound to be stressed out."

"True. I'm glad it wasn't us who missed the ship, because I'd be a basket case."

"Me too."

Barbara leaned her head back and closed her eyes. "When we get to Mexico, I'll give Mandy another call. I'd like an update on how they are doing."

Middlebury

Gideon left the upholstery shop and headed straight for the Freys' house. His stomach churned as he thought about getting the phone number for the bed-and-breakfast. He needed to know how Mandy was doing. "Sure don't understand why she hasn't called me, though," he muttered, pedaling as fast as he could. Since it wasn't raining or snowing today, he'd ridden his bike to work.

It was hard to think positive thoughts right now, with his girlfriend being so far away. Once he talked to Mandy, Gideon hoped he would feel a little better.

Approaching the house, he parked his bike near the porch and set the kickstand. Then taking the steps two at a time, he knocked on the door. Several minutes went by. When no one answered, he knocked again. He figured Mandy's father, who managed a meat-and-cheese store, would be home from work by now. Even if he wasn't, Mandy's mother should be around.

Gideon knocked again, with a bit more force. "Hello! Anyone at home?" Still no answer.

Thinking someone might be in the barn, he headed in that direction. When he stepped inside, he saw Mandy's brothers, Mark and Melvin, mucking out the horses' stalls. It seemed a little odd that Isaac and Miriam had given all their children names beginning with *M*. But then he remembered Mandy saying her dad wanted their daughter and son's names to start with *M* because his wife's name began with that letter.

Redirecting his thoughts, Gideon walked toward the stalls. "Hey, Mark. Hey, Melvin. Are your folks around?"

Mark, the older boy, crossed his arms. "Nope. Dad's workin' late this evening, and Mom went to see the chiropractor."

"Oh, I see." Gideon leaned against the stall door. "I came by to get the phone number of the place where Mandy and Ellen are staying in Hawaii. Would either of you know it?"

Both boys shook their heads.

"Sorry," Melvin said. "Guess you'll have to come back tomorrow."

"Oh, great," Gideon muttered under his breath.

Mark moved closer. "What was that?"

"Nothing. Tell your folks I stopped by and I'll drop by again when I get off work tomorrow."

"You okay?" Melvin asked. "You look kinda down-in-the-mouth."

"I'm disappointed." Gideon turned to go, calling over his shoulder, "See you boys later."

After mounting his bike, Gideon gripped the handlebars so tight his fingers began to ache. *This is ridiculous. I wouldn't have to get the number if Mandy had called me.*

Kapaa

"You have a beautiful garden, Luana." Mandy knelt on the grass beside a healthy-looking tomato plant. It seemed almost unbelievable all these vegetables could be growing in the middle of November. "It must be nice to be able to garden throughout the year."

Luana smiled. "I suppose we take it for granted."

"Have you always lived here on Kauai?" Mandy asked.

"No. Makaio and I were born and raised on the Big Island. We moved here to open the bed-and-breakfast a few years ago." Luana checked the leaves of a bean plant.

"Why didn't you open one there?"

"I suppose we could have, but after visiting Kauai several times, we fell in love with the island. And when the opportunity to buy this place came up, we couldn't resist." She moved over to the tomato plants and knelt down.

"It is beautiful here." Ellen spoke for the first time since they'd come outside. She'd been awfully quiet this afternoon. Mandy suspected her friend might be homesick.

"We do get some rain here, of course, but without it, the flowers wouldn't be so beautiful and it wouldn't be this lush and green." Luana pulled a few weeds. "If I had the choice of living any place on earth, I believe it would be here. In addition to liking the island, my husband and I love the opportunity to meet people from all over who come to stay at our B&B."

"I'm sure the people enjoy getting to know you, as well." Mandy held her hands loosely behind her back.

"I hope so. We do all we can to make our guests feel welcome."

The roar of a vehicle interrupted their conversation. An SUV with camouflage paint pulled into the parking area for guests. Mandy picked some grass off her bare foot, then stood at the same time as Ellen.

A few minutes later, a young man got out, carrying three egg cartons. Her mouth fell open. It was the same young man she'd met at Spouting Horn and seen again on Sunday at church.

Luana waved him over. "Aloha, Ken. I'd like you to meet Mandy and Ellen. They'll be staying with us until they're able to purchase tickets on a cruise ship to take them back to the mainland." She gestured to him. "Girls, this is Ken Williams. He and his family live nearby. They own an organic chicken farm, and they supply all the eggs and chicken meat we need."

"We've met before, haven't we?" Ken looked at Mandy and tipped his head. "I talked to you at Spouting Horn last week."

Mandy nodded, feeling unexplainably shy.

Ellen remained quiet.

"I didn't recognize you when I first got out of my rig, because when we met before, you wore an Amish dress."

Mandy's cheeks burned as she stared at her flower-print Hawaiian dress. "My friend and I were late getting back to the ship, and it left without us. So with our luggage still on board in the cabin we shared with two other friends, it left us with only the clothes we were wearing."

"I took Mandy and Ellen shopping, and bought them both nice muumuus," Luana interjected.

"I see." Ken shuffled his feet a few times then handed Luana the eggs. "These are for you. When you need more, let me know."

"*Mahalo*, Ken." She smiled. "I'd better take these into the house and get them put in the refrigerator."

"Would you like me to do it for you?" Ellen offered.

"No, it's okay. I also want to check on Makaio. He's doing some work on the other side of the house." Luana gave Ken's shoulder a tap. "If you're still here when I get back, you're invited to sit on the lanai with us for some coconut cake and iced coffee."

He pulled his fingers through his thick, tousled hair and grinned. "I may take you up on that offer. Can't stay too long, though. I still have several more cartons of eggs to deliver."

When Luana headed into the house, Mandy stood with her hands clasped behind her back. It felt awkward not to say anything, so she asked if Ken would like to take a seat in one of the lawn chairs under the shade of a tree.

"Sure. It'll give us a chance to get better acquainted," Ken replied.

Once they were all seated, Mandy glanced over at Ellen, hoping she would start a conversation, but she sat quietly, with a placid expression.

Mandy cleared her throat. "I—I saw you at church yesterday. You were on the platform, playing a ukulele."

"Yeah; I'm part of the worship team." Ken took his cell phone from his shorts' pocket and glanced at it, then put it back.

"Makaio plays the ukulele too," she added. "I'm surprised he's not on the worship team."

"He used to be, but he wanted some time off for a while." Ken kept his gaze on Mandy so long it made her ears heat up.

He probably thinks I look strange wearing a Hawaiian dress, even though my normal head covering's been replaced with the scarf Luana gave us.

Just then, Luana dashed around the side of the house with a panicked expression. "Help! Help! Makaio fell off the roof!"

Chapter 12

Luana paced the hospital waiting room, praying for patience. Her twenty-four-year-old daughter, Ailani, who was five months pregnant, sat in one of the chairs, picking at her cuticles—a nervous habit from her teen years.

Luana glanced at Ken, thankful he'd let Ailani know what had happened to her father. When the ambulance came and transported Makaio to the hospital, Luana rode along. Ailani's husband, Oke, was still at work, but he should be here soon.

"Tell me again, Mama." Ailani pursed her lips. "How did Papa fall off the roof?"

Luana stopped pacing and sat beside her daughter. "I'm not sure, but he was holding a Frisbee when he fell, so I assume he must have gone up there to get it." She glanced toward the nurses' station, wishing someone would come and tell them the extent of Makaio's injuries.

"I'm sure we'll hear something soon." Ken reached over and clasped Luana's arm. He always seemed to know what to say and had become almost like a son to Luana and Makaio. She hoped his parents appreciated the fine young man he'd turned out to be—always willing to help others, tender-hearted, hard-working, and a Christian in every sense of the word. *I hope the Lord sends Ken the right woman someday—someone who will make him as happy as he makes others.*

Luana's contemplations were halted when a doctor came into the room. "Mrs. Palu?" He moved toward her.

She nodded, rising from her chair.

"Your husband's leg is badly broken. He also has a slight concussion and numerous bumps and bruises. His leg will require surgery as well as a full cast, which he will need to wear for six to eight weeks. When Makaio is released from the hospital in a few days, he'll need to use crutches and not put any weight on his foot until X-rays show it's healed enough for him to walk on it."

Luana's shoulders drooped as she stared at the doctor in disbelief. If her husband couldn't be on his feet, how would he be able to help out at the B&B? And because she would need to care for him, she wouldn't have time to do everything necessary for hosting their guests. Ailani could help some, but she'd been quite sick to her stomach with her pregnancy and often didn't feel up to working, even part-time. The idea of hiring help flitted through Luana's mind, but with hospital bills to pay now, money would be tight.

"When can I see my husband?" she asked the doctor.

"You can go in now, before we prep him for surgery." The doctor turned and went out the door.

Luana rose from her chair. "Ailani, would you like to go in with me?"

Her daughter's brown eyes swam with tears. "Yes, Mama. I want Papa to know I'll be praying for him."

Luana looked at Ken. "Would you mind going back to the B&B to let Mandy and Ellen know how Makaio is doing and that I'll be here at the hospital for the next several hours? I need to stay until he's out of surgery and settled into his room. So it could be late before I get home."

Nodding, Ken rose from his seat and gave her a hug. "I understand your concern, but try to keep the faith. I'll be praying for Makaio, and you, as well."

Her lips quivered. "Mahalo."

As soon as Ken left, a nurse arrived to lead Luana and Ailani down the hall to see Makaio. The two women took seats, while another nurse prepared an IV for him.

"How are you feeling?" Luana scooched her chair closer to his bed.

"I'm a little fuzzy but better now than when we first arrived. I'm gonna need to get some fixing done on that leg of mine, though." He frowned, tears seeping from the corners of his eyes. "Sorry I slipped off the roof."

She placed her hand on his. "It was an accident, so don't give it another thought. I'm grateful nothing worse happened to you."

The nurse took Makaio's vitals. "You're in good hands, Mr. Palu. The surgeon will do his best to see that your leg heals as it should."

The nurses moved in and out for a while, but then the family sat together with no interruptions. He was scheduled for surgery as soon as the patient ahead of him came out. Luana would be glad when it was over.

After a while, another nurse came in and announced it was time to wheel Makaio into surgery. Luana and Ailani said their goodbyes and walked back to the waiting room with one of the nurses.

"We'll call you back when he's in recovery." The nurse motioned to a table with hot beverages. "There's coffee and hot water for tea, so feel free to help yourselves."

"I don't like waiting and wondering." With a watery gaze, Ailani ran trembling fingers through her shiny, black, shoulder-length hair. "It's hard not to worry about Papa."

"We need to pray and ask God to guide the surgeon's hands." Luana closed her eyes. *Lord, please help the doctor repair the damage done to Makaio's leg. I'm thanking You in advance.*

Kapaa

Mandy glanced out the living-room window and frowned. It seemed like she and Ellen had been waiting for hours to hear from Luana. They didn't know how badly Makaio was hurt or why he'd been on the roof. "Sure wish Luana would call," she murmured, turning away from the window. "It's hard to wait. I feel like we should be doing something, but I'm not sure what."

"We have no choice except to wait." Ellen handed Mandy a glass of guava juice. "It's a *schee daag*. Why don't we go out on the lanai and enjoy it?"

It was a pretty day, but Mandy wasn't sure she could enjoy it. At least, not until she knew how Makaio was doing. She took the offered glass and sipped a little juice. "I guess we can go outside, but we need to keep the door open in case the phone rings."

"The lanai is screened in," Ellen reminded, "so we won't be in the yard and should be able to hear the telephone."

"Okay." Mandy followed her friend to the enclosed porch and took a seat in one of the wicker rocking chairs. The simple motion of moving back and forth helped her relax.

Ellen sat motionless in her chair. "I wonder what Sadie and Barbara are doing right now. I sure miss them." She looked out toward the yard, where palm leaves swayed in the breeze.

"They are probably on the ship somewhere, eating ice cream, reading a book, or lounging by the pool. I'll bet they're both getting quite tan by now."

Ellen snickered, pointing at Mandy. "Have you looked in the mirror lately? Your face and arms are much darker than when we left Los Angeles eleven days ago."

Despite her apprehension over Makaio, Mandy squeezed her eyes together and laughed. "You're right. We've both gotten some color." She drank the rest of her juice and set the empty glass on the table between them.

Glancing into the yard, Mandy spotted a colorful bird. It looked like one of the cardinals they had back home, but this one had a red head, and the feathers on its body were gray and white. She stepped off the lanai for a better look, but the bird flew over her head and into a tree.

"What if Luana's not back in time for supper?" Ellen asked when Mandy joined her again. "Do you think she would mind if we fix ourselves something to eat?"

"I'm sure she wouldn't. She told us to help ourselves to anything we needed the day after we arrived here." Mandy wiped some moisture from her face. "It's warm out here. Maybe we should go back inside and turn on the air conditioner."

"We don't have air-conditioning at home, but we all manage during the warm summer months."

"True. Since it's been made available to us, we may as well make use of it, though." Mandy rocked in her chair.

Ellen's brows pulled in. "Now don't get too reliant on modern things. We won't have them available to us forever."

Before Mandy could respond, she noticed Ken's SUV pull into the yard. She leaped out of her chair, flung the screen door open, and ran out to greet him. "Do you have any news on Makaio?"

"Yes, I do. Just came from the hospital." Ken gestured to the porch, where Ellen still sat. "Let's take a seat, and I'll bring you up to speed."

Mandy led the way, and when they were both seated, Ken gave them the details on Makaio's injuries.

"Oh my!" Mandy touched her lips. "That poor man. I can't imagine how badly he must hurt."

"I'm sure they've given him something for the pain, and when he's in surgery, he'll be completely out." Ken's forehead wrinkled a bit. "Luana's worried about him, and so is their daughter."

"She mentioned Ailani, but we haven't met her," Ellen spoke up.

"I'm not surprised. She's expecting her first baby and has been having a tough time with nausea and swollen feet." Ken waved his hands in front of his face. "Sure turned out to be a warm day—even hotter than what was forecasted."

"Would you like a glass of juice?" Mandy offered. "Or we could go inside where it's cooler."

"Some juice would be great."

Ellen stood, pulling her hands down the sides of her dress. "I'll get it. Would you like another glass, Mandy?"

"Jah, danki."

After Ellen went inside, Ken turned to Mandy. "Were you speaking German to her?"

"I said, 'Yes, thank you.' It's a form of German. We call it Pennsylvania Dutch. Some also refer to our everyday language as German Dutch."

He leaned forward, resting his elbows on his knees. "Interesting. Would you teach me some Amish words?"

"I'd be happy to. Is there anything specific you'd like to know?"

"In a minute. I need to do something first." Ken sat up straight and pulled a handkerchief from his back pocket. "Looks like one of our birds left its mark on the shoulder of your dress." He wiped off the mess.

"Oh no." Embarrassed, Mandy touched her hot cheeks. "I was in the yard, admiring a colorful bird before you got here."

Ken gently rubbed the area, while Mandy sat, stiff as a board. "Don't worry. Think I got most of it off. You might want to spray the area with a spot cleaner, though, so it doesn't leave a permanent stain."

"Thank you, Ken. I appreciate it." Mandy spoke quietly.

"Okay now. How do you say the word *pretty*?" He stuffed the hankie back in his pocket.

"Oh, that's right. You wanted to learn some Amish words." Mandy felt so flustered, she'd almost forgotten. "That's an easy one. It's *schee*."

He smiled. "You look schee in that muumuu you're wearing."

Mandy felt warmth start up the back of her neck, spreading promptly to her face, adding even more heat. She wasn't used to anyone other than Gideon saying she was pretty. Clearing her throat, she quickly changed the subject. "How long will Makaio be in the hospital?"

Ken shrugged. "I'm not sure. Probably a few days. When he gets home, he'll have to take it easy for several weeks. The doctor doesn't want him to put any weight on his leg until it's healed well enough."

"I wonder how Luana will manage without his help." She wiped at the moisture on her forehead.

Ken leaned farther back in his chair. "I don't know, but I'm sure the Lord will provide what they need."

Ellen returned to the lanai with three glasses of juice on a tray. She'd no more than placed it on the small wicker table when another vehicle pulled in. A few minutes later, a middle-aged man and woman got out.

"Looks like you may have some guests. Was Luana expecting anyone to check in this afternoon?" Ken's question was directed at Mandy.

"She didn't say." Mandy swallowed hard. With Luana not here, she had no idea what to do. Running a bed-and-breakfast was different from waitressing. But apparently Ellen knew how to handle the situation, for she left the lanai and walked out to the couple. A few minutes later, she led them inside.

Mandy went over to assist her friend in welcoming the guests. *It's a good thing we're here,* she thought. *With Makaio unable to put any weight on his leg, Luana's going to need our help for a while.*

Chapter 13

After Ellen explained the situation to the guests who'd arrived, she picked up the guest book and asked them to sign it. In the meantime, she found their name in Luana's book, which also told what room the couple would be staying in. This wasn't much different than the routine of the B&B where she worked back home.

"We're sorry to hear Makaio's been hurt," said the woman, who identified herself as Sharon McIntire. "My husband and I stayed here last year and enjoyed getting to know him and his lovely wife." Her sincere expression revealed the depth of her concern. "If there's anything we can do, please let us know."

Ellen almost replied, "Danki," but answered instead, "Thank you. It's kind of you to offer."

"You must be new here." The man, who introduced himself as Carl, spoke up. "How long have you been working at the bed-and-breakfast?"

"I don't officially work here. My friend and I are filling in for the owners today." Ellen went on to explain how they'd missed the cruise ship and were staying here for the time being. "Luana and Makaio have been so kind to us. It's the least we can do to help them out."

They visited awhile longer, and then Ellen showed them to the Bird of Paradise Room. After leaving the couple alone to get settled in, she returned to the lanai.

Strange. I wonder where Mandy and Ken are. When Ellen peeked outside and saw Ken's vehicle, she knew he hadn't left. Opening the screen door and stepping into the yard, she spotted them crouched on the ground beside Luana's bountiful garden. They seemed to be deep in conversation, so she turned and went back into the house. Ellen couldn't help wondering how two people who barely knew each other could find much of anything to talk about.

"I can't get over all this garden produce." Mandy pointed to a head of butter lettuce. "It's November. Back home, our gardens are done for the year. We don't start planting again till spring."

"Do you enjoy gardening?" Ken tipped his head.

She nodded enthusiastically. "I like all the fresh produce we get in the summer, but it would be even nicer if we could grow it all year."

"It's one of the reasons I like living on this island so much." He fingered a cucumber. "Know what I wish?"

"What?"

"Wish I had my own organic produce business. I'd even like to try growing some things hydroponically." Ken let go of the cucumber. "I've never liked working on my folks' chicken farm that much. If my brother, Dan, was willing to take over the farm someday, I'd branch out and start my own business." Ken's eyes took on a faraway look.

"Isn't he interested in your family's business?"

Ken shrugged. "Dan's a surfer and likes to run off to the beach every chance he gets. Course I like to surf too, but not till after my work is done each day. Speaking of the beach, have you had a chance to visit one of our beaches?"

"Not yet. Ellen and I have been busy with other things. But I would like to go when I get the chance." When Mandy rose from the grass, she lost her balance and fell back. "Oh, my legs fell asleep."

"Let me help you." Ken held out his hand. Easily and quickly he stood, pulling Mandy to her feet. "Now about the beach, I'd be happy to take you there on my next day off."

"It would be nice, but we'll have to wait and see how things go with Makaio. Luana may need Ellen's and my help—especially now, having guests at the B&B." Mandy glanced at the house. "Speaking of which, I should go inside and see if Ellen got the new guests settled into their room."

"Okay. I should get going myself. My folks will be anxious for a report. I called them from the hospital before the doctor came in and told us about Makaio's injuries."

"I still can't believe he fell off the roof."

"Accidents happen when we least expect."

Mandy walked with Ken to his vehicle. After saying goodbye, she hurried into the house to find Ellen. *It would be nice to go to the beach. I hope Ellen and I can make it there before it's time to head home.*

On the Cruise Ship

During dinner that evening, the woman who sat at Barbara's left kept bumping her arm every time she reached into her purse to check her cell phone. Barbara tried to be patient, but then the woman picked up Barbara's glass of iced tea and took a drink. "Oops. Sorry about that." She set Barbara's glass down and scooted her chair over a bit.

Barbara managed a smile. She was sure the woman hadn't drunk from her glass on purpose.

Their waiter came by about that time and asked if he could get them anything.

"I'd like another glass of iced tea," Barbara replied.

He nodded. "I'll bring it with your dessert."

The tea and slices of coconut cake arrived a short time later. As she and Sadie enjoyed their dessert, Barbara smacked her lips. "This was another delicious meal. Should we do some laundry when we're done with dessert, or would you rather go to the lounge where the ventriloquist is performing?"

Sadie jiggled her brows playfully. "Now who would choose washing clothes over seeing a young man throw his voice?"

Barbara laughed. They'd seen the ventriloquist once before, but it would be fun to see his performance again. She and Sadie certainly needed a few laughs. Since Ellen and Mandy got left behind on Kauai, their conversations had been much too serious.

"Okay, it's settled." She placed her fork on the empty dessert plate and finished her iced tea. "Let's head up to the lounge and prepare to have our funny bones tickled."

After saying goodbye to the other people at their table, Barbara and Sadie headed for the lounge. Sadie took a deep breath and exhaled. "It's hard to believe we'll be in Mexico tomorrow. Our trip has gone way too fast."

"At least we'll be able to tour a bit before the ship sails back to Los Angeles." Barbara paused. "It'll seem strange, riding home on the train without our friends. We should get Mandy and Ellen's things packed up this evening."

"Jah. The only good thing about them not being here is we have more space to spread out in our cabin."

"I'd prefer having Mandy and Ellen with us right now."

Kapaa

When Luana arrived home from the hospital, she was surprised to see a car parked outside the B&B. She sat in her vehicle a few minutes, trying to recall if any guests were supposed to check in. After the ordeal she'd been through with Makaio, it was hard to make sense of anything. He would be out of commission for weeks—maybe months—making it difficult for them to run the bed-and-breakfast. But if they didn't remain open, it would hurt them financially—especially with hospital bills to pay.

Leaning her forehead against the steering wheel, she shut her eyes and prayed. *Lord, please help us through this difficult time.*

She lifted her head, remembering some repeat guests were scheduled to arrive. A middle-aged couple from Canada.

Luana pulled the visor down, checking in the mirror to see if there was a red mark from pressing her forehead on the wheel. Thankfully, there wasn't. *I need to get inside and check on things. I hope they're not sitting in the living room, waiting for me.*

When Luana entered the house, she found Mandy and Ellen in

the kitchen. Ellen was preparing a pot of tea while Mandy put some macadamia-nut cookies on a serving tray.

"I'm glad you're back. How's your husband doing?" Mandy closed the cookie container.

"Surgery was done on his leg, and when I left the hospital, he was sleeping." Luana put her purse in the closet and leaned against the counter. She glanced toward the hallway leading to the living room. "Are Mr. and Mrs. McIntire here? I saw a car parked outside and remembered they had booked a room and would be arriving sometime today."

"They're here." Ellen placed the teapot on the tray beside the cookies. "I had them fill out the guest book, then made sure they were comfortable in their room." She gestured to the serving tray. "We asked them to join us in the living room for refreshments. I hope you don't mind."

"Not at all." Luana sank into a chair, feeling a wave of relief. "I appreciate you taking over in my absence. I couldn't leave before Makaio was out of surgery and settled into a room. The doctor was pleased with how the surgery went today. My husband will have a long road ahead of him, though." She glanced at her watch. "Ailani should be home by now. Her husband, Oke, came to the hospital to see how Makaio was doing and take his wife home. Oke worries now that Ailani is expecting a baby." Luana rubbed her forehead. "You two haven't had the opportunity to meet them yet. Maybe after Makaio gets home from the hospital, we can have Oke and Ailani here for supper."

"That will be nice. Oh, before I forget, Ken came by earlier," Mandy said. "He told us about Makaio's injuries and that he'll need to stay off his feet for several weeks."

Nodding, Luana forced a smile. "But we'll get through this. The Lord will provide."

Chapter 14

$\mathcal{T}$he following day, Mandy entered the kitchen and found Luana sitting at the table, weeping. With a sinking feeling in the pit of her stomach, she hurried across the room, placing her hands on Luana's trembling shoulders. "Are you okay?"

"I thought I'd committed everything to God when I went to bed last night, but this morning our situation hit me full force." Luana sniffed. "With Makaio laid up and me having to take care of him, I'm not sure how I'll be able to handle things here by myself. Since our daughter is expecting a baby in the spring and has been having some difficulty with her pregnancy, the doctor says she shouldn't be on her feet too much. I won't do anything to jeopardize the health of Ailani or our future grandchild." She wiped her tears with a tissue. "Right now, we can't afford to hire any outside help, either."

Mandy took a seat next to her. "Ellen has experience working at a B&B back home, and we're both pretty good cooks. We could work for our room and board."

Luana sniffed. "I. . .I appreciate the offer, and it would help for the time being, but you'll be going home soon. Based on what the doctor stated about Makaio's condition, we're going to need help here for two or three months."

"We'll stay for as long as we're needed," Mandy blurted. Surely, Ellen wouldn't object. After all, it wouldn't be right to leave Luana and Makaio in the lurch.

Luana blinked. "But what about your families? They may not want you to stay here so long." She wiped at the tears still rolling down her cheeks.

"Once we explain the situation, I'm sure they'll understand." She gave Luana a tender hug.

Luana patted Mandy's back. "God bless you for your generosity. I feel better already."

"You're welcome." Mandy stood. "I'm going to our room to get Ellen now. Then we'll fix breakfast for your guests. After we eat, we'll call our folks and let them know we will be staying here longer."

Ellen was about to put her headscarf on when Mandy entered the room. "We need to talk." She flopped down on the end of the bed.

"What is it?" Ellen asked. "You appear to be *engschtlich.*"

"I'm not anxious, but I am concerned about Luana." Mandy clutched the folds of her muumuu. "When I went to the kitchen, she was crying."

"She's no doubt upset about Makaio."

"Jah, but it's more than that. When Makaio comes home, Luana is worried because the care he will need won't give her enough time to do everything here to keep the bed-and-breakfast running." Mandy paused and moistened her lips with the tip of her tongue. "So I said we would help out in exchange for room and board. I hope you're okay with it."

Ellen slowly nodded. "We can do it for a little while, but remember, we won't be here much longer. As soon as our folks send the money and we can book passage, we'll be going home."

"Makaio won't be able to help Luana for two to three months, so I told her we'd stay as long as we're needed."

Ellen's mouth fell open. "But we can't, Mandy. Why would you commit to such a thing? We both have jobs back home. If we don't get there soon, our employers will find someone else to take our place—assuming they haven't already."

Mandy stared at her hands as she continued to fiddle with her dress. "If my job at the restaurant is gone when I get home, I'll look for something else." She lifted her chin, eyes wide and almost pleading. "You can go if you want to, Ellen, but I'm staying here until Makaio is back on his feet. He and Luana have been good to us, and I won't leave them during their time of need."

Ellen couldn't believe her friend was willing to risk losing her job for people she barely knew. Then again, Mandy had always tried to help anyone with a problem. *It wouldn't be right to leave my best friend here. Besides, staying to help Luana and her husband is the Christian thing to do.*

Ellen pressed her palm to her cheek. "Okay, you're right. I shouldn't have been so hasty."

"You mean you'll stay for as long as we're needed?"

"Jah, but if we're going to be here for an indefinite amount of time, I'd like to find a fabric store and look for a simple dress pattern and some plain material."

Mandy pointed to Ellen's dress. "What's wrong with what you are wearing? We can always buy more Hawaiian clothes, you know."

Ellen shook her head. "I'm not comfortable wearing a muumuu. The print is too bold. If Luana has a sewing machine, I'd feel better making a few plain dresses."

"If she doesn't, maybe the fabric store would let you borrow a sewing machine and make your dresses there."

"Maybe." She blinked. "What about you? Don't you want to make a dress like what we're used to wearing at home?"

Mandy shrugged. "I'm comfortable in the muumuu and don't see the need."

What's gotten into my friend? Has she forgotten her Amish roots? Ellen's muscles tightened.

"Let's go. We need to help Luana fix breakfast." Mandy hurried from the room.

Ellen started to follow but paused at the door, closing her eyes. *Heavenly Father, help Makaio to heal quickly so Mandy and I can go home.*

✦──── ❋ ────✦

Middlebury

Gideon whistled as he headed for the phone shack to call Mandy. He'd gone by her folks' house after work today and finally gotten the number where she and Ellen were staying. It seemed like forever since they'd been together. He could hardly wait to hear her voice. Even more, he couldn't wait for Mandy to come home.

When Gideon stepped into the small, chilly building, he took a seat on the wooden stool and quickly made the call. A woman's voice came on a few seconds later. "The Palms Bed-and-Breakfast."

"Is Mandy Frey there?" he asked.

"Gideon, is that you?"

"Sure is. Who am I speaking to?"

"It's Ellen. Mandy's upstairs, making one of the guest beds. Hang on. I'll get her."

Gideon doodled on the notepad next to the phone while he waited. It seemed strange Mandy would be making a guest bed. *Maybe Ellen meant she's making the bed she slept in last night. But if that's so, shouldn't the hired help do it?*

Finally, Mandy came on the phone. "Hello, Gideon. How are you?"

"I'm fine. More to the point, how are you? I heard from your daed that you and Ellen missed the boat."

"We did. The ship moved on, which left us stranded." She cleared her throat. "We're thankful to be staying at a bed-and-breakfast with a nice Hawaiian couple who are Christians."

"So how come you didn't call me?" Gideon wrote Mandy's name on the notepad in front of him. "I had to get this number from your mamm."

"Things have been a bit hectic on our end." She paused. "But it's no excuse. I'm sorry, Gideon. I should have called you."

He leaned his head against his hand, releasing a soft breath. "It's fine. I'm relieved to hear your voice." Gideon's face felt uncomfortably warm. He liked hearing the sound of her voice, even if it wasn't as clear over the phone. "When are you coming home, Mandy?"

"Not for a while."

"I'd be happy to pay part of your passage."

"It's nice of you, Gideon, but we can't go anywhere right now."

"Why not?"

"The man who owns the B&B fell off the roof and broke his leg, which means he won't be able to help his wife manage the place. So Ellen and I volunteered to help out until he's back on his feet."

"It was kind of you to offer, but can't they find someone else?" Gideon gripped the receiver. This phone call was not going well at all.

"We're working for room and board, because they can't afford to hire anyone right now. Sorry, Gideon, but I need to go. Someone is knocking on the back door, and since I'm the only one in the kitchen, I need to answer it."

"Okay. I'll talk to you again soon, Mandy. Take care."

Gideon hung up but remained in the phone shack, rubbing the bridge of his nose as he reflected on their conversation. It was just like sweet Mandy to do a charitable deed, but now he had no idea when she'd be home. How were they supposed to keep their relationship going when she was thousands of miles away?

Kapaa

Ken pulled his motorbike up to the B&B, anxious to find out how Makaio was doing. When he stepped onto the lanai, where Mandy and Ellen sat snapping green beans, he smiled. "Looks like Luana put you to work. Is she here?"

"No. She got up early this morning and went to the hospital to see Makaio." Mandy motioned to the chair across from them. "You're welcome to sit and visit while we snap beans."

"If you have an extra bowl, I'd be more than happy to help with that." He seated himself near Mandy and began rocking.

"I'll get one." Ellen rose from her seat and returned with a plastic bowl and more beans, which she handed to Ken. "Here you go."

He took the bowl and placed it in his lap. "Thanks, I think." He chuckled then reached into his pocket and pulled out a business card. "On a more serious note, if you two need anything while you're here, don't hesitate to get in touch with me. Here's my phone number in case you need to call."

"Actually, there is something," Ellen said as Mandy took the card. "We'd like to make a trip to a fabric store. Would you be able to give us a ride—maybe later, after Luana gets back?"

"I'd be glad to take you, but I don't have time today. Would tomorrow be soon enough? I'll have the day off."

Mandy nodded. "Of course. We can work it in around your schedule."

"How long do you plan to be here?" Ken asked as he began snapping the beans in half. He didn't work as quickly as she or Ellen, but Mandy figured Ken hadn't had as much practice.

"We'll stay for as long as we're needed," she replied. "I'm sure we won't be working all the time, though, so it will give us a chance to see more of this beautiful island during our free time."

"I'm glad you'll be staying longer." He rocked too far back, and when he let go of the bowl, his hands went for the arms of the chair. The plastic bowl slid off his lap and bounced on the tile floor. "Oh no! I'm sorry." He jumped up and crouched by the rocking chair, grabbing for the beans. Some had even gone under the rocker.

"It's okay." Ellen dropped down beside him and started picking up beans. Once they had them all, she stood and took the bowl inside to wash them.

Ken smiled at Mandy. "Well, that was sure an icebreaker. Now we can get better acquainted. As I mentioned yesterday, I'd like to show you some special places. We can go to the beach, and if you like flowers, there are some really nice tropical gardens."

"I would enjoy either of those places. This island feels like paradise to me." Mandy stretched her arms out wide. "I wish there was an Amish community on Kauai. I could get used to living here."

Chapter 15

The following day while Ellen walked through the fabric store to look at material and patterns, Mandy stood near the front door with Ken. "It was nice of you to take time out to bring us here. I'm sure you had other things to do on your day off."

"I can't think of anything I'd rather be doing than helping two friends." Grinning, he winked at Mandy. "One of these days, I'll take you and Ellen for a tour of our farm and to meet my folks. Oh, just a second. My phone is buzzing." Ken pulled it out of his pocket. "Yep. My friend Taavi is trying to call me." He stepped aside. "Hey, buddy. What's up? That sounds like fun, but I'm in the middle of something right now. I'll call ya back later." He hung up and moved closer to Mandy again. "Sorry for the interruption. Taavi's one of my friends. He's a good surfer and was letting me know there's gonna be some prime wave action today. But I'd rather be here right now, getting to know you better."

Mandy felt the heat of a blush spread like fire across her cheeks. It was nice Ken wanted to know her better. Even though she'd known him less than a week, Mandy felt as though they were kindred spirits. *Maybe it's because he likes gardening and enjoys the beauty of God's creation,* she told herself. Of course, Gideon appreciated many things God created, but he had no interest in flowers, trees, or vegetable gardens. Whenever they were together, he talked more about his horse than anything. She shifted her purse to the other shoulder. *I shouldn't be comparing the two men.*

"Aren't you going to browse through the material?" Ken asked, pulling out a pack of gum.

"No, I'm not planning to make a dress." Mandy looked down at the green muumuu she'd bought with her own money yesterday. "I have two Hawaiian dresses now, and they work fine for me. I only came to the fabric store in case Ellen needs my opinion on anything."

Ken stared at her strangely, but made no comment. Several seconds passed before he spoke again. "Would you like a piece of gum?"

"No, thank you."

"Who's keeping an eye on the B&B this morning?"

"Ailani is there, but only to answer the phone. She won't be doing any physical work."

"Good to hear. What about Luana? Is she at the hospital with Makaio?"

"Yes. She left soon after we served our B&B guests their breakfast."

With wrinkled brows, Ken folded his arms and leaned against the wall. "Sure hope he won't have to be in the hospital too long. It will be better for Makaio and Luana once he's home. He'll be more comfortable in his own surroundings, and she won't have to run back and forth to the hospital."

Mandy shifted her weight to the other foot. "When my younger brother, Milo, got hit in the head with a baseball last year, he had a pretty severe concussion. Our folks had to hire a driver to take them to and from the hospital every day for a week."

"Is your brother okay now?"

"He's doing fine. No repercussions from the accident, and I'm grateful."

"Accidents happen so quickly." Ken sighed. "One minute, everything is fine, and the next minute something unexpected occurs. A person can become severely injured. I like to surf, and it can be dangerous too."

Mandy winced, fiddling with the straps on her purse. *Why would anyone choose to take part in a dangerous sport?*

"You need to know how to swim if you're gonna surf—or at least know how to tread water real well. It helps going to a beach that's patrolled by lifeguards. That's a stipulation my parents drummed into my brother and me." His mouth twisted grimly. "Another thing is watching out for other surfers in the water and trying not to get hit by someone or even by your own board. I've seen it happen many times."

"Surfing sounds exciting but also frightening."

Ken shifted his gaze away from her a few seconds, then looked back, clasping his chin with his fingers. "It can be, but the fun outweighs my fears." He took a step closer. "Say, I have a question."

"What is it?"

"I thought Amish people traveled by horse and buggy."

"We do." Mandy rested her hand on her hip. "Why do you ask?"

"When your brother got hurt, how come your parents hired a driver to take them to the hospital?"

"We usually only take the horse and buggies ten miles or so from our home. Farther away, and especially into the bigger cities, means we need to hire a driver."

"Interesting." He rubbed his chin.

She grew quiet as their conversation came to a lull. Ken kept looking at Mandy though, causing her face to warm. It was almost as though nothing existed except the two of them standing by the door. Even the sounds inside the store seemed to cease. Her throat constricted. For some reason, she couldn't look away.

It appeared as if Ken might be about to say something, but Ellen walked toward them with a bolt of beige material. "I found the color I want, but I need your opinion on a pattern."

"Okay." Mandy wiped moisture from her face.

"Think I'll wait outside in my rig while you two finish shopping." Ken looked toward the parking lot. "Take your time, though. I'm in no rush."

Mandy glanced over her shoulder, watching Ken go out the door. *He's such a nice person. I only wish. . .* She turned and followed Ellen to the back of the store, refusing to let her thoughts get carried away. *It must be the heat,* Mandy told herself. *I'm not thinking clearly today.*

"This is a nice enough hospital, but I'm anxious to go home." Luana's husband frowned. "I'll sleep a lot better in our own bed too."

"It shouldn't be too much longer." Luana placed her hand on Makaio's arm. "You ought to enjoy all the attention you're getting here while you can, and don't forget all the good food they've been feeding you."

"Your cooking is much better than hospital food. Guess I shouldn't complain though. I'm happy to be alive." Makaio closed his eyes a few seconds, before opening them again. "How are we going to manage the B&B with me unable to walk right now?" He winced as he gripped the bedsheets and tried to sit up. "We're starting into our busiest time of the year. You'll need my help more than ever."

"What's done is done, so there's no need to fret." Luana asked him to lean forward a bit and plumped up his pillows. Then she took a seat in the chair beside his bed and reached out to clasp his hand. "I have some good news."

"Please share it with me. I've had enough negative news since I fell off the roof."

"Mandy and Ellen have agreed to help out in exchange for their room and board." She gave his fingers a reassuring squeeze. "You need to quit worrying and relax so you can get better. You're not doing yourself any good by getting upset."

"You're right, and the Amish women's help is appreciated, but they won't be here much longer. As soon as they're able to get tickets, they'll be on a ship taking them back to the mainland." He reached for his glass of water and took a drink.

"No they won't. Mandy and Ellen have agreed to stay with us for as long as we need them—until your leg has healed and you can take over your responsibilities again."

"Why would they do it, Luana? They barely know us."

"Because they care and want to help." She smiled. "They're putting their Christianity into practice."

Makaio fell back against the pillow and closed his eyes. When he opened them again, Luana saw tears. He looked at her and asked, "Remember, when you believed God sent those young women to us for a reason?"

Her throat constricted, and she could only manage a slow nod.

"I'm certain now that it was so they could help us during our time of need."

Luana squeezed his fingers gently. "You may be right. But whatever the reason, I'm thankful Mandy and Ellen are staying with us."

Ensenada, Mexico

"Do you see the green, white, and red Mexican flag greeting us near the cruise terminal?" Sadie pointed at the huge flag waving in the breeze.

Barbara lifted her hands over her head to stretch her arms. "I could see it for some distance as we approached the harbor."

"I heard someone say Ensenada is a major cruise ship destination and thousands of tourists come here ever year." Sadie reached into her tote and removed her camera. Then she took a picture of the Mexican flag. "First Street is supposed to be another busy spot for tourists, so we ought to check it out."

"I'm glad we're sticking with a tour group today," Barbara commented. "I wouldn't want to be stranded in Mexico. The people speak a language we don't understand. It could be a little frightening."

"That wouldn't be a problem. Our tour guide mentioned most of the people who live here—especially those selling their wares—understand English."

"Even so, I'd be umgerrent if the ship left us behind, like what happened to Mandy and Ellen."

Sadie nodded. "You're right, so we shouldn't venture too far on our own today."

"I'm going to call Mandy when we get back to the ship and see how she and Ellen are doing," Barbara said as they began walking up Avenida Lopez Mateos, the main tourist street of Ensenada, lined with paved, red brick sidewalks. "I'll bet they're as eager to get home as we are."

"Jah, but unfortunately their luggage will reach their homes before they ever do."

"That's right. We're in charge of extra suitcases." Barbara's lips compressed. "Seeing that they make it off the ship and then onto the train could be a challenge, since we'll have our luggage to deal with as well."

"I'm sure we can manage." Sadie pointed to a store up ahead. "Let's go in there and see what souvenirs we can find." They paused to look at some colorful Mexican blankets and sombreros. "If nothing else, I'd like to buy a few postcards and maybe a handmade basket. After we finish shopping, I want to try one of those fish tacos I've heard others on the ship talking about."

Barbara's nose itched, so she paused to rub it with her finger. She hoped she wasn't allergic to something in the air. "I'll pass. Don't think I'd enjoy eating fish in a soft-rolled taco shell. I may try a regular ground beef taco if we can find any."

"I'm sure they're available." Sadie's next step caused her to stumble on the slippery brick. Suddenly, she was flat on her back.

Chapter 16

Albuquerque, New Mexico

*H*ow nice it is to finally be heading home." Sadie shifted in her seat, trying to find a comfortable position. "I only wish we could get there sooner." Normally, the *clickety-clack* of the train's wheels against the tracks would lull her to sleep, but not today. They'd only been riding the train since yesterday, and already she was tired of sitting. Her biggest problem was her bruised tailbone from the fall she'd taken in Ensenada. Fortunately, the only thing that had been seriously hurt was her pride. If she'd broken a bone, she may have ended up in the hospital and missed the ship when it left Mexico. Then she'd have been in the same predicament as her friends who were stuck on Kauai.

"Are you doing okay?" Barbara's anxious expression showed the extent of her concern. "You took a pretty hard fall on that brick sidewalk the other day. You must still be quite sore."

"I am, but I can deal with the pain. I'm having a hard time sitting, though."

"Should we go up to the café car and get a snack to eat? It might do you some good to walk awhile."

"Maybe in a little bit. Right now I'm trying to enjoy the scenery, even though my body is screaming to get up." Sadie pointed out the window. "I'm watching for some wildlife, like we saw on the train as we were heading to California near the beginning of our trip."

"We did see a lot of deer, as well as some turkeys, antelope, and coyote. I hope we spot some elk this time." Barbara leaned against the window and released a sigh. "I wonder what Mandy and Ellen are doing right now. Sure wish I could have talked to Mandy longer the other evening, but she said they were busy so she couldn't talk long. I'm still surprised they'll be staying longer than planned. I wonder how their families are dealing with this."

Kapaa

Ellen and Mandy had been working hard, keeping things at the B&B well organized and running smoothly. Makaio had come home from the hospital, but since he couldn't be on his feet, he'd been watching a lot of TV. It bothered Ellen because she wasn't used to having a television in the house, much less dealing with the blaring noise. Luana kept after Makaio to keep the volume down—especially when they had B&B guests. But the sound crept up as soon as she left the room, like it had this afternoon.

Ellen peeked into the living room and saw Makaio sleeping with the remote in his hands. She wouldn't dare take it from him, as she'd seen Luana do last night when Makaio fell asleep in his chair. He wasn't too thrilled when his wife woke him, either, and Ellen didn't want to upset him.

Since all their guests had gone out for the day and wouldn't be bothered by the noise, Ellen closed the living-room door and went to the kitchen, where Luana was showing Mandy how to make Hawaiian teriyaki burgers.

"Yum. It smells good in here." Ellen moved close to the counter, watching as Luana mixed soy sauce, sesame oil, ginger, and several other ingredients into the ground beef.

Luana looked at Ellen and smiled. "My husband loves this kind of burger."

"Speaking of Makaio, he's asleep right now."

"With the TV on, no doubt."

Ellen nodded, and Mandy, who stood nearby, winked at her.

"I'm not surprised." Luana lifted her gaze to the ceiling, while making a little clucking sound. "Normally he doesn't watch much TV. But now he has nothing else to do but sit, and I fear he will become addicted to it."

Mandy leaned toward the bowl and sniffed. "If these burgers taste half as good as they smell, then I may end up with an addiction."

They sat down to eat lunch a short time later and enjoyed pleasant conversation during the meal. Luana seemed a bit more relaxed since Makaio was now home. She even told them about some silly things he'd done years ago. "My husband can be a character at times." Luana laughed.

They had no sooner finished the meal than Ken showed up. Grinning from ear to ear, he asked if Mandy and Ellen would like to go watch the surfers with him.

"I would," Mandy responded with an eager expression. "It sounds like fun."

"How about you, Ellen?" Ken asked.

"Actually, if Luana doesn't need me for anything, I'd planned to get started on making my new dress this afternoon."

"You girls have been busy here all morning," Luana said, "so you deserve some time off to do your own thing."

"Why don't you and Ken go without me?" Ellen suggested.

Mandy's forehead wrinkled. "Are you sure?"

Ellen nodded.

"Okay then. Give me a few seconds while I get some things from my room to take along." Mandy hurried off but returned promptly with her sunglasses and a bottle of sunscreen.

"Why don't you put your things in here?" Luana handed Mandy a colorful tote decorated with palm trees.

"Thanks." Mandy and Ken said their goodbyes and headed out the door.

Ellen turned to Luana. "Would you mind if I use your dining-room table to cut out my dress pattern?"

"Not at all. While you're working on the pattern, I'll get Makaio some coffee and a burger. I looked in on him a while ago, and he's awake now."

On the way to the beach, Mandy and Ken pulled into the drive-through at a fast-food place, ordered drinks and some Maui onion chips, and then continued on their way. It was fun riding in Ken's camouflaged SUV.

As they approached the beach, Mandy's heart raced with excitement. Frothing white waves rolled in over the aqua-blue ocean, which in places appeared to be a beautiful turquoise. Being on an island, where the water could be seen from most places, was truly amazing.

Ken parked the car and shut off the engine. "Are you ready to watch some action?"

"Oh yes! I'm sure it will be exciting." Mandy hopped out and grabbed the floral-print tote she'd borrowed from Luana, while Ken took out a blanket and their snacks.

As they walked toward the water, Mandy's sandals sank into the soft sand, and she noticed the pretty golden color.

Ken pulled off his flip-flops. "Ah, now this feels more like it." He picked them up and pointed at Mandy's feet. "How 'bout you?"

Smiling, she did the same. The sand felt warm as the grains sifted between her toes. "I couldn't agree more."

"Let's pick a spot to sit and relax. My buddy, Taavi, is out there right now in the blue." Ken pointed to one of the surfers.

They walked farther down the beach to get a better view of the ocean. It was difficult for Mandy to walk properly, since her bare feet kept sinking in the sand. She lowered her head. *I probably look foolish, wobbling with every step.*

"How about here? This looks like a good spot for us to sit." Ken spread the blanket on the sand, and they both took a seat.

Watching the action on the water, Mandy was spellbound. Some surfers disappeared in the tube of a wave, then reappeared at the other end. She couldn't imagine how they kept upright on a surfboard, nearly swallowed up by the ocean, and seemed to have no fear.

A young Hawaiian man paddled in toward shore, lying on his stomach on a colorful surfboard. "Hey, how's it going, Ken?" he shouted after stepping out of the water and setting the board down.

"Not bad. The waves are lookin' pretty good today. Come on over! I wanna introduce you to my friend."

Hauling his board up the beach a ways, the young man came over to where they sat.

"Taavi, this is Mandy."

"Hey, it's nice to meet you." He knelt beside Mandy and shook her hand.

"Hi, Taavi. It's nice meeting you too."

"I take it you aren't going out there today?" he asked, looking at Ken.

Ken shook his head.

Taavi snickered. "It's okay. Leaves more waves for me to enjoy."

"Yep. You can have all the waves you want today." Ken looked at Mandy and winked.

They talked for a while, and then Taavi picked up his board and headed back into the surf. He paddled a good distance, and when the wave began, he was up on his feet, moving swiftly along in front of it. The way he sliced through the water, with the ocean's momentum, was incredible.

They continued to watch Taavi and others who were surfing the huge breaks in the water. *I wonder what Ellen is doing right now,* Mandy mused. *She's missing out on everything.*

"A nickel for your thoughts." Ken nudged her arm gently.

"I was thinking how Ellen is missing out on this beautiful beach and the fun going on in the water."

"I never get tired of coming to the beach. Makes me glad I'm living in Hawaii." He reached into his pocket and pulled out a pack of gum. "Would you like a piece?"

Smiling, she took one. "Thank you, and thanks again for paying for the drinks and chips we got at the drive-through."

"You're welcome." He put the gum back in his pocket.

Mandy watched as two surfers rode a wave a little too close to each other. It was one of the largest waves she'd seen so far. Neither guy seemed willing to give up his spot.

"Boy, they're too close!" Ken stood about the time the two guys collided with each other. They both splashed into the water and disappeared in the waves. Unfortunately, one of the surfers was Taavi.

"Sure hope no one got hurt. I'd better go check." Ken raced toward the water.

Mandy's heart pounded. She got up from the blanket, hoping for a better view. Holding her hands tightly against her sides, she prayed, *Lord, please help Ken's friend and the other fellow to be okay.*

Both guys surfaced. The people on shore seemed relieved, as everyone clapped. Taavi and the other surfer paddled to shore on their boards. When the fellow Taavi had collided with came out of the water, it appeared that his nose was bleeding. Ken took a look at him, then Taavi and turned to wave at Mandy.

A few minutes later, Ken ran back to her. "The other guy must have gotten clipped in the nose by his board, but it's not serious."

Relieved, Mandy took her seat again. She was glad no serious injuries had occurred. She directed her gaze toward the water, watching the young guy lying on the sand pinching his nose. Someone handed Taavi some tissues, and he took them over to the injured fellow. Then he headed in their direction.

"A great day for this sport." Taavi grimaced. "As you can see, accidents occur, no matter how much practice one's had."

"Does this happen a lot out here?" Mandy adjusted her scarf, keeping it from slipping off her head.

"It's random. Some people can go a long time and not get hurt. But sometimes it can sneak up on you, like it did for us today."

"Is his nose broken?" she questioned.

"Didn't look like it. He'd know if it was, since he's had it broken before." Taavi plopped down on the sand.

Ken sat on the other side of Mandy, pulled out his cell phone, and brought his knees up to his elbows. "Looks like I missed a call from my mom. Guess I'd better see what she wanted." He hopped up from the blanket and began to pace, kicking the sand a few times while he walked. "Hi, Mom. Yeah, we're still at the beach. Umm. . . I'm not sure when I'll be there."

Mandy tried not to eavesdrop, but it was hard not to hear what Ken was saying, with him only a few feet away.

"How are you liking Hawaii, Mandy?" Taavi asked.

"It's nice. You live on a beautiful island."

"Yeah, it's great. So where ya from?" He combed back his wet hair with his fingers.

"My friend Ellen and I are from Middlebury, Indiana. We're staying with Makaio and Luana Palu and helping out at their B&B until he's back on his feet again."

"Yeah, I heard about his accident. Makaio's a nice guy. Too bad it happened."

Mandy nodded.

"You're a long way from home. It's nice of you to hang around so you can help out. Wouldn't be easy on Luana, tryin' to do everything by herself."

"We're glad to do it, and I'm hoping during our free time we can see a few places on the island."

"Where's your friend today? Didn't she want to come to the beach?"

"Ellen had something she wanted to get done."

"Did I miss much?" Ken plopped down beside Mandy again.

"Not really. Mandy and I have been getting acquainted." Taavi pointed toward the water. "Now would ya look at that? The guy I collided with is already in the water and up on another wave."

They visited awhile longer, until Taavi said goodbye and headed back out to the water with his board.

Ken glanced briefly at Mandy and smiled, before leaning back and resting his elbows behind him.

She returned his smile, and as a gentle breeze blew across her face, she found herself savoring the moment and wishing she could freeze time so she could remain here forever.

Chapter 17

Elkhart, Indiana

On Monday, November 18, as the train pulled into the station, Barbara's heart began to race. They'd only been gone twenty-one days, but it seemed so much longer. "Oh look! It's snowing." She pointed out the window. "Now, that's a pretty homecoming."

Other passengers commented on the snow. Two young boys had their faces pressed against the window, fogging up the glass. One of them drew a smiley face with his finger.

"What a contrast from the blue skies and sunshine we had in Hawaii," Sadie commented. "All the hardwood trees have their winter look—gray and bare of leaves."

"Jah," Barbara agreed. "But the white pines are sure pretty. Their soft green needles, with a light sprinkle of snow, reminds me of the holidays fast approaching."

Sadie grunted, rising from her seat. "It's gonna be hard to get used to cold weather again. In some ways, Mandy and Ellen are lucky they got stranded on Kauai."

"I can't believe you would say such a thing." Barbara stood and reached for her carry-ons. "I'm glad to be here, and I bet they're missing home as much as we were."

"I'm happy to be here too. I only meant I'll miss the nicer weather and our friends get to enjoy it longer than we do." Sadie pulled on her heavy shawl and picked up her tote bags and purse. "For me, it will seem more like the season, especially with Thanksgiving and Christmas around the corner. I can't imagine those holidays without cold temperatures and a bit of snow."

"I suppose you're right," Barbara agreed, pulling her jacket closed at the neck. When they'd left Indiana at the beginning of their trip, it had been chilly, so they'd taken their jackets and sweaters along. But they'd never worn them in Hawaii except on the Big Island when they visited the volcano and a few times on the ship. The colder weather would take some getting used to.

The two boys Barbara had been watching earlier tried to get around Sadie in their eagerness to get off the train. Their mother called out to them, but one of them managed to squeeze past. In the middle of trying to collect all their things, his mother hollered for him to wait. Barbara and Sadie moved aside so the boy's mother and younger brother could join him.

When Barbara stepped off the train, she spotted her parents right away. Sadie's mother and father were there too. Hugs and smiles were given all around, and more than a few tears were shed. Once their suitcases, as well as Mandy's and Ellen's, were taken off the train, they loaded everything into their driver's van.

"It's a shame Mandy and Ellen aren't with you." Barbara's mother wiped at the tears beneath her eyes. "I talked to Mandy's mamm the other day, and she misses her daughter."

Before they climbed into the van to leave for home, Barbara squeezed her mother's hand. "I'm sure they miss their folks too." Snowflakes fell onto her eyelashes, and she had the urge to stick out her tongue to catch a few of the crystals. "It's good to be back. I had a great vacation, but there's no place like home."

Middlebury

I can't believe Barbara and Sadie are getting home today, but Mandy won't be with them. Gideon fretted as he headed down the road with his horse and buggy toward his mother's store. *Maybe calling her and explaining how hard it is to be without her would get Mandy home sooner. I should be at the train station right now, greeting my* aldi, *instead of here, wishing it were so.*

"Wow!" Gideon nearly jumped out of his skin when a car coming up on him tooted its horn. Being deep in thought, he'd allowed his horse to drift over into the other lane. He redirected the animal to the right side of the road.

After the car drove by, Gideon leaned back in his seat and tried to relax. But the knowledge of Mandy still being in Hawaii stuck in his craw.

"I need to quit stewing about this," Gideon mumbled. *Complaining and rehashing won't bring Mandy back any sooner. I shouldn't be thinking so much when I'm driving my horse and buggy, either. If I'm not careful, I could end up in the hospital, seriously injured.*

The roads were still bare, even though it had started snowing. He felt safe giving his horse the freedom to trot and was soon pulling up to the hitching rail at the quilt-and-fabric store.

When Gideon entered the building, he found his mother behind the counter cutting material for Ellen's mother, Nora. He figured she probably missed her daughter and wished she had arrived home today too. Gideon wanted to say something but decided it might be best to keep quiet. No point pouring vinegar on the wound. Nora wouldn't want to be reminded of her daughter's situation any more than he did Mandy's.

"I'm heading to the back room to unload those boxes you mentioned would be coming in today," he announced when Mom glanced at him.

She smiled and gave a quick nod, then kept right on cutting.

Gideon hurried to the back of the store, nearly bumping his elbow on one of the shelves. As he stepped into the storage room, he spotted four large boxes filled with bolts of material. With Barbara gone almost a month, and Mom being shorthanded, Gideon often came by the store after he got off work to help out. Mom had mentioned hiring someone during Barbara's absence but in the end decided to try and get by. If Gideon hadn't been helping a few hours each day, Mom may have changed her mind.

Focused on the task at hand, he opened the first box and pulled out several bolts of material, all in different shades of green. After placing them vertically on the proper shelf, he went back and got some more. Soon every box was empty, so he headed up front to see what else Mom wanted him to do. As he approached the counter, the front door opened, and Barbara stepped in.

"Wie gehts?" he asked, surprised to see her. He hadn't expected she'd be at the store so soon. "How was your trip?"

Barbara's blue eyes twinkled like fireflies dancing on a sultry summer night. "It was amazing! I can't begin to describe the beauty of Hawaii."

"Welcome back." Mom stepped around the counter and gave Barbara a hug. "Was it hard to leave the warm weather and return home to snow?"

"A little." Deep dimples formed in Barbara's cheeks when she smiled. "I did enjoy my vacation but missed my family, so I was ready to come home." Her shoulders drooped a bit. "I'm only sorry Ellen and Mandy couldn't be with Sadie and me today. It was exciting to have our parents waiting for us at the train station this morning."

Gideon's jaw clenched. *Mandy should have been with you, and I ought to have been there waiting to greet her.* He was giving in to self-pity again but couldn't seem to help himself.

Mom gave Barbara's shoulder a pat. "I missed you. Not only for your help here at the store, but for the enjoyment we have when we visit during slow times."

"I agree." Barbara glanced at Gideon, then quickly back at his mother. "Is my job still waiting for me, or have I been replaced?"

Mom shook her head. "You're too good of a worker to be replaced."

"Can I start back tomorrow, or would you rather I wait till Monday?"

"If you're up to it, tomorrow would be fine." Mom looked at Gideon. "Did you get all those bolts of material put out?" Shifting her weight, she rested her hand on the counter.

"Jah. Came up to see what else you might want me to do."

She reached under her glasses and rubbed the bridge of her nose. "Let's see. I suppose you could stay behind the counter while I take a much-needed break."

"I don't mind, as long as no one comes in needing material cut."

Gideon's forehead wrinkled. "I wouldn't be any good at that."

Barbara chuckled. "For goodness' sake, you work with upholstery all day. I would think you'd be an expert at cutting material."

"Nope. I don't do the cutting. That's Aaron's job. I take care of doing the books and waiting on customers, 'cause I'm the one good with numbers."

Mom tapped her foot, the way she did when her patience grew thin. "I'll tell you what, Son, if someone comes in needing material cut, you can come get me."

"Okay." Gideon waited for his mother to head to the back room, then he stepped behind the counter in her place.

"Would you like me to stay until she comes back?" Barbara offered. "If a customer comes in and wants some material cut, I'll do it for you."

"Are ya sure? I mean. . ."

She held up her hand. "I'm more than happy to do it."

"Danki." Gideon grinned. *Barbara's sure nice. No wonder she and Mandy are friends.*

Kapaa

As Mandy checked each of the rooms in the B&B, making sure they were prepared for the next guests' arrival, she thought about similarities between the Amish and Hawaiian people, such as their family values and desire to live a simpler life. She was also fascinated with Luana's beautiful quilts, displayed throughout the bed-and-breakfast. Every guest room had a different quilt on the bed and a lovely wall hanging. The Hawaiian quilt patterns were different from Amish quilts, but similar in some ways.

She leaned over and touched the pretty green-and-white quilt on the king-sized bed in the Bird of Paradise Room. Like most Amish quilts, the tiny hand-stitches were evenly spaced and barely visible. Once again, she found herself wishing she could take one of these magnificent quilts home.

Maybe Luana would like to have an Amish quilt, Mandy thought. *I could ask Gideon's mother to make one for her when I get home. In exchange, perhaps Luana would part with one of her quilts or even a quilted wall hanging.* She shook her head. *No, I shouldn't expect too much. Most likely, each of the quilts here at the B&B are special to Luana. It wouldn't be right to ask her to part with any of them.*

Pushing her thoughts aside, Mandy left the room and shut the door. Luana's daughter and son-in-law would be coming for dinner soon, and she needed to help Luana and Ellen in the kitchen.

That evening, everyone sat around the dinner table, enjoying the chicken chowder and haystack Mandy and Ellen had prepared for them. The delicious aromas reminded Mandy of home. *I wonder what Gideon's doing right now.* Chicken chowder was one of his favorite soups. Mandy had fixed it for him several times since they'd begun courting. *I should make the soup again when I get home and invite him over for a meal.* She placed her napkin in her lap and bowed her head for silent prayer.

"This chowder is good." Ailani and her husband, Oke, spoke at the same time.

"We're glad you like it." Mandy looked at her friend and smiled. When they'd been putting the chowder together this afternoon, she'd told Ellen she was sure everyone would enjoy it. Since it was a traditional Pennsylvania Dutch recipe, Ellen wasn't sure the Hawaiian family would like it as much as they did.

Makaio, who had insisted he hobble to the table on his crutches unassisted, was gulping down his second bowl. "This is different from what I'm used to, but I have to say, it's sure good."

"Don't eat too much," Mandy teased. "There's still a Dutch apple pie coming for dessert."

"Yes, and Makaio, where are your table manners?" Luana scolded, shaking her finger. "You sound like a puppy lapping milk."

Everyone laughed, including Makaio. "Sorry. The soup is so tasty, I couldn't help it. Bet the pie you made will also be good." He looked at Luana and grinned before taking another bite.

"You two young women are spoiling us with your good cooking. I won't know what to do when you leave—except maybe put my husband on a diet." Luana laughed, then reached over and touched Mandy's arm. "I can't begin to tell you how much I appreciate you both being here and helping out."

Mandy sighed. As much as she wanted Makaio's leg to get well, she was in no hurry to leave Kauai. She wondered if God had a special reason for allowing them to become stranded on this island.

Chapter 18

Middlebury

"I don't know what to do anymore," Gideon mumbled, clutching his shirt to his heart. "I feel like I'm losing her." He left the phone shack and headed up to the house. It was the second day of December, and Barbara and Sadie had been back two weeks, but in all those days, he'd only talked to Mandy once. Each time he called, she was either busy doing something at the bed-and-breakfast or had gone someplace. He'd finally gotten ahold of her, but it hadn't gone well. Mandy seemed distant—like her mind was someplace else. When he'd asked when she might be coming home, she wasted no time telling him she and Ellen were still needed there. It almost seemed as if she didn't want to come home.

I need to quit dwelling on this. He kicked a clump of snow with the toe of his boot. *Think I'll head over to Mom's store and see if she needs help with anything.*

"I've said this before, but I'll say it again, Barbara, I'm glad you're back working in the store again."

Barbara chuckled as she carried a bolt of material to the counter for a customer who was still shopping. "It's good to be back, Peggy. I enjoy my work here." She glanced around the room. "I haven't seen any sign of Gideon today. Do you know if he's planning to come by?"

"I'm not sure." Peggy looked toward the battery-operated clock on the far wall. "Maybe he had to work later than usual at the upholstery shop. When he does come by, it's usually earlier than this."

"I'm hoping to get the chance to talk to him about Mandy." Barbara folded some material from a customer who had changed her mind.

Peggy's eyebrows rose. "Is something wrong with Mandy?"

"No, nothing like that. She's fine physically. I'm worried about her attitude."

"What do you mean?"

"Well, I spoke to her last night, and—" Barbara stopped talking when another customer came in.

"We can talk later," Peggy whispered. "I'll take care of the counter, if you don't mind putting some more white thread on the notions shelf. I can't believe how many spools we've sold in the last two weeks."

"I'll take care of it right away." Barbara headed to the back room to get the box of thread. As she turned to leave the room, Gideon stepped in, bumping her shoulder.

"Oops, sorry. Didn't realize anyone was in here," he apologized.

"It's okay. No harm done." Barbara's face warmed as she stepped aside so he could enter the room. "Mind if I ask you something?"

"Sure." Gideon took off his hat and tossed it aside.

"Have you heard from Mandy lately?"

"Jah. Talked to her this morning." He dropped his gaze. "The conversation didn't go well."

"I'm sorry to hear that. I spoke with her last night." She ran her hands down the sides of her dress. "I'm worried about her, Gideon."

"Same here." Frowning, he looked up. "She won't be coming home for Christmas."

"She told me the same thing." Barbara leaned against the cabinet where some of the extra notions were stored. "Mandy and Ellen are doing a good deed by helping out at the B&B while the Hawaiian man is recuperating." She drew in a quick breath, wondering if she should share her concerns with Gideon.

"You're right. It's a charitable thing they're doing, but it seems as if Mandy likes being there a little too much."

"I agree. All she wanted to talk about was all the wonderful things she's seen so far on the island, and Mandy even mentioned. . ."

Gideon took a step toward her. "What else were you going to say?"

"Mandy admitted she wished she could stay on Kauai forever. Of course, I'm sure she didn't mean it. She's probably caught up in the excitement of being there, where the weather is warm and all the tropical flowers and trees are so pretty. I felt the same way when I was there, although I did miss home and looked forward to returning."

"You don't think Mandy will decide to stay in Hawaii, do you?" Gideon clasped Barbara's wrist, sending a strange tingling sensation all the way up her arm.

Disappointed when he let go, she tried to reassure him. "I'm sure she and Ellen will come home as soon as Makaio is better. From what Mandy said, his leg is slowly healing, but he needs to stay off it right now."

"Sure hope you're right. I hate to say this, but Mandy seems different. When we talked this afternoon, I had a horrible feeling she's forgotten where she belongs."

"With all she and Ellen have gone through, they've had to adjust to a new environment. Once she gets home, things will go back to what they were before our trip." Barbara moved back toward the door. "Guess I'd better get the spools of thread put out. Don't lose hope, Gideon. Mandy will be home soon."

As Barbara headed for the notions aisle, she glanced back and saw Gideon carrying a larger box out of the room. *How could Mandy treat her boyfriend like this? Doesn't she realize how worried he is and how much he misses her?* She placed the box of thread on the floor. *If Gideon was my boyfriend, I would have come home by now. Mandy and Ellen are doing a good deed, but I'm sure the Hawaiian couple could have found someone else to help out at their bed-and-breakfast.*

Kapaa

"Where are you going?" Ken's mother asked when he grabbed a cardboard box and started for the back door.

"Over to the B&B. I'm taking them more eggs and poultry. Remember when Luana called and asked for those?"

Mom nodded. "You've been over there quite a bit lately, Son, and staying longer than normal. What's grabbed your interest all of a sudden at Luana and Makaio's place?"

Heat crept up the back of Ken's neck. "Nothing, Mom. I'll be back as soon as I can." It was one thing to admit he was looking for excuses to go there, but another thing to acknowledge the reason why. Ken was not going to admit he was interested in Mandy or that he looked for any excuse to see her. Not that it mattered. She'd be leaving as soon as Makaio's leg healed, and then he'd probably never see her again. Besides, they were worlds apart. She'd return to her plain Amish life in Indiana, and he would remain here on Kauai, taking care of chickens. So there was no point in telling Mandy how he'd begun to feel about her.

"Whew! It sure can get humid here." Mandy wiped the perspiration from her forehead with a handkerchief. "I wonder if it's going to rain." She and Ellen had spent most of the afternoon pulling weeds in Luana's garden. It hadn't been so bad when they'd first come out, but as the sun grew higher, the heat increased, along with the muggy air. "This isn't the kind of weather they're having back home. Isn't it strange to be doing this type of work in December?"

Ellen nodded.

"Think how nice it would be if we could garden all year. Our lives would be a lot different, jah?"

"You're right." Ellen paused for a drink of water. "Speaking of home, how did your conversation with Gideon go?"

Mandy swatted at a pesky fly buzzing her head. "Not well. I could hear the disappointment in his voice, and he seemed offended. In fact, when I told him we wouldn't be back for Christmas, he got kind of huffy."

"It's no wonder, Mandy. He misses you."

"I miss him too, but we're needed here right now."

Ellen sighed. "The hardest part of being gone from home for me is missing Christmas with my family."

"I'll miss my family, as well, but we can celebrate the holiday with Luana and Makaio, like we did Thanksgiving. To me, they're starting to feel like family." Mandy thought about the delicious turkey dinner Luana had prepared with their help. In addition to Ailani and Oke joining them, Luana had invited the four guests at the bed-and-breakfast to enjoy the holiday meal with them. Mandy was impressed with her hospitality and kindness. It was one more similarity to the way her Amish family and friends reacted to those who visited their homes.

"I don't know about you, but I'm more than ready to take a break." Ellen set her small shovel aside, stood, and flexed her back. "Let's go inside and see if Luana needs us to do anything else."

"If not, maybe we can do something fun before supper."

"What do you want to do?"

"Why don't we go to the beach? You haven't been there yet, and it's a perfect day with no wind at all."

"I don't know." Ellen's eyes blinked rapidly as she tapped her chin. "With the sun being so hot, we might get burned."

"We have our sunscreen." Mandy gathered up her weeding utensils and was almost to the house when Ken's rig pulled in.

"Aloha!" he called after he got out of his SUV. "I brought some eggs and poultry."

Mandy waited for him to join them on the grass. "Luana will be glad, because we're getting low on eggs."

"I can take the box inside to her," Ellen offered.

"You don't have to. I'll take it myself." Ken smiled. "What have you two been up to this afternoon?"

"Weeding, but now we're ready for a break." Mandy returned his smile.

"I could use one myself. How'd you like to join me for a hot dog and some shave ice?"

"Is it really called *shave ice*, or did you leave off the *d*?" Mandy questioned.

"Nope. Here in Hawaii, it's known as shave ice."

Mandy smiled at Ellen. "Seems like we learn new things about Hawaii all the time."

Ellen nodded quickly before making her way to the house.

"So do you want to get something to eat with me?" Ken asked.

Mandy nodded. "Could we go to the beach for a bit when we're done eating? Ellen hasn't been there yet since we arrived on Kauai."

"Not a problem. As soon as I give the eggs to Luana, I'd be happy to take you both there."

As Ellen walked barefoot along the shoreline with Ken and Mandy, she noticed how well they got along. The way they laughed and talked nonstop, walking close to each other, made it almost seem as if they were a courting couple. Of course, how could it be? Mandy's boyfriend was waiting for her back home.

When Ellen stepped into the water, she couldn't get over how warm it felt. The waves lapped against her ankles as the sand moved slowly away, tickling her bare feet.

"Hey, look at the seal over there!" Ken pointed as the creature swam out of the water and came onto the beach.

"Do you see many seals here?" Mandy asked, reaching into her satchel for her camera.

"Not all the time, so it's worth a few pictures."

They watched the seal awhile, then moved down the beach, visiting and walking in the surf. The edge of Mandy's dress had gotten wet, and Ellen noticed hers had too. It was hard to guess where the water would hit her legs as it rolled onto the beach. The breeze blowing on her face felt good, as the sun warmed her exposed skin.

"Hey, come take a look at this." Ken stopped walking and bent down to scoop something off the sand.

"What is it?" Ellen moved closer.

"It's a piece of coral." Ken held it out. "You'll find pieces like this in many places on the beach."

"It reminds me of a head of cauliflower, only it's tan instead of white." Ellen reached out to touch it.

"We should each take a small piece," Mandy suggested. "Then, when we return home, we can have part of the island with us."

Ellen felt a bit of relief. *At least Mandy is talking about going home. I hope this means she has no crazy ideas about staying here on Kauai. If she did, there would be a lot of disappointed people back home.*

Chapter 19

*J*ve said this before, but I can't begin to tell you how much I appreciate your help." Luana examined a vase as she, Mandy, and Ellen went through some things she planned to sell at her two-day yard sale, which would start the next day. "You both have been a God-send to us."

"We're glad to do it." Mandy hoped they would make enough money to help with Makaio's hospital bills. He had health insurance, but it didn't cover all his medical expenses. Luana had mentioned they'd also receive some aid from their church, and several people had brought things over for them to sell at the yard sale. It did Mandy's heart good to see how the people from Makaio and Luana's church had rallied to help them out financially. It reminded her of how things were done at home when an Amish church member had a need.

"You have a lot of nice items here." Ellen held a photo of pink primroses.

"The picture you're holding used to hang in one of our guest rooms, but we replaced it sometime ago with a painting a friend made for us." Luana sighed. "Unfortunately, we can't keep everything. Since the primrose picture is a reproduction I found at our local thrift store, it doesn't have any real sentimental value." She picked up a small photograph. "This, on the other hand, has a lot of sentimental value."

"What is it?" Mandy leaned toward Luana as she handed her the photo.

"It's a picture of the quilt Makaio and I received as a wedding present from my parents." Sighing, she lifted her hands and let them fall into her lap. "It's been missing since we moved here from the Big Island."

"It looks like a beautiful quilt." Mandy looked closer at the picture. "The detail is beautiful, and I like the blue and white colors."

Tears welled in Luana's dark eyes as she nodded. "My mother made it. She even sewed Makaio's and my initials in one corner of the quilt." After Mandy handed the picture back to her, Luana stared at it with a somber expression. "I fear my mother's precious wedding gift may have been thrown out or accidentally given to charity before our move."

Mandy clasped Luana's hand, gently squeezing her fingers. "It's hard to lose something meaningful."

"It is, but life moves on, and I try to remember not to focus on *things*." Luana smiled. "Our relationship to God and people is what truly counts."

Friday morning, things were hectic at the B&B. Every room was booked, and Luana had to make sure breakfast was ready for her guests, as well as check that everything was set up as it should be for the yard sale later on. Fortunately, it wouldn't be open to the public until ten, which gave her enough time to feed her guests first. She was thankful Ellen and Mandy had offered to go outside right after breakfast, in case anyone showed up early.

When Makaio first woke up, he'd complained about his leg bothering him, but now, as they sat down for their morning meal, he shared with their guests some information about Kauai and said he'd be willing to answer any questions about island living.

"One thing you should be aware of is the vog," Makaio announced, reaching for his cup of coffee.

"What's a vog?" Ellen asked, as she served more coffee to their guests.

"I'd like to hear about this, as well," a middle-aged woman from Oregon said.

"The vog is sort of like fog, only it's from the volcanic ash on the Big Island." Makaio's nose twitched. "Depending on the intensity of the ash, it can bother some people, causing sneezing, congestion, and burning eyes."

"I hope it doesn't occur during our time here," the woman said. "I have enough problems with allergies and such."

"Hopefully, you won't have to deal with it." Luana gestured to the bowl of miso soup, along with some chopped green onions, small cubed tofu, and steamed white rice. "Miso soup is from Japan. Some people on this island enjoy having it for breakfast."

"Not me," Makaio announced with a shake of his head. "I prefer Spam and eggs."

Luana rolled her eyes. *Some things never change.*

From the minute the yard sale opened, until a few minutes before it was time to close up for the day, things had been busy.

"We did well today. I think there were some tourists browsing the tables. They seemed interested in the jewelry and wooden knickknacks I had for sale." Luana smiled. "Thank you, Ellen and Mandy. I couldn't have done it without your help. I'm glad Ailani was up to staying with her father while we were out here in the yard today too."

"We were happy to help." Ellen picked up a roll of plastic. Then she and Mandy covered everything on the tables and furniture in case it rained during the night.

"Luana, I have a question. What kind of birds are those?" Mandy pointed to several small birds on the lawn. "They look like miniature doves."

"You're right, they are. They're zebra doves, and you'll find them all over the Hawaiian Islands."

"They sure are cute," Ellen commented.

"Yes, but they can be quite brazen—especially when there's food around. When we eat outside, I've seen them swoop right down and, if we're not looking, steal whatever's on our plates." Luana yawned. "Oh my. This is one night I wish I didn't have to fix supper." She rubbed a sore spot on her back. "I'm exhausted."

"Don't worry about supper," Mandy said. "Ellen and I will take care of it. Why don't you go inside and put up your feet? We'll be in to get things started as soon as we gather up the empty boxes."

"Mahalo." Luana gave them both a hug and hurried into the house, thankful yet again for everything the young women had done.

"Do you have a problem with me staying over at the B&B awhile and joining them for supper?" Ken asked when his mother handed him a box of food she'd prepared for him to take over. "No doubt, they'll ask me to stay."

With hands on her hips, the small wrinkles around her eyes deepened. "Really, Ken? I thought we talked the other day about you spending so much time over there."

"I'm not a kid, Mom." Ken raised his voice slightly, to make a point. "In case you forgot, I'm twenty-three years old."

"No, I haven't forgotten."

"And it's not like I'll be shirking my duties here, 'cause I'm done for the day. It's Dan's turn to feed and water the chickens this evening." He shifted the box in his arms.

"I'm well aware of that. I just think—"

"Go ahead and say it, Mom; you think I'm spending too much time at the B&B."

"Is it about those Amish girls? Are you interested in one of them?"

"I've gotta go, Mom. This food will be getting cold if I don't head out now."

"All right. We can discuss this some other time." Mom reached out and touched Ken's hair. "When are you planning to get a haircut? You're starting to look like a shaggy dog."

"I like my hair this way." Ken swung his head side to side, hoping to make a point. "See you later." He turned and hurried out the door.

The sun felt intense on his shoulders as he headed to his vehicle. *I shouldn't have gotten defensive with Mom. I'll apologize when I get home. Are my feelings for Mandy so obvious? If I had admitted the way I've begun to feel about her, what would Mom have said?*

Ken's parents had only spoken to Mandy and Ellen a few times at church. Maybe it was time they got to know them better.

"This chicken casserole your *makuahine* made for us sure hits the spot." Makaio licked his lips. "Be sure to tell her mahalo."

"I will." Ken reached for a piece of bread and spread some guava jelly over it.

Having learned a few Hawaiian words, Mandy understood *makuahine* meant "mother," and *mahalo* was the word for saying "Thank you." Thanks to Luana, Makaio, and Ken's teaching, she'd learned how to count to ten in Hawaiian, as well as say the days of the week and months of the year. When she returned home, it would be fun to teach these words to her family.

"How'd the yard sale go today?" Ken asked Luana, before glancing briefly at Mandy.

"It went well. We made several hundred dollars and are hoping to do equally well tomorrow. I opened a hall closet a while ago and found a few more things to add to one of the tables for tomorrow's sale. I might look around the house some more after dinner and see if there's anything else I can get rid of." Luana looked at Makaio. "How about selling some of the Hawaiian shirts you've outgrown?"

He shook his head. "No way! I'm not parting with any of my shirts. I can still wear most of them, you know." Makaio stuffed a fork full of casserole in his mouth and winked at her.

"Back home, our yard sales draw a lot of folks too." Ellen reached for her glass of mango flavored lemonade. "It's amazing what people will often buy."

Mandy nodded. "Some folks' unwanted stuff ends up becoming someone else's treasure," she added.

"Wish I could have been here to help, but I had deliveries to make and was gone most of the day." Ken picked up his glass.

"We're glad you're here now and could join us for the evening meal." Luana handed Ken the bowl of fruit salad Mandy and Ellen had made.

"Same here." He grinned at Mandy, and she felt the heat of a blush cascade over her face.

Every time Ken looked at her, she felt something undeniable pass between them. *Maybe it's my imagination or wishful thinking.* She glanced at Ellen, wondering why she'd been so quiet. Except for the comment about yard sales, she'd been rather silent since they'd sat down at the table. *Maybe she's tired. We did have a pretty full day.*

Ken leaned closer to Mandy as he passed her the dish of purple sweet potatoes. "I was wondering if you and Ellen would like to take a tour of my parents' chicken farm after church on Sunday. Afterward, you can stay for dinner."

"Seeing how the chickens are raised would be interesting." Mandy looked at Ellen. "Don't you think so?"

"I suppose, but we might be needed here to help Luana with the Sunday meal."

"It won't be necessary," Luana was quick to say. "You two have been working hard lately; you deserve to enjoy a meal at the Williamses' place." Luana fingered the yellow plumeria tucked in her hair. "I want you to go and have a good time. We'll be fine on our own a few hours."

"It's settled then." Ken took a drink. "I'll look forward to seeing you both on Sunday."

Mandy looked forward to it as well—more than she cared to admit.

"How's your leg feeling, Makaio?" Ken asked.

"Not so bad, but I'll be glad when the cast comes off." His nose scrunched as he looked down at his leg. "I'm gettin' awful tired of sitting around, doing nothin' but watching TV all day."

"You don't have to watch TV." Luana's eyebrows raised.

"What else is there for me to do? I sure can't do any work."

"You could work on a word search or crossword puzzle." Smiling, Luana squeezed his arm. "I read somewhere those are good for stimulating a person's brain."

"It's my leg needing help, not my brain. And to make matters worse, my leg itches like crazy."

As Mandy ate the rest of her meal, Luana and Makaio's playful bickering caused her to think about her parents. *Dad can be stubborn and sometimes moody whenever he's faced with a challenge or when Mom wants him to do something he doesn't want to do. But they love each other, and as Dad sometimes says, "It's okay to disagree."*

There'd been times when Gideon acted moody, like the last time they'd spoken on the phone. *He's upset because I'm still in Hawaii.* Mandy's gaze went from Makaio to Luana. *If he could meet these wonderful people, maybe he'd understand.*

Chapter 20

$\mathcal{L}$ook at the glorious sunrise God has given us this beautiful Sunday morning!" Mandy exclaimed as she stood at the bedroom window. "You won't see anything at home comparable to this."

Ellen moved over to stand beside her. "It is lovely, but we have sunrises in Indiana too."

"Not rising from the ocean." Mandy opened the window. "I wish we had a view of the water from here. But then, it might be hard to get anything done. I'd want to stay at the window and admire the ocean all day." She drew a deep breath. "You can even smell the lovely fragrance of the flowers on the breeze. How much more *fehlerfrei* can it get?"

"You know, Mandy, not everything in Hawaii is perfect." Ellen's sharp tone was a surprise.

Raising her eyebrows, Mandy looked at her friend. "Course not, but it's what I dreamed of, and even more. Ever since my cousin told me about her trip to Hawaii, I've wanted to come. I like it here on Kauai." Hugging her arms around herself, Mandy moved away from the window and flopped down on her freshly made bed. "I'd love to live here, in fact."

"You're not serious, I hope."

"Jah, I am."

"Well, I hope your fancy for this island fades in the near future, because we'll be heading back home as soon as Makaio is in good shape again."

"I'm well aware." Mandy pulled her long hair aside, but instead of securing it into a bun, she let it hang loosely across her back. "I wish I could wear my hair down sometimes."

"You mean like when you're going to bed?"

"Jah."

Ellen stared. "Are you forgetting our Amish customs?"

"Of course not, but. . ." Mandy stood. "Never mind. I was only thinking out loud." She quickly pulled her hair into a bun at the back of her head and set her head covering in place. "Guess we'd better help Luana with breakfast so we'll be ready for church when Ken picks us up."

Ellen followed Mandy across the room, stepping in front of her. "Before we go, there's something I'd like to ask you."

Mandy halted, nearly colliding with her friend. "What is it?"

"Is it the island you've fallen in love with, or is it Ken?"

"I'm not acquainted well enough with Ken to declare any love for him, but. . ." Mandy turned her head to the side, unable to look at Ellen. "In all honesty, I do enjoy being around him. And if he were Amish. . ." Her voice trailed off. "Never mind. You wouldn't understand."

"You're right, I don't understand. But I do understand one thing. You're not the same person who began this journey with me. You rarely talk about home or Gideon anymore. And now you're wishing to live in some fantasy world, imagining what it would be like to live here on Kauai." Ellen paused, "Whether you're willing to admit it or not, I believe you have feelings for Ken, and they go beyond friendship."

Mandy's throat tightened as tears welled in her eyes. "It doesn't matter how I feel about him, because once we leave here I'll probably never see Ken again."

"Too bad Luana and Makaio couldn't join us for church," Ellen whispered as she and Mandy took seats inside the sanctuary. "When Makaio said he wasn't feeling up to going, one of us should have volunteered to stay with him so Luana could go."

"Maybe, but he'd probably rather have his wife stay with him instead of one of us." Mandy glanced at the platform at the front of the church, where Ken had gone to tune his ukulele. This morning he wore a pair of tan-colored slacks and a blue shirt with white palm trees on it.

Most of the men attending this church dressed casually, in light-weight clothes, such as shorts and Hawaiian-print shirts. Even some of the women wore shorts or capris. Mandy felt out of place in her Amish dress and white head covering. Of course, she would have been uncomfortable wearing a muumuu, since she'd never worn anything other than her traditional Amish dress while attending church at home. For some reason, though, here on Kauai, she felt like stepping out of her comfort zone.

When the musicians started playing at the front of the church, she focused on learning the new song the worship team sang. It still seemed strange not to sing traditional Amish hymns found in the *Ausbund*. However, she enjoyed many of the choruses she'd already learned at this church. A couple of times, Mandy tapped her foot in time with the music, until Ellen looked at her in disapproval.

Mandy had been away from home so long, she'd lost track of which weeks were off-Sundays for her home church district. On those days, her family usually visited a neighboring district, and on a few occasions stayed home and had private devotions. *I wonder what church district my family will attend today. If Mom and Dad were here right now, I bet they'd feel out of place—especially with the music and the casual way people dress.*

Ellen felt a bit uncomfortable with the loud music, but she enjoyed the message the pastor preached near the end of the church service. He mentioned how sometimes God provides for His people in surprising ways, as He did the Israelites when they were hungry. He sent them manna from heaven.

When the ship left without us, God provided for Mandy and me by guiding us to a place we could stay and giving us the privilege of helping Luana and Makaio in their time of need. Ellen shifted on her seat. *I need to stop feeling sorry for myself because I'm so far from home and do whatever I can to make the best of my time here on Kauai.*

They would be going with Ken to his parents' home after church for a meal and a tour of their poultry farm. It would be interesting, and another opportunity to do something fun. At times, Ellen felt as if she were intruding, but she was glad he'd invited both of them, and not Mandy alone. It would give her a chance to keep an eye on things and make sure a serious relationship wasn't developing between Ken and Mandy.

"Thank you for a delicious meal, Mrs. Williams." Mandy leaned back in her chair after they'd finished eating dinner.

"Yes, thank you." Ellen placed her napkin on the plate.

Ken's mother smiled. "You're welcome. Oh, and please call me Vickie."

"And I'm Charles, but you can call me Chuck." Ken's father reached over and affectionately patted his wife's arm. "We don't stand on formalities around here. I'm only sorry you didn't get to meet our youngest son. He's having dinner at a friend's house today."

"No worries. You can meet Dan some other time." Ken pushed away from the table. "Are you two ready for a tour of our poultry farm?"

"You can show it to us after we help your mother with the dishes." Ellen stood, reaching for her plate.

Vickie waved her hand. "It's okay. Charles will help me. He's always been good about doing the dishes."

He smiled and nodded. "Go ahead, Son. Show your guests around the place."

Ken escorted Mandy and Ellen outside and immediately began to explain about poultry farming. "You're probably aware of this already, but the chickens we raise for eggs are called 'layer chickens,' and the chickens which are raised for their meat production are called 'broiler chickens.' Literally billions of chickens are being raised throughout the world as a good source of food from their eggs and meat." He gestured to the chickens roaming about their acreage. "Here, we grow our chickens organically, using the free-range method. Commercial hens generally start laying eggs at the age of twelve to twenty weeks. By the time they are twenty-five weeks, they are laying eggs regularly."

Fascinated, Mandy watched the chickens run around, squawking and pecking at the ground. "Do they stay out all night?"

"Nope. Only during the day. At night, they're kept inside our chicken houses to keep them safe from predators and unfavorable weather. Our indoor facilities need to have an adequate drainage system, good ventilation, and appropriate protection from winds, all types of predators, and excessive cold, heat, or dampness. This system also requires less feed than cage and barn systems." Ken pointed to the buildings they housed the chickens in. "The poultry manure from the free-range chickens is used as fertilizer for our garden and fruit trees."

"Is there something specific that sets organic poultry growing and traditional growing apart?" Ellen questioned.

"Yes. The main differences between the traditional free-range poultry farming and organic farming is that with the organic method, a certain species of poultry bird are raised in small groups with low stocking density. The organic system also has some restrictions in the use of synthetic yolk colorants, water, feed, medications, and other feed additives. We feed our chickens high quality, fresh, and nutritious food to ensure their good health, proper growth, and high production."

"In addition to providing Luana and Makaio's B&B with eggs and poultry, who else buys what you raise?" Mandy lifted her head to meet Ken's gaze.

"We sell to the local farmers' markets, and also some of the bigger supermarkets on the island." He smiled. "People are always looking for locally raised, organic eggs and poultry."

"Thanks for explaining everything, Ken." Mandy wiped her forehead. The day had turned out to be quite warm.

"We'd better go back inside where it's cooler," Ken suggested. "But before we go, would you like to see our swimming pool?"

"With the ocean so near, I'm surprised you have a pool," Ellen stated.

"I actually prefer to swim in the ocean, but Mom likes the pool because there's no sand." Ken led them to the pool on the other side of the house. "You two are welcome to come use it any time."

"The water looks inviting, but I'd rather not."

"Really? How come?"

"Mandy doesn't know how to swim," Ellen interjected.

Mandy's heart beat rapidly as she turned to Ellen. She couldn't believe her friend had blurted that out. "Ellen. . ."

"No problem there. I'd be more than happy to give you a swimming lesson. I'm not bragging, but if anyone can teach you how to swim, it's me." Ken pointed to himself. "I've had lifeguard training, so I promise I won't let you drown. Oh, and if either of you needs a swimsuit, I'd be happy to take you shopping." As if the matter was settled, he started walking toward the house.

Mandy swallowed a couple of times as she scanned the outlying areas of the pool. It was stunningly landscaped with a different array of flowers, thick with blossoms. They formed a private border, cut off from the rest of the Williames's property. There was no grass in this section of the yard. Instead, large pieces of slate in different shapes and sizes covered the entire area, right up to the water's edge. A table and chairs sat in the far corner, and in the other was an open fire-pit, surrounded by several more chairs. The kidney-shaped pool and its aqua-blue color looked inviting, with the sparkling water so clear, she could see the bottom. On the end where the water was a deeper blue, a diving board jutted out. Even as nice as it was, Mandy wasn't sure she had the nerve to let Ken teach her how to swim. Just thinking about being in the water, especially over her head, sent a chill up her spine.

Middlebury

Gideon wasn't sure how he'd made it through church or the meal afterward. One thing he was certain of: he couldn't wait to get home. For the last two days he'd felt fatigued and irritable, but figured it was due to missing Mandy. Today, however, he realized he might be coming down with something. His forehead felt unusually hot, and his throat had a twinge of soreness.

As soon as I get home, I'm going to take a nap, because I'll bet I've got the flu, he told himself as he climbed into his buggy and gathered up the reins.

Gideon was glad church had been held at a neighboring farm, so he didn't have far to go. As crummy as he felt right now, he wasn't sure he could go more than a mile.

His horse picked up speed as soon as they approached his folks' house. Gideon didn't have to direct the animal down the driveway, because Dash galloped there by himself.

Gideon unhitched the horse, using all the strength he could muster, and let him run free in the pasture. Since they hadn't gone far, the horse hadn't worked up a lather. He would put the buggy away later on.

Plodding through what snow was left in the yard, Gideon made his way to the house. He stopped and leaned against the porch post, listening to a woodpecker tapping nearby. After scanning the yard, he located the bird in a dead tree.

Gideon's head pounded. Still, he remained where he was, watching the woodpecker at work. The red-headed bird skillfully tapped at the loose bark, searching for bugs underneath. As a chunk of the tree's bark broke away, Gideon looked a little closer, realizing the bird must have worked on this particular tree before. Not only were there pieces of bark scattered all around, but small piles of wood particles covered the ground like sawdust on a lumberyard's floor.

Gideon jumped when his mother's voice startled him. "I'm surprised to see you back already." Since Mom had stayed home with a cold this morning, she greeted him at the door. "Ach, Gideon, what's on your face?"

"What is it?" He pressed his palms against his warm cheeks. "I'm not feeling well. I need to go lay down."

She touched his forehead. "You're running a *fiewer*, and from the looks of those little bumps on your face, I'm sure you have the *wasserpareble*."

"The chicken pox? Oh, no! This is not what I need!"

Chapter 21

Kapaa

After all the rooms had been cleaned and the beds were made, Ellen took a walk outside to enjoy the sun for a bit. As she moved around the yard, breathing in the fragrance of the plumeria, with their pretty yellow petals, she smiled. The birds were happy, singing and fluttering overhead in the palms and other trees in the Palus' yard.

Moving toward Luana's vegetable garden, she watched the bees buzzing busily around the toppling cherry tomato plants. Ellen couldn't help reaching out to pluck a perfectly ripe piece of fruit. She looked at it a few seconds, enjoying the feel of the sun-warmed tomato in her hand, before popping it in her mouth and savoring the fresh, rich flavor. *Nothing compares to homegrown food from the garden,* she thought, heading back to the house.

Ellen entered the kitchen and went to look at the wall calendar. It was hard to believe, but in eleven days it would be Christmas. Never had she felt so homesick. Being away from her family this time of the year made it even harder. She had to admit, though, Thanksgiving hadn't turned out too bad.

She groaned inwardly, trying to convince herself to make the best of the situation. *Christmas will probably be nice, but it won't seem like the holidays without snow. I'm sure back home they'll have a beautiful white Christmas.*

Heaving a sigh, she moved away from the calendar and poured herself a cup of herbal tea. The delicious aroma of macadamia nut wafted up to her nose as she brought the mug to her lips.

I need to quit feeling sorry for myself and get busy on the Christmas cards I want to send to my friends and family back home. Ellen set her teacup down.

145

She had a few letters to write, as well.

Ken had invited them to see some sights on the island after he'd gotten off work this afternoon, but Ellen didn't want to go. She'd promised to help Luana decorate the B&B for Christmas, which she planned on doing as soon as she finished her cards and letters.

Ellen went to her room and found the supplies she'd picked up at the craft store the other day. Mandy had bought some too, and they'd decided to use the same colors and rubber stamps to create their cards.

At the kitchen table, Ellen set everything out. She began by cutting the different-sized colored papers to stamp and glue together. *I hope Mandy works on hers soon, or she won't get them sent out in time. I know she enjoys seeing the sights with Ken, but she's been shirking her duties lately.*

Ellen liked helping Luana and meeting the guests. It reminded her of being at the B&B where she'd worked at home. Plus, she had established a friendship with Luana and enjoyed their talks. It was the one thing she would miss the most when they returned to Indiana.

"I can't wait for you to see Opaekaa Falls," Ken said as he drove Mandy up Kuamoo Road. "From the overlook, you'll have a spectacular view. The falls are at their best in full sunlight, so I'm glad you were free to go with me this afternoon."

"I'm looking forward to seeing it." Mandy didn't know if her enthusiasm was for seeing the falls or even more of being with Ken. He sure loved the islands, and she was falling in love with Hawaii too. Mandy felt energized here. Every morning when she awoke, she could hardly contain her eagerness to see what new discoveries awaited.

"Oh, and if you're wondering about the fall's name," Ken added, "*Opae* is the Hawaiian word for shrimp, and *ka'a* means 'rolling'. It dates back to days when shrimp roamed the river and were seen rolling in the raging waters at the base of the falls. Also, across the road from the falls overlook is another lookout over the Wailua River Valley. From there you can get a good look at where *Raiders of the Lost Ark* was filmed."

Mandy's forehead wrinkled. "*Raiders of the Lost Ark?*"

"Yeah. It's a movie. You do go to movies, right?"

She shook her head. "Some Amish young people go to movies during their *rumschpringe*, but—"

"What's a rumschpringe?"

"It's a time of running around, before we make a decision about whether we want to join the Amish church or not."

Ken crossed his arms. "What if you don't join the church? Would you be shunned?"

"No." Ken's question caught Mandy off guard. She couldn't blame him for not knowing how shunning worked in the Amish community, but it was a bit unsettling to talk about because many English people had the wrong idea.

"Shunning is a form of church discipline," she explained. "It's meant to bring a wayward member back into fellowship with the church and body of believers." She clasped her hands together, struggling with her own desires. "I have not yet joined the church. If I decide not to, I won't be shunned."

"How come you haven't joined?" He glanced at her quickly, then back at the road ahead.

"I'm not sure it's the right thing for me." Mandy struggled for words, but as Ken pulled his rig into the fall's parking lot, she spoke again. "My parents are expecting me to join, and they'll be disappointed if I don't, but in the end, the final decision is mine."

"I see. Well, I hope you make the right decision." Ken turned off the engine, hopped out, and came around to open the door for her. "When we leave here, I'll drive you up to Wailua Falls. It's a double-tiered waterfall, and if we're lucky and the sun is at the right angle, we'll see a beautiful rainbow extending from the base of the falls in the mist. Wailua Falls is about eighty-five feet high—although some people say it's twice that height—and it drops into a thirty-foot-deep pool. During high flow, the falls often have a third tier."

Mandy took a deep breath. "There's so much I didn't know about

Kauai, but I'm excited to find out."

She followed Ken over to where several others stood along a chain-link fence, and peered out toward the falling waters. "It's so beautiful." Mandy readied her camera to take some snapshots.

A lady next to them turned and asked if they'd like a picture together with the falls behind them. Before Mandy could reply, Ken spoke up. "Thanks. That'd be great."

The woman took a few pictures, then handed the camera back to Mandy and moved aside.

I wonder how the photos will turn out. Mandy gazed at the falls spilling over the ledge behind them. *Does that lady think Ken and I are a courting couple? Do I dare admit, even to myself, that I wish it were so?*

"I appreciate you helping me with this." Luana took another ornament from the box as Ellen helped her decorate the Christmas tree. "I'd meant to do it sooner, but with the yard sale and taking care of Makaio, there hasn't been time."

"Believe me, I'm enjoying myself." Carefully, Ellen touched the needles of the tree. "What kind of tree is this, Luana?"

"It's a Norfolk Island pine. In Hawaii, some people order trees from the mainland, but we've always gotten ours here on the island, where they grow."

"Mandy doesn't realize what she's missing out on today." Ellen frowned. "Too bad she didn't stay and help us. But then, she hasn't been acting herself lately."

"It's all right. Ken was anxious to show her some sights, and you could certainly have joined them if you'd wanted to."

"Someone needed to stay and help with this." Ellen picked up a shiny glass ornament and hung it on the tree. "I've never decorated for Christmas before, so this all seems a bit strange to me."

Luana's mouth opened slightly. "You don't put out any decorations?"

"Only the Christmas cards we receive, and a few candles. Our focus at

Christmas is on Jesus and how God sent His only Son to earth as a baby so He could later die on the cross to become our Savior."

"It's our focus too, which is why I display this in a prominent place." Luana gestured to the Nativity set she'd placed on one end of the check-in table.

Ellen touched the baby Jesus figurine, running her finger across the smooth porcelain surface. "It's lovely."

"Do you get together with family and friends to share a meal on Christmas Day?"

"Yes, but sometimes we have to choose other days, close to the holiday, to have our family meal. Since our families are large, we can't always be together at the same time."

Luana smiled, reaching for an antique star ornament to hang on the tree. "It doesn't matter what day we celebrate, as long as we spend time with our *ohana*."

"*Ohana* means 'family,' right?"

"That's correct. Our family is important to us."

"Mine is to me, as well." Ellen stepped back to see how the tree looked. "I can smell the pine scent," she murmured.

"I like putting the tree in here for our guests to enjoy. I imagine my husband will come in and check things out when we're finished decorating. He's like a big kid at Christmas." Luana chuckled. "Normally, Makaio helps me decorate the B&B. He usually gets a new ornament for our tree every year too. The reason he didn't come into the living room while we're doing this is because it's hard for him to sit and watch when there's work to be done. He's quite comfortable sitting on the lanai this afternoon, drinking iced tea and reading the paper." She plugged in the string of lights, then stood off to one side, no doubt to admire their work. "I love the pretty colors and how the lights play off the shiny ornaments."

"It looks very nice, and the lights do make it stand out." Ellen added another wooden ornament to the tree—this one had palm trees painted on it. "I've never had a broken bone, but I imagine it's hard for Makaio to sit around when he was used to being so active."

"Yes. Makaio is not a patient man when it comes to being idle."

They continued to visit as the room was transformed. "You may have noticed," Luana said, "there are poinsettias blooming in many yards in our area. They're not potted, but grow quite large and bloom around this time of the year."

"Actually, I haven't noticed." Ellen smiled. "But I did observe the red-and-green leis you've put around the candles."

After they finished decorating, Luana suggested they go to the kitchen and bake some special Christmas cookies her mother used to make when she was a girl.

Mandy's heartbeat picked up speed when she and Ken climbed aboard the small boat that would take them up the Wailua River to see Fern Grotto. She had worn her lavender muumuu. It blended well with the tropical flowers she'd seen near one of the waterfalls.

"I think you're gonna enjoy the ride up to the grotto," Ken said as they sat on one of the wooden benches on the right side of the boat. "The scenery is beautiful."

"I can already see that," she responded as the boat pulled away from the dock.

"This is the only navigable river in Hawaii. It's fed by Mt. Waialeale, one of the wettest spots in the world. During the two-mile trip upstream, we'll be entertained with songs and stories of old Hawaii." He raised his eyebrows playfully. "You can even participate in a hula lesson if you like."

Mandy's face heated. "I don't think so. It's not something I'd be comfortable doing."

"It's okay. I was only teasing."

As they started up the river, Mandy was amazed at the beautiful mangrove trees lining the river's banks, as well as the colorful foliage. *If only we had something like this back home.*

When the boat reached the Fern Grotto landing, they took a short nature walk through a lovely rainforest. As they approached a fern-covered lava cave, the highlight of their tour, Mandy's breath caught in her throat. Colorful tropical plants grew in and around the cave. Their tour guide explained the grotto was one of Kauai's geological wonders and had formed millions of years ago. At one time the cave was open to the public, but it was no longer accessible.

They stood admiring the grotto for several minutes as the musicians who'd also ridden on the boat sang a few songs. Mandy felt as though she was in the middle of a fairytale.

As they began the walk back to the boat, Ken halted and leaned close to her ear. "You look nice in that dress, but there's something missing."

"Oh? What's missing?"

Mandy's heart beat a little faster, and her face warmed when he picked a Hibiscus flower and stuck it behind her right ear.

"Wearing it this way means you're not married." Unexpectedly, he reached out and took hold of her hand.

At a loss for words, all she could do was manage a smile. She'd had a fantastic time and wished the day didn't have to end. *Does Ken have feelings for me? Does he suspect how I've begun to feel about him? It would be wrong for us to become involved when we live so far apart—not to mention, he's English and I'm Amish. Besides, I don't think Mom and Dad would approve. Then there's Gideon—how would he feel if I broke up with him and didn't join the church? Oh, so many questions.*

Chapter 22

Middlebury

Except for a few remaining scabs on his arms, Gideon was pretty much over the chicken pox. He'd hated being sick and missing time from work, but at least he didn't have to deal with the itching anymore. When the pox had flared, he'd given in to the temptation to scratch on more than one occasion. Remembering the ordeal made his skin crawl. *I'll probably be left with some scars.* He let out a snort as he sat at a table in the back of the upholstery shop to eat his lunch.

"It's good to see you working again." Jim Nicolson sat beside Gideon and opened his lunch pail. He was the only English man working at the shop.

Gideon nodded. "The morning went by fast. Can't believe it's time for lunch already."

"So you're feeling all right now?"

"Physically, I'm fine, but emotionally, I'm a wreck."

"What's the problem?" Jim took out a sandwich and pulled off the cellophane wrap.

"My girlfriend, Mandy. She's still in Hawaii." Gideon grunted, slowly shaking his head.

"Is that so? Figured she'd be back by now."

Gideon poured coffee from his thermos into a cup. "She and her friend Ellen got stranded on the island of Kauai, so now they're helping out at a bed-and-breakfast there."

"To earn some money for their trip home?"

"No. The man who owns the B&B fell off the roof and broke his leg. Mandy and Ellen are helping the man's wife run the place while he's laid up." Gideon finished his coffee then dug into his lunch container and removed his tuna sandwich. Not one of his favorites, but busy as she was, Mom had taken time to make lunch for him this morning, so he would eat it without complaint.

"Sounds like a charitable thing they're doing."

"Yes, and I can't fault her for it. But she won't be here for the holidays, and it won't seem like Christmas without her."

"Any idea when she'll come home?"

"Nope. It's hard enough I haven't seen Mandy in a long time, not to mention we missed being together at Thanksgiving. But there's something else that's been nagging me even more."

"Oh?" Jim bit into his bologna sandwich.

Gideon poured another cup of coffee. "Mandy rarely ever calls me."

"Why don't you call her? Do you have the number there?"

"I have called, but she's usually too busy to say more than a few words. Sometimes she's not there at all." He frowned, rubbing his arm where a few scabs remained. "Once when I called, I was told she was out with someone named Ken, who was showing her around. Do you think she's avoiding me?"

"I wouldn't worry too much, Gideon. Your girlfriend probably wants to enjoy the beautiful island." Jim stared off for a moment. "Years ago, I was on Oahu for a short while. I'm sure it's changed a lot since then. It was a nice place to visit, but the cost of living is high—at least, compared to what we're used to here in Middlebury." He leaned back in his chair, sipping from his can of soda. "When do you expect your girlfriend to come home?"

Gideon shrugged, turning his palms up. "All I know is when she finally gets here, I'll be relieved." He couldn't help thinking about this fellow, Ken. Was he merely a friend showing them around the island, or could he be interested in one of the girls? If so, he hoped it wasn't Mandy.

Better not let my thoughts get carried away, he scolded himself. *Jim's probably right. I shouldn't be worried.*

Peggy and Barbara had kept busy at the fabric store from the time it opened until well past noon. Now it was time to take a break.

"It's nice we've slowed down for a while," Barbara commented. "This morning was so hectic we could hardly catch our breath."

"You're right. When the tourists locate this store, they spread the word and others come in. They take their time looking around too, and often find plenty of trinkets to take home." Peggy pointed to the nearest shelf. "That's why I've added more variety in the store, like purses, shoes, and some small home decor."

"I have to agree. In fact, I've been eyeing a purse over there myself."

Peggy tilted her head. "Oh? Which one?"

"The black purse with a little tan on it."

Peggy left for a moment and returned with the handbag. "Consider it yours. It'll be a bonus for the hard work you've been doing around here." She handed the purse to Barbara and gave her a hug.

"Danki." Grinning, Barbara put the purse straps over her arm.

"You're welcome to eat your lunch in the back room or sit here with me." Peggy motioned to the stools behind the counter. "One of us needs to stay up front in case any customers come in."

"I'll put my new purse away then get my sandwich and join you. It's not much fun to eat alone."

"I agree." Peggy pulled her lunch box out from under the counter while Barbara went to the back room to get hers. When she returned, they sat at the small table behind them, keeping the counter free for customers' purchases.

"How is Gideon doing these days?" Barbara asked after their silent prayer.

"He's feeling much better. In fact, today is his first day back at work."

"I had the wasserpareble when I was a child." Barbara crinkled her nose. "My mamm put stockings over my hands at night so I wouldn't scratch those itchy pox. One time, my arms itched so intensely I took the stockings off and scratched." She lifted her right arm and pointed to a scar. "Here's proof I should have listened to Mom."

Peggy sighed. "Even though Gideon is old enough to know better, he did his share of scratching too. I'm sure he'll have at least one bad *moler* to prove he scratched."

Barbara unwrapped her sandwich. "It's strange he never came down with the chickenpox when he was a boy."

"It is odd, especially because my other five *kinner* all had them. Walter and I always figured he must be immune." Peggy shook her head slowly. "Boy, were we ever wrong."

"Since Gideon is older now, I'll bet he was a lot sicker with the pox."

"Jah. He was one sick puppy the first week or so."

"I've been praying for him." Barbara's tone was sincere. She had asked about Gideon every day since he came down with the chicken pox.

Peggy frowned. *Then there's Mandy, stranded on an island and rarely bothering to call my son. Yet Gideon seems determined to talk her into joining the church and marrying him. I wish he'd reconsider.*

"Your sandwich looks good." Peggy blew on the chicken noodle soup still steaming in her thermos.

"It's chicken salad." Barbara took another bite. "If you like, I'll bring you some tomorrow."

"Sounds good. And I'll have some molasses cookies for us too. I plan to make a few batches this evening for our bishop's wife. There'll be plenty to share."

"I'm looking forward to taking classes in the spring so I can join the church," Barbara added. "Will Gideon be joining too?"

"He wants to, but I believe he's waiting on Mandy so they can be married."

"I thought so." Barbara's shoulders slouched a bit as she ate her sandwich.

Peggy touched her arm. "You mentioned awhile back that you were worried about Mandy, but our conversation was interrupted. Is this something you'd like to talk about now?"

Barbara shook her head. "It was nothing, really. I just wish she and Ellen were home."

Peggy didn't pursue the conversation, but she had an inkling Barbara was holding something back. *Could she possibly have feelings for Gideon herself, or is she missing her friend?*

Massaging the back of her neck where it felt a bit stiff, she continued to reflect on things. *Why couldn't my son have taken an interest in someone like Barbara? Sure wish mothers could pick out their son's wives. This girl is so caring and sweet. She's almost like a daughter to me.*

Kapaa

Mandy stood near the edge of the pool, trembling and breathing hard. She couldn't believe she'd let Ken talk her into this. Worse yet, it was awkward wearing a skirted lavender swimsuit. For modesty, she'd put a T-shirt over the top, but that didn't help her nerves. Ellen wore a similar swimsuit, only hers was dark blue. Yesterday, Ken drove them to one of the shops in town, and they'd bought the most simple-looking, modest swimsuits they could find.

Ellen was able to swim quite well and had already gotten into the water and begun doing the backstroke. While they were on the cruise ship with their friends, she would effortlessly skim through the water. Mandy envied her friend for making it look easy. She wasn't sure she could even get in the pool. All she could think about was when she'd struggled for air after her brother pulled her into the water when she was a girl. Her fear of drowning was almost paralyzing, and to this day, the trepidation gripped her. Mandy would never forget feeling certain she would drown. If not for their dad coming along and rescuing her, she probably wouldn't be here right now.

"Ready to give this a try?" Ken's deep voice, up close to Mandy's ear, caused her to jump back.

This is so embarrassing. Maybe agreeing to let him teach me to swim wasn't the best idea. She coughed, cleared her throat, and coughed again. *Maybe I should have told Ken why I'm afraid of the water.*

"You okay?" Squinting, he looked at her with obvious concern. "Are you coming down with a cold?"

"No, I. . .I'm a bit nervous right now."

"You have nothing to fear. I've taught people how to swim before, so I know what I'm doing." Ken jumped in the pool. "Hold onto the ladder and come on in. The water on this end of the pool isn't over your head."

Mandy's legs shook as she stepped onto the ladder. *Lord, help me be able to do this.*

As her feet touched the water, Ken's strong hands grasped her waist. "Easy now. . .You're doing fine."

Mandy wasn't sure if it was the nearness of him or the cool water on her legs, but a shiver went up her spine. When her feet touched the bottom, the water was as high as her waist. She turned her head toward Ken, but for assurance, kept one hand behind her, touching the ladder.

"Okay, now." Ken looked at her with an air of confidence. "Let yourself get used to the water."

All Mandy could do was shake her head as she gripped the ladder tightly.

"See there." Ken pointed to the middle of the pool. "Those markers painted on the side of the pool are to let us know where it starts getting deeper. The pool slopes downward and then levels off to a depth of eight feet."

"I don't want to go there," Mandy whispered.

"Don't worry, we have all this area to work in, and we'll stay at this end as long as you like." Ken pointed to the shallow end where they stood. "For now, though, why don't you walk around and put your arms out to the sides? Then move them in front of you, back and forth, letting the water roll over your hands and through your fingers. Keep repeating the motion until you feel more comfortable."

Mandy did as Ken instructed. All the while, he stayed beside her, doing the same motion.

The water felt almost like velvet as it softly whooshed through her fingers. After a while, Mandy smiled at Ken, feeling a little more at ease.

"Would you mind telling me why you never learned to swim?"

She drew a quick breath and looked away from him. One of her greatest dislikes was expressing any form of weakness, yet with Ken she felt vulnerable. Mandy tried sorting out her thoughts, but they kept getting scrambled by *what if*s. She didn't want Ken to think her reason for not wanting to swim was silly. Even though the incident happened when she was a child, it still greatly affected her.

"You don't have to tell me if you'd rather not." Ken's voice penetrated her thoughts. "I figured talking about it might help calm your nerves."

A wave of heat rushed through Mandy's body, yet it wasn't from being flustered. It was more pleasant and comforting, like sipping on warm cocoa during a cold winter's evening. The familiar sensation briefly reminded her of being back home with her family. Mandy wasn't one to vent about her problems, but her family was always there for her whenever she needed someone to talk to. Having this sort of feeling around a person she'd only known a little while was odd. *Do I trust Ken enough to share my thoughts? Perhaps telling him would be the right thing to do.* "Well, the truth is. . .I'm afraid of the water."

Mandy waited for him to respond and was surprised when he gently nudged her shoulder. "Then what made you decide to visit Hawaii, with so much water around?"

Heat flooded her cheeks. Ken was obviously confused by such a contradiction. "Just because I can't swim doesn't mean I don't enjoy staring out at the ocean. I'm okay with being around water, as long as I'm not expected to swim in it."

"All right. Makes sense." Ken looked directly at her, but the smile he wore seconds ago slowly diminished. "So why are you afraid of the water, if you don't mind me asking?"

It was difficult, but Mandy managed to explain the event that took place during her childhood. She stumbled a bit while she spoke and had a difficult time finding the right words to use, mostly because she was worried what Ken would think after she finished. Her gaze met his, but he wasn't laughing. His eyes appeared relaxed, reflecting somberness and concern.

"I'm sorry you went through that, Mandy." His voice was soft, and he spoke slowly, which was unusual since he was always so energetic. "It's frightening to think you could have drowned."

"It was, and I should've told you earlier why I didn't want to try swimming again."

"If you're having second thoughts about this, you don't have to do it. I won't force you to learn how to swim."

Mandy turned her head, noticing Ellen in the water, still swimming on her back. *I've gone plenty of years without swimming. Am I really going to let my fear stop me from learning now?*

The muscles tightened in her arms as she looked up at Ken. "No, I want to do this. I need to overcome my fear."

"Okay. You did well with the first part. Now we're gonna try something else."

"What do you mean?" Mandy eyed the ladder on the other side of the pool, wishing she had it for support.

"You need to trust me on this," Ken urged. "Take my hands and let me guide you around, only when I start walking backward, I want you to let your feet float behind you and start kicking."

"You won't go to the deep end, will you?" Mandy's eyes widened.

"Trust me, Mandy. We're only staying in the shallow end. And if you feel uncomfortable, we can stop anytime."

She did as Ken asked. Before long, as he pulled her from one side of the pool to the other, she found herself rather enjoying the feeling of gliding along on her stomach. *This isn't so bad. In fact, it's kind of fun.*

"Now, I want you to go one step further." Ken reassuringly squeezed her hands, keeping his backward motion. "As I pull you, keep kicking your feet, but also lower your head a bit more so your chin is skimming the water."

Nervously, Mandy complied. She was used to the water's coolness now, and it actually felt good as the bright sun shone down on them.

"You'll be a fish in no time, Mandy." Ellen smiled and waved as she stood on the end of the diving board.

"Be careful, Ellen." Mandy glanced at Ken after watching Ellen dive and go beneath the surface, hardly splashing any water at all. "I'll probably never be able to dive like Ellen, let alone feel comfortable if my feet can't touch."

"Never say never," Ken encouraged. "Look how good you're already doing."

"I have to admit, this is the first I've been in water this deep since I was a little girl."

"I have great confidence in you." Ken stopped while Mandy let her feet touch the bottom. Wiping the water from her chin, she missed Ken's touch when he let go of her hands. "That's why I'm going to ask you to keep trusting me. I wouldn't suggest you do anything I didn't think you could do."

"Okay. I. . .I trust you, Ken." Mandy took a deep breath. "You're good at this. Did you ever think of giving swimming lessons fulltime?"

"I taught children at one of the resorts here on the island for a while, but it took a lot of time away from helping my family at the chicken farm. So I only taught for one summer. It was fun, though."

"I know from experience, it's best to learn to swim when you're young. And I regret not pursuing it when I had the chance to learn from my dad."

"Don't look back Mandy. You're here now, and that's what counts. The next thing I'm going to ask you to do is lean over and put your face in the water."

Mandy gulped. "But. . .but I won't be able to breathe."

"You'll hold your breath while your face is in the water, then count to ten and lift your head to take a breath. Once you're able to put your face in the water, you can learn to float without assistance."

"I–I'm not sure I can." Mandy glanced at the other side of the pool, where Ellen continued to swim, this time with her face in the water. She made it look so easy as she kicked her feet and lifted her arms easily in and out of the water. It was the first time since they'd become stranded on Kauai that Mandy had seen Ellen enjoying herself so much.

"It may help if you hold on to me again." Ken grasped Mandy's hand. "Now take a deep breath, close your eyes if you're more comfortable, and put your face in the water."

Mandy grimaced. *That's easy for you to say. You already know how to swim, and you're not afraid of the water.*

Wanting to please Ken and hoping he wouldn't think she was a fraidy-cat, she took a deep breath and dunked her head under the water. But she couldn't muster the courage to open her eyes.

"Good job!" Ken grinned when she lifted her face out of the water. She noticed his face was wet too. "Now do it again; only this time, try opening your eyes."

Mandy did as he asked. Once her eyes got used to the stinging sensation, it wasn't so bad. She grinned when she saw Ken under the water, looking right at her. Then quickly, they surfaced together.

"Okay, now, I want you to grab the edge of the pool. When you put your face in the water, stretch out your legs and kick."

Again, Mandy did as Ken instructed. After she'd done it awhile, he showed her how to float on her back while stabilizing her head. If not for his gentle coaching, she never could have done as he asked. Mandy trusted Ken and felt sure she was in good hands.

"You're getting the hang of it, Mandy. Great job!" Ellen shouted.

Mandy was pleased with her friend's compliment. It made it easier to press on with the lesson.

"Ellen's right. You're doing very well." Ken gave her a thumbs-up. "A few more visits to my folks' pool, and you'll be swimming like a mermaid."

Mandy wasn't sure, but with Ken teaching her, she felt hopeful about learning to swim. In fact, she was beginning to think she could do almost anything with him at her side. Even though she had fought it, she was beginning to see Ken as more than a friend, and home filled her thoughts less often.

Chapter 23

Middlebury

Christmas didn't often fall on a Sunday, but today was one of those years it did. As Barbara sat on a church bench inside her uncle Nate's barn, she glanced at her friend Sadie, who sat to her left, and then to her sister Libby, on the right. The weather was quite chilly this morning, but the barn was kept warm by her uncle's woodstove. It was good to be with the people closest to her. *Too bad Mandy and Ellen aren't here.*

Sadie must have been deep in thought, staring into space, while drumming her fingers on the inside of her arm. Was she also wondering about their friends?

Ever since she'd arrived home, a day hadn't gone by when Barbara's thoughts didn't end up hundreds of miles away. It was hard enough to believe she'd been to Hawaii, let alone to think about Mandy and Ellen on a tropical island without any family. *I wonder what our two friends are doing right now. Are they wishing they were home with their families?* Barbara glanced out the window and saw it was beginning to snow. *Are Mandy and Ellen missing the cold, snowy weather, or are they content to be where it's warm?*

Barbara reflected on the last conversation she'd had with Ellen, when she'd mentioned how she and Mandy attended a church on Kauai. No doubt, they would attend services there today and then take part in whatever kind of celebration the Hawaiian couple had in their home.

I wonder if my friends feel out of place. I sure would. It must be hard for Miriam and Isaac, having their daughter so far away—especially during the holidays. I'm sure Mandy's brothers miss her too, since it's the first Christmas their entire family isn't together. Same for Ellen's parents and her siblings.

I'm thankful I can be with my family for Christmas. I can't imagine being stuck on an island, far from home, with people I'd only met a little over a month ago.

She glanced at the men's side of the room and spotted Gideon, wearing a grim expression. Barbara's heart clenched. *I wish he didn't look so sad. He must miss Mandy something awful today.*

Gideon had a hard time concentrating on the bishop's message. Christmas was supposed to be a joyful occasion, but he wasn't in the holiday spirit, even with the pleasure of seeing a few snowflakes falling this morning. Going to church and celebrating with his family afterward wasn't the same without Mandy. He'd called her the night before to wish her a Merry Christmas, but like before, she was busy and couldn't talk long. She'd been polite, of course, and explained they had company at the B&B, but it almost seemed as if she was looking for an excuse not to talk to him.

Maybe I'm being paranoid. With Mandy so far away and me not knowing when she's coming home, it's easy to conjure things up in my mind that may not even be true. I miss her so much, I can't think straight anymore.

The bench Gideon sat upon seemed more uncomfortable than usual. Or was it only because he felt so miserable? Scooching around to find a comfortable position didn't help, nor did stretching his legs out in front of him.

He sighed and instinctively reached up to touch the small indentation on his right cheek, caused from scratching an infected pox. This was not going to be one of his better Christmases.

Kapaa

"I'm glad we were able to go to church today," Ellen whispered as she and Mandy took seats in the sanctuary. "But it would have been nice if Luana and Makaio could have come with us."

"They wanted to, but Makaio still isn't doing well with his crutches, so he figured it would be better to stay home."

Ellen's stomach tensed as she heard the word *home*. Every year she looked forward to spending Christmas with her family. Not being with them today was heartbreaking. She turned to her friend. "Do you think he's ever going to be well enough to help Luana again so we can go home?"

"Of course he will. But is going home all you ever think about?" Mandy's brows furrowed. "Can't you enjoy our time here on Kauai for as long as it lasts?"

Ellen bristled. "The things you say shock me sometimes. It's Christmas, Mandy, and I miss my family. You should miss your family too."

"How can you even suggest such a thing?" A pained expression gathered on Mandy's face, and then she lowered her head. "I do miss everyone back home, but I'm trying to make the best of our situation." She slowly lifted her head. "And what about Luana? Would you want to leave her in a bind? I would hope not. It isn't the way we were taught."

"No, of course not. I only meant—"

"*Shh*. It's time to get quiet." Mandy motioned to the front, where the worship team had assembled.

The pastor stepped up to the podium and tapped on the microphone. The sound boomed through the speakers. Startled, many people jumped.

Red-faced, he grinned sheepishly. "Sorry. I didn't mean for that to happen. Would everyone please stand for a word of prayer?"

Luana sat on the sofa, gazing at the twinkling lights on their Christmas tree. Makaio was asleep in his recliner, with his Bible in his lap. He'd had a restless night, and soon after they'd read scripture together this morning, his eyelids had grown heavy. It was all right. He needed his rest. Luana's only regret was they couldn't go to church with Ellen and Mandy. Makaio was disappointed too, and had become impatient, complaining about not being able to climb a ladder to decorate the outside of the house with colored lights.

She understood her husband's edginess. After six weeks of wearing the cast, he had been excited to get the thing off. But when he'd seen the doctor two days ago, he was told he would need to wear it another two weeks to be sure the leg healed properly. Luana never let on, but she'd been hopeful for Makaio. Eight weeks was a long time to be wearing a cast.

She leaned her head back and let her mind drift to the many Christmases she'd spent as a young girl on the Big Island. Some years, her parents got together with other family members in one of their homes. Other times, they would gather at one of the beaches for a picnic. Anywhere with her loved ones felt like home.

She laughed faintly, thinking about her uncle Randy. He always showed up wearing a shell lei around his neck and a Santa hat on his head. Of course, he made sure it was his job to hand out all the Christmas presents to the children who were there. He used to tell them stories about how Santa Claus rode in a red canoe pulled by dolphins, and then they all sang, "Here comes Santa in a Red Canoe." Songs such as "Christmas in Hawaii" and the Hawaiian version of "The Twelve Days of Christmas" were accompanied by ukulele or a guitar.

As soon as Ailani and Oke came over and Mandy and Ellen returned from church, they would share a meal. Afterward, if Makaio felt up to it, he would play his ukulele while they sang Christmas songs for their holiday gathering.

Sighing, Luana stood and headed for the kitchen. The tantalizing smell of ham slowly heating in the oven reached her nose and caused her stomach to growl. It was tradition to have coconut pudding for dessert, but instead, she'd made a pineapple upside-down cake.

I'll miss those young Amish women when they return to the mainland, Luana thought. Even though she hadn't known them long, they'd become almost like family to her. *Maybe someday, if we can find someone to take over the bed-and-breakfast for a few weeks, we can go to Indiana to meet Mandy and Ellen's families. Visiting Amish country would be an interesting way to spend a vacation. We'd have to make sure we went during the warm summer months, because I don't think I could get used to the cold or snow.*

"Who's ready for dessert?" Luana asked, carrying a pineapple-upside-down cake into the living room shortly after their afternoon meal.

Oke smacked his lips. "It looks 'ono,"

"I agree. It does look delicious."

Ellen turned her head and gave Mandy a strange look. "You understood what 'ono means?"

Mandy smiled. "In addition to the Hawaiian Makaio's taught me, Ken's also shared a few more words and phrases."

"I should have guessed." Ellen got up from her chair. "Would you like some help serving the cake, Luana?"

"I can manage, but if you'd like to bring in the coffee and hot tea, I'd appreciate it."

"I'll come with you." Mandy hopped up and followed Ellen into the kitchen. Then she tapped Ellen's shoulder. "What did you mean in there, when you said you should have guessed Ken taught me some Hawaiian words?"

Ellen picked up the teapot and turned to face her. "I only meant that since you've been seeing him so much lately, I wasn't surprised he'd taught you to say the Hawaiian word. Why are you so touchy?"

"It's the way you sounded, I guess. Ken's been very helpful, and he's become a good friend. And may I remind you, he's been kind to you too." She set the coffeepot on a tray and got out the cups. "I never expected when we began our trip to Hawaii that I'd come to understand so many Hawaiian words, much less learn how to swim. I didn't think I'd ever conquer my fear of the water, but I'm grateful to Ken for making it happen."

Ellen gave her a hug. "Believe me, I'm happy for you. Getting over your fear of the water was a huge step. Trusting Ken to teach you how to swim was even greater. Now when we go on picnics during warmer weather at home, we can swim in the pond near the back of my folks' property. I'm looking forward to enjoying the summer months next year."

"Jah, and I can't wait to surprise my brothers."

A knock sounded on the back door, so Mandy went to answer it. She was surprised to see Ken on the lanai, holding a large paper sack.

"*Mele Kalikimaka*." Grinning, Ken stepped inside. "I come bearing gifts."

"Merry Christmas to you too." Mandy's heartbeat picked up speed, as it always did when she was with Ken. "I'll tell Luana and Makaio you're here, and that you've brought gifts for them."

Ken set the sack on the table. "The presents are for you and Ellen. Since this is your first Christmas on Kauai, and you're no doubt missing home, I wanted to do something special for you."

"Mahalo. It was a thoughtful gesture." Mandy looked at Ellen, raising her eyebrows to stress her point of Ken being good to Ellen too.

Ellen moved over to the table. "Yes, thank you, Ken, for thinking of us."

Mandy felt bad when he pulled two wrapped packages from the bag. "I wish I had something to give you."

"Your friendship is the only gift I need." Ken's sincere smile nearly melted Mandy's heart.

"Go ahead, open it." He handed her one of the gifts and gave the other one to Ellen.

Mandy's fingers trembled as she tore the wrapping paper off and opened the box. Her breath caught in her throat when she discovered a framed photo of a gorgeous sunrise. "Oh Ken, did you take this picture?"

"Sure did." He beamed.

Mandy wanted to shout at the top of her lungs how much she appreciated the gift, but she spoke softly instead. "It's wonderful. Thank you so much."

"You're welcome." Ken pointed to the other present. "Ellen, your gift is almost the same, except it's a sunset. I took them both the same day."

Smiling, Ellen opened her gift. "Thank you, Ken. Now when we go home, we'll have another slice of Hawaii to take with us, along with the coral you found for us on the beach."

I wish I didn't have to go home, Mandy thought for the umpteenth time. *But at least I'll have the picture the woman at the falls took of Ken and me. I'll keep it hidden in one of my drawers to remind me of what I'm missing.*

Chapter 24

I'm glad my husband got his cast off yesterday," Luana commented as she, Mandy, and Ellen got breakfast ready for their guests the second Saturday of January. "Unfortunately, he's like a crab with sore pinchers, because now he's faced with several weeks of physical therapy. He commented right away in the doctor's office how nice it was to finally have it off." Her forehead creased. "That man of mine grinned and said, 'Now I can scratch where I couldn't before, and it feels so good to have that added weight gone.'"

"Hopefully, it won't be long before his leg is good as new." Ellen placed a pitcher of pineapple juice on the tray, which she set on the table.

Mandy glanced at the calendar, wondering how much longer it would be before Makaio could resume his duties at the B&B. She wanted his leg to get better, but oh, how she would miss this wonderful place. In all her life she'd never been anywhere like Kauai, where she felt such peace.

"How are your swimming lessons going?" Luana asked, scattering Mandy's thoughts.

"Fairly well." Mandy smiled. "I'm getting more confident in the water and can even do the sidestroke and tread water a bit. Oh, and I'm getting used to putting my face under water, which is one thing I could never imagine being able to do. My family back home will be surprised at this accomplishment. They've tried to coax me to try swimming, but I've always refused."

Luana stirred the steaming eggs she'd begun cooking in a large frying pan. "If anyone could teach you to swim and feel confident in the water, it would be Ken. Besides being a good swimmer himself, he's kind and patient."

Mandy agreed wholeheartedly. Ken had never once pushed her to do anything she didn't feel comfortable with. He seemed to spread kindness to everyone he met.

"Are you two looking forward to the luau Ken is taking you to tonight?" Luana asked as she filled a platter with scrambled eggs.

"I certainly am." Excitement bubbled in Mandy's chest. "It should be quite interesting."

Ellen, looking less enthused, placed a pitcher of orange juice on the platter beside the pineapple juice. "I had planned to stay here and write some letters to family back home, but Mandy and Ken talked me into going."

"You won't be sorry." Luana stepped to the middle of the kitchen and did a little dance. "You'll see hula dancers, a fire dancer, and lots more great entertainment. And the food at a luau is downright delicious." Her eyes sparkled.

Watching Luana, Mandy and Ellen both giggled. "Did you ever hula dance?" Mandy asked.

"When I was a little girl I used to practice dancing in front of my bedroom mirror; with the door closed, of course. Then, during my teen years I took lessons and got pretty good, if I do say so myself." Luana chuckled and did a few hand motions to one side and then the other.

Mandy looked forward to attending the event, but even more, she was eager to spend time with Ken again.

Shipshewana, Indiana

Saturday was Gideon's day off, and he'd been running errands for his mother all morning. It was twelve o'clock and time to stop for lunch.

After entering the café inside Yoder's Complex and placing his order at the counter, he spotted Barbara sitting by herself. Stepping up to her table, he placed his hand gently on her shoulder. "Mind if I join ya, or is this seat taken?"

Turning her head quickly, Barbara gasped. "Ach, Gideon, I hadn't realized you were here."

"I've been running errands for my mamm this morning and decided to stop for something to eat. Sorry if I startled you." He gestured to the empty chair. "Is it okay if I sit at your table?"

She smiled. "I'd be pleased if you joined me."

Gideon took a seat. "Have you eaten already?" He noted she only had a glass of iced tea in front of her.

"No, I'm waiting for my order." She rested her hands on the table.

"Same here. I just put mine in." Gideon leaned forward. "Were you shopping too?"

"Jah. I was looking for a birthday present for my sister Fern."

"Any luck?"

Barbara nodded before taking a sip of her drink. "I found a puzzle for her, featuring a beautiful black horse. All she talks about is raising horses when she grows up."

"It's good Fern knows what she wants, especially at her young age."

"I like horses too, but not enough to raise them."

"Same here, although I've never considered giving up my job to do something like that. It would be an adventure."

"It certainly would." Barbara smiled.

Gideon sat quietly, suddenly at a loss for words.

"Have you heard anything from Mandy lately?" Barbara asked.

"I had a conversation with her on Christmas Eve. She was busy, though, so we didn't talk long." Gideon's posture sagged. "I can't help wondering if she's forgotten what we had. If a girl cares for a guy, she should be eager to talk to him." Frowning, he placed his straw hat on the table.

"Mandy may have been busy. There's a lot involved in running a bed-and-breakfast. No doubt she and Ellen have plenty of work to do." Barbara reached over and touched Gideon's arm.

"I suppose, but she can't be working all the time. You'd think on Christmas Eve. . ." Gideon's voice trailed off when both his and Barbara's meals were brought to the table. Was there any point in talking about this right now? It wouldn't change the facts. He appreciated Barbara's sympathy, but he wasn't sure she fully understand how badly he felt.

"Why don't we stop for a bite to eat?" Sadie suggested when she and her mother finished shopping at Yoder's Hardware.

"Good idea," Mom responded warmly. "I'm hungerich."

When they entered the restaurant, they placed their orders, then moved into the room where all the tables were set up. Sadie glanced at a table on the other side of the room and drew in a sharp breath. Gideon and Barbara sat together, and Barbara's hand was on his arm. *What? Why are they here together?* Her skin tingled as she wondered how Mandy would feel about this.

"Go ahead and find a table, Mom. Anywhere is fine with me. I'm going over to say hello to Gideon and Barbara, but I'll join you soon."

"Oh, okay. Don't be too long, though. I'm sure our food will be here shortly."

Sadie hurried across the room and stopped in front of her friend's table. When she said hello, Barbara pulled her hand away from Gideon's arm and stared at her with a wide-eyed expression.

"I'm surprised to see you," Sadie said. "Don't you usually work at the quilt-and-fabric shop most Saturdays?"

Barbara nodded. "I worked this morning, but surprisingly, things were slow, so Peggy said I could take the afternoon off."

Sadie glanced at Gideon. "Have you heard anything from Mandy recently?"

"Talked with her briefly on Christmas Eve but haven't heard from her since. How about you?"

"No. My plan was to call her on Christmas Day, but we had a big family gathering and time got away from me."

"The last time I spoke with Mandy was yesterday." Barbara spoke up. "She told me she's been learning to swim. She also mentioned that she and Ellen would be attending a luau this evening."

Gideon looked at Barbara and frowned. "Guess you were wrong about her workin' all the time." He leaned his elbows on the table. "I'm happy she's learned to swim, but Mandy seems like she has plenty of time for all kinds of things—except talking to me."

Sadie felt bad for Gideon, but at the same time, she hoped nothing was occurring between him and Barbara. Mandy would be devastated if she came home and found out he'd become interested in one of her friends while she was gone.

I wonder if I should talk to Barbara about this. Sadie bit her lip. *Regardless, now is not the time.*

Lihue

"Are you two ready to experience an evening you won't forget?" Ken asked as he led Mandy and Ellen to a table near the stage. He'd upgraded their reservations so they could have better seats.

"Yes, definitely!" Mandy looked down at the lovely flower leis she and Ellen had received when they'd entered the grounds. She was glad they'd both worn a muumuu tonight, rather than their Amish dresses. It made them blend in more with the crowd, even with the scarves they wore pinned at the back of their heads.

"The *imu* ceremony was interesting," Ellen commented.

Ken nodded. "Yes, and you'll enjoy eating some of the tasty pork during the meal we'll be eating soon. Since we have VIP seats, our table and the others closest to the stage will be called to the buffet table first."

"You shouldn't have spent the extra money." Mandy spoke softly. "We would have been satisfied to sit at any table."

Ken leaned closer to Mandy, touching her arm. "I wanted you to have the best seats so you could see the show up close and be transported to ancient Polynesia during the time of their migration to the islands." He pushed his seat back and stood. "Now, can I get either of you a glass of Hawaiian fruit punch while we wait for our meal?"

"I'd like one," Mandy replied. "But if you show me where to go, I can get it myself."

"Nope. You two are my guests this evening, and I'm going to wait on you." He looked at Ellen. "Does some punch sound good to you?"

"Yes, please."

Ken left the table and returned with two glasses of punch, which he handed to Ellen and Mandy. Then he went back and got one for himself.

A short time later, someone came and told them it was time to go to the buffet table.

"This reminds me of the buffet we serve at the restaurant where I work in Middlebury," Mandy whispered to Ellen as they took their plates and began dishing up. "Only the food's a lot different here."

"Be sure you try some of this to go with your kalua pork." Ken pointed to the container marked *Poi*. "It's made from the taro plant."

Mandy wrinkled her nose. "Luana told me about poi. She said it tastes rather bland."

"It's more of an acquired taste, but I think it's pretty good; especially when I dip the pork into it."

"Think I'll pass and have some purple sweet potatoes."

They continued down the line, filling their plates with stir-fried vegetables, teriyaki chicken, pan-seared filet of ono fish, tossed green salad with papaya dressing, taro rolls, and steamed jasmine rice. Mandy's mouth watered thinking how good it would all taste. As they passed the dessert bar, she noticed rice pudding, coconut cake, and pineapple upside-down cake, as well as several kinds of tropical fruits. She would wait until she'd eaten the main meal to get dessert, in case she was too full to enjoy it.

When they returned to the table, they bowed their heads for a silent prayer. As they ate their meal, Ken told them about the Kilohana Plantation, where the luau was being held. "There's a train ride you can take around the 105-acre historic plantation," he explained. "We could have ridden it this evening if we'd gotten here earlier, but I wasn't able to quit work in time."

"It's okay." Mandy forked a piece of pork. "What we're doing now is exciting enough."

"Maybe we can take the train ride another time." He pointed to the poi on Ellen's plate. "What do you think of it?"

"It is rather tasteless but not too bad. You should have tried some, Mandy."

"I might some other time." Mandy put another piece of pork into her mouth, enjoying the tender, succulent morsel. "Right now, I'm enjoying this moist, delicious meat."

When the meal was over and they'd finished dessert, the lights lowered and the entertainment began. Mandy sat mesmerized as an incredible tale unfolded through dance, song, and the rhythm of Tahitian drums. The story showed the depths of one family's great effort as they sought courage and vision to carry them on a voyage from Tahiti to Hawaii.

She sat in rapt attention as the theatrical luau ended with a dream scene featuring fire poi balls and the traditional fire knife dance. The world seemed to slow down as she thought about the difficulty of leaving the only home they'd ever known and traveling to a land far away to begin a new life. She'd been away from her family more than two months. Could she remain on Kauai, knowing she may only see them on rare occasions? It was a question never far from her thoughts these days.

Chapter 25

Saturday, January 16

I am sitting here on the beach with Ellen, watching Ken surf. It's frightening to see him out there in those giant waves, yet it's exciting too. How he manages to stand up and keep his balance on the board is beyond me. If I tried that, I'd be knocked into the water for sure.

Mandy placed her journal inside the tote bag she'd brought along and drew a deep breath. It had been several days since she'd written anything in it because they'd been so busy at the B&B. It felt wonderful to sit here now, enjoying all the sights and smells around her. This morning, when Ken stopped by and asked if she and Ellen would like to watch him surf, Luana had insisted they go, saying she could manage on her own for a few hours.

Turning to face Ellen, sitting on the blanket beside her, Mandy observed the plain dress Ellen had made. Except for church, Mandy hardly wore her Amish clothes anymore. The muumuu was comfortable and modest. Wearing it made her feel as if she belonged on Kauai. She had to admit, even though Ellen didn't have the exact pattern for an Amish dress, she'd done a good job with what she'd had to work with. She hoped her friend wouldn't hold it against her because she'd strayed from their traditional dress. Sooner or later, Mandy would have to change back to her customary clothing. If she were to arrive home wearing a muumuu, her family would be stunned and no doubt displeased.

"Luana's such a nice lady," she said, setting aside her thoughts. "Just think, if we hadn't missed the ship, we'd never have met her and Makaio."

Ellen nodded.

"It was good of her to let us have time off this afternoon to spend time on the beach. And look at the beautiful water. It stretches out as far as the eye can see." Mandy adjusted her sunglasses so they wouldn't keep slipping on her nose where she'd put sunscreen.

She focused her attention on Ken when she noticed him talking with two young women on the beach. She assumed he must know them fairly well, for the dark-haired woman wearing a navy-blue swimsuit stood close to Ken, with her hand resting on his arm. Mandy felt a twinge of jealousy but reminded herself that she had no claim on him. They were only friends and would be saying goodbye, most likely for good, when she left Hawaii.

Refocusing, she noticed that Ellen's mind seemed to be elsewhere as she watched a stray dog digging frantically in the sand close to the surf.

"What's the crazy *hund* doing?" Mandy chuckled as the shaggy mutt continued to dig and spin around in circles.

"I don't know, but he's certainly energetic. Determined too." Ellen laughed as the critter threw clods of wet sand into the air.

"The dog's not the only energetic one." Mandy pointed to the frothy water. Ken was paddling out from the shore. "It amazes me the way he paddles out with his board, then stands up and rides those big waves back in. I'd be exhausted if I tried that, not to mention making a fool of myself."

"But now you could swim, or at least stay afloat."

"No way! I'm not a strong enough swimmer yet. Even if I was, I wouldn't have the strength or nerve to do what Ken does."

"Me neither. It takes a lot of practice to master the art of surfing. Fortunately, where we live, we don't have to worry about such things. Swimming in my folks' pond is good enough for me." Ellen grabbed a handful of sand and let it sift through her fingers.

Swimming in a little pond won't be near as exciting as paddling around in the ocean, Mandy thought, but she didn't voice the sentiment to her friend. She looked back at Ken and the enormous wave forming behind him. She sat up straight as the current swelled like a huge wall coming up from the ocean floor. This was the biggest wave she had seen. Ken turned and obviously saw it as he readied himself on the board. She instinctively stood up, watching Ken use his arms to paddle as the wave approached. In no time he was on his feet, riding the water's crest as if it was as easy as riding a bike. Ken rode the wave beautifully and crouched a bit on his board as a huge curl formed alongside of him. Then quickly, he disappeared, as if the water had swallowed him up.

Not far from where Ken was last seen, another surfer was engulfed in a separate tube of water. Mandy covered her eyes, peeking through her fingers to watch as the surfer lost his balance. The power of the water flipped him into the air, and then he landed on the backside of the swell. He seemed to be okay after retrieving his board and simply waited for another wave to ride.

Mandy kept watching and silently said a prayer. *Please Lord, keep Ken safe and don't let him fall off the board.*

Ellen stood up too. "I can't see Ken anymore, can you?"

"No." Mandy held her breath for what seemed like many minutes, looking for any sign of him. It wasn't like she hadn't seen this type of surfing when Ken took her to the beach a while back, but this was different. It was Ken out there in the unrelenting ocean.

She was about to run down to the water's edge—to do what, she didn't know. A sigh of relief escaped her lips as Ken, still on his board, emerged, skimming skillfully out of the curling wave. She watched in awe as he continued surfing the swell until it weakened and brought him in to shallower water.

Ellen sat back down and Mandy followed. "Wow, he had me scared for a minute." She smiled when Ken raised his hand to wave at them. Then he turned back toward the ocean.

"He seems to know what he's doing," Ellen said. "Look at him. He's going back out for more. I have to say, a huge wave like the one he rode would have been enough for me. Imagine being in a wall of water like he was. Makes me shudder, even thinking about it."

"Me too."

"Do you think that silly hund belongs to anyone?" Ellen pointed to the dog again. "I don't see his master anywhere."

"Maybe whoever he belongs to is up the beach a ways and the dog wandered off." Right now, the animal was of little interest to Mandy, as she breathed deeply to quell her rapidly beating heart. She watched Ken float casually on his board to wait for another wave to swell. A short time later, he came out of the water, laying his surfboard on the sand. The dog raced over to him, barking and wagging his tail.

"What do ya want, boy? Wanna play?" Ken bent down, grabbed a stick, and flung it into the water.

The dog bounded in after it, swam back, and dropped it at Ken's feet. *Woof! Woof!*

"So you do wanna play, huh?" He picked up the stick and threw it again, a little farther out in the water.

Once again, the dog retrieved it, looking up at Ken as if begging for more.

"Okay, one more time, boy, and then I'm done. I need to go rest awhile." He tossed the stick, and as the dog swam out to it, Ken plodded up the beach and dropped onto the blanket beside Mandy.

"Do you know who owns the dog?" she asked.

"Nope. I'm guessing he's a stray."

"He was digging furiously in the sand a while ago," Ellen spoke up. "It was comical to watch him—especially when he looked over this way, with sand on his nose."

"For sure, he has a lot of energy." Ken chuckled.

"After watching you in those waves, I'd say the dog isn't the only one with a lot of energy." Mandy tilted her head. "What kind of dog do you think it is?"

He shrugged. "Hard to tell. Looks like a mixture of terrier and spaniel."

"Did you enjoy riding the big waves?" Ellen asked.

"Yeah. It's me at the mercy of the ocean. It's a rush—kind of hard to describe."

All Mandy could do was shake her head. She didn't want to let on how scared she'd been when Ken got lost for a few seconds in the wave.

"Would you like a glass of cold hibiscus tea?" Ellen reached for the cooler they'd brought along. "I imagine you're pretty thirsty by now."

"Sure. I'd appreciate something cold to drink."

"How about something to eat?" Mandy offered, relieved Ken was back on dry land. "We brought along some Maui onion chips, as well as some of Luana's macadamia nut cookies."

"They both sound good."

Ellen poured the iced tea, while Mandy got out the food. When they started to eat, the dog bounded up, barking and wagging his tail.

"The poor pooch looks hungry." Mandy broke off a piece of her cookie and held it out.

"Oh, oh, now you've done it. We'll never get rid of the mutt." Ken smirked as he reached out and scratched behind the critter's ears. "We're gonna have a friend for life."

"I guess so." Mandy giggled. "Maybe we should ask some of the people here on the beach if the dog belongs to anyone."

"I'll do it as soon as I finish my snack." He gave the dog a few chips. Although there was nothing left in Ken's hand, the mutt continued to lick the salt off his fingers. "From the way the pooch gobbled it up, I'm guessing he hasn't eaten in a while. One more reason to believe he's a stray." He stood and wiped his hand against his black tank top before Mandy could think to hand him a napkin. "Wouldn't be surprised if someone didn't drop the dog off somewhere and he wandered down to the beach in search of food."

Mandy hated to think anyone would do such a thing, but even back home some dogs ended up to be strays, abandoned by their masters. If this dog was homeless, it was a shame, because he seemed so smart, not to mention friendly and playful. She wished they could take him back to the B&B, but Luana didn't have any pets and probably wouldn't appreciate having a dog hanging around pestering her guests.

As if he could read Mandy's mind, Ken looked over at her and smiled. "If I don't find the dog's owner, I'll take him with me—at least till I can find him a good home."

She smiled too, thinking once more what a nice person he was.

"Oh, great. Looks like the vog is creeping in." Ken pointed to the haze blowing toward them.

"Could that be why my eyes are itching all of a sudden?" Mandy asked.

"Wouldn't be a bit surprised. I'll go ask around about the dog, and then we should probably get going before the vog becomes any worse." Ken stood and started down the beach, with the dog trailing along.

"If the hund doesn't already have a home, I bet he'll find one with Ken," Ellen remarked.

Mandy was about to comment, when a round of sneezing overtook her. *Achoo! Achoo! Achoo!* "Oh, dear, my eyes itch worse now too." She reached into her tote for a tissue.

When Ken returned, he took one look at Mandy and suggested he ought to take her home. He pointed to the dog. "Guess the mutt's coming with me for now, 'cause nobody I talked to knows where he belongs."

Mandy smiled, despite how miserable she felt. She was glad Ken would be taking the dog. It wouldn't be right to leave the poor animal alone on the beach.

Luana went out to the lanai to visit with Makaio awhile, but the telephone rang. "I'd better get it." She handed him a glass of freshly made lemonade. "It could be Ailani calling about the doctor's appointment she went to this morning."

She hurried back to the kitchen and picked up the receiver. "The Palms Bed-and-Breakfast." When she realized it was someone asking about the availability of a room next month, she grabbed the guest book to check for vacancies. She gave the woman the available dates and details, then took down her information, including a credit card number to hold the reservation.

After Luana hung up, she returned to the lanai with a glass of lemonade for herself. "It wasn't our daughter, but we do have another guest scheduled for the first weekend in February."

"Good to hear. We need all the business we can get, especially with many of my hospital bills still unpaid." Makaio's brows furrowed. "I'll be glad when the doctor says my leg's healed sufficiently and I can resume my regular duties here. I feel like a burden to you when all I do is sit around. Think I've put on a few extra pounds too." Patting his stomach, he took a sip of lemonade. "Good tasting. You make it just the way I like."

"Mahalo." She leaned over and kissed his cheek. "And you're not a burden. You'd do the same for me if I were the one laid up. It's part of the commitment we made to each other when we got married."

"True. I only wish—"

"And don't you worry. You'll lose those extra pounds when you're up and about again." Luana patted his cheeks. "I'll see that you do." The phone rang again, and she stood. "Hold your thoughts. I'll be right back."

Middlebury

Gideon hoped when he called Mandy this time, she'd be free to talk. He missed her and wanted to know she was missing him too. Right now, he felt insecure feelings creeping in—the ones that told him Mandy wasn't his girlfriend anymore.

He chided himself for thinking this way and took a moment to shake off his doubts before making the call. After pausing at the door of the phone shack a few seconds, Gideon stepped inside and took a seat on the wooden stool. Then he punched in the number for the B&B. Mandy's birthday was coming up soon, and he wanted to tell her that he'd sent a gift and a card. The phone rang several times before a woman's voice came on the line. "Aloha! This is the Palms Bed-and-Breakfast."

"This is Gideon Eash. Is Mandy there? I'd like to speak with her, please."

"Oh, I'm sorry. Mandy isn't here right now. She's at the beach with Ken. She mentioned something about surfing."

"What did you say?" Gideon was sure he must have misunderstood. No way would Mandy have gone surfing. She couldn't even swim.

"I said, Mandy's at the beach. Ken took them surfing."

A chill shot up his spine. If she'd been foolish enough to try surfing, then her life could be in danger. The sport was dangerous—even for a strong swimmer, which Mandy definitely was not. Then another thought popped into his head. *Mandy's with that guy named Ken again. Just who is this fellow, and how close have they become?*

"Would you please tell her Gideon called and that I'll try to call again on her birthday? Oh, and let her know to expect a card and a gift from me."

"What day is Mandy's birthday?" the woman asked.

"January twenty-eighth. She'll be twenty-one years old."

"Thanks for letting me know. We'll be sure to do something special to help Mandy celebrate her birthday."

Gideon's jaw clenched. *It should be me helping Mandy celebrate, not people she barely knows. She was off someplace with him before when I called.* A rush of adrenaline coursed through his body. *Seems like she spends a lot of time with this fellow. Sure hope I have nothing to worry about.*

Kapaa

By the time Mandy and Ellen arrived back at the B&B, Mandy's nose was sore from blowing it so many times. She'd been sneezing a lot, and her eyes had become even itchier than they were at the beach.

"Is something wrong, Mandy?" Luana asked when they entered the kitchen. "You look like you've been crying."

"I've been sneezing, and my eyes are red and itchy." She brought her hand up to her right eye and rubbed it. "This started while we were on the beach and got worse as Ken drove us back here."

"I'll bet it's the vog." Luana handed Mandy a tissue. "I'll give you an allergy pill and then you should go lie down for a while."

Ellen gave Mandy's shoulder a tender squeeze. "See, not all things in

Hawaii are perfect. You'd have to deal with the vog all the time if you lived here."

"Not all the time," Luana corrected. "Only when the wind blows the ash over from the Big Island."

Mandy sighed. "Guess there's good and bad in everything. Wherever you go, no place is perfect." She pushed her shoulders back and smiled. "Even with the vog, I still enjoy being here on Kauai."

Chapter 26

*O*h my, this is a surprise!" Mandy exclaimed when she entered Luana's dining room and saw a decorated cake with her name on it. A pink tablecloth, with brightly colored balloons and the words *Happy Birthday* printed around the edge, covered the table. Paper plates and matching napkins had also been added. "How did you know today was my birthday?" Before Luana could respond, Mandy nudged Ellen's arm. "I'll bet you spilled the beans."

"Nope. It wasn't me."

"It was the young man who calls to speak with you so often." Luana covered her mouth. "Sorry, but I forgot to tell you he called the day you and Ellen went to the beach with Ken. He wanted to let you know he was sending a card and gift for your birthday."

Mandy scratched at her cheek where a mosquito had taken a bite. "That's strange. I haven't received anything from Gideon in the mail. The only birthday cards I've gotten were from my parents and from Barbara and Sadie." She sighed. "I wish you could have met our other two friends who made the trip to Hawaii with us. I'm sure you would have liked them."

"If they're anything like you two, we definitely would have liked them." Makaio motioned to the birthday cake in the middle of the table. "Mandy, why don't you make a wish and blow out your candles so we can all eat some of my wife's yummy coconut cake?"

"Not yet." Luana shook her head. "We won't cut the cake until Ken gets here."

"Ken's coming over?" Mandy couldn't hide her pleasure.

"Yes. He'll be here as soon as he's done eating supper." Luana gave a playful wink. "I believe he has something for you."

Mandy grinned. She looked forward to seeing Ken.

She thought about the dog they'd found on the beach and how Ken had taken it home. He'd named the mutt Rusty, and it had taken a liking to Ken's mother right away. Now the critter was her constant companion.

"I have a present for you." Ellen handed Mandy a floral gift bag. "Happy birthday."

Mandy reached inside and felt some fabric between her fingers. She raised it up and discovered a green, Amish-style dress. It wasn't what she'd expected, and it was difficult to show appreciation—especially when she'd told Ellen previously how content she was wearing a muumuu.

"It's for our trip home," Ellen explained. "Since you have only one Amish dress, you'll need a change of clothes."

Mandy hadn't even thought about her clothing for the trip. Ellen was right. She would need more than one plain dress. She hugged her friend. "Danki for your thoughtfulness in making the dress for me. It must have been hard to sew it without me finding out."

"Not really." Ellen smiled. "Whenever you went shopping with Luana or somewhere with Ken, I worked on it. I'm thankful she has a sewing machine."

"Here's our gift to you." Luana handed Mandy a large box covered with paper in a design of tropical birds. "There are actually two gifts inside—one from Makaio and one from me."

Mandy tore off the paper and pulled the lid aside. The first thing she saw was a set of lovely potholders and an apron to match. Each had different Hawaiian flowers on them. "Mahalo, Luana. Did you make these?"

"Yes, I did. When Ellen began working on her dresses, it put me in the mood to sew."

"Keep looking, Mandy." Makaio motioned to the box. "There's something from me."

She pulled a layer of tissue aside and gasped when a beautiful ukulele came into view. "Oh, my. . . This is too much!" She stared at the instrument in amazement.

"It's not brand new," he explained. "It's a used one I picked up at a yard sale a few years ago, but it's in great shape, and I thought you might like it."

"I certainly do. Thank you both so much." Mandy gave Luana and Makaio a hug. Then she picked up the ukulele and started strumming the strings. Even though musical instruments were not used during an Amish church service, some Plain people, including her father, played the harmonica or guitar for personal enjoyment. She looked forward to many hours learning to play this wonderful birthday present.

"Sorry I haven't shown you how before," Makaio apologized. "Either I've not felt up to it or you've been busy. But I would like to teach you before you return to your home on the mainland."

"Oh, would you? I'd like that so much. Maybe we could make some time for it each evening."

"Good idea." He glanced at the cake and then at Luana. "Are you sure we can't cut the cake and eat it now?"

"Don't even think about it." Luana shook her finger at him. "Why don't you give Mandy a ukulele lesson while we're waiting for Ken? Then maybe you won't think about dessert."

Makaio and Mandy took seats on the living-room couch, and he showed her the three main chords used for playing the ukulele. "They are C, F, and G7," he explained, demonstrating with his own instrument, as Mandy held hers.

She positioned her fingertips on the strings in the way he showed her and was soon strumming a short tune.

"I'm impressed," Makaio said. "You catch on quick."

"I do have a bit of music experience from playing my battery-operated keyboard."

"Mandy caught on quickly to swimming too." Ellen took a seat beside her. "But then, she's always been good at whatever she sets her mind to do."

"You're good at whatever you do, as well." Mandy gestured to the dress Ellen made for her. "I've never been able to sew as well as you."

"We all have our talents," Luana remarked. "God made everyone special, and each of us is unique."

A knock sounded on the door, and Luana went to answer it. When she returned to the living room, Ken was with her. He wasn't carrying a gift, and she wondered if Luana had been mistaken when she'd mentioned he might give her something. It didn't matter, though. His presence was gift enough.

"Happy birthday, Mandy." Ken smiled and moved toward the couch.

"I guess Luana must have told you I was turning twenty-one today."

"She sure did, which is why I wanted you to have something special for your birthday." Ken swung out the hand he'd been holding behind his back. It was holding a beautiful garland of flowers that he draped around Mandy's neck.

She touched the soft pink-and-white orchid petals. "Mahalo, Ken." She'd never received a bouquet of flowers before, and this was even more special.

"I have something else for you." Ken reached into his shirt pocket and pulled out a brochure, which he handed to her.

"What's this about?" she asked, eyeing it curiously.

"It's information on a whale-watching cruise." He smiled widely. "I booked us to go on one tomorrow, early afternoon. You're invited too, Ellen," he quickly added.

"Oh my!" Excitement swelled in Mandy's chest as she studied the brochure. "I never thought I'd get to see any whales while I'm here." She looked over at Luana, who sat in the wicker rocking chair across from her. "Won't you need Ellen and me to help out tomorrow? It wouldn't be fair if we left you with all the work to do."

"It's okay," Luana assured her. "You can take care of any work needing to be done in the morning. Going on a whale-watching cruise is special, and I wouldn't want either of you to miss it."

Tears welled in Mandy's eyes, and she blinked to keep them from spilling over. "This has been a special birthday. Thank you all so much."

"You're welcome," everyone responded.

"So now, let's head on back to the dining room and have some of Mandy's birthday cake." Makaio rose from his seat. "After waiting so long, I may even have two pieces."

Mandy snickered, and Luana poked her husband's belly. "If you don't watch it, you'll have no choice but to get rid of some of the shirts you've outgrown when we have another yard sale."

Makaio slipped his arm around her waist as he grabbed his cane. "Well, if you weren't such a good cook, I wouldn't have so many temptations."

Thank You, Lord, for my special Hawaiian friends, Mandy prayed, *and for allowing me to be here on my twenty-first birthday.*

Middlebury

Gideon had awakened during the night and realized he'd forgotten to call Mandy in the evening to wish her a happy birthday. He'd tried earlier today, but all he'd gotten was the B&B's answering machine. He couldn't leave a message, though, because their mailbox was full. He'd planned to call before going to bed, thinking it would be around dinnertime on the island, but exhausted after a long day at work, he'd fallen asleep on the sofa.

He pushed himself up and rubbed his face. "Why didn't Mom or Dad wake me before they went to bed?" he muttered, running his fingers through his hair.

Swinging his feet over the couch, Gideon thought about Mandy. *Sure hope she isn't upset with me for not wishing her a happy birthday. What if she thinks I forgot?* He massaged his forehead and groaned. *Maybe she's been too busy to notice.*

Port Allen

The following day, Mandy's heart pounded as Ken helped her and Ellen board the catamaran that would take them on the whale-watching tour. This was one of the most exciting things she'd done since leaving home. She'd brought her camera along, and if they saw any whales, she hoped to get some good shots.

"I hope the water doesn't get choppy," Ellen commented as she took a seat. "I don't do well on a boat in rough weather."

"You should be okay." Ken patted Ellen's shoulder. "If things get a little rough, remember to keep your focus on land, not the waves."

Before they set sail, the captain and his crew asked all the passengers on board to give their full attention to a safety briefing, letting everyone know where the life jackets were located and how to put them on. A member of the crew explained that the vests had a light attached, and when it got wet, the light would come on to help the Coast Guard locate the person in the water. This bit of information frightened Mandy somewhat. The thought of being in the middle of the ocean, even with a life jacket, made her tremble. Being in a swimming pool with her feet touching the bottom was different than being in the big ocean and not being able to see what was under her.

Another crew member let everyone know where the galley was and said snacks, as well as fresh water and soda, would be available.

Mandy whispered to Ken that she and Ellen had been through a similar safety briefing when they'd first boarded the cruise ship. "It was on a much larger scale, of course," she added, "because there were so many passengers."

As the boat moved out, things went along well. Mandy enjoyed the warmth on her skin and beautiful scenery along the way.

"Over there is the Na Pali Coast." Ken pointed to the emerald-green pinnacles towering above the shoreline. "The only land access to this rugged terrain is through an eleven-mile trail. The path crosses five different valleys and ends at a secluded beach. It's one of the most challenging hikes, with narrow sections and muddy soil from so much rainfall. Also, when the streams get high, they're extremely dangerous to cross."

The splendor of it all almost took Mandy's breath away. "It's amazing."

"Look, there!" Ellen shouted.

Mandy turned in the direction her friend pointed and saw an enormous whale surface, thrusting its tail into the air. "Wow! Look how big it is!"

Soon, more whales appeared. Mandy pulled her camera from the tote bag and started snapping one picture after the other. "Without pictures to show, no one back home would ever believe this," she told Ellen.

"The whales come to our warm waters from Alaska this time of the year. They reproduce and give birth," Ken explained. "It's the reason you see so many of them."

"It makes good sense." Mandy chuckled. "Even the whales want to get out of the cold and come where the waters are warmer."

"What kind of whales are they?" Ellen asked.

"They're humpback whales," Ken replied. "They can grow up to sixty feet in length, and their lifespan averages fifty years."

Everyone on the catamaran grew silent. Mandy watched a gray whale with a white underbelly breach suddenly to the surface then fall heavily back below the water's depth. Another whale broke smoothly out of the ocean, spouting before it started under again. Before disappearing, the whale slapped its huge tail, as if it was waving to them. Cameras started clicking to capture the special moment.

"Humpback whales can be quite entertaining." Ken grinned. "Here in Hawaii, when they arrive, it's regarded as a homecoming, because they're considered the original locals."

As the boat continued on, the ocean became a bit choppy. It didn't take Mandy long to realize Ellen wasn't doing well.

"I feel nauseous, like I did on the cruise ship when the water became rough." Ellen moaned, holding her stomach.

Mandy looked over at Ken, then back to Ellen, who was beginning to cough.

"Oh, no, I'm going to vomit." Immediately, Ellen leaned over the railing and emptied her stomach.

Mandy stood close by, gently patting her friend's back. She wished she had some motion-sickness drops to put behind Ellen's ears. Of course, they hadn't helped her much when she'd become seasick on the cruise ship.

"I'll get a bottle of water to rinse her mouth," Ken volunteered.

"Thank you." Until now, Mandy had forgotten how sick her friend had been before. But that morning in the cabin with Ellen rushed back to her, like it was yesterday.

Ken returned with a bottle of water. "I'll give her this whenever she's ready."

Another whale showed itself, this one quite close to the boat. In her excitement to capture a picture of it, Mandy leaned over the rail. She was on the verge of snapping the photo when a wave hit the catamaran, causing Mandy to lose her footing. She nearly lost her balance, but Ken caught her in time. "That was close." He placed his hand around Mandy's waist and held her to his side. "Are you okay?"

Her face radiated with heat. "I'm fine."

Just then, Ellen got sick again. When Mandy reached out to comfort her, she loosened her grip on the camera and it plunged into the water. "Oh, no! My camera!" she wailed. "I've lost all the wonderful pictures I've taken on this trip."

What started out to be a glorious day and had suddenly turned sour. Not only was poor Ellen pale and trembling, but now Mandy had no photos of Hawaii to show her family or friends back home. What a disappointment. The only pictures she would have of Hawaii were her memories.

She stared at the choppy waters, struggling not to give in to tears. *I guess the memories I've made here are something to be thankful for. It's more than I would have had if Sadie, Barbara, Ellen, and I had never made this trip.*

Chapter 27

*T*he last Sunday in February, Mandy was awakened by a fierce whooshing sound coming from outside. Something hit the outside of the window. Wind gusted hard against the B&B. Nature whistled as a storm held firm over the area.

"Is it windy out?" Ellen sat up in bed, yawning and rubbing her eyes.

"Jah, sounds like the wind to me." Mandy clambered out of bed and pulled the curtains aside. "Oh my! Come look at this, Ellen. You should see how the trees are swaying. Some are bending so much I'm afraid they might split. And look, palm branches are scattered everywhere."

Ellen joined her at the window. "I've never witnessed such strong winds before. The rain is actually blowing sideways!"

"It should be fully light out by now, but see how dark it still is. Those clouds look nasty." Mandy shivered. "You don't suppose it's a hurricane?"

"It could be, I guess. Maybe we should see if Luana and Makaio are up. If so, they may be in the kitchen by now."

The girls hurried to get dressed, and by the time they entered the kitchen, the lights in the B&B had gone out.

"We have no power, and how long it'll be out, I can only guess," Makaio grumbled from where he sat at the table. "I can't watch TV now, either."

Luana looked over at the girls and winked. "No television playing in the background most of the day... How sad is that?"

Mandy stifled a giggle.

Makaio drummed his fingers on the table. "So much for the Spam-and-egg breakfast I was hoping for this morning. And what are we supposed to serve our guests, who no doubt expect a hearty meal?"

Luana placed both hands on his shoulders. "It's not a problem. We've been through this before. I have plenty of fresh fruit to offer, as well as cold cereal and bread."

"Who wants bread when you can't toast it?" He glanced at Mandy and Ellen. "We won't be going to church today, because if the power's out here, it's most likely out there too. Besides, it's dangerous to go out in weather like this."

"My husband's right. A person could get hit by a falling branch or, worse yet, by a coconut falling from a tree. You certainly don't want to get clunked in the head by one of those." Luana moved to the refrigerator and took out a bowl of mixed berries. "We should be thinking positive and hope the electricity will be back on soon."

"In the meantime, what can we do to help?" Ellen asked.

Luana gestured to the pineapple sitting on the counter. "One of you can slice the *hala kahiki* and arrange it on a platter. The other can get the cereal out, along with a container of milk."

As Ellen went to get a knife out of the drawer, Mandy repeated the word for pineapple over and over in her mind. She was happy her vocabulary had grown with the Hawaiian words she'd learned so far.

"If we're stuck having cold cereal this morning, let's have it with coconut milk instead of regular milk," Makaio suggested.

"I'll get it out in case someone wants to try it, but I'm guessing most of our guests will want to stick with cow's milk."

"Coconut milk's healthier, but I guess not everyone realizes it." He pushed his chair aside and headed for the refrigerator. "Think I'll have a glass of it now, in fact."

Mandy couldn't help noticing how Makaio still limped as he walked. His therapy sessions were going well, but sometimes he tried to do too much and it set him back—like yesterday, when he'd tried to move something too heavy. Before she could ask if he would like her to get the coconut milk, he'd already taken it from the refrigerator.

"Do storms this bad hit Kauai often?" Ellen asked as she began cutting the pineapple.

"We get a fair amount of wind and rain, but severe storms, strong enough to knock out the power, don't happen often." Luana added several slices of papaya to the berries she'd placed on a large platter. "When they do, we're sometimes left without power for several hours."

"Right." Makaio poured some coconut milk into a glass and took a drink. "Last year, around this time, we lost power during a storm, and it didn't come back on for two whole days."

Luana fanned her face. "The temperatures were in the eighties, and it was impossible to cool the house down without air-conditioning."

"We're used to the heat and humidity during the summer," Ellen put in. "Since we Amish don't have electricity in our homes, we've never had air-conditioning to cool things down."

"Many Hawaiian natives and others who live here don't have it, either. They rely on the trade winds," Makaio explained. "The main reason we have AC is for the comfort of our guests, who aren't used to warmer weather. It would be nice if we could afford a generator for our establishment. Then we'd have some power to run lights and the refrigerator." He took another sip of coconut milk and set the glass back on the table.

Mandy stared out the window, watching the rain still falling quite heavily. Puddles quickly formed in the lawn, and pelted flower blossoms were scattered about. "What do you do for lights when the power goes out?" she asked, going to the cupboard to get the boxes of cereal for breakfast.

Luana pointed to the battery-operated candles sitting on a shelf across the room. "Makaio has a large lantern, also powered by batteries. It's good for many hours and puts out quite a bit of light. Our biggest challenge is cooking, but with the use of the barbecue grill, we manage to get by."

Mandy realized Ellen was right about things not being perfect on Hawaii, but like the Amish, the Hawaiian people knew how to survive without electricity.

By eight o'clock that evening, the winds had died down, but the power at the B&B had not been restored. They all sat around in the living room with battery-operated candles for light while Makaio gave Mandy another ukulele lesson. After only a month's worth of practice, she'd gotten quite good at playing the instrument.

Ellen sat close to one of the larger candles and wrote a few letters to send home. She continued to write until the soothing music caused her eyes to grow heavy. In an effort to keep awake, she sat up straight and arched her back before picking up her pen. By nine o'clock, everyone but Mandy and Ellen had gone to bed.

"Sure wish we could have gone to church today." Mandy relaxed against the back of the couch. "I missed the music and looked forward to seeing Ken."

Ellen looked up from her letter writing. "Nothing else? What about the pastor's message?"

"Of course I missed his sermon. I only meant—"

"You don't have to explain, Mandy. If you ask me, you're getting a little too attached to Ken."

"I am not. We're good friends, and nothing more." Mandy abruptly stood. "I'm tired and going to bed. Are you coming?"

"I'll be there as soon as I finish this letter to Sadie. I'm bringing her up to date on how we're both doing."

"Say hi for me too, please." Mandy picked up the flashlight Makaio had given her earlier and hurried from the room.

Ellen liked how quiet the B&B was right now. Their only two guests were pleasant and had retired to their room a short time ago. Awhile later, a knock sounded on the door. Since Ellen was the only one up, she went to see who it was. Seeing Ken through the peephole, she opened the door.

"Sorry for coming by so late. I meant to drop by earlier to see how you all were doing after the crazy storm, but I ended up helping my dad and brother pick up tree branches and other debris once the winds died down."

"We're all okay." She opened the door wider and offered him a seat.

Ken glanced around the dimly lit room. "Where is everyone?"

"They went to bed awhile ago." Ellen kept her voice down so as not to wake anyone.

"Even Mandy?" His tone revealed disappointment.

"Yes." Ellen figured Mandy hadn't had time to get undressed yet, but she wasn't about to tell her Ken was here. She'd no doubt come rushing out of their room, and they would sit and visit while Ellen played chaperone.

Ken stepped back toward the front door. "Well, I guess if everyone's okay, I'll head back home. Tell Mandy hi for me, and I'll talk to her soon."

Ellen cleared her throat, gathering up the courage to tell Ken what he needed to know. "Has Mandy told you she has a boyfriend back home?" She looked at him squarely, resting her hand on her hip.

"No, she's never mentioned it." He tipped his head.

"His name is Gideon, and once Mandy joins the church, they will no doubt get married."

"Oh." Ken shuffled his bare feet across the tile floor a few times. "It makes sense that someone as nice as Mandy would have a boyfriend waiting for her back home. I'm sure she will make Gideon a wonderful wife."

Before Ellen could form a response, Ken turned and rushed out the door.

Ellen stared at the candle flame flickering close to her. She felt bad telling Ken about Mandy's boyfriend, but something needed to be done to discourage him from pursuing a relationship with her. She didn't want to hurt his feelings and had come close to calling him back. Her resolve won out, though. *I did it for Mandy's sake, as well as Ken's.* Ellen bit her bottom lip. *I had to make sure he didn't have any ideas of trying to sway Mandy to stay in Hawaii. It was time to break them apart, before one or both becomes too serious about the other. When Mandy is happily married to Gideon, she'll be glad she returned to Indiana and left her Hawaiian fantasy life with Ken behind.*

Middlebury

"I hate to do this to you," Sadie whispered to Barbara in the middle of their young people's singing, "but I've developed a *koppweh* and need to get going. You'll either have to leave with me or find another way home."

"I'm sorry you have a headache." Barbara patted her friend's arm. "If you don't mind, I'd like to stay for the rest of the singing. I'm sure someone here will be willing to give me a ride home."

"Danki for understanding." Sadie gathered up her things and headed outside to her horse and buggy.

Barbara felt a bit selfish for staying instead of accompanying Sadie, but Gideon was here tonight, and she hoped for the chance to speak with him. She enjoyed the opportunity to socialize and sing with Amish friends too.

After the singing wound down, most of those who'd attended lingered for a while, visiting and snacking on leftover cake and cookies.

Gideon surprised Barbara when he sought her out. "Where's Sadie? I noticed the two of you sitting together earlier." He flashed her a smile.

"She came down with a koppweh and went home. Of course, I have no ride now, but I'm sure I'll find someone heading my way who'll be willing to give me a lift."

"Your house is on my way, so I'd be happy to offer you a ride."

Barbara smiled. "Danki, Gideon. I appreciate it so much." Her cheeks warmed.

As they headed for home a short time later, Barbara struggled with her feelings. She'd begun to care for Gideon as more than a friend, but she was sure he didn't feel the same way about her. *There's no hope of us being together, because Mandy will be coming back soon, and he's in love with her.*

Barbara would never intentionally do anything to come between Mandy and Gideon, but if by some chance, things didn't work out for them, she might find a way to reveal her feelings to him.

Chapter 28

ilani had a baby girl two days ago. They named her Primrose, after Luana's favorite flower. The birth was not easy, but it was quickly forgotten once the precious baby was born. Because Ailani was still weak from the long labor she endured, she and Oke will be staying at the B&B until she's strong enough to take care of the infant on her own.

It was nice to make cookies yesterday for all of us to enjoy. Makaio and Luana left earlier today to run some errands. They also had a doctor's appointment to see how Makaio's leg is doing.

Mandy hoped things would go well for Makaio today. Luana had been so patient throughout his recovery.

She set her journal aside and smiled at Ellen, who sat beside her at the kitchen table, drinking a cup of lavender tea. "You know what, Ellen?"

Blowing at the steam swirling up from her cup, Ellen raised her eyebrows. "What, Mandy?"

"Seeing Ailani's baby makes me long for a child of my own." Mandy got out the soft cinnamon cookies and bit into one.

"I'm sure you'll have a baby someday—after you and Gideon are married." Ellen sipped the fragrant tea. "This lavender honey I added is quite good."

"I have to agree." She reverted back to Ellen's comment about her and

Gideon. "What if we don't end up getting married?"

Ellen tapped Mandy's shoulder. "Of course you'll get married. Why do you think he's waiting for you to join the church? You have nothing to worry about. Once you get home, things will work out."

"But what if I decide not to join the church?"

"Not join? And do what, Mandy—stay here in Hawaii and marry Ken? Is that what you're hoping for?"

Mandy bit her lip so hard she tasted blood. "No, I. . ." Unbidden tears sprang to her eyes. She'd suppressed her emotions so long she felt as if she could burst. "It's not like that."

"What do you mean?"

"Except for church, I don't see much of Ken anymore." Her throat felt sore when she spoke. "Something's changed. I can't imagine what I did, but it seems I may have said or done something to offend him. We were getting along so well before, but now I don't know."

"He's probably busy helping out at his parents' chicken farm."

Mandy drew in a few slow, steady breaths. "How busy could he be? He always had time to come by before. Ken hasn't even brought any eggs in a while. His brother's been making the deliveries." She clenched her fingers. "I feel like he's avoiding me for some reason."

"Maybe you're overthinking things, Mandy."

She tapped Ellen's arm. "Have you seen Ken recently? And if so, did he say anything to you about me?"

"Umm. . .no." Ellen pushed away from the table and rose. "Think I hear the baby crying. I'm going to see if Ailani needs any help."

Before Mandy could comment, her friend made a hasty exit. *Strange. Is Ellen trying to avoid talking to me about Ken?*

As Ellen stepped into the living room, where Ailani sat rocking her baby, a feeling of guilt weighed heavily on her.

"Is everything okay?" Ailani asked. "It sounded like you two were having a disagreement."

"Oh, that. Mandy's a little worried about why Ken hasn't been around much lately."

"He's probably busy helping at his parents' farm right now."

"Yes. I told her the same thing." Ellen took a seat. She wasn't about to reveal to anyone, especially Mandy, what she'd told Ken the other evening.

She wondered how her best friend could be thrown off her normal path. Mandy had a nice boyfriend back home, waiting for her return. Ellen figured it was up to her to help Mandy see the light, but maybe she'd been wrong. Perhaps she should have kept her nose out of things.

Mandy is hurt because Ken hasn't been in touch with her lately, and it's my fault. If I hadn't told him about Gideon, he'd still be coming around. Her jaw clenched. *But Ken needed to know he has no future with Mandy, so I did it for both their sakes.*

Ellen felt sure things would be as they once were after they returned home. Her friend might miss Ken and everything she liked about Hawaii, but in time it would seem like a distant memory. In some ways, it was good Mandy had dropped her digital camera in the ocean during their whale-watching cruise. Having the pictures she'd taken would only have served as a reminder of what she'd left behind on Kauai. *I don't like admitting this, but I'm glad her camera is at the bottom of the ocean, never to be seen again. Those pictures would only keep her memory of Ken alive.*

Pushing these thoughts to the back of her mind, Ellen moved across the room to offer her assistance to Luana's daughter. "You look tired. Would you like me to hold Primrose for a bit?"

Ailani nodded. "I'd appreciate it. Since Mama took Dad to physical therapy, and Oke's at work, I've had full responsibility for the baby, and no matter what I do, she won't stop fussing." She appeared to be overwhelmed as she looked at Ellen with quivering lips.

Ellen's heart went out to the young woman. "Why don't you go lie down awhile? I'll take care of Primrose till your folks get back."

"Mahalo." Ailani rose from her chair and handed the precious bundle to Ellen.

After Ailani left the room, Ellen walked out to the lanai, while gently patting the baby's back. She heard water running in the sink and knew Mandy must be washing dishes in the kitchen.

It was a breezy afternoon, with comfortable temperatures—the kind of day one enjoyed being outside. After several minutes, Primrose stopped crying, so Ellen took a seat on the glider, softly humming as she rocked. The warmth of the baby and the infant's gentle breathing as she was lulled to sleep stirred something in Ellen's heart.

I understand why Mandy would want a baby of her own. I'd like one too, but if it's meant to be, it'll happen in God's time. Mandy has a better chance at having a boppli *than I do.* She swallowed against the lump in her throat. *At least she has a boyfriend back home, eager to marry her. I don't even have a suitor. Maybe someday God will send the right man into my life.*

Middlebury

Sadie's stomach churned as she stepped into the phone shack to call Mandy. She hoped to unburden her worries, and the sooner the better. In the last few weeks she'd seen Gideon with Barbara a couple of times, not to mention hearing he'd taken her home from the singing a few Sundays ago. If Mandy didn't get home soon, Gideon might start courting Barbara or someone else.

Sadie wanted to speak with Barbara about this too, but every time she started to bring up the subject, she lost her nerve. One time, she'd casually mentioned to Barbara about seeing Gideon a lot, but her friend made light of it, saying they were only good friends and he needed a sympathetic ear. Barbara said she was concerned, because with Mandy having been gone so long, Gideon was beginning to lose hope.

To make matters worse, the last time Sadie had spoken to Ellen on the phone, she'd learned Mandy had been seeing a lot of a young man named

Ken. Ellen didn't say whether Mandy had fallen in love with this fellow, but she sounded concerned because Mandy was gone from the B&B so much.

"None of this would be a problem if they'd stuck with me and Barbara instead of heading out on their own when the ship docked at Kauai. We should have insisted they join our tour group that day," Sadie mumbled as she punched in the number for the bed-and-breakfast.

The phone rang a few times before someone picked up. "The Palms Bed-and-Breakfast."

"Mandy?"

"Yes. Is this Sadie?"

"Jah."

"It's nice hearing from you. How are things in Middlebury?"

Sadie shifted on the wooden bench, trying to find a comfortable position. "Everyone's fine, but—"

"Good to hear. Ellen and I are doing well here. We're busier than ever." Sadie couldn't get a word in edgewise, so she let Mandy continue.

"Luana and Makaio's daughter had a baby girl two days ago. She and her husband are staying at the B&B so she has more help until she gets her strength back." Mandy paused briefly, but before Sadie could respond, she rushed on. "The baby's so little, and you should see all her dark hair. Oh, and they call her Primrose. Isn't that a sweet name?" Her voice sounded so enthusiastic.

"I guess so; it's kind of tropical sounding, but certainly nothing like our traditional Amish names."

"Amish parents don't always give their babies traditional names anymore, Sadie. I know an Amish couple who named their little girl Doretta, and I think it's a lovely name."

"You're right, and so is Primrose. I only meant. . ." Sadie cleared her throat. "Have you heard from Gideon lately?"

"Not for a week or so. I'm sure he's quite busy. He sent me a birthday card and gift, but I never got it."

"Maybe it got lost in the mail."

"Jah. That's most likely what happened."

"Have you talked to Barbara lately?" Sadie questioned.

"No, but then if she had called, I would have been too busy to talk very long."

"I see." Sadie licked her lips. She was quickly losing her nerve. "I saw Gideon and Barbara the other day, and I think—"

"What did you say, Sadie? I can hardly hear you anymore. The connection must be bad."

Maybe it's a sign I'm not supposed to say anything. Sadie tapped her fingers on the wooden shelf where the phone sat. *I probably shouldn't say anything about Barbara and Gideon right now. It may be best to keep my concerns to myself and wait to see how things go when Mandy gets home.*

"Sorry, Sadie, but I have to hang up now. I heard a car pull in and need to see who it is."

"Okay. Take care, and I hope to see you soon."

When Sadie hung up, she leaned her head against the wall and sat several seconds, wondering if she should have called Mandy at all, for nothing had been accomplished as far as Gideon and Barbara was concerned. It was nice to hear Mandy's voice, though. It seemed like she and Ellen had been gone forever.

Kapaa

Mandy peeked out the window and saw Luana and Makaio getting out of their car. Makaio had a big grin on his face as they walked up to the house. She went to the back door and opened it for them. "How'd the physical therapy session go?"

"It went well." Luana, all smiles too, pointed to Makaio. "Tell her the happy news."

"I had a good report today." His smile widened. "I can finally return to most of my duties here, which I kind of knew already. I've been feeling fine and did some gardening yesterday while you girls baked cookies."

Makaio paused. "We hate to see you go, but when you're ready, I'll go on the Internet and help you book your tickets."

Although eager to see her family and friends again, Mandy felt a sense of disappointment. This place and these people had become home to her. It wouldn't be easy leaving her special Kauai friends, whom she'd come to know and love.

Chapter 29

*F*riday, April 15, was Mandy and Ellen's last night on Kauai. Luana and Makaio had planned a going-away party for them, and Ken had been invited. Mandy's emotions ran high, feeling both happy and sad. Seeing him tonight, knowing it was the last time they would be together, nearly broke her heart. She wished she was free to share her feelings with him, but she would never be so bold. Besides, Ken had not given her any reason to believe he had feelings for her other than friendship—although after he'd looked at her a certain way or done something thoughtful, she'd wondered if he saw her as more than a friend. But that was before he'd stopped coming around so much.

It's better this way, Mandy thought as she sat between Ellen and Ailani on the couch. *I'll be returning to my Amish life, and he'll stay here with his family, like before I came to Kauai.*

She glanced across the room, where Ken sat in a chair, talking with Makaio and Oke. Ailani took pictures of everyone in the room, while Oke held the baby. Mandy noticed every once in a while, Ken looked in her direction, then glanced quickly away. Would he miss the friendship they'd established or forget about her soon after she was gone? He'd kept his distance these past several weeks and hadn't said much to her tonight. *If I only understood why he's stayed away, at least nothing would be left unsaid.*

Tears welled in her eyes, and she fought to keep them from falling onto her cheeks. In some ways, she wished he hadn't come. It may have made it easier. On the other hand, she was glad for the opportunity to see him one last time. If Mandy still had her camera, she would have taken a picture of him.

"We're certainly going to miss you both." Luana's statement pushed Mandy's thoughts aside. "I hope you'll call or write so we can keep in touch." Her eyes misted. "Maybe someday you can visit Kauai again, or we might go to Indiana to see you."

"It would be nice, but another trip for me would be expensive." Mandy was barely able to speak around the lump stuck in her throat. She'd known almost from the minute she and Ellen first arrived at the bed-and-breakfast that it would be hard to leave, but she'd never expected it would be this difficult to say goodbye. Of course, back then, neither of them had an inkling they'd be staying for several months. If not for Makaio's accident and Luana needing help at the B&B, they would have gone home long ago.

"I have something for both of you." Luana rose from her seat and left the room. When she returned, she handed Mandy and Ellen two quilted potholders and pillow shams, all sewn with colorful Hawaiian print material.

"They're beautiful. Mahalo," Mandy whispered tearfully.

Ellen, also with tears in her eyes, nodded. "Yes, we appreciate your thoughtfulness."

"Now don't forget to take home the ukulele I gave you." Makaio spoke up. "You've learned the basics, so now all you need to do is practice. It won't be long and you'll be playing as good as me." He looked over at his wife and smiled.

Mandy could only manage a nod. Every time she played the Hawaiian instrument, she would think of Makaio, as well as Ken because he also played the ukulele. Of course, she would also have the sunrise picture Ken had given her.

"Hold up your gifts so I can get your picture. These will be nice to put in my scrapbook." Ailani smiled. "I've enjoyed getting to know you. Mahalo for helping my ohana while Papa's leg was healing and for taking care of me and Primrose when we came home from the hospital." She bent to kiss the top of her baby's head.

"You're welcome." Mandy smiled. "It was our privilege to help your family."

Ellen nodded. "We appreciate all that's been done for us too."

"I have something for both of you." Ken stood and made his way over to the couch. Then he handed Mandy and Ellen each a paper sack.

"How about you young people sitting on the sofa together so Ailani can take your picture after you've opened Ken's gifts?" Luana suggested.

The two friends scooted over and Ken took a seat beside Mandy. Even though they weren't talking much, she was grateful to be in his company this evening.

Mandy opened her gift and fought for control when she pulled out a lei made with kukui nuts. "Mahalo, Ken," she murmured. "This looks like the one you've worn a few times when we did some things together."

"It's the same one. I wanted you to have it as a symbol of our friendship, and so you would remember your time here on Kauai."

How could I ever forget it—or you? Mandy kept her thoughts to herself but nodded to Ken. She wished she could freeze this moment. Having him here, receiving his heartfelt gift made it even harder to leave tomorrow. Ellen, on the other hand, had made it clear she was ready to leave Hawaii and get home to her family.

Ellen opened her gift and revealed a pretty shell lei. "Thanks, Ken. It was nice of you to think of us."

"Okay, ladies, hold up those gifts, and everyone smile." Ailani snapped a few pictures before returning to her seat.

"What's for dessert?" Makaio asked.

"I made an angel food cake with strawberries and whipping cream, in honor of our most special guests," Luana replied. "I'll get it ready to serve right now."

"I'll give you a hand." Ellen rose from the couch.

Oke came over with Primrose, who'd begun to fuss, and handed her to Ailani. "I think she needs her *makuahine.*"

Makaio wandered out to the kitchen, and soon Luana announced it was time for dessert. Ken got up with Oke and Ailani, and they headed for the dining room.

Mandy remained seated a few minutes, closing her eyes to hold back the tears threatening to spill over. She wished she and Ken could spend a few minutes alone, but it was probably better they didn't. She couldn't be so bold as to ask if they could take a walk outside, and he had certainly not suggested it. Once more, she consoled herself with the fact that this was how it was supposed to be. The Hawaiian words *a hui hou,* which meant "until meeting again," floated through her mind, but she didn't voice them because deep down she knew she would probably never see Ken again.

Saturday, April 16

Ellen and I boarded the ship a few hours ago. After our evening meal, we'll be heading for the Big Island. Ellen's excited, but I have mixed feelings. We missed the opportunity to see the volcano and other things Barbara and Sadie got to view before their voyage home, but leaving Kauai is so difficult for me. I will miss Luana and Makaio, but Ken most of all. Even though we have no future together, it didn't make it any easier for me to part ways with him.

Mandy wondered if Ken would miss her. She knew Makaio and Luana would—especially with all the hugs Luana had given Ellen and Mandy when she drove them to the docks. The tears Makaio's wife spilled with their goodbyes were proof enough. The Palus were such a special couple.

Mandy thought about tomorrow and how she'd miss going to church in Kapaa. She would not be able to see Ken up front with the rest of the worship team. She'd miss the inspirational songs of praise, the pastor's encouraging message, and even the brightly colored Hawaiian clothes many people wore.

She looked down at her Amish dress. Her muumuu was packed away now, and it saddened her a bit, knowing she wouldn't have any reason to wear it again. She'd probably show it to her family, and then it would be put in a drawer to be looked at from time to time as a reminder of her days on Kauai.

Ellen had been eager to board the ship and talked about the delicious meals they would have on the cruise liner. She was also looking forward to seeing the volcano that Sadie and Barbara had seen before heading for the mainland.

After Ellen finished freshening up before dinner, Mandy quickly closed her journal. She didn't want her friend to see what she'd written. She was fairly certain Ellen had suspicions about her feelings for Ken and didn't want to discuss the matter. Talking about it and thinking about it were two different things. Mandy's feelings for Ken were all she could think of right now, even though she tried to squelch them. The image of his face was constantly on her mind, not to mention how he'd looked at her when they finally parted last evening. If Ken had taken her into his arms, even for a casual hug, she didn't know what she would have done. Truthfully, she wished he had. Would she have been able to let him go?

Mandy closed her eyes, finding it hard to forget their final, silent goodbye. She'd walked with Ken to his vehicle, while the rest of them stayed inside. The short walk felt like miles, instead of a few feet. The silence between them was deafening. She'd studied every feature of his face. As he gazed into her eyes, she silently screamed, *Please, Ken, ask me to stay.* When he reached out to take her hand, it may as well have been a kiss. Coming from Ken, even this simple act of friendship had sent her heart soaring. The look on his face before he turned and got in his SUV nearly tore Mandy's heart apart. As difficult as it was, she kept silent and let Ken walk out of her life. He was English. She was Amish. What more could either of them say?

My fantasy is over now, she reminded herself. *It's time to face reality and focus on my life back home. Mom, Dad, and the rest of my family are waiting for me, and so is Gideon.* She massaged her forehead, continuing to mull things over. *Do I care for Gideon as much as I did before? Will Ken become a distant memory when I see Gideon again? Guess I won't know for sure until I see him again.*

Middlebury

"I'm glad spring is here," Peggy said Monday afternoon as she opened her store's front window and drew in a deep breath. "Can you smell the fresh air?"

Barbara nodded from where she sat behind the counter on a wooden stool. "It smells like clean towels when they've been hung outside to dry."

"On afternoons like this, I wish I could be home working in my garden, instead of cooped up in this stuffy store. When I sell the store someday, I'll be able to spend more time in my garden and do other things I enjoy." Peggy remained at the window a few minutes, then moved toward the door. "Since there are no customers at the moment, I think I'll go outside and take a short walk. I'll keep an eye on the door, and if any customers show up, I'll hurry back inside."

"Go ahead. Take your time." Barbara motioned to the bolts of material lying before her. "While you're gone, I'll put these away."

"Danki, Barbara. Don't know how I'd get along without you." Peggy smiled. "You're a hard worker. It's a comfort to have someone I can depend on."

Barbara's face warmed. "I love working here and want to do a good job for you."

"Well, keep doing what you're doing, and you'll have a job here for as long as I own the store." With a parting wave, Peggy went out the door.

I hope she doesn't sell this business anytime soon. Barbara fingered a quilted potholder lying on the counter. *Wish I could buy the store when she decides to sell, but there's no way I can afford it.*

Sniffing the warm breeze coming through the open window, Barbara's thoughts wandered back to Peggy's other comments. She felt the same way as Peggy did about spring. It affected her soul, making her feel more alive. Springtime seemed to put the spirit of youth in people, young and old alike. The drudgery of cold winter months, long and gray, faded as each vivid new bloom brightened the landscape. Even from inside the store, Barbara could hear the birds singing and the leaves rustling in the gentle breeze. There'd even been a bee in the store earlier, which she'd quickly shooed out the window. Saying goodbye to the winter blues was something Barbara didn't mind at all. Spring was also a time when hearts seemed merrier, and the spirit of love seemed to be felt everywhere.

Will I ever be fortunate enough to find love? If I never get married, I'll continue working here as long as Peggy owns the store. Barbara picked up two bolts of material and carried them to the shelf where they belonged. She had started back to get the others when Gideon entered the store, smiling widely. "Did you hear the good news?"

"What good news?" She picked up another bolt of material, holding it under one arm.

"Mandy and Ellen are on their way home."

"Oh? I hadn't heard. When will they be here?" Barbara tried to sound nonchalant, but internally, she was shaking.

"It'll be a few more days. I talked to her daed yesterday. The man who owns the B&B where they stayed is doing better now and can take over his job again. The cruise ship Mandy and Ellen are on was supposed to leave Kauai Saturday night." Gideon leaned on the counter. "Of course, it won't go directly to Los Angeles. It'll stop at another Hawaiian island for a good part of a day, then move on to stop in Ensenada, Mexico, before docking at the port in L.A. From there, they'll catch a train to bring them the rest of the way home." Gideon's smile widened. "Isn't it exciting, Barbara? Just think, by this time next week I'll be reunited with Mandy. Then we can start making plans for our future. I can hardly wait."

Barbara hadn't realized she'd been holding her breath until she felt the need to breathe. "That's wunderbaar." She forced a smile. *Mandy is a good friend, and I look forward to seeing her again, but once she gets home, I won't be seeing Gideon as often. He won't need a sympathetic shoulder to cry on, and Mandy might not appreciate me spending time with her boyfriend. I need to set my feelings for him aside and try to be happy for them.*

Chapter 30

Saturday, April 23

Ellen and I are on the train, heading toward our final destination. It's been difficult sitting all day and then sleeping in seats, but we didn't have enough money to pay for a sleeper car this time. Poor Ellen is especially glad to be off the ship, as the waters were quite rough coming back to the mainland, and she got seasick again.

Mandy paused from writing in her journal to glance out the window. Several buffalo were silhouetted against the setting sun. It was amazing to view such big animals grazing on the plains.

Shortly after noon, they'd left Albuquerque, New Mexico, and entertained themselves playing a few games until it was time for supper. Now, while Mandy caught up on her journal writing, Ellen nodded off.

Mandy had written in a previous journal entry about the things they'd seen on the Big Island. The volcano was interesting, but after being on Kauai, she couldn't help comparing the two islands. The area near the volcano on the Big Island looked so barren and full of lava rock. Although curious about the volcano, Mandy kept thinking about the beauty of Kauai. Even now when she closed her eyes, she visualized swaying palms, lovely flowers, and sandy beaches.

She thought about her Hawaiian friends—especially Ken. He'd looked so handsome in his Hawaiian shirt the evening he'd taken them to a luau. And even more handsome when he'd come to say goodbye the night before they'd left Kauai. Memories of the times they'd been together would stay with her forever.

Ken was so patient and kind when he taught me to swim, Mandy mused. *I could trust him with my fear of water, and he helped me relax and keep trying.*

At times, Mandy wished she'd never met Ken. But she was grateful for the opportunity to get to know him. *If only I could have the best of both worlds—the Hawaii life with Ken, and my Amish life with. . .*

Her thoughts swept her back to when their ship departed Kauai's tropical paradise. She'd stood on the deck, tearfully watching until the island became a tiny dot against the huge horizon and then faded away. The farther away they got, the sadder Mandy felt. The ocean's vastness seemed to swallow her up, leaving a huge hole in her heart.

Desperately needing to focus on something else, Mandy turned to the journal page she'd written the day the ship stopped at the harbor in Mexico. Since she didn't have her camera anymore, it was important to fill her journal with as many remembrances as possible. She jotted in a short note about something she'd forgotten to mention—seeing several sea lions on the rocks and platforms. The creatures looked silly, flapping their flippers as they carried on with loud barking.

Mandy remembered her amazement at seeing so many brightly colored buildings in Ensenada. Some were chartreuse. Others were painted in bright pink, green, and blue. They were certainly in sharp contrast to the plain white of most Amish homes where she came from. It was interesting how each culture varied in their architecture, style of living, and food choices. Many things had been different in Hawaii than what she was used to at home.

Different is good when you fall in love with it, though. Mandy drew a deep breath and closed her eyes. *Maybe I ought to follow Ellen's example and sleep.*

Monday, April 25

We're in northeast Indiana and almost home. The scenery alongside the tracks looks familiar. Mom and Dad will be waiting in Elkhart for me to get off the train. I wonder if Gideon will be there too.

Hoping to quell her nervous stomach, Mandy reached for the tote bag at her feet, placing her pen and journal inside. She glanced at Ellen, whose nose was pressed against the window like an eager child. No doubt she was anxious to get home.

"You know something?" Mandy lightly tapped her friend's arm.

"What?" Ellen turned to look at her.

"Since we've been gone so long and both lost our jobs, we'll need to start looking for some other employment as soon as possible."

Ellen groaned. "I sure hope we can find something."

"I can still do volunteer work at the thrift store in Shipshewana, but since the restaurant in Middlebury replaced me with someone else, I won't be returning there unless one of the other waitresses ends up quitting for some reason."

"Maybe your daed will have an opening at the meat-and-cheese store."

"I've worked there before and didn't like it much. I'd rather be waitressing, where I can visit with people." Mandy sighed, maneuvering in her seat to get more comfortable. "But I guess if it's all I can find, I'll do it, because I want to pay Mom and Dad back the money they spent on my cruise ship and train tickets to bring me home from Hawaii."

"I plan to pay my folks back too." Ellen clasped Mandy's hand. "I'm sure we'll both find something, even if it's not our first choice for a job."

Elkhart

When Mandy stepped off the train, she spotted her parents right away. Ellen's folks were there too, but she saw no sign of Gideon. She'd expected him to be at the train station, waiting for her. Giving Mandy little time to think about it, Mom quickly enveloped her in a hug. "It's good to have you home, Daughter. We've missed you so much!"

"I missed you too." Mandy hugged Dad next, blinking happy tears from her eyes. Despite missing her friends on Kauai, it truly was good to see her family again.

"Do you have any luggage besides what you're carrying?" Dad asked.

"We each have a small suitcase Luana and Makaio gave us," Ellen spoke up.

"I'll walk over with your daed to get it." Dad hurried off.

Ellen leaned close to Mandy and whispered, "Where's Gideon? I'm surprised he's not here."

Feeling a bit guilty, Mandy replied, "Maybe he's upset because I didn't give him much of my time whenever he called while we were on Kauai. He may think I was trying to avoid him. Perhaps he doesn't want to court me anymore."

"I couldn't help overhearing, Mandy," Mom interjected. "I seriously doubt he would think such things. Every time Gideon has seen your daed, he's asked about you, and he said on many occasions he couldn't wait for your return. I am fairly certain he had to work this afternoon. I wouldn't be a bit surprised if he doesn't drop by our house this evening."

Mandy's emotions swirled as she thought about seeing him again. Would she still have feelings for Gideon, or had they faded when she met Ken?

Middlebury

Since Gideon had been at work when Mandy's train arrived in Elkhart, he hadn't been able to greet her at the station. It had been disappointing, but at least now that work was over he could stop by the Freys' house to welcome her back.

Filled with a mixture of excitement and apprehension, he clutched his horse's reins so tightly the veins on his hands stuck out. Maybe it was good his horse, Dash, was taking his sweet time. What if Mandy wasn't excited to see him? What if during her absence she'd changed her mind about being his girlfriend? Gideon didn't think he could deal with her rejection—especially after waiting all those months for her return. It would be one thing if she'd been here and they'd drifted apart, but if the miles separating them caused Mandy to forget what they once had, Gideon would be distraught. After all, he hadn't wanted her to go in the first place but had no way of stopping her. Of course, he had foolishly given Mandy his blessing, which he saw now as a big mistake.

"Take a deep breath and calm yourself," he mumbled, guiding his horse up the Freys' driveway. "In a few moments you'll see Mandy face-to-face."

After Gideon tied Dash to the hitching rail, he reached inside the buggy and took out the gift he'd bought for Mandy. He was especially eager to give it to her, since the birthday present he'd sent in January had apparently gotten lost in the mail.

Racing for the house, he took the porch steps two at a time and lifted his hand. But before he could knock, Mandy's brother Melvin opened the door.

"I heard your horse whinny and knew we had company." The boy looked up at Gideon and grinned. "Figured you came to see Mandy."

Gideon gave a quick nod. "Is she here?"

"Jah. She's in the living room, teaching everyone some words she learned from her Hawaiian friends." Melvin stepped aside. "Go on in. Bet she'll be glad to see ya."

Gideon followed him into the living room, where he found Mandy sitting on the couch, with her mother on one side, and her brother Mark on the other.

He cleared his throat and took a step forward.

"Look who came to see you, Mandy." Melvin pointed to Gideon.

Mandy stood and a bit awkwardly reached out her hands. "It's nice to see you again."

"It's good to see you too. Welcome back." He clasped one of her hands and put the paper sack he held in the other. "I brought you a little welcome-home gift."

"Danki, but you didn't have to." Mandy's gaze darted from Gideon to her little brother and back again. She seemed nervous, reminding him of a skittish colt.

"I wanted to give you something. Go ahead and open it."

Mandy opened the sack. When she withdrew a pair of binoculars, her eyebrows lifted.

"I remembered how much you've enjoyed watching the birds in your yard. With spring being the time so many birds are around, I thought. . ."

"It's a nice gift, Gideon. Danki for thinking of me." Mandy's expression relaxed as she motioned to the only free chair in the room. "Please, take a seat."

Course I would think of you. I thought about you every day you were gone. Gideon sank into the chair. *This isn't how I'd planned to welcome you home, Mandy. I'd hoped we could spend some time alone this evening, and I could express my feelings without others listening.* He shifted uneasily, grasping the arm of the chair. *Maybe I should offer to take her for a buggy ride. It would give us a chance to spend some time alone. But then, her folks might think I'm rude and that I want her all to myself. I'm sure they're eager to visit with her too.*

Staring at a stain on the hardwood floor, Gideon continued to fret, unsure of what to say or do. He'd never felt awkward around Mandy before; but then they usually didn't have all of her family sitting in the living room, staring at them.

As if by divine intervention, Mandy's mother stood and gestured to the other room. "Mandy, why don't you go with me to the kitchen and bring out some refreshments? Oh, and Gideon, if you'd like to join us, you can fix the kaffi. As I recall from your previous visits, you know just the right amount of grounds to put in the pot."

"Jah, sure, I can take care of the coffee." Gideon followed Mandy and her mother into the kitchen. He still wasn't alone with his best girl, but at least he didn't have her dad and three younger brothers staring at him. Gideon had noticed that Mandy's older brother, Michael, wasn't here this evening. He figured Michael and his wife, Kathryn, must have other plans and couldn't be part of their family gathering. Or maybe they'd be here later. Surely they would also want to greet Mandy.

While Gideon got the coffee going, Mandy cut up some apples and arranged the slices on a platter. She glanced at him a few times but didn't say a word. Her silence made him feel even more uncomfortable. She used to be so talkative when they were together.

"I'll take the cookies I made earlier into the other room." Miriam smiled, giving her daughter's arm a tap. "After the kaffi is ready, you and Gideon can bring the fruit and coffeepot in." She picked up the cookie tray and some napkins, then hurried from the room.

I wonder if Mandy's mamm left us alone on purpose, so we could talk. Sweat beaded on his forehead as he moved closer to the counter where Mandy stood. "I've missed you greatly, and I'm so glad you're back."

"I missed you and all my friends too."

Friends? Is that all we are, Mandy?

He shuffled his feet a couple of times, searching for something else to say that might break the tension. "So, how was Hawaii? I heard you liked it there a lot."

Her eyes lit up for the first time since he'd arrived. "Oh, I did. I liked everything about Hawaii, except for the vog."

"What's a vog?"

"It's sort of like fog, only it comes from the volcano on the Big Island. It was worse than normal for a few days while Ellen and I were staying on Kauai, and it bothered my allergies. Fortunately, it didn't last long, and it never occurred again during my stay," she quickly added.

"I see." Gideon didn't know why, but he was at a loss for words. It may have been his imagination, but things seemed even more strained between them—almost like they were strangers. He couldn't put his finger on it, but he noticed a change in Mandy. She was dressed the same way as she had before, but her enthusiasm in seeing him just wasn't there. It seemed as if her mind was someplace else.

Should I give her a hug or kiss? It might help break the barrier between us. Heart pounding, Gideon stepped up to Mandy and boldly drew her into his arms. He lowered his head, and was about to kiss her, when she pulled away and reached for an orange. "Maybe I should cut some orange slices to go with the apples."

He couldn't help noticing her cheeks had turned red. The old Mandy would have hugged him back and would certainly not have pulled away from his kiss. The young woman standing before him was not the same person as she had been before her trip. Gideon had a sinking feeling the old Mandy had been changed by her experience on Hawaii. The question was, could he bring her back?

Chapter 31

Kapaa

*K*en glanced at the calendar on his cell phone. It was hard to believe the first Saturday of May had come around so quickly, or that Mandy had been gone two weeks. Ever since Ellen told him Mandy had a boyfriend back home and they might be getting married, Ken had felt strange. He'd begun to have feelings for Mandy, although he had never let on to her. It was hard, but after learning about her boyfriend, he'd kept his distance from her. In all the time they'd been together, Mandy had never mentioned having a boyfriend back home. But then, was there any reason for her to, since Ken hadn't known her that long? Maybe in time she would have opened up more. Since she was Amish, Ken had felt from their first meeting he needed to tread lightly.

Strange how his feelings for her came on so quickly. He'd had girlfriends before, but none he cared about as much as Mandy, and in such a short time too. Ken must have read Mandy wrong, though, because he'd begun to think she had feelings for him too. *Maybe it was wishful thinking. Most likely, she only saw me as a friend. Truth is, we are worlds apart.*

When he'd run into Makaio at the grocery store the other day, Ken found out Mandy had been in touch with Luana. She'd called the B&B soon after she got home. This meant Luana had Mandy's phone number. Ken fought the desire to ask for it, so he could give Mandy a call. But talking to her, knowing he wouldn't see her again, would only add to his frustrations. It was better for both of them if he made no effort to contact her and cut the friendship off clean.

There's no point in me dwelling on all this, Ken berated himself. *Mandy's back home where she belongs, and I'm here, in a place I hope to always call home.*

Ken's cell phone rang. Seeing Taavi's name pop up, he answered right away. "Hey, buddy, what's up?"

"The surf—that's what." Taavi chuckled. "How 'bout grabbing your surfboard and meeting me on the beach?"

Ken didn't feel much like going, but maybe it would improve the mood he was in. "Yeah, okay. I'll see you there in half an hour."

"The waves are a bit strong," Taavi called as Ken carried his surfboard across the sand to where his friend sat. "Maybe it's not such a good idea to go in. Might have been a mistake to come here today. Sorry for wastin' your time."

Ken shook his head determinedly. "Those monster waves don't frighten me. A little struggle in the water might help release some of my tension."

Taavi's brows furrowed. "Don't be stupid, man. There's no point taking any chances—especially if your mind is on other things."

"Come on, Taavi, you've surfed in waves higher than these, and not so long ago, either."

"Yeah, but I'm not comfortable going out there right now."

"Suit yourself. I'll take my chances." Ken carried his board into the water and paddled out to where the waves were breaking. Plenty broke near him, but none he could ride. As he sat on his board, bobbing in the water's rhythm, Ken glanced in the direction of the beach. He noticed quite a few surfers milling around with their boards, but only a few were in the water with him. *Oh, well. At least I won't have to worry about plowing into someone.*

Suddenly, a gigantic wave formed behind him. *Okay, here we go!* He worked his arms to catch a swell. When he stood up, everything seemed to be going fine as his board glided smoothly on the water's surface. He glanced toward the beach and pictured Mandy sitting on the sand, watching and waving to him. Then, before Ken had time to react, a massive wall of water engulfed him. It felt like he'd been smacked by a huge hand as he tumbled off the board and went under. The force shoved him deeper and deeper, somersaulting him into the ocean's blue depths. Over and over he rolled, trying to comprehend which way was up.

When the sea finally lost its grip, Ken knew he didn't have much time. Holding his breath and kicking as hard as he could, he followed the bubbles rising toward the surface. Ken saw light as he got closer to air, which by now he desperately needed. *Only a little farther. Keep going. You're almost there.*

Ken felt a hand grip him under the arm and soon realized it was Taavi pulling him onto his board.

"Are you okay, man?" Taavi took a deep breath of air, and Ken did the same. "You had me scared for a minute when your board made it to shore without you on it."

"Guess you were right about not going out there with those angry waves." Ken choked and coughed water out of his lungs. "Should have stayed on the beach with you."

"Doesn't matter. You're here now, and you're okay."

Together, they paddled back to shore on Taavi's board.

"Should never have even tried surfing today. It was stupid of me." Ken groaned, falling onto the sand, exhausted from the ordeal. "I've been kind of depressed lately and thought it might help."

"Want to talk about it?"

Ken shook his head. "Not now, anyhow."

To Ken's relief, Taavi didn't question him any further. Talking about his feelings for Mandy seemed pointless and would only make him feel worse. He needed to forget about her and move on with his life. It was time to start fresh.

"It doesn't seem the same around here without Ellen and Mandy," Luana said as she and Makaio enjoyed chilled pineapple juice together on the lanai. "Ken isn't coming around as much anymore, either."

Makaio nodded slowly. "I've noticed it too. The last couple of times the eggs were delivered, Ken's brother Dan brought them over. The last time I saw Ken was at the grocery store. He asked if we'd heard anything from Mandy."

Luana set her glass on the wicker table between them. "My guess is he misses her."

Makaio quirked an eyebrow. "You mean, Ken?"

She tapped his arm. "Of course I mean Ken. Isn't that who we were talking about?"

"I mentioned his brother too."

She pushed a piece of hair behind her ear and secured it with a decorative comb. "Didn't you ever notice the way Ken looked at Mandy?"

"Well, now that you mention it, I did get the impression he thought she was nice."

"It was far more than that. They had eyes for each other. There's no mistaking it."

Makaio waved his hand in her direction. "Maybe you thought there was a spark between them because you're such a romantic."

"I am a romantic, which is why I can tell when two people have a special connection."

"But didn't Mandy mention having a boyfriend back home?"

Luana nodded. "His name is Gideon. He called here to talk to her several times."

"Well, there you go. If Mandy has a boyfriend, then she wasn't interested in establishing a relationship with Ken. I bet she only saw him as a friend."

"No, it was more, but it doesn't matter now because she's gone, and Ken will no doubt find someone else." She picked up her glass and took a drink. "I'm still analyzing the situation, so please bear with me. I understand Mandy has a boyfriend back home, but she was always so excited when Ken showed up. I could see her eyes light up."

"Come to think of it, I remember that too."

"And she hardly spoke of her Amish boyfriend, but she couldn't say enough about Ken. It's my guess they tried to squelch their feelings for one another, knowing Mandy would eventually leave the island."

"You could be right."

"I believe Ken has been staying away from here lately to help himself cope." Luana took another sip and set her glass on the table. "He'd probably think about Mandy every time he came through our door."

"Well, they're both young and may have stars in their eyes, but I bet it won't be long and they'll be over this puppy-love thing." Makaio leaned over and gave Luana a kiss. "I say, let's leave it in the Lord's hands. He knows what's best for Mandy and Ken."

A car pulled into the yard, and Luana stood. "Looks like our daughter is here, and she brought the baby. I'll go out to greet them and bring little Primrose inside so her grandpa can hold her."

"I need to walk, so I'll come with you." Makaio grinned. "Last one there's a rotten egg."

Middlebury

It was Saturday, and Gideon had the day off. He'd arrived at the meat-and-cheese store where Mandy was working in hopes she would be free for lunch.

When he stepped inside, he spotted her near the back of the store, stocking shelves. "Hey, how are you doin'?"

She looked up at him and blinked. "I'm okay. I didn't expect to see you here today."

"Came to see if you'd be free to join me for lunch."

She glanced at the clock on the far wall. "Guess it's noon, but I only get an hour for lunch, so I'm not sure I'd have enough time to go out anyplace. Besides, I brought a sack lunch from home today. It's a nice day, so I planned to eat out back at the picnic table."

"I could buy some beef sticks and cheese and sit out there with you." Gideon didn't want to pass up this chance to spend a few minutes with Mandy. Except for the evening he'd dropped by her house and at church last Sunday, he hadn't had the chance to see or talk with her.

She smiled up at him. "If you'd like to join me for lunch, I'll get my food and meet you out by the picnic table."

"Okay, see you there." Gideon hurried over to the cooler where the cheese was kept and selected a bag of yellow curds, as well as a carton of chocolate milk. Then he picked out a teriyaki beef stick and paid for them at the register. He took his sack full of goodies outside and sprinted around back, where he found Mandy sitting at the picnic table by herself. *Whew! At least I'll have her all to myself.*

He took a seat across from her, and after their silent prayer, they both took out their lunches. As they ate, they talked about the nice weather they'd been having, but it didn't take long before the conversation lagged.

Desperate for an answer to the question nagging him for some time, Gideon blurted, "Who's Ken?"

Mandy's eyes opened wide. "How do you know about him?"

"I don't know anything about him, but one day while you were in Hawaii, I called the B&B to talk to you and the lady mentioned you were at the beach with Ken."

Mandy's cheeks colored. "It's. . .uh. . .nothing to worry about. Ken and I were only friends. He was Ellen's friend too."

"Oh, okay." Not quite satisfied with her answer, he continued probing. "You don't seem the same since you came home. You're almost a different person."

"I felt different when I was in Hawaii. You can't believe how beautiful and serene it is there."

"You're right. I can't, 'cause I've never been and probably will never have the opportunity to go."

"I didn't think I'd have the chance to go, either, but I did, and I'm glad. It was the opportunity of a lifetime, and I'll never forget the friends I made on Kauai." Mandy had a faraway look in her eyes, and it bothered Gideon. Her thoughts should have been here, with him, not on some tropical island.

"Is everything all right between us, Mandy?" Gideon dared to ask. "I mean, are you and I still. . ."

His words were cut off when Mandy's dad came around the corner of the building. "Sarah's been at the cash register all morning and needs a break. Would you please take over for her, Mandy?"

She was immediately on her feet. "I'll be right there, Dad." Looking at Gideon, Mandy offered him a brief smile. "I'm sorry for cutting our conversation short, but I've gotta go."

"It's okay, but before you do, would you be free to come over to my house for supper this evening? Mom plans to make her wunderbaar fried chicken, and she always fixes plenty."

"I appreciate the invitation, Gideon, but I promised Ellen, Sadie, and Barbara I'd go out to supper with them. We've been wanting to get together and talk about our trip to Hawaii and haven't had a chance before now, since we're all working different schedules." Mandy gathered up what was left of her lunch and put it inside her tote.

"It's all right; I understand. We'll talk again soon."

After Mandy returned to the store, Gideon remained at the picnic table for several minutes. The sun felt good shining directly on his back. He took his hat off and ran his fingers through his thick hair. Hearing a whinny, he glanced at his horse stomping the pavement where he was tied to the hitching rail. Gideon wasn't ready to leave yet and sat awhile longer. Any other time, Mandy would have lingered a few minutes before returning to the store, but things had changed between them. There was no doubt about it.

Watching a hornet on the table not far from where his arm rested, Gideon took his hat off and shooed it away. When the bee flew closer and hovered near his face, he whacked it again, relieved to see it fly off.

What can I do to make things right? He was at a loss as to what to do next. *One thing's for certain—I miss the old Mandy and want her back.*

Chapter 32

The moon, hanging low in the east, was barely visible when Barbara came out of the house. *Thank goodness the days are getting longer.* She glanced at the sun, still high in the western sky, before climbing into the buggy. Daylight was a few hours from fading, and depending on how long she and her friends lingered at the restaurant, she might even get home before dark.

Barbara had decided to take a back road, so she'd left a little early. Traffic this time of year, especially on a Saturday, could get rather heavy. She wasn't in the mood to put up with impatient drivers when they got behind the buggy. The last thing Barbara needed was her horse getting spooked, especially the way she was feeling right now. Barbara always enjoyed spending time with her friends, but this evening she felt a bit uneasy. It would be bad enough to try and hide the nervousness, let alone eat with the butterflies in her stomach.

As the buggy pulled out onto the road, she heard her dog barking in protest. "Not this time, Duke. Where I'm going, they don't allow pets." Barbara smiled, thinking how her German shepherd loved going for buggy rides.

Keeping her attention on the road, she asked herself, *Will I be able to hide my feelings for Gideon from Mandy tonight?* She and Gideon had become good friends while Mandy was in Hawaii. Barbara found it easy to talk to him—even if most of their conversations were about Mandy.

Barbara's friendship with Mandy was important too. They'd been good friends a long time. The last thing she wanted to do was break Mandy's trust. But how could she deny her feelings for Gideon? *I must keep them to myself and guard my heart so neither I, nor anyone else, gets hurt.*

Barbara turned her attention to the scenery along this stretch of road. While her horse, Gaffney, trotted at a comfortable pace, she enjoyed looking at the fields that had been planted a few weeks ago and were now sprouting the first leaves of corn and soybeans. Apple and cherry blossoms added colors of pink and white among the red and deeper rosy hues of azaleas and rhododendrons.

Barbara smiled when she saw a hen turkey, followed by a dozen of her poults, scurrying into some underbrush. She sighed, wondering if she would become a mother someday.

Shipshewana, Indiana

"It's nice we can be together this evening." Sadie smiled across the table at Mandy. "We've all been so busy we haven't had time to visit since you and Ellen got back from the islands."

"It's good we were able to get a table for four at this restaurant," Ellen responded before Mandy could comment. "Saturdays are always busy, especially with so many tourists in town."

Looking around, Barbara smiled. Being here before five o'clock helped, because the supper crowd hadn't arrived yet.

Sadie looked at Mandy again. "I can't believe how tanned you got while you were gone. You must have enjoyed the sun quite a bit." She turned to Ellen. "Looks like you got some rays, as well, although Mandy's skin is even darker than yours. Guess I'm a little envious of you two getting to be in Hawaii enjoying warm weather the whole winter. But I'm glad you had a good time."

"Thanks." Ellen picked up her menu. "I'm glad the Lord watched over us throughout the extended trip."

"I believe God allows things to happen to us, and He kept you there long enough for a purpose," Barbara stated.

"I agree." Ellen smiled. "That purpose, of course, was helping out at the B&B, and we were both happy to do it. Right, Mandy?"

Mandy barely nodded as she stared at the menu. For some reason, nothing appealed. After working all day at her father's store, she should be hungry. She glanced at the waistline of her dress, noticing how baggy it looked. Mandy hadn't mentioned it to anyone, but since returning home, she'd lost five pounds. The reason for her loss of appetite had to do with missing the friends she'd made on Kauai. Her heart wasn't in much of anything she did lately. In the waking hours, her thoughts were filled with things she saw and did on the island. When she went to bed, she dreamed of being back there. If only she hadn't dropped her camera overboard, she would have gotten all those pictures printed by now and put in a scrapbook. Instead, she came home with only souvenirs and memories of their trip. Over time those memories would begin to fade, which bothered Mandy the most, as she didn't want to forget the faces of the special friends she'd made.

She thought of all the pictures, resting on the ocean floor: Ken and her at the falls; the exciting luau; all the times spent on the beach; and the photos she'd taken in Luana and Makaio's yard. Such a great loss. At least among the nice gifts she'd received from the Palus, she had three other mementos that meant a lot to her—these were from Ken. Mandy kept them in one of her dresser drawers underneath the muumuu dresses she'd worn during her stay on Kauai. Each night in the quiet of her room, she'd retrieve them to look at before going to bed. To some, they may only seem like trinkets from Hawaii, but because the coral, lei, and sunrise picture had been gifts from Ken, they held deep meaning for her. It was good she didn't have pockets in any of her plain dresses; otherwise she would have carried the kukui nut lei close to her each day.

"It's your turn now." Ellen gave Mandy's arm a gentle tap. "The waitress is waiting to take your order."

"Oh, sorry. I must have been spacing off." She glanced at the menu one more time, then ordered a spinach salad.

"Don't you want anything else?" Sadie's forehead wrinkled. "A salad's not going to fill you much."

"I'm not in the mood for anything else." Mandy grabbed her glass of water and took a sip. Maybe coming here for supper wasn't a good idea, especially if her friends scrutinized everything she did. Mandy's conscience pricked her. *No one's actually been scrutinizing me. I'm being too sensitive.*

After the waitress left the table, Sadie took a photo album from her oversized purse and placed it on the table. "These are the pictures Barbara and I took during our trip to the Hawaiian Islands. I thought you might enjoy seeing some of the things we saw along the way."

Mandy swallowed hard. It was difficult to look at the lovely photos without feeling envious. "It's nice you have them to keep your memory of Hawaii alive."

"Don't you have pictures?" Barbara asked. "You bought a digital camera before we left for our trip to Hawaii. I would imagine you took many photos while you were on Kauai."

"I did, but the camera fell overboard when Ellen and I were on a whale-watching cruise."

"It was my fault," Ellen interjected. "I got seasick, and when Mandy tried to comfort me, she lost her camera."

"Such a shame." Sadie pursed her lips. "If you want copies of any of my photos, I'd be happy to have some made."

Mandy gave a brief shake of her head. "The pictures I had were mostly taken on Kauai, and there's no getting them back." She released a heavy sigh. "I felt such peace when I was there." Being home was good, but it wasn't like Hawaii. Mandy still felt as though a part of her remained on the island.

"Don't you feel peace here at home?" Barbara tipped her head, looking strangely at Mandy.

Mandy felt trapped and wasn't sure how to respond. "Well, I only meant. . ."

"It's okay." Ellen came to her rescue. "Being in Hawaii was peaceful for me, as well. There were so many beautiful flowers, colorful birds, and swaying palm trees. Luana and Makaio's bed-and-breakfast was peaceful too, and they made us feel so welcome."

"They're good Christians," Mandy said. "I don't know what we would have done if strangers we met hadn't taken us to the B&B the evening we became stranded."

"I can only imagine how frightened you both must have been." Sadie cast a sidelong glance at Barbara. "How do you think we would have handled it if we'd been in such a situation?"

Barbara shrugged. "I'm not sure. As it was, we were scared not knowing at first what happened to you both."

"May I take a closer look at your album?" Ellen asked.

"Certainly." Sadie handed it to her just as the waitress came with the drinks they'd ordered.

"You have some nice pictures." Ellen turned each of the pages, pausing often to comment.

Mandy glanced at them too. Seeing photos from the Big Island, Maui, Oahu, and especially Kauai, caused her to tear up. Barbara must have noticed, for she reached across the table and placed her hand over Mandy's. "Are you all right?"

"Just missing Hawaii." She looked away from the album. "Let's talk about something else now, okay?"

Sadie's brows squished together. "But I thought our meeting was to compare notes about our trip."

"It's fine. We can talk about it if you like." Mandy twisted the napkin in her lap. Once their meals came, maybe the conversation would change.

Barbara looked over at Ellen. "Before we say any more about Hawaii, I've been wondering how your new job is going. Do you like being a housekeeper at the hotel in Middlebury?"

"It's all right," Ellen replied, "but I preferred working at the B&B before we left for Hawaii. Of course," she added, "I work additional hours at the hotel, which means earning more money."

"How about you, Mandy?" Sadie questioned. "Do you like working at the meat-and-cheese store?"

"It's okay, but I enjoyed my previous job of waitressing more." She reached for her glass of iced tea and took a sip. "At the restaurant, I could visit with customers as well as the other waitresses during my breaks. We don't have nearly as many employees at my daed's store, and there's not a lot of excitement."

"You won't have to work there forever," Ellen stated. "Once you and Gideon are married, you can quit working at your daed's store and become a fulltime homemaker."

"Have the two of you set a wedding date?" Barbara leaned slightly forward.

"No, and since I'm not taking classes to join the church this spring, Gideon hasn't asked me to marry him. For now, at least, I'll keep working while I live at home."

"Oh, I see." Barbara leaned back in her seat.

Is that a look of relief on Barbara's face? Mandy wondered. *Could she be interested in Gideon? Does he have feelings for her? I can't help but wonder what happened during my absence. Maybe I'm overlooking something. If Gideon became interested in Barbara, surely he would have told me.* She pursed her lips. *I still care about him, but my feelings aren't as strong as they were before I met Ken.*

When their meals came, they prayed silently, then talked about some things going on in their area. By the time they were ready to order dessert, the conversation returned to Hawaii.

"Have you heard from Luana since we've been home?" Ellen asked Mandy.

"Only once, when I called to let her know we'd made it okay."

"I've been meaning to write them and say thank you again for everything they did for us, but other things have taken up my time."

"I'd have to say you two did a lot for the Hawaiian couple, as well," Sadie interjected. "You sacrificed by not returning home right away so you could help out when Makaio broke his leg."

"I didn't see it as a sacrifice." Mandy shook her head vigorously. "I enjoyed helping out. And by staying longer, Ellen and I were able to see a lot more things on Kauai then we ever expected. Also, thanks to our friend Ken, I learned how to swim, which I thought I'd never be able to do."

"That's wunderbaar, Mandy." Barbara's tone was enthusiastic. "Now you can go swimming in the ponds and lakes around here with the rest of your friends."

I'd rather go swimming in Hawaii, Mandy mused. Then another thought came to mind. *Would it be wrong for me to move to Hawaii and begin a new life? What would my family say if I did? Could I be happy living so far away?*

Since she hadn't joined the church yet, Mandy was free to choose what she wanted to do with the rest of her life, but going back to Hawaii would be a major decision, affecting everyone in her family, as well as Gideon.

Mandy determined to give it more time. *I haven't been home long enough to know for certain if this is the life I'm meant to have.*

Chapter 33

Middlebury

*E*xcitement welled in Mandy's soul when she went to the mailbox the first Saturday of August and found a letter from Luana. She hurried back to the house and went straight to her room to read it privately.

Taking a seat on the end of her bed, Mandy tore open the envelope. It had been awhile since she'd heard any news from Hawaii, and she was eager to hear how everyone was doing.

The first part of Luana's letter was about her granddaughter, Primrose. Mandy read every word as though it was meant to be savored. The baby had grown several inches and started to roll over on her own. Luana said it pleased her to have Ailani working part-time at the B&B again. She brought Primrose with her, of course, and Makaio and Luana took turns watching her while their daughter made up the guest rooms each day. Mandy tried to visualize what the baby looked like and wished Luana had enclosed a picture.

Luana also wrote about the nice weather they'd been having and how well things were doing in her garden.

Mandy smiled, remembering how she had enjoyed spending time in Luana's garden, even when the weather turned hot and humid. Watching the gentle sway of palm leaves, listening to the birds sing, and breathing in the delicate scent of the tropical flowers in the yard filled her senses. She giggled, remembering how a cardinal had left its calling card on her muumuu.

Mandy stopped reading for a minute, while her mind wandered further. *I wonder how Ken is doing. Oh my, I wish I could stop thinking of him.*

As she turned the letter over to continue reading, a sudden coldness hit the core of her being. Her voice trembled as she read the next line out loud: "I ran into Ken's mother the other day when I was at the farmer's market. Ken has been seeing someone and is planning to get married in November."

Mandy's vision blurred as she stared at the words. *Could Ken have been seeing someone the whole time Ellen and I were on Kauai and not mentioned it? Maybe it was one of those young women I saw him talking to on the beach the day he'd been surfing.* She shifted uneasily on her bed. *Or it could be someone he met after we left—perhaps one of the young women on the worship team at his church.*

Mandy's shoulders sagged as she reached up to rub her throbbing temples. She couldn't help feeling disappointed by this news, but she consoled herself with the knowledge that it was better this way. Ken obviously didn't care for her the way she did him, or he would have contacted her after she'd come home. Her throat constricted. *And he wouldn't be marrying someone else in November if he'd felt any love for me.*

Mandy finished reading Luana's letter, then with a heavy heart, tucked it inside a box in her closet where she kept mementoes. Glancing down, she spotted the ukulele Makaio had given her, leaning against the closet wall. Holding the instrument the way she'd been taught, she took a seat on her bed again and began to play a song he'd taught her. The longer she played, the more her heart yearned for Ken and the things she'd discovered on the island.

A long-distance relationship with him wouldn't have worked, and since neither of them was free to leave their homes and families, it was all for the better. He had a fiancée, and she had Gideon. The brief encounter she'd had with Ken while visiting Kauai was like the vog. It swept in one day and was gone the next. Mandy had recovered from her allergic reaction to the vog. She hoped she could set aside her feelings for Ken, as well, and reestablish the relationship she'd once had with Gideon.

Ellen carried the laundry basket outside and set it under the clothesline. It was a beautiful sunny day—not too hot and not too muggy, which made it perfect clothes-drying weather. She was about to pick up a pair of her dad's trousers when Sadie rode into the yard on her bike.

"This is a nice surprise." Ellen smiled. "Are you here for a visit or only out for a ride?"

Sadie parked her bike and joined Ellen by the clothesline. "I've been meaning to talk to you about something, so I'm glad you're here this morning."

"Okay. We can chat while I hang the clothes, or take a seat at the picnic table under the shade of the maple tree when I'm done."

"I'll help you hang the laundry. When we're finished, we can sit and talk." Sadie picked up a towel and clipped it to the line.

Once all the wash swayed gently in the breeze, they both took a seat at the picnic table.

"What did you want to talk to me about?" Ellen asked.

"Barbara and Gideon."

Ellen blinked rapidly. "You mean Mandy and Gideon?"

"No. I'm talking about Gideon and Barbara."

"What about them?"

"I've seen them together several times since Barbara and I got back from Hawaii." Sadie paused. "Gideon even gave Barbara a ride home from one of the young people's singings a few months ago."

"Was this before or after Mandy and I arrived home?"

"It was before, but I saw them together again last night."

"Where?"

"At the benefit auction in Shipshewana. They were sitting next to each other during most of the bidding."

Ellen sucked in her lower lip. "Was Mandy there too?"

Sadie shook her head. "I figured she'd be with Gideon, but when I asked him about her, he said she had a koppweh and didn't feel up to going."

"I didn't go, either. Mom had a dress she wanted to make, so I stayed home to help with it." Ellen fiddled with the ties on her head covering. "Do you think Gideon's interested in Barbara?"

Sadie shrugged her shoulders. "Whether he is or not, I believe she's interested in him. While you and Mandy were on Kauai, Barbara talked a lot about Gideon. She kept saying how sorry she felt for him and that if he was her boyfriend, she'd have come home right away."

Ellen mulled things over. "Well, as you know, Mandy hasn't taken classes with us to join the church."

"Jah, and I'm surprised. If she and Gideon are making plans to be married, she'll need to get baptized and join." Sadie rubbed the side of her neck, her tone uncertain. "Maybe things aren't going well with them because of Barbara."

Ellen shook her head. "I don't think it's Barbara's fault. Mandy lost interest in Gideon while we were in Hawaii."

"Are you sure?"

"Jah. She rarely talked about him, and whenever he called, she didn't talk long at all." Ellen paused, wondering if she should say more.

"Wonder why? I've always heard absence is supposed to make the heart grow fonder."

Ellen took a deep breath and sighed. "Mandy became infatuated with a young man named Ken. He came over to the B&B to deliver eggs and chicken, and it didn't take long before he started taking Mandy—and sometimes me—out to see some of the sights on Kauai."

"Did Mandy tell you she had feelings for Ken?" Sadie questioned.

"Not in so many words, but I could see it in her eyes when they were together and whenever she talked about him."

"Was he interested in her?"

"I believe he was. That is, until I. . ." Ellen dropped her gaze as she clasped her hands together in her lap.

"Is there something else you were going to say?"

"Jah." It wasn't easy to admit what she'd done, but she needed to get it off her chest. "One evening after a bad storm, Ken came by the B&B to see if everyone was okay. Luana, Makaio, and Mandy had gone to bed, so Ken and I visited a few minutes." Ellen's voice cracked. "We talked about Mandy, and in order to discourage Ken from pursuing a relationship with her, I told him Mandy had a boyfriend waiting for her back home, and they were planning to be married."

"You did the right thing. If I'd been there, I would have told him that too. It would be horrible for Mandy's folks and everyone else she's close to if she'd stayed on Kauai and married an outsider."

"The time Mandy and I had in Hawaii was good, and I'm glad we had the opportunity to experience it, but it wasn't our world—the one we were born into and have become a part of since we were *bopplin*." Ellen lifted her chin. "Mandy's future is here with Gideon. We need to make sure no one—not even our friend, Barbara—comes between them."

Sadie's forehead wrinkled. "We can pray about the situation and maybe interject our opinion if asked, but the future of our friends is in God's hands, not ours."

Gideon shook his horse's reins to get him moving faster. He was on his way to Mandy's to take her for a buggy ride and felt anxious to get there. In the months Mandy had been back from her trip, things had been strained between them. She'd often had some excuse not to see him when he suggested they do something together. Since she'd agreed to his invitation this evening, he hoped things would go well. Her distant attitude certainly wasn't from a lack of him trying. Gideon had invited her out several times, as well as to his folks' for supper. When Mandy first returned from Hawaii and seemed so distracted, he'd figured it would take a little time before she readjusted to life at home. But it seemed to be taking forever, causing him to have more doubts. He and some of Mandy's other friends hadn't joined the church yet, deciding to wait until fall, and hoping Mandy would be part of their group.

Think positively, Gideon told himself as he started up the Freys' driveway. *If things go well tonight, Mandy may agree to take classes in the fall. Then she could join the church and we can be married. It's something to hope for, at least.*

Gideon pulled up to the hitching rail and was pleased when Mandy came out of the house right away and climbed into his rig.

"It's a nice night for a buggy ride," she commented, seating herself beside him. "When the sun goes down, I'll bet we'll see lots of twinkling stars."

"I'll bet too." Gideon grinned at her, and a warmth spread through him when she gave a pleasant smile. *So far, so good.*

As they traveled the back road between Middlebury and Shipshewana, Mandy grew silent, but Gideon kept trying to engage her in conversation. She wasn't the talkative person she used to be. Before her trip to Hawaii, Mandy always thought of things to say. At times, she could be a real chatterbox.

Barbara talks to me more than Mandy does. Gideon glanced her way and frowned when he realized her eyes were shut. *Is she thinking about me or someone else? Could Mandy have fallen asleep?*

Mandy had a hard time staying awake. The gentle sway of Gideon's buggy and the rhythm of the horse's hooves clip-clopping along the pavement were enough to put anyone to sleep.

"Would you like to stop by the Hitching Post for some frozen yogurt?" Gideon asked when they arrived in Shipshewana.

"No, thank you. I ate too much of my mamm's zesty meatloaf for supper and don't have room for anything else. But if you want to stop for some, I'll sit and watch you eat it."

"No, it's okay." Gideon snapped the reins. "Let's keep riding." He turned his rig around and headed back in the direction of Middlebury.

Is he taking me home? Does he think I'm bored? Mandy sat up straight. "How are things going with your job at the upholstery shop? Do you still enjoy working there?"

He nodded. "I've been helping out at my mamm's quilt-and-fabric shop some too."

"Bet she appreciates it, but I'm surprised you have the time."

"I go there after work some afternoons."

"I figured with Barbara working at the store, your mamm wouldn't need more help."

"She gets pretty busy sometimes. Seems there's always something I can do to help. How do you like working for your daed?"

"It's okay, but I'd rather work at one of the local restaurants."

"Why don't you then?"

"There haven't been any openings since I got back."

They rode a short ways in silence, then Gideon guided his buggy onto a dirt road and pulled back on the reins. "Whoa!"

"What are we stopping for?" she asked.

"I. . .I've missed you, Mandy, and I'm hoping we can get back what we once had." Before Mandy could form a response, Gideon pulled her into his arms and kissed her. Although firm and gentle, like his kisses had always been, it didn't feel right to her. The kiss lacked the emotion she remembered from Gideon's kisses. *Maybe it's me. I'm not the same person I was before Hawaii. No matter how hard I've tried to get them back, the feelings I once felt for Gideon aren't there anymore. How can I verbalize this without hurting him?*

Mandy was the first to pull away. Unable to look at Gideon, she murmured, "I'm not going to join the church this fall, Gideon, so you're free to pursue someone else if you like."

"What?" His mouth hung open.

"I'm not sure if the Amish life is right for me, and it's not fair to keep you waiting." She placed her hand on his arm and gave it a gentle tap. "You're a good friend, and I don't want to hurt you, but I can't make any promises at this time."

"I can wait till you're sure." His tone sounded sincere.

"Please don't. You deserve to be happy."

"You make me happy, Mandy. You always have." He clasped her hand.

"Will you at least pray about things and give it more time before you make a final decision about not joining the church?"

"Okay, but I can't make any promises." Mandy closed her eyes. *So much for trying to express my feelings to Gideon. I should have made things more clear. I doubt we'll ever get back what we once had.*

Chapter 34

$\mathcal{T}$he first Sunday of October, Mandy sat on a backless wooden bench in her brother Michael's barn, watching as Gideon, Barbara, Sadie, and Ellen were baptized and received into fellowship in their Amish church. They had waited until fall, hoping she would join too, but she'd let them all down.

It was a beautiful autumn morning, and the doors of the barn had been left open on both ends, allowing a comfortable breeze to waft through. A fall-like aroma hung in the air, and Mandy breathed deeply of its earthy scent. When a rustling sound caught her attention, her eyes were drawn toward the entrance. A scattering of early fallen leaves had been captured in the draft and made their way inside, swirling in circles across the barn floor. Mandy's gaze followed the dancing leaves until they disappeared and whooshed out the opposite door.

When someone sneezed, Mandy hunched her shoulders and focused on her friends up front. She remained that way until her brother's new puppy barked from outside, seemingly disgruntled for not getting any attention. Michael had surprised his new bride with a little basset hound a few weeks after they were married and said he'd chosen that type of dog because they were good with children. The puppy was adorable, and it was comical to watch it tripping over its own floppy ears. Mandy suspected by next year sometime she'd probably be an aunt. At least one happy event might be happening in the year to come.

A feeling of guilt swept over her. It felt awful to disappoint Mom and Dad by not being one of the candidates for baptism this morning, which meant no open door for her to be married in the Amish church anytime soon. Her friends were disheartened too. Part of Mandy wanted to be free to explore her feelings and decide what she wanted to do with the rest of her life, but she also was drawn to joining the Amish fellowship. It was like being on a teeter-totter: up and down, up and down, as she tried to decide what to do. Should she have taken classes and joined the church with her friends? She couldn't answer that question right now.

Mandy stared at her hands, clasped firmly in her lap. *But I wasn't ready.* Next spring was a long way off, and unless something happened to change her mind, she would follow through with her decision to join the church then—for her family's sake, if nothing else.

As Gideon took his seat after being baptized and welcomed into fellowship with the church, he glanced quickly in Mandy's direction, noticing how forlorn she appeared, looking down at her lap. He felt disappointed she hadn't been part of their group today—especially when they had all waited until fall, hoping she would join them. Even harder was trying to come to grips with her reason for not taking classes and joining. Was it because she wanted to do something different with her life, or had Mandy refused to take classes because she didn't want to marry him? Gideon had committed himself to the church and wondered if Mandy ever would. She seemed like an outsider looking in—living among them, but not one of them.

Back in August when he'd taken Mandy for a buggy ride, her mood at times seemed cheerful. He'd felt enthusiasm one minute and disappointment the next—especially after she'd told him he was free to find someone else. *Maybe I should have listened to her then, instead of holding out false hope.*

His gaze went to Barbara. *Would she be a better choice for me?* Gideon had enjoyed his conversations with her during the time Mandy was gone. Barbara was attractive, had a sweet spirit, and most important she wanted to be Amish. But Gideon saw some problems: He didn't know how Barbara felt about him, and he wasn't sure whether Mandy had any feelings for him anymore. Likewise, he felt unsure of his feelings for Barbara and Mandy. He'd never been so confused.

Gideon had noticed how well his mother and Barbara got along.

While Barbara was in Hawaii, Mom had mentioned several times how much she missed her. Furthermore, both of his parents had expressed concern because Mandy would not join the church. Mom even went so far as to say no son of hers should be made to wait around indefinitely for a young lady who didn't want to commit to the Amish way of life. He felt the pressure building but fought it off, needing to be cautious. Gideon didn't want any regrets where Mandy was concerned. Everything needed to be prayed about, allowing God to work things out.

Before directing his attention back to what the bishop was saying, Gideon made a decision. If Mandy didn't join the church next year, he would give up on their relationship and stop seeing her. In the meantime, regardless of what Mandy told him, he would try a little harder to get back what they once had.

At lunch following the church service, Ellen took a seat beside Mandy. "Is the dress you're wearing the one I made you in Hawaii for your birthday?" she asked.

"Jah, it's the green one." Mandy's expression was somber.

"Something doesn't look right with it." Ellen pulled at the material. "The dress looks as if it's hanging on you and doesn't fit like it should. I was certain it fit you properly when you wore it home from Hawaii."

"I may have lost a little weight since then," Mandy admitted. "But don't worry, I'm sure I'll gain it back and the dress will fit perfectly again."

"That makes me feel better, and I'm glad it wasn't because I measured wrong." Ellen looked at her friend long and hard. "I wish you could have been with us today when we went forward to be baptized. It was a meaningful occasion."

Mandy nodded. "I'm sure, and I'm happy for all of you."

"Why didn't you take classes with us? You've never truly explained."

"Jah, I did. I told you before. I don't feel ready." She drank some of her lemonade.

"When will you be ready?"

"How do we know when we're ready for anything? Maybe I'll take classes next spring, but I'm focusing on the now. I want to keep working and saving money, because I still haven't paid my parents all they spent for the ticket that brought me home from Kauai." Mandy squinted against the sun streaming into the window and scooted over a little to avoid it.

"What about Gideon? Do you think he will wait for you that long? He most likely wanted to be married this fall."

"Please, Ellen." Mandy's brows furrowed. "Don't make me feel any guiltier than I already do."

"Guilty for not joining the church or making Gideon wait?"

"I'm not sure." Mandy's voice lowered. "To tell you the truth, I'm not sure of anything anymore."

"I can tell." Ellen pushed the pickle on her plate around with her fork. "You're not the same person you were before we went to Hawaii. We've been home over five months, and by now you should have gotten over. . ." Ellen stopped talking when she noticed several women at the table looking their way. Now was not the time or place to express her feelings to Mandy. She would do it another day, when they could talk privately.

Barbara glanced at Mandy and Ellen, wondering what they were talking about. The two had their heads together, speaking in low tones. Then they stopped talking altogether, barely looking at one another.

During the church service this morning, it had been difficult for Barbara to concentrate on the preacher's message. She kept thinking about Mandy and how she'd disappointed all of them by not joining the church. *Gideon, most of all,* she thought. *I wonder if she'll ever decide to join, and if so, will Gideon wait for her or find someone else to court? I wish it could be me, but I doubt he sees me as anything more than a friend. If Mandy would break things off with him, I might have a chance.*

"Are you going to the young people's singing tonight?" Sadie nudged Barbara's arm, scattering her thoughts.

"Umm. . . I guess so. Are you planning to go?"

"I wouldn't miss it." Sadie smiled. "This will be our first singing as church members."

"Did you ever have second thoughts about joining the church?" Barbara whispered, leaning closer to her friend.

"Absolutely not. I've always looked forward to joining. Even as a little girl I knew what I wanted." Sadie chuckled. "I used to pretend I was the bishop, and I'd baptize my dolls."

Barbara laughed. "You were that eager?"

"Jah." Sadie nodded in Mandy's direction. "It saddens me to think you, Ellen, Mandy, and I made the trip to Hawaii together, but only three of us became members of the church today. From the time we were girls in school, I thought we'd all join together."

"I thought so too." Barbara sighed. "A link was truly missing in what should have been a happy occasion for all of us this morning."

"Before we went to Hawaii, did Mandy give any indication she might not join?"

Barbara shook her head. "At least not to me. She may have mentioned something to Ellen, though. They're pretty close."

"I bet Mandy's folks are deeply hurt their only daughter hasn't committed to becoming a baptized church member. My parents would certainly be upset if I never joined."

"Do you think Mandy will end up leaving her Amish roots altogether?"

Sadie shrugged. "Could be. After talking to Ellen about the way Mandy acted when they were staying with the Hawaiian couple on Kauai, nothing would surprise me."

"She's told me a few things too." Barbara pursed her lips. "The one I feel the most sorry for is Gideon. Mandy's been unfair, making him believe she would return from Hawaii and join the church, then staying longer than planned and not joining after she got home." She lowered her voice even more. "He deserves to be happy."

"Maybe he'll find happiness with someone else."

"You think so?" Hope welled in Barbara's chest.

"Anything's possible. Especially since things don't seem to be going well between him and Mandy these days."

A feeling of guilt settled over Barbara, for hoping Mandy and Gideon broke up, but she couldn't help wishing if things didn't work out between them, Gideon might turn to her. *He'd have to be blind not to see I have feelings for him. Every time he's around, I break out in a cold sweat. And sometimes when he talks to me, I feel like I can't speak without stuttering or saying something foolish.* She squeezed her eyes shut, thinking how nice Gideon looked in his Sunday best today. It was all she could do not to stare at him. *If I were in Mandy's shoes, I'd hang on to Gideon and never let him go.*

Chapter 35

*B*y early January, Gideon had finally accepted the fact that his relationship with Mandy was over. Even if she did join the church this year, there was no hope of them being together. It hadn't been easy at first, but if he wanted to move forward with his life, he had to make this choice. He'd tried to continue courting Mandy for a while after he'd joined the church, but the feelings they'd once had for each other weren't there anymore. Fortunately, their parting wasn't bitter, and they'd agreed to remain friends. That wasn't to say he'd erased the last couple of months from his mind. The feelings deep in his heart would take effort and time to overcome, especially with the holidays still fresh on his mind.

Thanksgiving and Christmas had been difficult, since Mandy hadn't spent either holiday with him. But with the help of his family, Gideon had made it through. After Christmas dinner, he and his brother Orley had taken a walk outside, and Gideon had taken the opportunity to unburden his soul. He'd explained the changes in Mandy since she returned from Hawaii and mentioned how she kept drawing further from him. Orley helped Gideon admit to himself the relationship was ending and that he shouldn't pursue Mandy anymore. If he wanted to remain friends with her, the best thing was to set her free. At the same time, Gideon would also be free to pursue a new relationship when the time was right. He'd taken his brother's advice, and by New Year's had come to terms with things and felt ready to focus on the future.

Gideon had asked Barbara to attend a singing with him this evening and was on his way to her house right now. He and Barbara had always gotten along well. Since she worked in his mother's store and they saw each other often, he felt comfortable around her. The sparks weren't there like they had been with Mandy in the beginning of their courtship, but maybe in time deeper feelings would come. Meanwhile, he enjoyed the stronger friendship developing between them. Gideon and Barbara saw eye-to-eye on many things, and most importantly, she had no desire to be anything but Amish. If things progressed with them, he'd probably end up asking her to marry him. "Think Mom would be happy if Barbara became her daughter-in-law someday," Gideon murmured.

As if in response, his horse whinnied and his ears perked up. The gelding acted frisky, prancing along the snow-covered road, blowing out his breath in steady streams as Gideon urged him forward.

Gideon had dressed warmly this evening, with a heavy jacket and gloves. Mom had given him a quilt to place across their laps. She'd also provided a thermos of hot chocolate, saying to make sure they kept warm, because the temperature was supposed to dip down this evening.

Gideon's thoughts returned to courting Barbara. Next week a group of young people planned a get-together that would include ice skating and a bonfire. He and Barbara would join them. He looked forward to the winter sport and having quality time with his new girlfriend.

Barbara's heart pounded as she stood at the living-room window, watching for Gideon's horse and buggy. Hours earlier, she'd debated on what dress to wear. Mom had stepped into her bedroom while she was trying on dresses and suggested Barbara wear a blue dress because it brought out the color of her eyes.

Barbara turned from the window when her mother entered the living room. "I'm a little naerfich tonight," Barbara admitted.

"I remember during my courting days, I was so nervous my knees sometimes knocked." Mom gave Barbara a hug. "I worried someone would notice, but no one said a thing."

"My knees aren't knocking, but I feel like I've got butterflies in my stomach."

Mom smiled. "You'll be fine, Daughter."

Barbara kept it to herself, but every time she and Gideon were together she found herself falling harder for him. She was amazed they'd become a courting couple. She'd thought for sure he would end up marrying Mandy.

Of course, Gideon hasn't proposed to me, and maybe he never will. He might only see me as a good friend—someone to fill the void since he and Mandy broke up.

Barbara took a seat on the couch. She remembered how when Gideon first asked her out, she'd asked Mandy how she felt about it. To Barbara's surprise, Mandy had given her blessing, stating she didn't have romantic feelings for Gideon anymore.

She sighed. *I can't believe Mandy would give up what she and Gideon once had, but I guess she has her reasons.* Barbara was glad she could freely express, at least to Sadie, how she felt toward Gideon. Until he declared feelings of love for her, she would remain quiet. But if the day ever came he asked her to marry him, Barbara's answer would be yes.

Shipshewana

On Monday morning, Mandy's day off at the meat-and-cheese store, she headed to the thrift shop where she volunteered one day a week. She enjoyed working there. It broke up the week and gave her something to look forward to. She couldn't wait to see what had come in since the last time she'd volunteered her services. All kinds of housewares and clothing were normally donated. Mandy would sort through the boxes and bags and then clean or repair what was needed.

She snickered, thinking about the wigs that had come in a few weeks ago. It would be comical to wear one of them while dressing up for a skit of some kind. Another time she'd opened a box of dishes, but many of them were chipped so they couldn't be put out.

Mandy pulled her thoughts together when the vehicle she rode in slowed down and turned the last corner before the thrift store. It had begun to snow pretty hard, and she breathed a sigh of relief when her driver dropped her off in front of the store.

Mandy shivered as she stepped through the door. "Brr. . . It's sure cold out there." She stomped her feet and brushed crystal flakes from her shoulders. "The snow's coming down harder," she told Mary Jane Bontrager, the woman in charge of the store for the day.

Mary Jane crinkled her nose. "We probably won't get too many customers. Only the brave or someone desperately seeking a bargain would be likely to come out in weather like this."

"I did." Mandy snickered. "But then, I enjoy my work here. It's a nice change of pace."

"I like it too." Mary Jane gestured toward the back of the store. "Someone brought in several boxes of used items last week, but I haven't had time to go through any of it. Would you mind sorting?"

"Sure, no problem. I'll begin as soon as I hang up my jacket and outer bonnet and put my lunch tote away."

Mandy moved swiftly for the back room. Once she'd put her things away, she located the boxes and got right to work. The first box was filled with children's toys, so she put them in two piles and would take care of cleaning them as soon as she sorted the items in the other boxes.

The clock clicked close to noon, and Mandy was about to stop and eat lunch, when she discovered something in the third box that nearly took her breath away. She studied the beautiful blue-and-white quilt. It didn't look like a traditional Amish quilt when she opened it the whole way. This one reminded her of the photo she'd seen of Luana and Makaio's quilt while staying at their bed-and-breakfast. After inspecting the covering closely, she discovered the initials *L* and *M* sewn in one corner of the quilt. Although it seemed impossible, Mandy wondered if by some miracle this could actually be Luana and Makaio's missing quilt. *But how would it get all the way from Hawaii to Indiana?*

Mandy knelt on the floor beside the cardboard box, holding the quilt. Gazing at the beautiful Hawaiian design put a lump in her throat. She felt a strong need to purchase this quilt, even if it wasn't Luana's. She couldn't imagine leaving it here in the store for someone else to buy, and she felt sure they would. An item this lovely wouldn't last long.

Carrying the quilt up to the front counter, Mandy held up her find. "What price will you put on this?"

Mary Jane studied the covering a few seconds, pursing her lips. "I'm normally the one who prices things here, but. . . Oh, I don't know. The quilt's design is unusual, especially for around these parts. Why don't you decide on a price? You have an eye for finely made quilts, so you can probably price it as well as I could."

Mandy shook her head. "You don't understand. I want to purchase this quilt. It reminds me of Hawaii, and it looks like the picture of a quilt that used to be owned by someone I met on Kauai."

"I'll tell you what. Since it means so much to you, why don't you give a donation to the store for whatever you can afford? Then the quilt will be yours."

Mandy didn't have a lot of money, but she'd been saving up since she began working at her dad's store. "Would a hundred dollars be fair?"

Mary Jane gave an affirmative nod. "Consider it yours."

Holding the covering close, Mandy's heart swelled. She'd replaced her digital camera a few months ago, so when she went home this evening, she would take a picture of this outstanding quilt and send it to Luana. If, by some miracle, it turned out to be her and Makaio's quilt, Mandy would make sure it was returned to them, even if it meant taking it there herself.

Mandy smiled. *Now wouldn't it be something if I got to go back to Kauai and could present something so special to Luana and Makaio? I hope and pray this is truly the lost quilt they received on their wedding day.*

Chapter 36

*B*undled in a heavy jacket, thick brown scarf, and matching gloves, Mandy stepped outdoors, where a strong wind continued blowing from overnight. Hopefully it would ease up soon, like it was supposed to. Making her way down the slippery driveway, she pulled her scarf up to the bridge of her nose.

Shivering against the cold, she opened the mailbox and pulled out a stack of mail. Thanks to the gloves she wore, her grip wasn't so good. Before she could react, a gust of wind whipped it right out of her hands and sent the mail flying down the road. She raced after it, trying to hold her balance as she slipped and slid in the snow. She grabbed one letter, but ended up bending it. "Oh, great! Come on, Mr. Wind. You're supposed to be calming down by now."

Mandy removed her gloves and managed to pick up the rest of the mail as the wind subsided, almost instantly. She stopped and looked around. *Guess the wind must have heard me.* She giggled. After thumbing through the retrieved items, she saw only a few bills and some advertising catalogs. It had been almost two weeks since she'd sent Luana a letter with the picture of the quilt she'd found at the thrift store. So far, there'd been no response. She hoped her letter hadn't gotten lost in the mail. If Luana had received it, she should have responded by now. Even if she thought the quilt wasn't hers, surely she would have written back.

Meandering back and being careful not to fall, she inhaled a breath of frosty air. Looking out across the field and the tree line adjacent to their property, Mandy paused for a minute to watch a steady stream of smoke, almost fog-like, wafting slowly in the afternoon's breeze. No doubt someone up the road had stoked their woodstove. The whitish haze was a stark contrast against the bare dark trees at the far end of the field. At least the stronger winds had finally settled down.

Winter had its own fragrance. Even snow sometimes smelled like rain. One thing she could always count on this time of the year was the pleasant aroma of wood smoke in the air. As much as she missed Hawaii, if she lived there she'd probably miss some things about winter here.

As Mandy approached their phone shack, she stopped to check for messages. The chilly wind picked up again, as quickly as it had stopped, causing the falling snow to pelt Mandy's face. She found welcome relief inside the small wooden building, despite its lack of heat.

Taking a seat on the cold metal chair, Mandy pressed the answering machine button. The first two messages were for her father, and the third one was for Mom. Mandy waited for the fourth message to come up. Her heartbeat quickened when she heard Luana's voice.

"Mandy, this is Luana Palu. I received your letter, and I'm so excited. After comparing the picture you sent me with the one I showed you of our missing quilt, I've concluded that the one you found is almost certainly Makaio's and mine. I can't begin to imagine how it could have gotten all the way from Hawaii to Shipshewana, Indiana. You finding it has to be more than a coincidence. I see it as a God-sent miracle."

Tears welled in Mandy's eyes and spilled over onto her cheeks as Luana's message continued. "If you would be willing to send me the quilt, I'll gladly pay you for it, and also reimburse your postage. Please give me a call as soon as you can."

When the message ended, Mandy remained in the phone shack several more minutes, feeling elated with this awesome news and thinking things through. She could box up the quilt and mail it tomorrow, but it might take a few weeks to get there, or might never make it at all. Apparently it had taken nearly two weeks for her letter and picture to reach Hawaii, or she would have heard from Luana sooner.

I'd rather take it there myself. Mandy moistened her chapped lips with her tongue. *Mom and Dad won't approve of me flying, even though I haven't joined the church, but I'm going to talk to my cousin Ruth and see if she will help me book a flight to Kauai.*

South Bend, Indiana

Mandy's heartbeat quickened when, one week later, she sat in the airport, waiting to board her plane. Flying was a new experience for her, and traveling alone for such a distance made it even more frightening. Yet her excitement over making this trip to Kauai overrode the nervousness. She could hardly wait to see Luana and Makaio's expression when she took their quilt from her suitcase and presented it to them. She'd never dreamed she'd have an opportunity to visit Hawaii again, let alone hand-deliver their lovely wedding quilt.

Mandy reflected on her parents' reaction when she told them Ruth had not only booked her flight to Kauai but also loaned her part of the money for a round-trip ticket. Mom was stunned and begged Mandy not to go. Dad said it was Mandy's choice. He not only gave her time off from work, but he encouraged Mandy to do what she felt was right.

It's not like I'm going to stay there forever. She gripped the handle of her carry-on bag. *I'll only be staying at the B&B two weeks. Then I'll return home, and everything will go back to normal.*

Mandy's flight would go to Detroit, Michigan. From there she would change to a plane taking her to Los Angeles, and another plane would fly on to Lihue, Hawaii. The airport in Lihue wasn't far from where the cruise ship docked when she and Ellen got stranded on Kauai.

She smiled inwardly, thinking about Ellen's response when she'd told her about finding the quilt and the plans she'd made to take it to Kauai herself. Ellen had clasped Mandy's hand and cautioned, "Don't miss your plane on the day of your return flight or I'll have to come and get you. Of course, since joining the church, I won't be allowed to fly unless it's an emergency."

Mandy had giggled and replied, "If I get stranded again, you'll be the first person I call, because it will be an emergency."

"Will you see Ken while you're there?" Ellen's furrowed brows revealed concern.

"No, he got married in November, so it wouldn't be right for me to seek him out. I'll be enjoying my time with Luana and Makaio, though, and it'll be fun to see how much little Primrose has grown."

"Please give them my best." Ellen's sincere hug told Mandy her friend had sent her off with a blessing. Even Sadie, Barbara, and Gideon wished her well, saying they would pray she had a safe trip.

It's nice to have good friends, Mandy thought. *Both here and in Hawaii.*

On the plane, Mandy sat with her nose pressed against the window, in awe of all she saw. Flying wasn't nearly as frightening as she'd imagined. In fact, she rather liked it.

When the airplane first took off, she'd seen what looked like miniature buildings and vehicles below, but as the pilot took them higher into the sky, the buildings were replaced with nothing but white, fluffy clouds, giving the appearance of cotton. In some places, the edges of the clouds were lit up by the sun's reflection. It was so different than watching clouds from the ground. Some were tall and billowy, like pillars against the bluest of skies, and others so distinct she could imagine touching them.

"Beautiful," Mandy whispered, briefly closing her eyes. Being up this high gave her an inkling of how it must be for God looking down on the world He created.

Mandy's eyes snapped open, and she clenched her fingers when a vibration went through the plane. Quickly, she looked out the window again but saw nothing amiss.

"Is this your first time flying?" the elderly lady beside her asked.

"Yes, it is." Mandy smiled. "Can you tell?"

The pleasant woman nodded slightly.

"This is all so new to me. Since the minute I took a seat, I've been intrigued with everything going on." She extended her hand. "Sorry, I should have introduced myself earlier. I'm Mandy Frey."

"Nice to meet you. I'm Charlotte Lowell." She shook Mandy's hand. "I felt the same way on my first flight many years ago. The bumps and vibrations we might be feeling are nothing to worry about. It's only a bit of turbulence."

Mandy felt herself relax. On this, her first opportunity to fly, she felt as if God had put this nice lady beside her on purpose.

Please keep us safe as we make this journey, she silently prayed. *And watch over my family and friends while I'm gone.*

Kapaa

"Your feet are gonna start to ache if you don't sit down and relax," Makaio told his wife. "Mandy's room is ready, and it won't be time to pick her up at the airport for two more hours. So you may as well join me for a glass of mango lemonade and some of those macadamia nut cookies you made this morning."

Luana shook her head. "Those cookies are meant to be a treat for Mandy when she gets here. They're one of her favorites."

"Doesn't mean we can't eat a few of them now." Makaio stepped up to Luana and kissed her cheek. "*E hele mai*—come and take a seat."

Luana sighed. "Oh, all right, but we're only drinking the lemonade. If I set out any of the cookies, you won't be able to stop at one. Pretty soon, the whole jar will be gone." She went to the refrigerator and took out the pitcher of lemonade, placing it on the table, along with two glasses. After taking a seat, she poured for both of them.

"Ah, this hits the spot." Makaio drank half his drink then paused and smacked his lips. "Yep, that's real good stuff."

Luana glanced at the clock again. "Where do you think she is now?"

"Who?"

She swatted his arm playfully. "Mandy. Who else?"

He shrugged. "Somewhere over the Pacific Ocean headed toward here. Probably two hours out if the plane's on time."

"Maybe we should head for the airport now. She's supposed to arrive at 8:21 p.m., and I want to make sure we're there on time to pick her up."

Makaio rolled his eyes. "It takes less than thirty minutes to get to the airport from here."

"But traffic could be bad. You know how it gets sometimes coming out of town."

"You're right, but it's usually worse when people are getting off work or heading out to a luau or some other function." He gestured to his watch. "Let's wait another half hour."

"Okay." Luana leaned back in her chair and tried to relax. The last time she'd been this excited was when she became a grandma. She'd missed Mandy and looked forward to seeing her again. To add to her excitement, she could hardly wait to see the quilt Mandy had found. It still didn't seem possible it could be her and Makaio's wedding quilt.

No matter how hard Luana tried to keep her emotions in check, the thought lingered: *What if it isn't our quilt after all? If not, it'll feel like we've lost it all over again. But then, how many quilts would have the initials* L. M. *sewn in the corner, as the picture of the one Mandy found showed? Well, in a short time, my questions will be answered and we'll know for sure.*

Chapter 37

The minute Mandy entered the baggage claim area, she spotted Luana and Makaio, both wearing eager expressions. She ran toward them, excitedly. Before any words were spoken, Luana's warm hug encompassed Mandy.

"It's so good to see you," they said in unison.

Then Makaio stepped forward and pulled Mandy close. Tears flooded her eyes, and she gulped on a sob. In some ways it felt like she'd been gone longer than nine months. In another way it seemed as if she'd never left at all—most likely because there hadn't been a day when her thoughts hadn't returned to the islands and the people she'd come to know and love. Oh, how she had missed the warmth and beauty of Kauai. Even more, she'd missed spending time with her Hawaiian friends. It would probably be harder to leave this time, but at least she'd have fourteen full days to spend with Luana and Makaio before returning home.

"Let's get your suitcase." Makaio pointed to the revolving conveyor belt where her checked luggage would be coming.

As Mandy stood waiting for her suitcase to appear, she took in the sights around her. She saw the familiar landscape of the hills in the distance and felt a warm breeze coming through the open areas in front of the building.

"There it is!" she shouted, when her luggage appeared. "The one with the green ribbon tied to the handle."

Once Makaio retrieved her luggage, the Palus led the way to their car. Before getting in, Mandy paused and lifted a silent prayer: *Thank You, Lord, for bringing me here safely.*

"How were your flights?" Luana asked as Makaio directed the vehicle onto the main road.

"A little bumpy sometimes, but it didn't bother me much—especially when the nice lady sitting beside me helped calm my fears." Mandy rolled down the back window a crack and breathed in the fresh, balmy air, feeling her whole body relax. "I could get used to traveling by plane. It's so much quicker," she commented, resting deeply against her seat.

"Were you nervous making connections?" Makaio asked.

"A little at first, but my cousin Ruth has flown before, so she told me what to expect." Mandy put the window down farther and held on to her head covering.

"You didn't break any church rules by flying, I hope." Luana looked over her shoulder with concern.

"No, because I have not yet joined the Amish church—although, my mother wasn't too happy about me coming."

"She didn't want you to return our quilt?" Luana's tone was one of surprise.

"Mom wanted me to mail the quilt, but I felt better returning it to you in person."

"Speaking of the quilt," Luana said, "I can hardly wait to see it. I'm almost one hundred percent sure from the picture you sent that it's the same one we were given as a wedding present."

Mandy smiled. "One of the first things I'll do when we get to the B&B is open my suitcase."

Kapaa

When Mandy entered the bed-and-breakfast, she felt as though she was at home. With the exception of a few new plants in the living room, everything looked exactly as it had when she and Ellen left last April.

"We have the Primrose Room ready for you. Is that okay?" Luana asked.

"Yes, it'll be perfect. Speaking of Primrose, when will I get to see your sweet baby granddaughter?"

"Ailani will be coming to work tomorrow. She always brings the baby with her." Luana picked up a framed picture sitting on a side table. "Can you believe how much my granddaughter has grown?"

"She's adorable."

"Yes, we feel truly blessed."

It was tempting to ask how Ken was doing, but Mandy figured it wasn't a topic that should be discussed, since as far as she knew, he'd gotten married back in November. Even though she no longer dwelled on the feelings she'd once had for him, occasionally she thought about the friendship they'd established and hoped he was doing well.

Makaio set Mandy's suitcase on the floor. "Should I take this to your room now so you can unpack your things?"

"You can leave it there for the moment. I'm going to open it now and take out the quilt."

Mandy went down on her knees and unzipped the suitcase. Then she lifted the covering out and handed it to Luana.

Makaio inhaled sharply, and Luana gasped, clasping her hands to her chest. "It. . .it's our beautiful wedding day quilt!" She lifted one corner and pointed to the initials. "See here—*L. M.*" Tears gathered in her dark eyes and dripped onto her cheeks. "I truly never thought I would see this again, much less that it would be found in such an unexpected place."

Makaio slipped his arm around his wife's waist, then gave Mandy a wide grin. "*Mahalo nui loa*—thank you very much."

Wiping away her own tears, Mandy barely managed to say, "You're welcome."

It did her heart good to see and actually feel how much they appreciated receiving this quilt. Luana and Makaio showed Christ's love to others as they entertained strangers almost on a daily basis. It was her utmost pleasure to see them get something in return. She thanked God for allowing her to be instrumental in getting their beloved Hawaiian quilt back where it belonged.

"We can talk more about the quilt after you're settled in," Luana suggested. "I'm sure after your long day of travel, you must be exhausted."

"I am a little weary," Mandy admitted. "It's hard to believe I started out this morning in Indiana and arrived here on Kauai before the day was out."

"While Makaio is putting your suitcase and carryall in your room, I'll put some water in the teakettle, and we can have a little snack out on the lanai before it's time for bed. It'll be good to catch up with each other's lives." Luana winked at Mandy. "Oh, and I made your favorite macadamia nut cookies."

Mandy moistened her lips. "Sounds wonderful."

The following morning when Mandy woke up, she took her purple muumuu out of the suitcase and slipped it over her head. While she was in Hawaii she would dress like she had during her previous stay. Once Mandy joined the church, which she felt obligated to do, there would be no opportunity to wear the dress again. It was like one last fling during her rumschpringe days. *At least I'm not doing anything totally crazy or wild like some young people do*, she thought, looking at herself in the mirror.

It was tempting to go outside, pick a pretty flower, and put it behind her right ear. Instead, Mandy secured the black scarf she'd brought along to the back of her head in preparation of going to the kitchen to help Luana with breakfast. It would be like old times, except this morning she was the only guest in the house. Luana had mentioned last night that they didn't have any other B&B guests scheduled for the next two days. Mandy had already determined when those guests checked in, she would help out by making beds, cleaning rooms, and offering to do anything else that would help Luana. It was the least she could do in exchange for the free room they'd offered her. Makaio had tried to reimburse Mandy for the amount she'd paid for the quilt when she'd found it at the thrift store. But she'd been adamant, saying the money she'd paid should be considered a gift.

Mandy lifted the window to enjoy the Hawaiian breeze and listen to the birds' sweet melodies coming from the trees. A flash of gray and white appeared, landing on a branch. The red-headed bird looked like one she'd seen once before in the Palus' yard. *Weerit, churit, weerit, churit,* it chirped.

"Hey, I should be the one scolding you." Mandy giggled, remembering how a bird looking a lot like this one had left its calling card on her muumuu. Even the memory of Ken wiping the splotch from the shoulder of her dress held a special place in her heart.

When good smells from the kitchen began to waft upstairs, Mandy quickly closed the window. *I need to quit thinking about Ken and see if Luana needs help with anything.*

Mandy's nose twitched when she entered the kitchen and smelled a sweet aroma. "Something smells familiar." She peered over Luana's shoulder and studied the batter in a large bowl. "Is it my favorite mango-flavored pancakes with sweet coconut syrup?"

Nodding, Luana smiled. "It's one way I can thank you for bringing our quilt back to us."

"It was my pleasure, and I'm happy it all worked out. I will carry the memory of giving it to you for the rest of my life." Mandy slipped into a colorful apron. "Now what can I do to help?"

"Nothing really, unless you want to. . ." A knock at the door interrupted Luana. "Would you mind seeing who that is, Mandy? I'm about to start cooking the pancakes, and I don't want them to burn." She reached over and grabbed the spatula from the pan.

"No problem." Mandy hurried across the room. Turning the knob, she opened the door. Heat flooded her face when she looked into Ken's blue eyes as he stood, holding a carton of eggs.

"Mandy!" His eyes widened. "I sure didn't expect to see you here this morning. What brings you back to Kauai, and how long will you be staying?"

Lightheaded, Mandy felt her heart beat so fast she could almost hear it echo in her head. Ken was as good-looking as she remembered, and his pleasant, deep voice still sounded the same. The only thing different about Ken was that he'd cut his hair, although it was still thick and curly. She had to catch herself to keep from giving him a hug. *But you mustn't even think such thoughts,* her conscience reminded. *He's a married man.*

"I found Luana and Makaio's lost quilt in a thrift store in Shipshewana, so I brought it back to them." She spoke quickly, trying not to stare at his handsome face and barely making eye contact with him.

"Wow! How about that!" He set the eggs on the counter and stared hard at Mandy. "I can hardly believe you're here. I've missed seeing you and—"

"How have you been? I'm looking forward to meeting your wife."

Ken tipped his head to one side. "My wife?"

"Yes. Luana wrote in a letter she sent me about you getting married last November."

Ken's eyebrows furrowed. "Me, married?" With his eyes fixed on Mandy, he brushed some hair off his forehead. "Oh, you must be talking about my brother, Dan. He got married in November."

"Oops! Guess I messed up and wrote the wrong name," Luana called from across the room. "I must have been preoccupied when I wrote that letter. Come to think of it, I was holding Primrose at the time."

Mandy's lips parted, but no words came out. So Ken was still single. It was difficult not to get her hopes up, but a longing welled in her soul like nothing before. *Could there be a chance Ken might. . . No. He only sees me as a friend. That's how it was before I left, and I'm sure nothing's changed.*

Chapter 38

*M*andy's legs trembled like they had when she and Gideon first started courting. Only Ken wasn't courting her. He merely stood staring at her with a wide smile. She could hardly believe he hadn't gotten married.

What does it matter? she asked herself. *I'll be returning home in two weeks and will start classes to prepare for joining the church this spring.* She shifted uneasily. *I wonder what would happen if I didn't join and stayed here instead.*

Mandy's thoughts swirled until she felt as if her head might explode. She remembered when Luana had told her how she and Makaio left their family and friends on the Big Island to begin a new life as owners of the B&B here. *Would it be wrong to leave my family and stay in Kauai permanently? I would miss everyone, but I'd go home for visits. It would be hard on my folks, though, especially Mom. She wants all her children living close, which I totally understand. If I was married and had children, I'd wish for the same thing.*

"Why don't you two go out to the lanai and get reacquainted?" Luana suggested. "After you've visited awhile you can join Makaio and me in the dining room for breakfast."

"I should help you," Mandy offered.

"No, it's fine. You're our guest here this time, and guests don't help with the cooking."

Mandy was tempted to argue, but Ken had already started out the door, so she thanked Luana and followed him to the lanai.

"I still can't believe you're not married," Mandy murmured, taking a seat beside him on the porch swing. "I thought maybe it was one of the young women you were talking to on the beach when I was here last year."

He shook his head. "No serious girlfriends for me. But speaking of marriage. . . Since you have a boyfriend in Indiana, I figured you'd be married by now." He took a step back. "You're not, are you?"

Mandy's mouth opened slightly. "No, I'm not married, but who told you I had a boyfriend?"

"Ellen."

"When?"

"Remember the night of the bad storm?"

Mandy nodded.

"Well, I stopped by here after it had subsided, to see how you were all doing. Everyone but Ellen had gone to bed, so she and I visited a few minutes. During our conversation, she mentioned you had a boyfriend back home and said after you joined the Amish church you would most likely get married."

A shock wave rippled through Mandy, and she grabbed the edge of the swing, fearing she might fall off. *Why would my good friend tell Ken about Gideon? Did she do it on purpose to make sure he didn't develop strong feelings for me? Could this be why Ken pulled away and didn't come around much after that night?*

"So what about your boyfriend?" Ken's question broke into Mandy's thoughts. "Has he asked you to marry him?"

Slowly, she shook her head. "I haven't joined the church. Gideon and I broke up awhile back." Mandy paused to draw a quick breath. "He's seeing someone else now."

Ken blinked. "Really? You're unattached?"

"Yes."

A wide smile stretched across his face as he moved closer and reached for Mandy's hand. "Would you be willing to let me court you? That's how the Amish refer to dating, right?" He looked deeply into her eyes.

"It is, and I would." Mandy swallowed hard. "There's just one problem; I will only be here two weeks, then I'll have to return to Indiana, because I bought a round-trip plane ticket."

"Is it refundable?"

"I don't think so. My cousin booked the ticket for me, and Ruth got the cheapest one she could find."

His fingers tightened around hers. "You can't leave in two weeks, Mandy. We need more time to court." Ken's tone sounded desperate and sad at the same time.

His look of sincerity brought a smile to her lips. *Ken cares about me. He always did. He only kept his distance because of what Ellen told him about me and Gideon.* Mandy felt torn. She wanted desperately to stay and develop a relationship with Ken, but staying longer would mean losing part of the money Ruth had loaned her for the plane ticket. It would also disappoint her parents. They were expecting her to return and take classes in the spring. Mandy didn't want to hurt them, but if she said goodbye to Ken again, her heart would break, even more than it had the last time she'd left Kauai.

"I need to pray about this." She gazed at his handsome face. "Can we talk about it again in a few days?"

"Of course, but I want to see you every single day you're here." He lifted his hand and gently caressed her face. "I've missed you so much."

Ken leaned closer, and Mandy felt in her heart he was about to kiss her, but Luana called them to breakfast. "Guess we'd better go eat." She rose from the swing. "I'm glad you came over this morning."

"Same here." Still holding Mandy's hand, Ken brought it slowly to his lips and feathered a kiss across her knuckles. She had a sense of what it was like to float, when together, they headed for the dining room. Mandy didn't know how things would turn out for her and Ken, but she was sure of one thing: she'd never been happier.

After Ken left, Luana noticed Mandy seemed quieter than usual. The bubbly spirit she'd exhibited earlier this morning had suddenly vanished. "Are you tired, Mandy? Would you like to go to your room and take a nap?"

"I'm not sleepy, but I would like to talk to you about something."

"Certainly. Why don't we take a seat in the living room where it's nice and cool? Ailani's car broke down, and since Makaio went to pick her and Primrose up, we should take advantage of our quiet time together." Luana chuckled. "If my precious granddaughter decides to start hollering, we won't be able to hear ourselves think."

"I'm looking forward to seeing her, though. I can't wait to take a few pictures of your grandbaby." Mandy followed Luana into the other room and took a seat in the rocking chair.

Luana sat on the couch across from her. "Now what was it you wanted to talk to me about?"

"I'm confused about Ken."

"What do you mean?"

Holding the armrests, Mandy got the rocking chair moving. "He wants to court me."

Luana tipped her head. "Court?"

"Yes. It's what the Amish call dating."

"Ah, I see. I'm beginning to understand why Ken didn't come around much after you left."

"Why is that?"

"He missed you. Coming here probably made him think about you even more." Luana smiled. "I suspected he'd fallen head over heels for you, but it wasn't my place to say anything. I figured once you went home, Ken would move on with his life and find someone else."

Mandy nodded. "I thought so too, and when you wrote and said he was getting married, I tried to accept the fact that a relationship between him and me was not meant to be."

"And now how do you feel?"

"Confused."

"About your feelings for Ken?"

"No, I'm clear about that. Seeing him again this morning and learning he isn't married made me aware my feelings for him hadn't changed." Mandy paused and lowered her head. "I'm in love with him, but I don't see how things could work out between us when I live so far away."

"Have you considered staying in Kauai?" Luana questioned.

Mandy nodded. "I love it here, but all of my family live in Indiana, and I need to consider them. I don't know if I could move here permanently without their blessing. I'm not sure I'd be truly happy living so far from them, either."

"The first thing you should do is pray about it." Luana reached for the Bible on the coffee table and opened it to a passage she had underlined some time ago. "Listen to what it says in Proverbs 3:5–6: 'Trust in the Lord with all thine heart; and lean not unto thine own understanding. In all thy ways acknowledge him, and he shall direct thy paths.'"

Mandy's chin quivered as she rose from her chair. "Mahalo, Luana. I needed the reminder."

When Ken returned home later that morning, he had a hard time concentrating on his work. Beautiful Mandy, whom he'd fallen in love with during her stay on Kauai last year, would be returning to the mainland again unless he could convince her to remain here with him.

What should I do, Lord? he silently prayed. *I want to be with Mandy, but I can't force her to stay. Her family is in Indiana—so far away.*

Fate could be a strange thing sometimes, if this was actually fate. Ken never thought he'd see Mandy again, especially when Ellen had told him about Mandy having a boyfriend and given the impression they'd be getting married. He'd tried so hard to forget her, but nearly every day Mandy's sweet face was vivid in his mind. Ken had even gone out on a couple of dates, but he couldn't get Mandy out of his thoughts. The few times he'd taken a girl out for dinner, his mind had been elsewhere. He'd finally given up, deciding it might be too soon to think about dating anyone. Maybe a few years down the road it would get easier.

Ken gripped the handle of the shovel he'd been using to clean the chicken barn. *Is it possible God used Luana and Makaio's missing quilt to bring Mandy back to Kauai? Maybe this is where she belongs.*

He took a seat on a bundle of straw, watching the chickens move about and hoping they might divert his spiraling thoughts. *What should I do? Mandy's met my parents and brother, and they got along well. I'd like the chance to meet her parents and siblings too. It'd be great to see the area she grew up in.*

As Ken sat pondering, one of the barn cats rubbed against his leg, jarring his thoughts. The cat purred then leaped into Ken's lap. "You're supposed to be keeping the mice down, not lounging around." He snickered and stroked the feline's ear. "Guess I shouldn't be sitting here, either."

Ken sat a few more minutes then placed the cat on the floor and stood. He picked up his shovel and opened the door to the large pen. He was about to start cleaning, when Taavi walked in.

"Hey, Ken! Thought I'd stop by to see if you wanna go surfing with me. The waves are looking real good today."

"Wish you would have called me instead of coming all the way out here." Ken set the shovel aside and reached into his pocket for his cell phone. "Oh, yeah, it's in the house on the charger." He slapped his forehead.

Taavi snorted. "Well, you answered your own question, buddy." He pointed to Ken's feet. "You sure look funny wearin' those clod-hopper boots."

"What? Do you think I'd wear a pair of flip-flops out here? No way!" Ken lifted his gaze to the ceiling.

"So what do you think about heading to the beach. You wanna go?"

"Any other time I'd jump at the chance, but I have work to do." Ken picked up Fluffy, his favorite chicken, and stroked the hen's feathers. "Not only that, but Mandy is back for a couple of weeks, and when I'm done working for the day, I'll be with her."

Taavi leaned against the wall. "You weren't the same after Mandy left last year. Fact is, you acted like a love-sick seal. So guess I won't be seein' much of you till she goes home again—unless, of course, you beg her to stay."

"I'll stop by soon or give you a call." Ken set the chicken on the floor.

"You might want to know how things turned out."

"Sounds good." Taavi thumped Ken's back. "Say hi to Mandy for me."

After his friend left, Ken contemplated the situation with Mandy. *Is her place really here on the island because she brought back Luana and Makaio's quilt? Or maybe,* he thought, grabbing the shovel again, *my place is in Indiana with her.*

Chapter 39

For the next ten days, Mandy and Ken spent every free minute together. In addition to him visiting Mandy at the B&B, he took her to see several sights she hadn't seen before. Today, Ken had some time off, so he'd booked a one-hour trip with the Wings of Kauai. He wanted Mandy to see the entire island from the air. This would be his special treat before she went home. Ken couldn't wait to see her surprised look when he told her about the island air tour. Hopefully, it would be something she'd remember for a long time to come.

Since Mandy's return to the island, Ken had removed his surfboard from the roof of his SUV. He figured there'd be no time for hanging out on the beach, nor did he want to waste a minute without Mandy at his side. He'd taken his vehicle to the gas station and through the car wash so that everything could be perfect for her.

Ken glanced at the passenger seat, where Mandy sat in his SUV, holding a camera. He was glad she'd gotten a new one and was enjoying taking photos. *But no photo can ever replace the real thing.* Ken reflected on how he had longed to see Mandy's sweet face during the months she'd been gone. She'd been in his thoughts daily, and his dreams at night. Having her sitting beside him now was an answer to prayer.

Ken had been praying about their situation and discussed it at length with his folks. As of last night, he'd finally come up with a way for him and Mandy to be together on a permanent basis, even though it meant giving up the dream he had of owning his own organic hydroponic nursery on the island he loved so much.

"Guess where we're going?" He waited for her response.

Tilting her head she looked at him. "I don't know. Where?"

"To the airport. I booked us an island tour with Wings over Kauai."

"Really? It sounds like fun. I'm looking forward to riding in a plane again. It should be fun to see the island from the air."

"It will be fun, but riding in a small plane will be a little different than the big jet you were on coming here."

"I figured it would be since it's so much smaller." She giggled. "No flight attendants to offer cold drinks and snacks."

"There will be water and soda pop on the plane, but the only passengers will be us, the pilot, and four others who signed up for the flight."

Smiling, she lifted her camera. "I'm anxious to get some pictures. I need something to take home to remind me of this trip."

For the first several minutes, Mandy sat with her nose pressed against the window on her side of the airplane. Due to distribution of weight, Ken sat next to the pilot, and the other passengers were in the back, with one middle-aged woman sitting across from Mandy.

Mandy's stomach flew up as the small plane took off, but she didn't mind. What an adventure it was to look down and see the layout of the land, with all its peaks and valleys. Everyone on board wore headphones so they could communicate with the pilot, as well as with each other. The plane flew out over the ocean, and the pilot called their attention to some whales. It was different seeing them from this perspective.

Mandy wished she and Ken were the only ones in the plane so she could speak to him freely, without others hearing their conversation.

As they continued on, several waterfalls came into view. One of them was the same falls she and Ken had visited last year, when the nice lady offered to take their picture. Of course, seeing it from above put a different slant on things. All the while, Mandy snapped more pictures.

When the Na Pali Coast came into view, she couldn't help exclaiming, "How amazing! It looks different than when we saw it by boat, but beautiful, nonetheless. Only God could have created something this spectacular."

Ken looked over his shoulder and smiled at her. Then he gave a thumbs-up.

I love him, she thought. *How am I ever going to leave here when it's time to go? I wish it were possible for me to stay. I'll miss Ken terribly when I return to my home on the mainland.*

Ken's heart pounded as he drove Mandy back to the B&B later that afternoon. He needed to tell her how he felt, but was unsure of her reaction.

"Mahalo, Ken, for giving me such a nice day." Mandy held up her camera. "I took enough pictures to help me remember my time on Kauai this time." She sighed deeply and leaned back in her seat. "I'm going to miss being in Hawaii, but I'll miss you most of all."

Pleased with her declaration, Ken couldn't wait any longer. He pulled off at a wide spot on the shoulder of the road. "There's something I need to tell you."

Mandy tipped her head. "What is it?"

He reached for her hand. "It may seem like it's too short for the declaration I'm about to make, but we spent a lot of time together when you were here before." He paused, searching for just the right words. "Every minute you were with me was special. Truth is, these last couple of days, we'd no sooner part than I'd began counting the hours till the next time we could be together."

"I felt the same."

Gently, he held her fingers. "I'm in love with you, Mandy."

Her eyes glistened with tears. "Oh Ken, I love you too. I began to feel it soon after we were formally introduced, but I feared so many things. With the distance between our homes, I didn't see how anything could work out."

"I didn't believe so for a while, either, but after praying and thinking everything through, I've come up with a plan."

"You have? What is it?"

"I'm going back to Indiana with you."

"To meet my family?"

"Yes, and also to look for a job so I can be close to you, because if you'll have me, I want you to become my wife."

"I would be honored to marry you." Mandy spoke in a soft, shaky voice. "But you can't move to Indiana. You have a job right here, helping your parents raise chickens. Life in Middlebury is a lot different than Kauai. There are no sandy beaches, palm trees, tropical flowers, or places to go surfing."

Mandy's somber expression concerned him. Was she having second thoughts about being with him?

"If you leave Kauai, you'll miss the island, as well as your family and friends."

"I'll have you, and I'll make new friends." Ken shifted in his seat, never taking his eyes off Mandy. "I've already talked to Mom and Dad about this, as well as my brother, Dan. He said he'd take over my responsibilities with the business, and Mom and Dad are fine with it too. They'll come visit whenever they can. My family wants me to be happy, and my happiness is with you."

"What about your dream of owning your own organic hydroponic nursery?"

"I'm willing to give it up to be with you. Staying in Hawaii and owning my own business may not be God's will for me. Truthfully, sometimes the things we think we want are not what is best for us."

"I believe you're right. I've been rather selfish thinking only of my own needs and longing for Hawaii, when I should have been asking God what is best for me."

Ken leaned forward and drew Mandy into his arms. Then he kissed her gently on the lips.

When they pulled apart, Mandy stared at him with a dazed expression. *Did I kiss her right? Should I have asked her first? Does she want me to go to Indiana with her?* Many doubts filled Ken's mind, but one thing he believed without question: the kiss felt right. In fact, it was perfect. And if Mandy's sigh was any indication, maybe she felt it too.

For a while they sat together, holding hands but saying nothing. Words weren't necessary as Ken looked into her beautiful brown eyes. The tiny flecks of green in Mandy's eyes looked even more vivid as traces of tears remained.

Ken traced her jawline with his fingers, then moved his hand to the back of her head. He didn't have to pull her close, for she willingly went toward him, and they kissed again. It was so sweet, Ken felt as though he were floating.

Mandy swallowed hard, then cleared her throat. Her cheeks were still flushed, no doubt from what they'd shared seconds ago.

"You're not thinking of joining the Amish faith, are you?" she asked.

Sorry to see the moment end, Ken breathed deeply. "I will if it's the only way we can be together."

"No, Ken. I cannot ask you to make such a sacrifice." Mandy paused. "It's a difficult transition that not many English people have been able to make." She smiled tearfully, gently touching his face. "I'd thought I would join the Amish church this spring, but it would only be to please my parents. I can be happy attending any church as long as it teaches God's Holy Word."

"What exactly are you saying?"

"From the time I was a young girl, I was taught it would be my choice to join the Amish church. Mom and Dad often said it wasn't a matter of what church you belonged to. What counts is what's in a person's heart and whether you choose to follow God." Mandy paused before she continued. "So, even though they may be disappointed because I'm not becoming part of the Amish church, they will be pleased I have found a Christian man. I only wish we could both live near our families. Hawaii's a long way from Indiana, and you had no plans to leave here until now."

"True." Ken took her hand. "But we can live in Indiana to be near your family and take our vacations on Kauai, where my folks live. It only takes a portion of a day to get here by plane, so we can go once or twice a year—maybe more if I should end up opening my own business in Indiana."

"When I first went to Kauai, I thought it was the island I loved, but

I've come to realize it wasn't the island, but rather the people I'd met while living there. I've also learned it doesn't matter what church we attend, as long as we are serving the Lord." She leaned her head on his shoulder. "I want to serve Him with you."

Epilogue

𝓜andy's heart swelled to overflowing as she stood at the altar beside her groom, preparing to recite her wedding vows. A meaningful life's journey was about to begin for her: not pure Amish, but still living a Christian life, ready to serve God.

She took a deep breath to steady her nerves, and then the vows flowed from her heart: "I Mandy, take you, Ken, to be my husband, secure in the knowledge you will be my constant friend, my faithful partner in life, and my one true love. On this special day, I affirm to you in the presence of God and these witnesses my sacred promise to stay by your side as your faithful wife, in sickness and in health, in joy and in sorrow, through good times and bad. I further promise to love you without reservation, comfort you in times of distress, encourage you to achieve your goals, laugh with you and cry with you, grow with you in mind and spirit, always to be open and honest with you, and cherish you for as long as we both shall live."

Tenderly holding her hand, Ken repeated his vows. As he spoke the words, Mandy listened intently while gazing into his vibrant blue eyes, filled with happy tears.

Thank You, Lord, for bringing this special man into my life.

When their vows concluded, Mandy stood beside her groom, listening to the song "Each for the Other" sung a cappella by three members of the church worship team.

As the trio sang "Each for the other, and both for the Lord," Mandy stole a look at the people who had come to witness their union this sunny but cold Saturday afternoon.

Mandy's folks sat on one side of the church, along with her brothers, Milo, Mark, Melvin, and Michael, as well as Michael's wife, Sarah.

Ken's parents; his brother, Dan; and Dan's wife, Sandy, sat on the other side of the church. It pleased Mandy that Ken's cousin Brock had been able to take over the responsibilities of the Freys' chicken farm so they could all be here for the wedding.

Mandy's best friends, Ellen, Sadie, and Barbara, were seated in the pew behind Mandy's family. Gideon sat beside Barbara, whom he planned to marry in the spring. Mandy was glad they could still be friends. Barbara was the better choice for him, since she shared his dedication to the Amish church.

They were meant to be together, Mandy thought, *just as Ken is the man God intended for me.*

She looked forward to spending their honeymoon in Kauai, where Luana and Makaio had promised to give them a wedding reception. When Mandy and Ken returned from Hawaii, they would begin making plans for the bed-and-breakfast they wanted to open. It would be an exciting adventure, although a bit frightening. But with God's help, she felt confident it would succeed. Like Luana and Makaio, she and Ken would minister to many people in the days ahead. . . .and perhaps entertain a few angels unaware.

Luana's Hawaiian Teriyaki Burgers

1½ pounds ground beef
1 small onion, chopped
1 egg
¼ cup soy sauce

2 cloves garlic, minced
½ teaspoon fresh ginger, minced
2 stalks green onion, chopped
1 tablespoon sesame oil

Combine all ingredients in large bowl; mix well. Form into patties. Fry, grill, or broil. For additional taste, serve with a slice of pineapple on top of each burger.

Mandy's Organic Chicken Chowder

2 tablespoons butter
¼ cup onion, chopped
1½ cups cooked chicken, cubed
1½ cups carrots, diced
1½ cups raw potatoes, diced
2 chicken bouillon cubes

1 teaspoon salt
⅛ teaspoon pepper
2 cups water
3 tablespoons flour
1½ cups milk

Melt butter in a 3-quart saucepan. Add onions and sauté until tender. Add chicken, carrots, potatoes, bouillon cubes, salt, pepper, and water. Cover and simmer until vegetables are tender. Combine flour and ½ cup milk in a jar. Shake until blended. Add to vegetables along with remaining milk. Cook on medium heat, stirring constantly, until mixture thickens. Yields 1¾ quarts.

History of Hawaiian Quilts

The introduction to sewing and quilt making came to Hawaiians from the wives of American missionaries in 1820. Patchwork quilts were made in the missionary boarding schools, where girls were taught to sew. Even though the missionaries are credited with teaching new concepts and techniques in quilt making, the development of the Hawaiian appliquéd quilts lies with the Hawaiian women. Many of the designs and methods they used are found only in Hawaii. Hawaiian quilt making became a form of self-expression during nineteenth-century westernization. Every stitch had a meaning and every part of the design a purpose.

Quilting frames in Hawaii were set close to the ground so quilters could sit on their handwoven *lauhala* mats. A wide variety of fill material for the quilts was used in Hawaii, including soft fibers from tree fern, cotton, wool, and animal hair. As three layers were stitched together. The quilters started at the quilt's center and worked toward the edges.

Quilts found on the mainland that are the most similar to Hawaiian quilts are appliquéd in the Pennsylvania Dutch tradition. Their quilts often consist of a central medallion appliqué that resembles the Hawaiian technique and repeats the same floral design in four large blocks. The Hawaiian women designed their quilts based on floral surroundings, legends, and innermost feelings of love. Every quilt had a purpose, and no two quilts were alike.

Discussion Questions

1. For some time, Mandy had a desire to visit Hawaii. Her boyfriend, Gideon, wanted her to stay but gave his blessing so she could pursue her dream. Have you ever wanted to do something so badly you didn't consider another person's feelings? Like Gideon, have you ever given someone your blessing, even though you felt what they were doing was wrong?

2. On the cruise ship, someone mistook Mandy and her Amish friends for nuns. Have you ever assumed something about a person based on their outer appearance?

3. Mandy was afraid of water and was unable to swim, yet she set her fears aside to go on the cruise to Hawaii. Have you ever wanted to do something so much you were able to set your fears aside in order to pursue your goal? Or have you ever held someone back from doing what they wanted, because of your own fears?

4. When Mandy and Ellen became stranded on Kauai, a caring Hawaiian couple took them in. Would you be willing to take in strangers at a moment's notice and make them feel welcome? If you have entertained strangers, how did it all work out?

5. Since Mandy's and Ellen's luggage was left on the ship, they only had the dresses they were wearing when they became stranded. Luana suggested they go shopping for a modest-looking Hawaiian dress. Mandy was content to accept the style of clothing on Kauai, but dressing that way made Ellen feel uncomfortable. How do you feel when you're subjected to uncomfortable situations? Do you conform or stay with what you believe is appropriate for you? Why?

6. When Makaio was injured, should Mandy and Ellen have agreed to stay on Kauai longer to help at the B&B, or would it have been better if they'd returned home right away?

7. After Barbara and Sadie returned to Indiana without their two Amish friends, Barbara found herself drawn to Mandy's boyfriend, Gideon. She did not act upon her feelings and kept them to herself. What would have happened if she had let him know how she felt? Have you ever been in a similar situation? If so, how did you respond?

8. Ellen realized Mandy was captivated by Hawaii and a certain young English man, so she intervened without Mandy's knowledge. Is there ever a time we should intervene if we feel someone we know is about to make a wrong decision that could change the course of their life? Should Ellen have gone to Mandy and discussed her feelings instead of going behind her back and attempting to manipulate the situation?

9. Even though Luana had lost a sentimental quilt, she didn't let it consume her. She moved on with a positive attitude. Have you ever lost something that had either monetary or sentimental value? What was the item, and how did you cope with the loss?

10. When Mandy returned home from Hawaii, Gideon saw a change in her. It was almost as though they were strangers, and he didn't know how to get back what they'd once had. Life is full of changes, some good and some bad. How do you deal with a friend or loved one who has changed?

11. Gideon's mother, Peggy, was unsure of him choosing Mandy for a wife. However, instead of meddling, she prayed about it, allowing God to work things out for her son. What happens when we allow God to work in our lives, rather than taking matters into our own hands?

12. Mandy's desire to live a different life from the one she'd always known was hard for her family and friends to accept. If you had a child who wanted to serve God in a different church than the one in which they were raised, how would you respond?

13. Did you learn anything new about the Amish by reading this story? If so, what was it?

14. Were there any Bible verses mentioned in this story that spoke to your heart? If so, what were they, and how did they bolster your faith?

THE
Hawaiian
DISCOVERY

Dedication

To our special friends from Kauai—Nathan & Rebecca Cotter,
Tristan Dahlberg, and Randy & Primrose Rego.
May God bless each of you.

Cast thy burden upon the LORD,
and he shall sustain thee.
PSALM 55:22

Prologue

Middlebury, Indiana

$\mathcal{E}$llen Lambright finished sweeping the kitchen floor and paused from her work to brew a cup of tea. Since the Pleasant View Bed-and-Breakfast currently had no guests, she and her friend Mandy had spent most of the day giving each of the guest rooms a thorough cleaning. While they worked, Mandy's husband, Ken, made a few repairs on the front porch.

Mandy and Ken had purchased the B&B two years ago, soon after they were married. They'd hired Ellen to help out, since she'd had previous experience working at another bed-and-breakfast in the area. Ellen enjoyed her job and was glad her friends' business had been doing well. Many tourists came to the area, looking for lodging, and information had quickly spread about their B&B. Mandy, having been raised in an Amish home, was an excellent cook. Ellen knew her way around the kitchen too. With their culinary skills, every guest woke up to a tantalizing breakfast.

As she sat at the table, sipping the soothing lavender tea, Ellen's thoughts took her back to Hawaii, where she'd had her first taste of what quickly become her favorite beverage. It seemed like yesterday when Mandy, Ellen, and their friends Sadie and Barbara went on a cruise to the Hawaiian Islands.

When Ellen and Mandy became stranded on Kauai, it turned into quite an adventure. Thanks to a caring Hawaiian couple who owned a bed-and-breakfast in the town of Kapaa, the young women were taken care of. It was during their stay on the island that Mandy fell in love with Ken, whose family owned a business raising organically grown chickens. At first, Ellen hadn't understood her friend's infatuation with Ken, but as time went on, she realized the couple had fallen in love. The most difficult part was trying to understand Mandy's decision not to join the Amish church. However, by the time Ken moved to Indiana and married Mandy, Ellen had accepted the changes.

A chilly January breeze blew outside, and Ellen rose from her seat to put a log on the fire in the adjoining room. Things had slowed down at the B&B since the holidays. But that was okay. It would give Ellen more free time to spend with her parents and siblings.

The phone rang. "Good evening," Ellen answered. "Pleasant View Bed-and-Breakfast."

"Hello. This is Vickie Williams. Is my son available?"

"Yes, he's around somewhere. Would you like me to see if I can find him?"

"Please do. It's urgent that I speak with him right away."

Ellen heard the anxiety in Vickie's voice. *I hope nothing bad has happened.* Just then she heard a noise in the kitchen and looked up.

"Oh, wait. Ken just came inside." Ellen held the receiver out to him. "It's your mother."

Ken reached for the phone. "Hi, Mom. How are things on sunny Kauai?" He shifted the receiver to his other ear. "What was that?"

Mandy moved closer to him.

"Oh, no!" The color drained from Ken's face as he lowered himself into a chair. "I'll book the next flight available. And don't worry, Mom. Just pray."

Ken hung up the phone and leaned forward, his face in his hands.

"What's going on?" Mandy put her hands on his shoulders. "What did your mother say?"

"Dad had a heart attack. He's in the hospital being prepped for surgery." Ken looked up, slowly shaking his head. "It sounds serious. I have to go to Kauai, Mandy. My folks need me right now."

"Of course they do, and I'm going with you." Mandy's brown eyes darkened as she turned to face Ellen. "Do you think you can manage the B&B while we're gone?"

"Of course." Ellen slipped her arm around Mandy's waist. "Now that it's winter, things are likely to be slow here anyway. So don't worry. Everything will be fine. It shouldn't be difficult to run the place by myself."

Chapter 1

Two weeks later

*E*llen was up by six and ready to face the day. After Mandy and Ken left for Kauai, she'd brought some of her things from home before new guests arrived. With people coming and going, someone had to be in the house at all times.

Once in the kitchen, Ellen fixed a piece of toast with apple butter and heated a cup of her favorite tea. She appreciated the door separating the kitchen from the dining room. The noise of her breakfast preparations would hopefully go unnoticed, and neither of the guests would be disturbed.

Ellen nibbled on the toast and watched the sun slowly climb into the sky. *The Lord can surely create beautiful sunrises and sunsets. But I can't sit here all day, taking in the view. Ken and Mandy are depending on me, and it's time to start breakfast for the guests who arrived last evening.*

After she finished eating and had put the dishes in the sink, Ellen spotted the neighbor's cat darting through the yard with a sparrow in its mouth. *Poor little bird. Wish that feline would go after mice and leave our feathered friends alone.*

When the cat disappeared, Ellen double-checked the menu she'd planned for the middle-aged couple who'd checked in last evening. She would serve them scrambled eggs and sausage, sliced bananas mixed with vanilla yogurt, and blueberry muffins with sweet creamy butter. There were also two kinds of juice in the refrigerator.

She glanced at the clock. *I need to hurry.*

After spending most of the morning and a good chunk of the afternoon scurrying to get everything done before another set of guests arrived, Ellen felt tired. She went into Ken and Mandy's room, where she'd been sleeping since they left, to freshen up before her friend Sadie Kuhns arrived.

Two boxes of Christmas decorations sat in the corner. A few days after New Year's, Ellen had helped Mandy and Ken take down the simple holiday trimmings and box them up for next year. But in the rush to get Ken and Mandy packed and to the airport, some of the boxes didn't get put away. "In one of my spare moments, I'll need to get those in the attic."

Turning from the decorations, Ellen eyed the bed longingly. She wished she could take a short nap. But with Sadie coming soon, there was no time for rest.

Things hadn't slowed down as much as she'd expected, and Ellen had soon realized it would be difficult to run the place without Mandy's help. So she'd asked Sadie to help out whenever she could. Since her friend worked weekdays at the hardware store in Shipshewana, she was available most evenings and Saturdays.

Ellen smoothed a few wrinkles in the lone-star quilt covering the queen-sized bed. Mandy's mother had made it, as well as several others for the guest rooms. Most of the rooms were decorated with an Amish theme, so it was appropriate to have homemade quilts on all the beds.

Ellen glanced at the calendar on the far wall. It was hard to believe Ken and Mandy had been gone only two weeks. It seemed much longer. But it was a good thing they left when they did. Ken's father had died three days ago, and his mother and brother needed emotional support, as did Ken.

When Mandy had called the other day, she learned that Ken's brother, Dan, had taken their dad's death harder than anyone, and he could barely function. This meant most of the duties at the organic chicken farm fell on Ken's shoulders. Mandy had also mentioned that it could be a few months before they returned to Indiana. Ellen hoped they'd be back before spring. Things slowed down during the winter months, but tourists flocked to the area during the rest of the year, keeping hotels, B&B's, restaurants, and gift shops in Elkhart and LaGrange Counties very busy.

With only two guests in the house this morning, Ellen's load had been a little lighter. But this afternoon, another couple checked in, so Ellen was glad she could count on Sadie for extra help.

After changing into a clean dress and apron, Ellen stepped into the hallway. Glancing at her reflection in the entryway mirror, she saw the telltale signs of exhaustion beneath her blue eyes, in addition to worry lines creasing her forehead. Even her blond hair didn't look as shiny as usual. Truth was, Ellen wasn't sleeping well, and her energy level was at an all-time low. How much longer would it be before Mandy and Ken returned? Could Ken's brother handle the family business on his own, or would he end up hiring someone to help out?

Ellen hadn't said anything to Mandy, but she hoped Ken's mother might sell the organic farm and move to Indiana. Ellen couldn't imagine living so far from her parents and siblings. She figured it must be difficult for Ken too. Someday, when he and Mandy had children, it would be nice for the little ones if they lived close to both sets of grandparents.

Studying her reflection, Ellen tapped her chin. *I wouldn't want to be separated permanently from my family or friends.*

The months Ellen had spent with Mandy on Kauai had been difficult, despite the beautiful scenery surrounding them in every direction. Had it not been for the companionship of Mandy, as well as the kindness of Luana and Makaio Palu, Ellen would have given in to depression during their unexpectedly long stay. She'd always been close to her family and missed them terribly during the months she'd been gone. Ellen had developed a special bond with Luana. The generous Hawaiian woman was as beautiful on the inside as her outward appearance. Her caring, gentle spirit was exactly what Ellen needed, being so far from home.

Mr. and Mrs. Hanson stepped into the hall from their guest room, pulling Ellen out of her musings.

"We're going out to eat an early supper." Mrs. Hanson, a silver-haired woman in her midsixties, gave a rosy-cheeked smile. "Do you have any restaurant suggestions, Miss Lambright? This is our first time visiting the area, and we're not sure which establishment to choose."

"If you're looking to stay fairly close to the B&B, then I would suggest Das Dutchman Essenhaus. They have many good choices on the menu, as well as a buffet with a variety of delicious food. Of course," Ellen added, "there are several other nice places to eat as well."

"We appreciate the suggestion." Mrs. Hanson put her hand in the crook of her husband's arm. "Shall we seek out the closest restaurant, dear?"

He nodded agreeably, then called over his shoulder as they moved toward the door, "Thank you, Miss Lambright. When we get back, we'll let you know how we liked the food."

Ellen smiled as the pleasant couple stepped outside. Of course, most of the guests who came here were kind and polite. Ellen couldn't recall anyone saying anything negative during their stay at the Pleasant View Bed-and-Breakfast.

"Guess I'd better head for the kitchen and fix myself some supper." Ellen snickered as she padded down the hall to the kitchen. Since no one else was in the house, it didn't matter if she talked to herself. But she'd have to be careful not to do that when guests were present.

Soon after Ellen started washing her supper dishes, Sadie knocked and entered through the back door.

"Sorry for being late. I had some errands to run for my *mamm* after I got off work, and it took longer than I expected." Sadie's hazel eyes, with flecks of green, seemed to sparkle as she removed her heavy jacket and hung it over the back of a kitchen chair. Her pretty auburn hair couldn't be seen under the black outer bonnet she wore on her head.

"No problem." Ellen lifted a soapy hand. "As you can see, I haven't started the breakfast casserole I'm planning to serve to the guests tomorrow morning."

"I've eaten your delicious casserole before, and I'm sure they will enjoy it as much as I did." Sadie removed her outer bonnet, placed it on the chair, and picked up a dishcloth. "I'll dry and put the dishes away, unless there's something else you need me to do."

"I could use your help with the casserole, but let's get the dishes done first."

As Ellen and Sadie completed the task, they talked about the weather.

"It's sure nippy out there," Sadie said as she placed a plate in the cupboard. "Makes me wonder if it might snow yet this evening."

Ellen glanced out the window at the darkened sky. "I hope not. I have another set of guests coming in later, and the roads could get icy if it snows."

Sadie bumped Ellen's arm and gave a playful wink. "It is winter you know. Most people expect a little snow this time of the year."

"True." Ellen sighed. "I wonder if Mandy has been able to take a little time to enjoy the beautiful weather they're no doubt having on Kauai. I should have asked when she called the other day."

"I'm sure even though she's busy helping Ken's mother with things, she's been able to spend some time outdoors in the sun." Sadie reached for a glass to dry. "The balmy weather was the one thing I enjoyed most when we visited the Hawaiian Islands."

"Same here. Although the beautiful flowers and colorful birds made it special too." Ellen pulled the drain plug, letting the water out of the sink. "Well, that chore is done. Guess I'll set out the ingredients for the breakfast casserole." She made her way to the refrigerator and paused. "Unless you'd like to have a cup of tea before we start the preparations."

"That does sound nice. I'll put the teakettle on the stove." Sadie got the water heating, while Ellen placed two cups and some slices of banana bread on the table.

As they ate their snack and drank the tea, Sadie brought up the topic of Mandy again. "You don't suppose Ken and Mandy will decide to stay in Hawaii permanently, do you?"

Ellen shook her head. "I'm sure they have no plans of staying. If they did, Mandy would have said something when we last spoke." She reached for a piece of the moist bread and slathered it with creamy butter. "She did say Ken's mother really needs their help right now, so it could be a month or two before they return to Indiana."

Sadie raised her pale eyebrows. "That's a long time for you to run the bed-and-breakfast on your own."

Ellen pointed at Sadie. "You're here helping me, so I'm not completely on my own."

"But a lot of work will fall on you when I'm not able to be here. Have you considered hiring someone full-time? Maybe one of your sisters could help out."

"With the exception of my younger sister, they all have jobs, and Mom needs Lenore at home to help with chores." Ellen took a sip of tea and set her cup down. "Besides, so far I'm able to manage on my own. And once Mandy and Ken get back, we won't need anyone else."

"You have a point." Sadie fingered the edge of the tablecloth. "Let's hope they get back before too many people make reservations and you end up with more responsibility than you can handle. Not to mention that with me working at the hardware store all week and helping out here evenings and Saturdays, it could end up being too much for me too."

The phone rang, and Ellen excused herself and stepped into the hall to answer it. "Pleasant View Bed-and-Breakfast. Ellen Lambright speaking."

"Hello. This is Tammy Brooks, and I'd like to make a reservation. It will be for my husband and myself, as well as our little one. Do you have any vacancies for this Friday and Saturday night? We'll be attending my aunt's funeral Saturday morning, and we haven't been able to find suitable accommodations."

Ellen found it hard to believe that all the hotels and other B&Bs in the area could be booked, but she gave the woman the benefit of the doubt. The fact that the couple had a baby might be a problem, since the policy here was to rent only to adults. And she couldn't lie to the woman, because four of the six rooms were vacant this weekend.

"Umm. . .would you please hold on while I check on this?"

"Yes, of course."

Ellen set the receiver on the entryway table and rushed back to the kitchen. "There's a woman on the phone who wants to make a reservation for this Friday and Saturday night." She moved closer to Sadie. "The only problem is, they have a baby, and we're not set up to accommodate children here."

Sadie rubbed the bridge of her nose. "You could borrow a crib and set it up in the parents' room."

"*Jah*, but what about the policy of no children?"

"Did you tell her that?"

Ellen shook her head. "She sounded desperate for a place to stay, so I thought I'd get your opinion before I responded."

"What do you think Mandy would do if she was here?"

"I'm not sure, but I believe she might make an exception."

Sadie patted Ellen's arm. "Then my advice is to follow your convictions."

"Okay, I will. After all, it's only one little child. What could it hurt to let them stay a few days?"

Chapter 2

*E*llen was surprised when she heard a vehicle pull in at ten thirty Friday morning. Check-in for guests wasn't until three in the afternoon, and she wasn't expecting any deliveries.

Going to the front door, she watched as a young couple got out of a minivan. The dark-haired man opened the sliding back door and took a small boy out. As the family headed for the B&B, Ellen stepped out and greeted them on the front porch. Thinking they might be lost and in need of directions, she asked, "May I help you?"

"I'm Tammy Brooks, and I made a reservation with you earlier in the week." The blond woman gestured to the man beside her, holding the little boy's hand. "This is my husband, Ned, and our two-year-old son, Jerry. We're a few hours early, but if it's possible, we'd like to check in now."

Ellen rubbed her forehead, wondering what to do. The Brookses' room wasn't quite ready. Worse yet, their child was not the baby she had expected.

She continued to massage her temples. How would Mandy handle this is if she were here? She probably wouldn't have to deal with it, because she would have said no in the first place.

"Well, your room isn't ready, but I suppose it would be all right if you wait in the living room while I make the bed." She glanced at the little boy. "Will your son be okay sleeping in a crib? I set one up in your room, because when we talked on the phone you said he was a baby."

Tammy shook her head. "No, I said we have a little one."

"Sorry. I assumed you meant a baby." Ellen couldn't remember when she'd felt so rattled. She had gone against the "adult only" policy, and now she would be hosting a couple with a toddler, not a baby.

She opened the door wide and stepped aside so the guests could enter. "Please come in."

"I'll go out to the van and get our luggage." Ned looked at his wife. "You and Jerry need to get inside out of the weather."

"Yes, it is a lot colder here than I expected." Clasping her son's hand, Tammy led the blond-haired boy into the foyer. Ellen took their coats and hung them on the coat tree. They followed her into the living room.

"This home is lovely. I like the Amish theme." Tammy gestured to a quilted runner on the coffee table. "I guess it makes sense, with you being Amish, that you'd have this type of item here."

Ellen shook her head. "I can't take credit for any of the decor. My friend, Mandy Williams, and her husband, Ken, own the B&B. I just work here."

"Oh, then I look forward to meeting them." Tammy took a seat on the couch and lifted Jerry onto her lap. He leaned his head against her chest and stuck his thumb in his mouth.

"Actually, Ken and Mandy are in Hawaii right now," Ellen explained. "I'm in charge of the B&B until they get back."

Tammy heaved a sigh. "They're lucky. I'd give anything to be on vacation in Hawaii right now."

"They're not on vacation. Ken's parents live there, and his father died of a heart attack recently."

Tammy lowered her gaze, stroking the top of her little boy's head. "That's too bad. I'm sorry for their loss."

"Yes, it's been difficult for them."

"As I mentioned when I made our reservations, my aunt passed away. I'm sure there will be lots of tears shed during her funeral tomorrow."

Ellen slowly nodded. Saying goodbye to a loved one because of death or even miles of separation was never easy. She thought about the loneliness she'd felt when she and Mandy were in Hawaii, so far from their Amish family and friends. At one point, Ellen had begun to feel as if she was never going home. Mandy, however, seemed to adjust well to her Hawaiian surroundings. For a while, Ellen had wondered if her friend might end up staying on Kauai. She was glad when they both returned to their homes in Indiana. Then Mandy found Luana and Makaio's missing quilt by a strange coincidence, so she returned to the island for a time. That was when Ken proclaimed his love for Mandy and decided to move to the mainland so they could be married.

Ned entered the house with their suitcases, bringing Ellen and Tammy's conversation to an end. "It's clouding up out there." He cupped his hands and blew on his fingers. "Might get some snow while we're here."

"January and February are usually our snowiest months." Ellen rose from her chair. "If you'll make yourselves comfortable here, I'll get the bed made up and then show you to your room."

When Ellen returned to the living room, she spotted Ned in front of the fireplace with hands outstretched toward the heat, while his wife slouched on the couch with her eyes closed. Ellen figured the poor woman fell asleep. She was surprised to see little Jerry kneeling on the floor in front of the coffee table. The little guy had his mother's comb, and pulled it across the exposed part of the table.

Ellen gasped when she looked down and saw a gash in the wood. She was sure it hadn't been there before. *Oh, dear, how am I going to explain this to Mandy when she gets home? Should I say something to the boy's parents or let it go?*

She didn't have to think long, for Jerry's father turned around and grabbed the comb from his son's chubby little hand. "That is a no-no, Son. You're not supposed to get into your mommy's purse."

Ned didn't say anything about the scratch on the table. He either hadn't seen the mark or chose not to mention it.

Ellen decided not to say anything about the scratch, either. She would work on it later and try to buff it out. "The room is ready for you now."

Ned shook his wife's shoulder. "Wake up, honey. Our room is ready, so you can take a nap on the bed if you want."

Her cheeks colored as she looked up at Ellen and blinked a couple of times. "Sorry for dozing off. Guess I'm more tired than I realized."

"It's all right. If you'll follow me down the hall, I'll show you to your room."

When they entered the room with a king-sized canopy bed, Tammy commented once again on the Amish décor. "What a lovely quilt on the bed. Was it locally made?"

Ellen nodded. "The owner's mother, who is Amish, has made several quilts for the B&B. This one, however, my own mother quilted, so it's special to me."

Tammy fingered the stitching along the top of the covering. "It must have taken many hours to produce something this intricate. I can't get over how tiny and even the hand-stitching is. I do a little sewing, but could never tackle anything this big or with such a complicated design. What is this pattern called?"

"It's the log-cabin pattern."

Ned leaned close to the bed, as though scrutinizing the quilt. "Doesn't look like a log cabin to me."

"Oh, the design is there all right," his wife said. "You just can't see it."

Squinting, he shook his head. "You can't see what's not there."

Deciding it was time to end this conversation, Ellen pointed to the crib across the room. "Will that be adequate for your son?"

"Since it's a full-size crib, I'm sure it will be fine. We recently put Jerry in a small bed at home because he kept crawling over the rail and getting out of his crib." Tammy picked the boy up and carried him across the room. "I bet you could use a nap too, little man." As soon as she put him in the crib, he started to howl.

Ellen hoped Jerry wouldn't cry a lot while they were here. It would disturb the other guests, not to mention herself.

She turned toward the door. "I need to get some things done now, so I'll let you folks get settled in. Let me know if you need anything."

"Thanks, we will," Ned shouted above the boy's screams, which grew louder by the minute.

Ellen wanted to cover her ears as she exited the room. Had she done the wrong thing by allowing this couple with a child to rent a room? Well, it was too late to worry about it now. She'd make the best of things and hope little Jerry didn't cause too much of a disturbance while he and his parents were here.

Ellen woke up Saturday morning, rolled onto her side, and looked at the alarm clock on her nightstand. It read 6:00 a.m. A few seconds later, Ellen heard the old clock chime faintly from the other room, confirming the hour. She felt tired and out-of-sorts because Jerry's frequent crying kept waking her. She hoped the guests occupying two of the upstairs rooms hadn't been disturbed too. If word got out that the Pleasant View Bed-and-Breakfast was noisy, business could suffer. The one thing Ellen could do for her friends during their absence was to make sure their establishment ran smoothly and without complications.

After Ellen got dressed, she headed for the kitchen to get breakfast ready for her guests. This morning she planned to serve baked oatmeal, French toast, and a bowl of fresh apple, orange, and banana slices. Between the three items, Ellen felt sure everyone would have something they liked for breakfast. She would also serve apple and orange juice, as well as coffee and tea for the adults. For little Jerry and anyone else who wanted it, she had plenty of milk.

Ellen glanced at the clock on the kitchen wall. It was six thirty, and Sadie should be here any minute. She heard a soft knock on the back door and, opening it, found Sadie on the porch, holding a wicker basket.

"It feels good in here," Sadie said when she entered the kitchen. "The temperature dipped during the night, and the ride over with my horse and buggy was chilly. I half expected to see snow when I looked out the window this morning."

"Well, I'm glad you're here, because I could use your help with breakfast." Ellen kept her voice low so she wouldn't wake any of the guests.

"I saw three cars parked outside, so I figured you must be busy." Sadie put the basket on the table. "I made two apple pies last night. Thought you might want to serve them for breakfast this morning. They'd go nicely with the baked oatmeal you mentioned you'd be fixing today."

Ellen's mouth watered. "Yum. I love apple pies, especially this time of year. Maybe I'll forget about making French toast and serve the pies instead."

Sadie removed her outer garments and hung them up. "How'd things go after I left here last night? Did the little boy settle down and go to sleep?"

Ellen shook her head. "He fussed and cried well into the night. I probably didn't get more than a couple hours of sleep."

"I can tell. Your eyes look bloodshot, and there's no spring in your step." Sadie moved closer to Ellen. "Are you wishing now that you'd said no to the parents' request to book a room here?"

"Yes and no." Ellen rested her hips against the table. "It's nice to have more business in January, but at the same time..."

Sadie leaned closer to Ellen. "Sounds like someone is up already. I hear a muffled conversation down the hallway."

Ellen retrieved a bowl from the cupboard and placed it on the counter. "I wonder which guest is up."

"Oh, there you are Miss Lambright; I hoped you were up." Deep wrinkles formed across Ned's forehead. "I'm afraid we have a problem in the bathroom."

"Oh?" Ellen tipped her head. "What sort of problem?"

Ned glanced at the floor, and when he looked back at her, his cheeks reddened. "My son dropped my keys in the toilet then gave it a flush. Now they're stuck inside where I can't reach."

Ellen cringed. Walking along the beach in Hawaii sure sounded like a nice alternative about now.

Chapter 3

Island of Kauai
Kapaa, Hawaii

As Mandy approached the Palms Bed-and-Breakfast, she heard music drifting from the open windows and knew Makaio must be playing his ukulele. It brought back memories of times he'd taught her how to play the instrument. Makaio had even given Mandy a ukulele for her birthday when she and Ellen stayed with him and Luana. Mandy still played it during her free time, and the music always brought her back to the days spent on Kauai.

Stepping onto their lanai, Mandy set the box she held on a small wicker table. She was about to knock on the door, when it opened and Luana greeted her with a hug. "*Aloha*, my dear friend. How are you today?"

"I'm doing all right, but Ken's still having a hard time. Between dealing with his father's death and trying to keep the organic farm running, he's pretty stressed out."

"Isn't Ken's brother helping?" Luana asked.

Mandy shook her head. "Dan's taken his dad's death the hardest of all, and he's sunk into depression. His wife, Rita, said it's all he can do to get out of bed."

Luana's dark eyebrows rose. "Does that mean Ken is doing all the work by himself?"

"Pretty much. I'm helping him with the chickens as much as I can, and of course, doing inside chores to help Ken's mom. As you can imagine, neither of us has any free time." Mandy gestured to the box. "I brought the four-dozen brown eggs you requested."

"*Mahalo*. With all the guests we have scheduled in the next few weeks, the eggs will be gone quickly."

"Let me know when you need more. The layers are producing a lot right now."

"Good to know." Luana gestured to the wicker chairs on the lanai. "Do you have a few minutes to sit and talk? I have some fresh papaya and pineapple cut. It might be a nice pick-me-up."

Mandy moistened her lips. "That does sound good, but I can't stay long. Ken needs my help this morning, cleaning out the rest of the chicken houses."

Luana gently rubbed Mandy's back and shoulders. "You know what I think?"

"What's that?" Mandy felt her tension ease a bit.

"I think Ken's mother should hire someone to work on the farm. She'll have to do that anyway, once you and Ken go back to the mainland."

Sighing, Mandy sank into a chair. "It doesn't look like we'll be leaving here anytime soon. But you're right—Vickie should hire someone—if for no other reason than to help Ken right now. He's so tired at the end of the day that he can barely muster up the strength to kiss me goodnight."

Luana slowly shook her head. "That's not good. Why, you two are still basically on your honeymoon. Instead of wading through piles of chicken manure, you should both be swimming in the ocean and enjoying the mesmerizing sounds of the surf."

"I wish we could spend time relaxing on the beach, but as you know, that's not the reason we came to Kauai." Mandy gestured to the cardboard container. "Would you like me to take the eggs inside for you?"

"No, I'll do it." Luana picked up the box. "Just sit there and rest. I'll be back with some delicious fruit."

When Luana went inside, Mandy leaned her head back and closed her eyes. She drew in a deep cleansing breath of air, relishing in all the pleasurable scents from vegetation blooming in the Palus' yard. Back home, the only flowers around were the poinsettias left over from Christmas. So Mandy's senses were piqued by all the colors and fragrances on the islands.

The sound of birds chirping in the trees nearly lulled her to sleep. *Luana is right. I do need some time to relax. Ken needs it too. I bet he wishes he had time to go surfing with his friend Taavi.*

When Luana returned to the lanai, Mandy opened her eyes and

yawned. "It's a good thing you came back when you did, or I'd probably be counting sheep."

Luana tipped her head to one side and chuckled. "Silly me. I took you literally for a moment there." She placed a plate of fruit on the wicker table and handed Mandy a glass of guava juice. "I'm glad you had a few minutes to yourself. It's not good to work all the time."

Luana plucked a piece of pineapple off the plate and took a seat in the chair beside Mandy. "I spoke to Makaio when I was inside and asked if he knew of anybody who needed a job or might like to work at the Williamses' farm."

"What'd he say?" Mandy took a sip of juice.

"Not off hand, but if he hears of anyone, he'll be sure to let Ken or his mother know."

Mandy nodded slowly, before taking another drink of the succulent juice. She wished they sold guava juice in the stores at home, because their bed-and-breakfast guests would enjoy it as a nice change from the usual orange, apple, or grape juices she offered.

"How's Ellen doing these days?" Luana asked. "Is she managing the B&B on her own?"

"When I spoke to her earlier this week, she said she's been quite busy. But she's managing okay with our friend Sadie's part-time help." Mandy shifted in her chair. "Ellen ran into a little problem last week, though, when she rented a room to a couple with a two-year-old boy."

"So I'm guessing your bed-and-breakfast has an 'adult only' policy like we have here?"

"Yes, but Ellen made an exception and regretted it later. Would you like to hear what happened?"

Luana nodded as she nibbled on a piece of papaya.

"Well, in addition to scratching the coffee table in the living room with his mother's comb, the little guy dropped his father's keys in the toilet, and they got stuck."

"Oh, my! Were they able to get them freed without calling a plumber?"

"Yes. The boy's dad bent a coat hanger and fished them out." Mandy helped herself to a piece of pineapple. "Ellen was so apologetic. She thought

I'd be upset, but I told her not to worry. It could have happened if Ken and I had been there. We both like kids, so we would have probably made an exception and let the couple stay too."

Luana grinned. "Running a B&B does have its challenges. Believe me, over the years of owning this business, Makaio and I have faced many unusual situations. We are thankful each day for the Lord's help in everything we say and do."

"One thing is certain. You two are the kindest, most hospitable couple I've ever met. It's because of you that Ken and I decided to open our bed-and-breakfast in Middlebury."

"Well, thank you. It's nice to know we had a positive influence."

Mandy reached over and clasped her friend's arm. "You certainly have, and in more ways than one." She set her empty glass down and stood. "As much as I'd like to sit here all day and visit, you have things to do, and I need to get back to help Ken."

Luana rose and gave Mandy a hug. "Please keep in touch, and we'll let you know if we hear of anyone who might need a job."

Middlebury

"I'm glad you were able to take a little time off and join me and your *daed* for lunch today," Ellen's mother said as she sat at her kitchen table. "We don't get to visit much since Mandy and Ken left you in charge of their bed-and-breakfast. I think you're working too hard."

Ellen's father looked at Ellen and winked.

"I'm fine." She smiled, hoping to reassure her mother and thankful that Dad understood her position. Mom had enough going on with Lenore, Ellen's youngest sister, close to finishing up her last year of school. It seemed as if she worried about everyone in the family—including Dad and how hard he worked at his shoe store. She also fretted over Ellen's other two sisters, who were away in Sarasota waitressing at a restaurant until they returned in the spring. Ellen didn't want to cause Mom more concern.

"Sadie's the one who's working too hard, being at the hardware store all day and helping me out in the evenings and Saturdays. I don't know where she gets all that energy."

Mom took a sip of water. "I'm sure your friend does work hard, but you do too, and—"

"Now Nora, don't start mothering our oldest *dochder*," Dad spoke up. "Ellen's a grown woman. I'm sure she knows her limitations and can handle most any situation."

Ellen bit the inside of her cheek. "Actually, I do have a problem I can't seem to resolve on my own. Sadie hasn't been able to figure it out either."

"What's going on?" Dad leaned his folded arms on the table.

Ellen explained how the little boy had dropped his father's keys in the toilet. "Even though his dad managed to get them out, the toilet hasn't been running right since."

"Does it still flush?" Dad questioned.

"Jah, but it keeps running, unless someone jiggles the handle. And I sure can't expect any guests staying in that room to be subjected to the inconvenience."

Mom looked at Dad. "I bet you could fix it, Nathan. You've always been handy with things like that."

He nodded, running his fingers through the sides of his thinning reddish-blond hair. "I'll come over sometime later today and take a look-see."

"*Danki*, Dad. I'm sure if anyone can fix it, you can."

Ellen finished washing her supper dishes when Sadie arrived to help with preparations for breakfast the next morning.

"How'd your day go?" Sadie asked after removing her outer garments and hanging them up.

"It went well." Ellen dried her hands. "I had lunch at my folks' place, and my daed said he'd be over later today to check on the toilet that keeps running." She glanced up at the clock. "I figured he would be here by now, though."

"Maybe he got delayed at the shoe store. Sometimes customers come in a few minutes before the hardware store closes, and we have to stay open till they finish shopping."

"Jah, that could be what's happened. It wouldn't be the first time he's had to work late either."

A knock sounded on the back door. "I bet that's my daed now." Ellen hurried to the door, but when she opened it, she jerked her head back, surprised to find Ezra Bontrager on the porch, holding a tool box.

"Hello, Ellen." Ezra's cheeks reddened. "I'm guessin' I took you by surprise, showing up here when you expected your daed." He gave her a half-smile, glanced down at his boots, then looked back at her.

"I am a bit surprised," she admitted.

"Your daed's still at the shop, so I hope you don't mind, but I'm here to take a look at your *briwwi*."

"Oh, okay." Ellen felt a little funny about her dad's employee coming over to fix the toilet, but she needed it done, so she showed Ezra the way.

"You work in a nice place, Ellen." Ezra paused before entering the guest room. He glanced around, as though trying to take it all in, and then he stared at her a little longer than normal.

Ellen noticed Sadie poke her head into the room and give her a silly grin. Then she disappeared into the kitchen, hopefully, undetected by Ezra.

"Uh. . .thanks, Ezra." Her chin dipped down. "I like working here. I'd be disappointed if I ever had to quit."

"That speaks volumes to me." Ezra shuffled his feet. "I like my job too. Your daed's a good boss. I don't mind assisting him and enjoy the easy-going pace at the shoe store."

Ellen smiled. "Dad's mentioned several times how glad he is that you're working for him. He says you're a good worker."

"That's nice to hear." Ezra blushed as he looked down at his boots again. "Guess I'd better get busy fixin' your problem in the bathroom."

Ellen led Ezra into the small connecting bathroom and watched as he set his tool pouch in front of the sink. "It's sure a waste of water when a toilet runs all the time, and the noise it creates can get annoying," he commented.

"I'm glad it still worked after those keys got flushed, but I began to worry when it started doing this." She rested her hand against the door frame.

He flushed the toilet, jiggled the handle, and lifted the lid off the top.

"I think I know what the problem is, so you can go back to whatever you were doin', and I'll get to work."

"Okay. Let me know if you need anything." Ellen returned to the kitchen where Sadie mixed muffin batter.

"Did Ezra find the problem?" Sadie asked.

"I think he may have, but now he has to fix it." Ellen took a carton of eggs from the refrigerator. "Think I'll mix the eggs and milk now, so tomorrow morning all I'll have to do is cook and scramble the egg mixture."

Ellen and Sadie worked in silence until Ezra came into the room. "All done," he announced. "The briwwi shouldn't keep running anymore." Ezra glanced in Ellen's direction, giving her a shy kind of grin.

"Danki for taking care of it. How much do I owe you?"

He held up one hand. "Don't worry about that. Your daed said he'd take care of it, since I did him a favor by coming over in his place." He shuffled his feet once more. "Guess I oughta get going."

"Okay. Thanks again, Ezra."

"No problem," he mumbled before heading out the door.

Sadie snickered.

"What's so funny?"

"Didn't you see the way Ezra looked at you when you two chatted?"

Ellen shook her head. "I don't know what you're talking about."

"Oh, boy. . . How could you miss it?" Sadie snickered again. "I think Ezra's interested in you. Jah, I'm almost sure of it."

"No way!" Ellen took out a wooden spoon. "I've known Ezra since we were in school. Besides, he's two years younger than me."

"A few years one way or another doesn't mean a thing." Sadie poked Ellen's arm. "I wouldn't be surprised if Ezra doesn't ask your daed if he can start calling on you."

Ellen shook her head. "Even if Ezra wanted to, it'd be kind of hard for him to come calling on me when I'm here at the B&B working all the time."

"Well, you know what they say—'where there's a will, there's a way.'"

Ellen rolled her eyes. "Come on, Sadie. No more talk about Ezra Bontrager. Let's get to work."

Chapter 4

*E*llen sat at the desk in the kitchen, looking at the computer to confirm upcoming guests. It was hard to believe it was the last day of February. But on the other hand, the outside thermometer reading was a clear reminder that winter was far from over.

Ellen thought about the warm tropical breezes in Hawaii, and wondered if Mandy and Ken were outside, doing something fun today. They certainly deserved a little enjoyment. She knew from having visited the Williamses' organic chicken farm that the work could be tiring and demanding, so some relaxation was certainly needed on occasion.

Ellen remembered the day she and Mandy had gone over to swim in the Williamses' pool. She was a good swimmer and enjoyed herself, but poor Mandy, unable to swim at the time, feared the water. Ken volunteered to teach Mandy, and she caught on fairly quick. Those days had been fun and carefree, despite Ellen's longing for home.

Returning her focus to the upcoming B&B reservations, Ellen reflected on how things had been slow at the bed-and-breakfast the last few weeks. She wasn't complaining. It was only temporary and gave her more time to spend with family and friends. Last night she and Sadie had visited their friend Barbara Eash and enjoyed supper together.

Clicking the ballpoint pen in her hand, Ellen continued, deep in thought. *It's funny how things turn out in a way one never expects.* Barbara was happily married to Mandy's ex-boyfriend, Gideon, and they had a one-year-old baby girl they'd named Mary Jane. Had it not been for Mandy falling in love with Ken when they were stranded on Kauai, she might very well have married Gideon and be living here. Maybe not at this bed-and-breakfast, but somewhere in Middlebury.

Ellen turned off the computer and went to get a drink of water. As she stood looking out the kitchen window, the scene was breathtaking. Fresh-fallen snow coated everything in a powdery, glistening white, and big puffy clouds slowly parted to reveal an azure sky of blue.

A squirrel caught her attention as it bounded through the fluffy snow, leaving a small trail of tracks behind it. Then the critter stopped under a pine tree and stood on its hind legs to look around. His bushy tail was bent in a position reminding Ellen of a question mark.

I wonder what that little guy is thinking. Ellen watched as a slight whiff of breeze lifted and blew through the squirrel's thick gray tail.

Her gaze shifted higher in the tree, where she spotted something red. It was a beautiful cardinal sitting on the end of a pine bough, and even though muffled by the closed window, its *cheer, cheer, cheer* song reached her ears.

Ellen took the last gulp of water and gave one more glance out the window. "Oh my!" She watched in amazement as the cardinal flew off, sending a sprinkling of snow from the branch, down over the squirrel. Ellen giggled when the squirrel jumped up and took off running. "I'll bet that was cold. Wait till I tell Sadie about those critters."

It was moments like this that were fun to share. *Poor Mandy. She's missing all this winter beauty.* Ellen walked back to the desk and reached for the phone. *I need to call her and see how they are doing. They've been gone almost two months. Surely they must be ready to come home soon.*

Kapaa

"Mandy, you're wanted on the phone," Vickie called from the kitchen. "You can take it on the living-room extension."

Mandy set the dust rag aside and picked up the receiver. "Aloha."

"Hi, Mandy, it's Ellen. I haven't heard from you in quite a while and wondered how you are doing."

Mandy took a seat in the recliner. "We're getting by, just busier than ever it seems." She paused and took a drink from her bottle of Hawaiian filtered water. "I'm sorry for not keeping in better touch, and I'm glad you called. I planned to call you as soon as I finished helping Vickie clean the house. Luana and Makaio are coming over for a barbecue this evening, so we wanted to get the cleaning done before we started getting things out for the meal."

"Sounds like fun. I thought about you earlier. Do you have time to talk now?"

"Yes, I have a few minutes," Mandy replied.

"I'm glad you're taking time out to do something enjoyable. How are Makaio and Luana?"

"They're both well, and keeping busy with the B&B. Are things busy there too?"

"It's slowed down a bit, but I'm sure things will pick up with spring just around the corner. Oh, and we had some snow overnight. You should see how beautiful it is right now. Your yard looks like a pretty Christmas card."

Mandy sighed. Along with missing everyone back home, she missed Indiana's winter beauty. Making snow angels didn't compare to making them in the sandy beaches of Hawaii—not that she had any free time to spend along the ocean's shore.

"Any idea when you'll be coming home?" Ellen asked.

Mandy clasped her knees tightly together. The back of her throat ached, making it hard to swallow. She reached for the bottle and took a drink.

"Mandy, are you still there?"

"Yes, I'm here."

"Oh, good. Thought maybe we'd been disconnected. Did you hear my question about when you might return to Middlebury?"

"Yes, I did—it's just that. . ." Mandy's voice trailed off.

"What's wrong? You sound *umgerennt*."

"I'm not really upset. I just dread giving you this news."

"What news? Is everyone there all right?"

"We are fine physically, but everyone's emotions are still scattered all over the place."

Mandy twirled a piece of hair around her fingers, then touched the flower pinned behind her left ear, signifying she was married. "You see. . . well, the thing is. . . Ken and I have discussed this at great length, and we feel a responsibility to stay here and help out."

"I understand, but for how much longer?"

"Indefinitely. Ken's mother can't manage without us, and Ken's brother wants her to sell the farm, because he doesn't want to run it anymore. In fact, he's talking about moving to California, where Rita's parents live."

"That's too bad. Would Vickie consider moving to Middlebury with you and Ken?"

"No, she is determined to keep the place. It's all she has left to remind her of Charles, and she feels he would not want her to sell out." Mandy spoke quietly, hoping Vickie couldn't hear her conversation from the kitchen. The last thing she wanted to do was make her mother-in-law feel guilty for keeping them here.

"So in order for us to stay on Kauai, we'll need to sell the B&B there."

Silence on the other end. Mandy knew her friend wouldn't take this news well. "Ellen, please say something."

"I...I'm stunned. When you and Ken left for Hawaii, I never dreamed you wouldn't be coming home. I thought..."

"We thought we'd be coming back too. But our circumstances have changed, and we feel it's God's will for us to stay on Kauai."

"I understand about family obligations, but what about your family here? Your parents and siblings will be disappointed when they hear this news."

Mandy's vision blurred as tears sprang to her eyes. "I'm going to miss them all terribly, but Ken and I can't be in two places at the same time. Maybe someday Mom and Dad, or one of my siblings can take a cruise and come here to visit. I'm sure they would fall in love with the island the way I did."

"Maybe, but they won't be able to stay. Their home is in Middlebury."

Mandy drew a couple of deep breaths, hoping not to break down. *Why does Ellen have to make this so difficult?*

"I don't mean to be selfish, but it's hard to think I may never see you again." Ellen sounded like she too was close to tears.

"We'll come home for visits," Mandy assured her. "Ken will have to hire someone to help out on the farm, and even if Ken's not free to leave the island, I'll fly home whenever I can."

"I'm sure you both feel like you're doing the right thing."

"Yes. Oh, and there's a couple more items I need to mention."

"What's that?"

"You're the first person we've told about this. None of my family knows our plans yet." Mandy cleared her throat. "Would you please not share this with anyone until I've let everyone else know?"

"Sure, Mandy. So what was the other thing you wanted to tell me?"

"We'll be contacting a Realtor to sell the B&B, but we'd like you to keep running the place—at least until the new owners take over. When that happens, then maybe you can continue working there if you want to."

"Oh, I see."

"If you'd prefer, we can close the bed-and-breakfast while it's up for sale." Mandy held her breath, waiting for her friend's answer. She hoped Ellen would be willing to keep the place open. She and Ken needed the extra income to help them pay to ship their personal things from the mainland to Kauai, and she didn't want Ellen to be out of a job.

"If it doesn't sell quickly, I may have to hire someone to help full-time. Sadie's been most generous to assist me in her free time, but with her working at the hardware store, I can't ask her to keep doing it indefinitely. I'm surprised she keeps going like she does."

"I understand. Feel free to use your discretion about whether to hire someone to help you there. Since Sadie is still helping you, go ahead and tell her our news, but just keep it between the two of you, until we've told my family."

"Okay."

Mandy heard the door to the kitchen open and saw Vickie enter the living room. "Umm, I'm sorry, Ellen, but I'd better go. I'll call you again soon and let you know how things are progressing."

"All right. Take care, Mandy, and tell everyone, including Luana and Makaio, I said hello."

"I will. Bye, Ellen." Mandy hung up the phone and sat slumped in her chair. As much as she loved it here on Kauai, she would miss her friends and family back home. It was hard to tell her best friend the sad news and even harder to ask Ellen to keep all this information a secret for some days ahead. Mandy would call her folks tomorrow and let them know the new plan. She dreaded hurting her parents, but it couldn't be helped. This would be a big adjustment for several people in her life. But Mandy felt confident she was supposed to be on this island, so she would take one day at a time and trust God to guide her and Ken.

Middlebury

Ellen hung up the phone, leaned over, and bent into the pain. She couldn't imagine Mandy and Ken selling their beautiful bed-and-breakfast, much less making what could very well be their permanent home in Hawaii.

Ellen tried to soak it all in as the tears ran down her cheeks. When the B&B sold, she would probably be without a job, because the thought of working here without her friend, Mandy, was not pleasant. She never imagined this would happen. Just thinking about this change brought an ache to her heart. *Why do I have to lose one of my best friends? We had such a good thing here. Why, Lord?*

Ellen wept for several minutes and then forced herself to sit up. *It isn't right for me to be thinking only of myself. I could tell from talking to Mandy that she felt sad about selling the bed-and-breakfast. She and Ken are making a sacrifice to stay on Kauai and keep his parents' organic farm running. The least I can do is offer them my full support.*

Ellen reached for a tissue, dried her eyes, and blew her nose. Then another thought popped into her head. *Will I have to show the B&B to prospective owners, or will the Realtor Ken and Mandy hire do that? And if that's the case, how's it going to work if there are guests here?*

There were so many things to think about; it was hard not to feel overwhelmed. Ellen knew, however, that the best antidote for stress was prayer. So she bowed her head and closed her eyes. *Heavenly Father, You know what is best for Mandy and Ken, as well as Ken's mother and brother. I want to seek Your will in my life, so help me keep a positive attitude and remember to trust You in all things. Perhaps there is something better for me than working here at the Pleasant View Bed-and-Breakfast. Help me to be open to the plans You have for my life. Please watch over my dear friends in Hawaii, as they serve and trust You for their future.*

When Ellen opened her eyes, a sense of peace settled over her like being covered with a warm quilt. She didn't know what the future held for any of them, but felt confident that through it all, the Lord would be their guide.

Chapter 5

I still can't believe Mandy and Ken are selling this place," Sadie said Friday evening as she and Ellen put on their aprons, in preparation for baking.

"I know. The Realtor they contacted is coming by tomorrow morning to do a walk-through, which will help her figure out how much they can ask for the B&B." Ellen sniffed. "I'm trying to keep a good attitude, but I struggle not to cry every time I think about it. Everything went along so well, and now this."

"I don't understand why they couldn't keep the B&B and let you run the business like you're already doing." Sadie's chin jutted out. "A lot of people own a business in one state when they live in another. Besides, they might move back here someday. And if they sold the bed-and-breakfast, they'd have to start over."

"Mandy and Ken will need the money from this place when it sells to help out with their expenses staying on the island." Ellen pressed her palms against her chest. "I don't think they have any plans of coming back."

"I wonder if they'll come home for visits."

"Mandy said they would, but with a business to run, it will be difficult for them to get away very often."

"Maybe we could take another cruise and go see them sometime." Sadie's round face offered Ellen a hopeful-looking smile. "It's something to think about and maybe start planning for now."

"Guess we'll have to wait and see how it goes." Ellen gestured to the baking pans sitting on the counter. "In the meantime, we'd better start mixing, or the harvest loaf will never get done."

At ten o'clock on Saturday morning, a dark blue car pulled up the driveway of the Pleasant View Bed-and-Breakfast. It was Ken and Mandy's Realtor, and Ellen wished she didn't have to answer the door. The woman had phoned the night before, saying she'd be coming by this morning to do a walk-through of the B&B. While this was necessary in order to put the place on the market, Ellen dreaded the process. It was one more reminder that Mandy and Ken weren't coming back. Nothing would be the same without them.

If whoever buys the B&B lets me keep working for them, maybe I won't feel so bad, Ellen thought as she made her way to the front door. *At least I'll still be doing the kind of work I enjoy, and in familiar surroundings.*

Ellen put a smile on her face and opened the front door just as the woman stepped onto the porch.

"Good morning, I'm Polly Stapleton."

"Please come in. I'm Ellen Lambright." She opened the door wider and stepped aside.

Polly paused in the entrance until the door was shut. "I didn't realize this place was run by Amish. I'm sure the business does nicely in our tourist area."

"Ken and Mandy are English, but I am Amish."

"Oh, I see." Polly looked about the room.

"During tourist season the B&B does a good business." Ellen put her best friend's interest ahead of her feelings. She wouldn't say anything to detract from the sale of the home.

"The bed-and-breakfast is in a good location and quite easy to find." Polly looked at the floors. "Is this wood flooring throughout most of the house?"

"Yes. Ken and Mandy had the kitchen floor sanded and finished after they moved in." Ellen watched the Realtor write down the information.

"I understand there are six bedrooms in this house." Polly turned to face Ellen. "How many of them are actually used for guests?"

"Five. There are three bedrooms down, and three upstairs. The owners have their own room and bath on one end of the house, and the other two downstairs rooms are for guests. Each of the rooms has its own bathroom,"

Ellen added. She gestured to the living room. "Would you like to look in there first, or do you want to start with the bedrooms?"

"Let's start with the kitchen, then work our way through the rest of the house."

"Please excuse the disarray. I cleaned out the utensil drawer earlier and haven't quite finished the project," Ellen commented.

"No problem." Polly placed her expensive-looking leather purse on the side table.

Ellen led the way, her heart sinking. This walk-through made selling the bed-and-breakfast official, and her resolve to keep a positive attitude was weakening.

That evening, when Sadie showed up, Ellen's burden felt heavier. She tried to put on a happy face, but her friend saw right through it.

"Okay, what's wrong?" Sadie placed her hands on Ellen's shoulders. "I can see by the lines in your face and your slumped posture that you're upset about something."

"The real estate agent Mandy and Ken hired to sell the B&B was here this morning." Ellen sank into a chair at the kitchen table. "She'll put the place on the market within the next few days, and then it's just a matter of time before someone buys it." A deep sigh escaped her lips. "If I had enough money I'd purchase the B&B myself, but there's no way I could come up with a decent down payment, let alone make monthly payments. Even if I could afford to buy this home, it wouldn't be the same without our friend, Mandy."

"I understand the feeling. I'm not dealing well with this either." Sadie took a seat beside Ellen. "It's hard to accept change, isn't it?"

"Jah." Ellen's throat constricted. "It's difficult to trust God for my future."

Sadie rapped her knuckles against the table. "A few years from now we might both be married. Then we'll be focused on raising a family and feeling hopeful about our children's futures."

"Maybe so. Although right now, neither of us has a boyfriend, so marriage seems a long ways off—much less raising a family."

Sadie clasped her hands under her chin. "You may not have a steady beau now, but there's one young man who I believe would like to be your suitor."

"Who would that be?"

"Ezra Bontrager."

Ellen swatted the air. "Oh, not that again. If Ezra is looking for a woman to court, I'm sure it would be someone younger than me." She pushed her chair aside and stood. "Now let's get busy planning tomorrow's breakfast for the two guests that checked in this afternoon."

"All right, I'll change the topic for now." Sadie stood up and repositioned her *kapp*.

"What do you mean 'for now'?" Ellen's brows drew inward.

"Until Ezra is around here again, talking sweetly to you." Sadie giggled.

"Okay, you've had your fun." Ellen smiled and poked her friend's arm.

The phone rang, and Ellen picked up the receiver. "Pleasant View Bed-and-Breakfast." Since the computer wasn't on, she glanced at the guest reservation book lying next to the phone. Not fully trusting the computer's scheduling program, she used the book as a backup. "Yes, Mrs. Adams, the date you requested is confirmed. I have two rooms reserved for you and your family, and will look forward to seeing you next month."

When Ellen hung up the phone she looked over at Sadie and groaned. "What's going to happen if the B&B sells quickly? What if the new owners decide not to accommodate any of the guests that have reservations? They'll need time to settle in, won't they? What if they make all kinds of changes around here?"

"There, there, try to relax." Sadie patted Ellen's back. "You *druwwle* about things that may never happen. I'm sure whoever buys the bed-and-breakfast will be happy to have guests coming right away, because without people booking rooms, there would be no income."

Ellen moved her head slowly up and down. "You're right, Sadie. I do have a tendency to worry about things. I need to remember what Psalm 55:22 says: 'Cast thy burden upon the Lord, and he shall sustain thee.'" She smiled. "If necessary, I'll quote that verse every day to remind myself not to worry, but cast my burdens on the Lord."

Kapaa

"Are you sure you don't want something more to eat for lunch?" Mandy placed her hand on Ken's arm as they sat at the table on his mother's lanai. "You hardly ate a thing."

"The heat of the day's taken away my appetite," he replied. "I'm good with the fruit salad you served." Ken rose from his chair. "Besides, I want to check on those raised beds I built and see if I need to make any adjustments."

"That's fine, but could I say something first?"

"Sure. What's on your mind?" Ken sat back down.

"Since the B&B will be going on the market soon, I think it would be good if I go back to Middlebury and box up some things to be sent here. Most of our clothes are still there, as well as many personal items. I'd like to make plane reservations right away. Can you manage without my help for a week or two?"

"Yes, I'll manage. And you're right—we do need the rest of our clothes, not to mention anything else we don't want to sell with the B&B." Ken leaned over and kissed Mandy's forehead. "I wonder sometimes how I ever got along before I met you. The fact that you're willing to leave your family and friends on the mainland and relocate here to help mine speaks volumes."

She patted his arm. "My place is with you, Ken. Wherever you are is where I want to be." Remembering her wedding vows, Mandy whispered, "My sacred promise is to stay by your side as your faithful wife, in sickness and in health, in joy and in sorrow, through good times and bad. I further promise to love you without reservation, comfort you in times of distress, encourage you to achieve your goals, laugh with you and cry with you, grow with you in mind and spirit, always to be open and honest with you, and cherish you for as long as we both shall live."

Ken drew Mandy into his arms. "I thank the Lord for bringing you into my life. Had you and Ellen not become stranded on this island, I would never have experienced the joy of knowing you, my beautiful wife."

Mandy gazed into her husband's vibrant blue eyes. "I am thankful God brought you into my life as well. And I am confident that wherever we go and whatever we do, with you by my side and God at the center of our lives, we will find peace and happiness."

Chapter 6

Middlebury

*I*t's so good to see you." As soon as Mandy entered the bed-and-breakfast, Ellen gave her a welcoming hug. "It seems like you've been gone forever."

"I know." Mandy swallowed hard, hoping tears wouldn't let loose and she'd be unable to stop crying. Being back in Middlebury, in the home she and Ken had bought soon after their marriage, was bittersweet. As much as she loved Hawaii, it was hard to think about leaving her family and friends once again.

The prospect of selling the B&B was also difficult. Their lovely home had been on the market for two weeks, and so far they'd received no offers. At least with Ellen running things, the business would stay open for guests while it was for sale. Mandy hoped when a buyer came along that the people would continue using the home as a bed-and-breakfast.

"How long can you stay before you have to go back to Hawaii?" Ellen asked, following Mandy into the living room, after she'd taken off her coat.

"My return flight is in two weeks, so that should give me enough time to go through everything, get it boxed up, and sent off to Kauai." Mandy blew out a noisy breath. "It could be a while before either Ken or I will be able to come back for another visit, so I'll want to spend some time with my family and other friends while I'm here too." She moved close to the fireplace, rubbing her hands. "Brr. . . I've been enjoying the warmth of Hawaii long enough to forget how cold it can be here this time of the year."

Ellen nodded. "I assume you've already seen your folks?"

"Oh, yes. They hired a driver and met me at the airport in South Bend." Yawning, Mandy took a seat on the couch, and Ellen joined her. "Sorry.

I'm kind of tired."

"Well, you did just fly over the ocean and several states. You'll have to get used to the time change too."

"You're right about that. It took me a week to adapt to Hawaii time, and now I'm back here and will need to readjust." Mandy yawned again, although she wasn't sure it was only the trip making her tired. All the extra work she'd been doing to help Ken and his mother was enough to exhaust anyone. They all worked on the farm from sunup to sunset. And now she had much to do here, which would also be tiring.

Mandy looked around. "The place looks nice. You're doing a great job keeping it spotless."

"You know me. I like to make sure everything is in its place." Ellen smiled.

"You've always been more organized than me." Mandy lifted her hands and let them fall. "I'm sorry to put you through all this, Ellen. Having the Realtor come by and having to make sure everything looks good so she can show the B&B to potential buyers can't be easy."

"It's okay. I'm doing it for my best friend, so don't give it another thought." Ellen gave Mandy another hug. "I'm so happy to see you."

"Same here."

"Sadie suggested the two of us plan another cruise to Hawaii so we can visit you on Kauai." Ellen stared down at her hands, resting in her lap. "I'm not sure when that would be, though. She has her job at the hardware store, and I'm working here right now, so it would be hard for either of us to take a trip anytime soon."

"I understand." Mandy reached over and clasped Ellen's hand. "You're my best friend, and no matter how many miles separate us, I'll never forget you. We must keep in touch through letters and phone calls. It will help us know how to pray for each other."

"If I'm still working here, or someplace else where there's a computer, we could email each other."

"True. I hadn't thought of that. Now aren't you glad Ken taught us both some basic computer skills?"

"Jah, but I'm not sure I'll ever get really good at it. I'm still leery of pushing a wrong key." Ellen glanced toward the window. "Did you hear a horse whinny outside?"

Mandy tipped her head. "I think so."

Ezra could almost hear his knees knock together as he stood on the front porch of the Pleasant View Bed-and-Breakfast. Whenever he was in the same room with Ellen, he felt like a schoolboy with a crush on the teacher. Only Ellen wasn't his teacher. She was his boss's daughter, and a beautiful woman two years older than him. Every time he looked at her pretty blue eyes or shiny golden blond hair peeking out from under her kapp, his mouth went dry. Ezra was certain Ellen didn't realize his interest in her went beyond friendship, nor did Ellen's father. Ezra certainly would never have admitted it to anyone either. He'd be embarrassed if Ellen knew how he felt, and even more so if he asked to court her, and she turned him down.

He'd known Ellen since they were in school together, but because she was two years older, he'd never imagined them being anything but casual friends. *It's best I admire her from a distance and not let on for now, at least. If Ellen ever gives an indication of liking me, though, I might take the chance.*

Ezra remembered how one day when they were youngsters playing in the schoolyard, he'd gotten a splinter in his thumb and Ellen had removed it. Back then, they saw each other in church, but other than school and church, they'd never made contact. When Ezra became older and saw Ellen at a young people's event, he'd watch her and wish he had the nerve to talk to Ellen or ask her out. But he was too scared to approach the young woman and face rejection.

Pulling his shoulders back and drawing in a breath, Ezra knocked on the door. A few seconds later, Ellen answered.

He took a step to one side, and then two back, bumping the porch railing. "Oops." His cheeks warmed. *She must think I'm a klutz.*

"Guder owed." Ellen smiled. "What brings you by here this evening, Ezra?"

He lifted the paper sack in his hand. "I ate supper at your folks' house, and since your mamm knew I'd be comin' this way to go home, she asked if I'd stop in and give you this." Ezra handed her the sack.

"Let me guess. Mom made something for dinner with red sauce in it." Ellen looked at Ezra with a sly grin.

"Why, yes. Earlier, when your mamm invited me to stay for dinner, she asked what I liked." Ezra's cheeks grew warm. "I told her stuffed peppers was one of my favorites, but how did you know there was red sauce?"

"Because you have a smudge of it on your face." Ellen pointed to her own face to show him where it was on his.

"Oh, oh." Ezra licked a finger and went over the spot. "Did I get it?"

"Jah, good enough. And don't worry about it," Ellen added. "When that happens to my daed, he always says, 'I'm saving it for later.' Now let's see what Mom has for me."

Ezra watched Ellen peek into the bag while he absentmindedly rubbed his face again.

"Yum. Mom sent me some chocolate whoopie pies. These will be nice to share with Mandy."

"Will you be sending them to her in Hawaii?"

Ellen shook her head. "Mandy's here now. She came back to get her and Ken's personal things, because they're staying in Hawaii for good."

"Your daed mentioned that." Ezra turned sideways and gestured to the FOR SALE sign out front. "What are you gonna do once this place is sold?"

Ellen shrugged. "I'm not sure. It all depends on who buys it and whether they want me to continue working here."

Since Ellen hadn't invited him inside, Ezra figured it was time to go. "Guess I'll be seein' you, Ellen. Maybe at the next young people's singing."

She'd barely said goodbye, when Ezra leaped off the porch and raced for his carriage. "If Ellen had any interest in me at all, she'd have invited me in to taste one of those whoopie pies," he mumbled, releasing his horse from the hitching rail. Most B&Bs in the area didn't have a designated place for visiting horse and buggies, but this one did, which made it nice for Ezra or any other Amish person who might come by.

As Ezra climbed into his buggy and headed for home, he had a little talk with himself. It wasn't the whoopie pies he wanted, for Nora Lambright had served some of those after supper this evening. The truth was, he'd hoped Ellen might invite him in so he could spend a little more time with her. *Of course,* Ezra reminded himself, *I'd have probably tripped over my own tongue trying to make a sensible conversation.*

He snapped the reins. "Giddy-up there, Harley. Let's get home. My mamm's probably wonderin' why I missed supper tonight."

As Ezra headed down the road, he grimaced. *I can't believe I showed up with red sauce on my face. How embarrassing.*

"Who was at the door?" Mandy asked when Ellen returned to the living room.

"It was Ezra Bontrager. He had supper at my folks' place this evening, and my mamm asked him to drop off some chocolate whoopie pies for me on his way home." Ellen held up the paper sack. "In a little while, let's each have one with a cup of lavender tea." Ellen placed the sack on the coffee table and took a seat beside Mandy again.

"Isn't Ezra good friends with Sadie's brother?" Mandy asked.

"Jah, he and Saul have been hanging out with each other since eighth grade. And Ezra still works at my daed's shoe store."

Mandy nodded. "I've seen him there when I've gone to buy shoes. He's kind of quiet, but always polite." She pulled a throw pillow away from her back and scooched into the couch. "How old is Ezra anyway?"

"He's a couple years younger than the both of us, remember?"

"That's right. . . I'm surprised he isn't courting someone by now. Ezra isn't too hard to look at, and he's earning himself a fair living." Mandy turned toward Ellen. "He could make a nice young woman a good catch."

"So what do you think you'll go through first?" Ellen quickly changed the subject.

"I haven't decided yet. I'll make some decisions in the morning." Mandy pointed to the sack of whoopie pies. "I'm ready for some of those now. Should I go to the kitchen and fix us some tea?"

"No, that's okay. Please stay here and rest. I'll be back soon with the tea and some napkins." Ellen hurried from the room.

Mandy leaned against the sofa cushions and closed her eyes. Even though it'd be hard to leave this home again, her place was in Hawaii with Ken. For the next two weeks, she would concentrate on packing up all their belongings, knowing after that, she'd return to her loving husband.

Chapter 7

J can't believe I've been here a whole week already. There's so much to do yet." Mandy rubbed her forehead and groaned. "I don't know about you, but I'm exhausted."

"It has been a job, but between me and your family you've had plenty of help." Ellen gestured to the boxes on the floor in front of where they knelt. "We've emptied all of the closets, gone through the garage, and made a place for anything left over your folks could put in a yard sale or give away to family or friends."

"Yes, and what a relief. I'm glad all the furniture is staying with the B&B." Mandy closed another box and marked on the outside what it contained. "I never realized how much work it would be to go through everything and make a decision as to what to keep and what to give away." Her shoulders sagged.

Ellen wished Mandy didn't have to return to Hawaii, and that she and her husband would come back to stay. But under the circumstances, their choice was for the best.

Ellen stared down at the boxes. *This is difficult, letting go of a good friend. But I need to be supportive and strong. Mandy is relying on me.*

Mandy gestured to the open box, full of Ken's clothing. "Since the Realtor is bringing someone by at noon, I'd better close this up. We need to be out of here before they show up."

Ellen nodded. "I'm glad Sadie and Barbara are free today and can meet us for lunch. It's been a long time since the four of us got together for a meal and a nice visit."

"You're right." Mandy smiled. "I'm looking forward to it."

Shipshewana, Indiana

Even with the clouds hanging low and snow in the forecast, Ellen looked forward to being with her friends. Drawing in the aromas of cooking meats and deep fried foods as she and Mandy entered the Fireside Café in Yoder's Shopping Center, she realized how hungry she was.

"Sadie and Barbara are over there." Ellen pointed to one of the tables. "I wonder if they've ordered already."

"Let's go see." Mandy followed as Ellen led the way.

A busy waitress heading toward the kitchen with a tray full of dirty plates, stepped between the two girls, nearly running into Mandy. The woman's eyes widened as she stopped in her tracks. "Pardon me, miss."

"It's okay." Mandy spoke pleasantly.

As they approached the table, Barbara and Sadie stood up and hugged Mandy.

Ellen's heart clenched when she saw tears gather in her friends' eyes. She struggled not to cry too. Today might be the last time they'd be together for some time. Surely, none of them would be going to Hawaii anytime soon, so they'd probably not meet as a group again until Mandy was able to make another trip to the mainland.

"Have you two placed your orders yet? I'm famished." Ellen hoped to lighten the mood.

Sadie shook her head. "We wanted to wait till you and Mandy got here. That way they'd bring all our food out together. Oh, and by the way—everyone's lunch is my treat today." She pointed her finger at Mandy. "And no arguments, please."

Mandy gave a small laugh. "Have I ever won an argument with you?"

"Well, maybe once." The flecks of green in Sadie's hazel-colored eyes became more pronounced when she chuckled and poked Mandy's arm.

Mandy snickered in response.

"Shall we take turns ordering, or should we all go up to the counter at once?" Barbara pushed a small piece of her nearly black hair back under her white head covering.

"Here's how we're going to do this." Sadie pulled a notebook and pen from her black-and-white quilted purse. "You can all write down what you want, and then I'll go place our orders. It only makes sense, since I'm the one who'll be paying."

Sadie waited until everyone wrote down their requests, then she headed for the counter.

Mandy took a seat beside Barbara, while Ellen sat across from them.

"Where's your cute little girl today?" Mandy asked. "I was hoping I'd get to see her."

"I left Mary Jane with Gideon's mamm. She's cutting another tooth and is kind of fussy, so I figured it'd be best not to bring her along." Barbara's blue eyes brightened as she told how her one-year-old girl had learned to walk. "She never tried to crawl. She just pulled herself up at the coffee table one day and took a few steps."

Mandy laughed. "I'm looking forward to being a mother someday."

"Parenting is a lot of work," Barbara said. "But the rewards are many, and I wouldn't trade motherhood for anything."

Ellen couldn't help but notice the look of longing on Mandy's face. She and Ken had been married over two years. No doubt she'd hoped to be pregnant by now. Well, at least Mandy had found a good man. It didn't take a genius to see that she and Ken were deeply in love.

Ellen tugged on her lower lip as she shuffled her feet under the table. *I wonder if I'll ever fall in love and get married. I'd like to find my soul mate, raise a family, and grow old together. But maybe it's not meant to be. I might end up like my aunt Ruth, in her sixties and still single.*

Sadie returned to the table and sat beside Ellen. "This feels like old times, doesn't it, ladies?"

They nodded.

"How are things in Hawaii, Mandy?" Barbara asked.

"The weather was beautiful when I left Kauai a week ago, but Ken, his mother, and I have been so busy since his dad passed away that we've barely had time to notice. I can't imagine how the two of them are managing while I'm gone."

"What about Ken's brother?" Sadie asked. "Wasn't he helping his dad with the chicken farm while you and Ken lived in Middlebury?"

"Yes, he was, but after Charles died, Dan didn't want to work there anymore." Mandy fiddled with her purse straps. "A few days before I left Kauai, Dan and his wife moved to California, where her parents live. Fortunately, they were renting, not buying a house."

Barbara's dark eyebrows furrowed. "He left his mother when she was in need? I can't imagine anyone doing such a thing."

"His actions might seem strange, but Dan took his dad's death pretty hard. In fact, he could barely function for the first several weeks. He and his wife talked it through and decided the best way for him to deal with everything was to leave the island—at least for a time." Mandy pursed her lips. "It was hard on his mother to see them go, but Vickie seemed to understand. And she appreciates having Ken and me there to help with the farm."

Sadie's shoulders drooped as she heaved a heavy sigh. "Hawaii is so beautiful. When we were all there, enjoying our vacation, it felt like I'd had a taste of paradise."

"It's always seemed that way to me," Mandy agreed. "But losing Ken's father dampened our spirits. To tell the truth, we haven't had time to do much of anything fun since it happened."

"Losing a loved one is always hard." Barbara clasped Mandy's hand. "I'll remember to pray for you, Ken, and his mother."

Mandy smiled. "Thank you."

A waitress came with their food, and the conversation turned to other things. Ellen felt thankful for this opportunity to be with her friends, but she couldn't help wondering how things were going at the bed-and-breakfast. Would the people who looked at it make an offer?

Middlebury

Sunday morning dawned with a beautiful sunrise. Most of the snow in the area had melted, and a taste of spring was in the air. It put Ellen in a cheerful mood as she and Mandy headed down the road with her horse and buggy toward Gideon Eash's parents' house, where church would be held.

Seeing a FOR SALE sign as they went past a house took Ellen's thoughts in a different direction. The Realtor had called Mandy last evening, saying the couple who looked at the bed-and-breakfast realized they weren't ready to take on the commitment of running a business that would tie them down. Ellen wondered why they'd even bothered to look at the place if they understood all the work involved. It seemed like a waste of the agent's time, and the news had dampened Mandy's spirits. Selling the B&B would help her and Ken financially, and be one less thing to worry about as they focused on running Ken's father's business on Kauai.

Once more, Ellen wished she had enough money to buy their home. But apparently, it was not meant to be.

Fortunately, they hosted no guests right now, so she hadn't fixed the usual continental breakfast she prepared on Sundays when guests occupied rooms.

Ellen glanced at Mandy, sitting beside her in the front of the buggy with a faraway look in her eyes. "May I ask what's going through your mind right now?" Ellen took one hand off the reins and touched her friend's arm.

"Oh, reminiscing a bit." Mandy looked over at Ellen and smiled. "In some ways it seems like a long time ago that I drove a horse and buggy. In other ways, it feels like only yesterday when I sat in the driver's seat, guiding my horse down the road."

"Do you ever regret not joining the Amish church?" It was a question that had been on Ellen's mind for some time, but she'd never had the nerve to ask before.

"Sometimes, but I couldn't join the church and marry Ken, so I don't regret that. He's everything I've ever wanted in a husband, and I love him so much." Mandy spoke in a quiet voice.

Ellen nodded. "When you and I were stranded on Kauai, every time Ken came around, it was obvious that you two had fallen for each other." She relaxed her grip on the reins a bit, allowing her horse to pick up speed as they drew closer to the Eashes' place. "At first it upset me, because I was afraid if you two established a permanent relationship it would mean you'd become English and probably stay in Hawaii. But then, Ken chose to move here. So by the time you two got married, I'd accepted things and felt confident that even though we weren't both Amish, we could still remain friends."

Mandy's eyes glistened with tears. "And friends we shall always be. Our bond is as strong as if we were sisters."

Ellen couldn't argue with that. Ever since she and Mandy were children, they'd gotten along. As they grew into adulthood, their relationship had become even stronger. The distance between Hawaii and Indiana could never change that.

Chapter 8

Lihue
Kauai County, Hawaii

As Mandy's plane pulled up to the gate a little after three o'clock Tuesday afternoon, the FASTEN SEATBELT sign shut off. Passengers began assembling their belongings, whether from the overhead bins or under the seats in front of them. After retrieving her bag from the upper bin, Mandy remained in the aisle seat she had in coach. If she'd had the money for first-class seating, she would have been one of the first people off the plane. But that was okay. She was just glad to be home.

Mandy saw the flight attendant waiting by the door as a mobile bridge attached itself to the plane. She could hardly wait to see Ken. But the passengers ahead dillydallied down the aisle like slow cattle.

As she exited the security gate, Mandy heard a familiar voice call out to her. Her heart swelled and tears clogged her throat when she spotted Ken waiting. Mandy had missed her husband during the two weeks she spent in Indiana, but it didn't hit her how much until now. He looked so handsome in his blue-and-white Hawaiian-print shirt and navy blue shorts. Ken's skin had darkened in the two weeks she'd been gone, making his blond hair stand out even more.

"It's so good to have you home. I've missed you like crazy." He wrapped his arms around Mandy in a welcoming hug.

"I've missed you too." She stood on tiptoe and gave him a kiss, not even caring if they had an audience. *If I had joined the Amish church when my friends did, I would never display this much affection in public—even greeting my husband after an absence.* She glanced around. Several other couples were hugging and kissing. To them, she and Ken didn't look out of place or appear too forward.

They walked hand-in-hand to the baggage claim. As much as Mandy missed her family, being with her husband again was a reminder that here in Kauai was the place she needed to be. Whether in Hawaii or back in Indiana, when she was with Ken, it felt like home again.

In the baggage area, her husband picked off a suitcase from the conveyer belt. "I think this is your bag." Ken rolled the case up to Mandy.

"Nope, my bag is bigger and has a long scratch down the front." She giggled.

He slapped his forehead. "Oops, that's right. I'll go back and get the right one."

"Hang on. I'll go with you." Mandy smiled up at him.

"Well it's been a couple of weeks since I've seen the suitcase." He gave her a silly grin. "Anyway this bag is black and looks like all the rest."

Ken returned the case back on the moving belt, and soon after, a man came up and grabbed the bag. "I was wondering where my suitcase was." The man looked over his shoulder at Ken, as he darted off toward the car rental shuttles.

Mandy scanned the luggage and spotted her bag. "There it is Ken— next to that tan suitcase."

He grabbed the bag and rolled it over to her. "Now we have the right one."

Mandy unzipped the outer pocket. "Here's proof—my navy blue umbrella."

"If you hadn't caught my mistake, we could've taken the wrong suitcase home."

"That poor man would not have been happy." Mandy clutched Ken's arm as they headed for the parking lot.

"It was hard to be back in Middlebury again without you. Seeing our business for the last time and moving away from Indiana permanently was difficult too." Mandy let go of Ken's arm and clasped his hand.

"I figured it would be difficult. Wish I could've been there with you." He tenderly squeezed her fingers. "I appreciate all the hard work you did and that you hung in there until it was finished." His gentle voice was soothing to her soul.

"It would be nice to be able to be in two places at once."

"Yeah." Ken's blond hair blew in the breeze. "Sometime in the future we'll plan a trip to Indiana."

"I hope so. We both work hard, and it would be fun to go there for a relaxing vacation next time."

"By then the B&B will belong to someone else, and maybe we'll have our own house here. Mom's been good about letting us stay with her, but she needs her space—and so do we."

"I can't wait to pick out a permanent home together, but it can wait. There's plenty of room at your mom's house, so at least we aren't crowding each other." Mandy stepped aside while Ken opened the door of their camo rig and put her suitcase inside.

"Are you hungry? Should we stop somewhere for a bite to eat before we go home?" Ken asked.

Her heart skipped a beat when she looked into the depth of his eyes. "That would be nice. I didn't have much to eat on the plane, and the few snacks I brought along didn't fill me enough." She gripped his hand tightly. It felt warm and comforting. "A late lunch sounds great."

"Okay. Let's stop at the Lemongrass Grill in Kapaa. While we eat, you can fill me in on everything that's been going on in Middlebury."

Mandy smiled. "I will. And you can catch me up on everything that's been happening here during my absence."

Kapaa

Mandy stared at the menu their hostess handed them. So many mouth-watering choices. She enjoyed coming to this Pan-Asian eatery with pagoda-inspired décor.

Mandy had a favorite she'd ordered before, but today she might try something different. The server brought them ice water and asked what they'd like to drink. They both ordered iced tea with lemon, but since they weren't certain what they wanted to eat yet, the middle-aged waitress said she'd return in a couple of minutes.

"Would you like an appetizer, Mandy?" Ken asked. "We could share some lobster ravioli, if that sounds appealing."

Mandy licked her lips. "Sounds good."

When the waitress returned, she placed the iced teas by their napkins. Ken put in their appetizer order, and also the guava barbecued ribs for his entrée. Mandy ordered shrimp scampi—one of her favorite island meals.

While they waited for their food, Mandy filled Ken in on how things went with her family, as well as at the B&B. "Someone came to look at it while I was there, but they weren't interested in buying our business."

"The right buyer will come along." Ken leaned closer to Mandy and whispered, "I said this before, but it bears repeating. I missed you so much, and I'm glad the Lord brought you safely back to me. I can't imagine my life without you."

Sitting beside Ken, Mandy rested her head on his shoulder. "I feel the same way about you."

When their waitress brought the appetizer, Ken and Mandy bowed their heads for silent prayer. While Ken often prayed out loud, they sometimes prayed silently for their meals. Ken called it "praying Amish," since that's the way Mandy had grown up saying her prayers.

After their prayer ended and they'd begun eating the lobster ravioli, Ken told Mandy how things went on the farm. "The chickens are laying well right now." He blotted his mouth with the dinner napkin. "We've been keeping our regular stores supplied, as well as the Palm's Bed-and-Breakfast."

Mandy paused from eating to sip her water. "How have Luana and Makaio been doing since I've been gone?"

"As far as I know they're getting along well. My mom went over the other day with some eggs, and when she came back she said Luana's daughter, Aliana, is expecting another baby."

"I'm sure the Palus must be excited about having a second grandchild." Mandy smiled. She hoped it didn't seem forced. It was difficult not to be envious, when she wanted a baby so bad. But maybe there was a reason she hadn't gotten pregnant yet. With all the things at the organic farm keeping her busy, it was probably best that she wasn't expecting a baby right now. Someday, though, when the time was right, Mandy hoped she and Ken would become parents.

Middlebury

It was almost eight thirty in the evening when the doorbell rang. Ellen went to answer it, figuring the guests who had reserved two rooms were probably on the porch. Gwen Adams had called over an hour ago, saying their plane had gotten in late and they were waiting to pick up a rental car.

Ellen opened the door. A woman and a man with two teenage girls waited, each holding a suitcase.

"Hello. I'm Lew Adams." The man reached out his hand. "Glad we finally made it."

Ellen shook hands with the family. "Welcome to the Pleasant View Bed-and-Breakfast. Please, come in and I'll show you to your rooms."

When the family entered the living room, Mr. Adams looked around, as though studying every detail. "I noticed a FOR SALE sign out front," he said. "Would you mind telling me the reason you're selling the place?"

His wife nudged his arm. "I can't believe you asked that question, Lew. It's none of our business why this home is being sold."

His lips quivered slightly as his nose creased. "I want to know a few details. Figured you would too, since. . ." He stopped talking and turned to face Ellen. "How much are you asking for the business?"

"Actually, this home is not mine. I'm managing it for the owners who have moved to Kauai, Hawaii. You would need to contact their Realtor for details on the price." Ellen opened the drawer of the end table near the couch and took out one of Polly's business cards. "Here's her contact information."

"Hmm. . ." Mr. Adams studied the business card. "We're thinking of relocating to this area, and Gwen has often talked about owning a bed-and-breakfast." He looked at his wife. "What do you think, dear? Wouldn't it be nice to own a place like this?"

Before Gwen could respond, one of the girls spoke up. "I don't wanna live in a B&B, Dad. We'd have no privacy. Besides, what kind of cute guys live in this small town anyway?"

"Really, Susan, you're only concerned about your love life? Dad's idea sounds like fun to me," her sister commented. "In fact, it'd be a new adventure."

Susan rolled her eyes. "You would say that, Jill. You're eager to move out of Chicago and start over somewhere else." She sighed, then took her cell phone from her purse. "I'd miss all of my friends, school, and all the cool places to shop for the trendiest styles. Oh, and you have no idea how much work would be involved if Mom and Dad bought a bed-and-breakfast."

Jill folded her arms, squinting as she stood almost nose-to-nose with her sister. "How do you know about B&Bs and how much work is involved in running one? And why do you have to throw cold water on everything, Susan?"

"I don't, but you—"

Their father stepped between them. "We don't need to talk about this tonight. In the morning, though, I would appreciate the opportunity to walk through the whole house. If I like what I see, I may get in touch with the real estate agent for more details."

Ellen sucked in her breath. *If these people should decide to buy Ken and Mandy's B&B, I could be out of a job, because with two teenage girls, I doubt they'd need me to work here anymore.*

Chapter 9

*B*y the middle of May, Lew and Gwen Adams had moved into the bed-and-breakfast as its new owners, and Ellen was out of a job. The couple's daughters would be helping their parents during the hours they weren't in school. Ellen had graciously offered to explain how she'd been running things in Mandy and Ken's absence, but Mrs. Adams stated she had her own way of doing things and would figure it out.

A week ago, Ellen had moved back to her parents' house, but she still hadn't found another job. She'd driven by the bed-and-breakfast yesterday on her way to the grocery store in Shipshewana. The spacious home looked pretty much the same on the outside, but she had a hunch the inside may have changed.

Ellen saw new potted plants near the front flower bed, and more along the driveway. She wondered how much other vegetation the owners would add.

During the time the Adamses had stayed at the B&B, Gwen made it obvious that she was contemplating things she would change if she lived there. She never mentioned anything specific, but a few times Ellen caught her standing in the living room or dining room, looking around as though deep in thought.

Everyone does things differently, Ellen reminded herself as she put her head covering in place. *I need to stop pining for what obviously wasn't meant to be and move forward with my life.*

Right now, her immediate need was to go outside and get her horse and buggy ready for the trip to the Blue Gate Restaurant, where she would meet Sadie for breakfast. Since Saturdays were Sadie's day off, this was a good time for them to get together.

Shipshewana

"I'm not sure what you're having, but the breakfast buffet is what I'm leaning toward." Sadie looked across the table at Ellen and grinned.

"It would probably be good, but I'm not all that hungry this morning." Ellen glanced out the window, then back again. "I may have a bowl of oatmeal."

"Is that all? Don't you want to order some toast to go with it?"

Ellen shook her head, feeling a little put out with her friend's mothering. "Are you still depressed about losing your job at the B&B?"

"Jah. I probably shouldn't panic, because it's only been a week, but I haven't found anything yet."

"Well, not to worry. I may have the answer for you." Sadie leaned forward, resting her elbows on the table. "A part-time position at the hardware store has opened up. They'll be interviewing people today and Monday. If you're interested in working there, that is."

Ellen's lips pressed together as she thought about her options. Working at a hardware store was not at the top of her list, but no jobs were available at any of the bed-and-breakfasts or hotels in the area.

"I'll give it some thought, Sadie, but I probably won't put in my application today."

"How come?"

"I promised to run several errands for my mamm, and then I need to get home and help her and my younger sister do some gardening."

"Okay, but I'd make sure to go first thing Monday morning. You don't want to miss the opportunity for a job."

Once again, Ellen felt like Sadie was being too pushy. She most likely meant well, so Ellen made no comment.

Their waitress came, and Sadie chose the buffet, along with her drink.

Ellen chose a beverage, and was about to order oatmeal, but changed her mind. "Guess I'll have the buffet too. The line has gone down some. I hope there's still a good variety left."

Their waitress smiled. "It has been busy since we opened this morning, but don't worry. There's plenty of food waiting for you."

Ellen and Sadie got up and headed for the buffet. When they returned to the table, they offered silent prayers.

"Have you heard anything from Mandy lately?" Sadie picked up a piece of bacon.

"Not since last week when I called to inform her that the new owners had moved into the bed-and-breakfast." Ellen took a drink of water and swallowed hard. Thinking about how difficult it had been to leave a job she'd enjoyed made her stomach knot up.

Middlebury

"I can't wait to pick your sisters up at the train station in Elkhart Monday morning."

Ellen heard the excitement in her mother's voice. Ruby, who was twenty, and Darla, seventeen, had been working at a restaurant in Sarasota, Florida, all winter and were finally coming home. Normally the girls returned to Indiana in April, but this year they'd chosen to stay an extra month. Ellen couldn't blame them. The weather in Florida, similar to Hawaii, was beautiful this time of the year. If it hadn't been for her job at the B&B, Ellen might have tried to get a job for the winter in Sarasota too. At least Darla and Ruby hadn't had to deal with snow during the winter.

The girls would return to their jobs as waitresses at the Amish-style restaurant in Middlebury, where they would work until late fall.

I'm sure when I see my sisters they'll be sporting nice tans from all that Florida sunshine. They will probably look healthy compared to my pale face. Ellen filled a pot with water, set it on the burner, and lit the propane stove. She watched her mother grab the bread-and-butter pickles from the refrigerator. Mom liked to can them in the summer, and the family ate the delicious pickles year-round.

"I'll need to bring up some more *bickels* from the basement, since this is the last jar upstairs," Mom commented.

"I can get you some when I'm done peeling the potatoes." Ellen placed another peeled spud on the cutting board, quartered it, and tossed the pieces in a bowl with the others.

"No hurry, I'll get them after we eat dinner." Mom arranged the pickle slices on a glass tray. "Will you be free to go with us to pick up your sisters?"

Ellen was on the verge of saying she couldn't go because she'd be applying for a job at the hardware store Monday morning. But the interview could wait until Monday afternoon. Darla and Ruby would expect everyone in the family to greet them when they stepped off the train, and Ellen wouldn't let her sisters down.

Usually, the girls went to and from Florida on the Pioneer Trails bus. But they wanted to try something different and come home on the train this time.

Perhaps my sisters would like to go to Hawaii with me sometime, Ellen thought as she grabbed another potato. *If they like Sarasota, I'm sure they'd fall in love with the Hawaiian Islands. Maybe by the time we're all ready to go, Lenore will be old enough to join us.*

Ellen figured returning to Hawaii was a silly dream, but it was fun to have a goal, even if it never came about.

Mom put the jar of pickles away and checked on the meat simmering in a pan on the stove.

"Something smells good in here, ladies. What's for supper?" Ellen's father sniffed the air as he entered the kitchen.

"Lemon chicken and mashed potatoes." Mom pointed to some glass jars on the counter. "And canned green beans from last year."

"I got the recipe for the chicken when I was on Kauai with Mandy," Ellen interjected.

"Sounds real tasty." He jiggled his bushy eyebrows. "How soon till we eat?"

"The chicken's almost done, and Ellen has the potatoes boiling on the stove. All I need to do yet is open two jars of beans and get them heated." Mom smiled. "Lenore's in the dining room setting the table, so by the time you get washed up we should be ready to eat."

"All right then. I'll see you at the table." Grinning widely, Dad sashayed out of the room. He was in an exceptionally good mood this evening. Perhaps it had been a profitable day at the store.

"The table is set. What else can I help with?" Lenore came in and stood next to Mom.

"You can put the lemon chicken on a platter and cover it with foil to keep warm." Mom pointed to the spare tongs on the counter.

A short time later, supper was on the table. Everyone was about to sit down when someone knocked on the front door.

"I'll get it." Lenore hurried out of the room. When she returned, Ezra was with her.

"Sorry for the interruption." Tugging the brim of his hat, Ezra handed Dad his lunchbox. "You left the store without this." He shifted from one foot to the other. "Figured you might want to have it come Monday morning."

"Danki, Ezra." Dad pointed to an empty chair at the table. "If you haven't eaten yet, why don't you join us?"

Ezra gave his shirt collar a tug. "Well, I. . ."

"Come on, son. I bet you're *hungerich*."

"I can't deny my hunger, but I don't wanna barge in."

"There's always room for one more at our table," Mom spoke up. "If your mamm's not expecting you for supper, we'd be happy to have you join us."

"My folks went out to eat this evening, so I'm on my own. Figured I'd make a sandwich when I got home, but what your havin' smells a lot better than a hunk of bologna between two slices of bread."

"Come on, then, you can take the seat over there beside Ellen."

Ezra rubbed the back of his neck. "Jah, okay." A splotch of pink erupted on his cheeks as he made his way over and sat down awkwardly. For some reason, Ezra seemed a bit nervous this evening.

Lenore looked over at Ellen and rolled her brown eyes, but at least she didn't say anything. Ellen could almost imagine what her little sister might be thinking.

After everyone prayed, Mom picked up the first plate of food to pass around the table.

Ezra looked at Dad. "Your *fraa. . . Sie is en gudi Koch.*"

"You're right, Ezra. My wife's a real good cook." Dad motioned to Ellen. "And so is my oldest dochder, who cooked the chicken. Ellen will make a fine fraa for some lucky fellow someday."

Ellen's face heated. She wished she could make herself disappear. What was her outspoken father trying to do—get Ezra to become interested in her?

She squirmed in her chair as Ezra's dark eyes darted from side to side. *How embarrassing. I'll bet poor Ezra wishes he'd gone home and fixed a cold sandwich.*

Ellen glanced at her father, sitting at the head of the table with a smug-looking smile on his bearded face. *I hope Dad's not trying to play matchmaker. If so, he's barking up the wrong tree, for Ezra and I have nothing in common.*

Chapter 10

Monday morning Ellen awoke with a headache. The pain in her forehead was almost intolerable—like the car horn she'd heard blaring the other day across the street from the Blue Gate Restaurant. Even so, she wouldn't let it stop her from applying for a job at the hardware store or going to Elkhart to greet her sisters' train.

When Ellen stepped into the kitchen, Dad handed her a slip of paper. "When I went to the phone shack to check for messages, I found one for you. Wrote it down to make sure I got it right."

Ellen grimaced as she silently read the note.

"What's wrong?" Mom moved across the room and placed her hand on Ellen's shoulder. "You look umgerennt."

"The message is from Sadie. It seems the part-time position she told me about has been filled." Using the tips of her fingers, Ellen made tiny circles across her forehead. "Guess I'll have to keep on looking."

Dad poured a cup of coffee and handed it to Ellen. "If we had more work at the shoe store right now you could help out there, but for the past few weeks there's only been enough to keep Ezra and me busy."

Ellen shook her head. "It's okay, Dad. I'm sure something will open up for me soon." She handed the cup back to him. "Did you forget that I don't care much for *kaffi*? I usually drink *tee*."

"Oh, you're right." Dad reached under his hat and scratched his head. *"Ich bin allfatt am eppes vergesse."*

"You're not always forgetting something, Nathan." Mom chuckled, giving his arm a tap. "Only certain things you can't remember."

He nodded. "It's what happens when a person gets old. Sometimes I feel like *en aldi schachdel*."

Lenore poked her head into the kitchen. "You're not an old and worn-out cow, *Daadi*."

346

"Jah, I am. See here—I have the *runsele* to prove it." With a deep laugh, he touched the wrinkles on his forehead.

Ellen couldn't help smiling. Dad could be such a character at times. She felt fortunate to have good parents. They both tried to keep a positive attitude, even during difficult times.

I should try to be more cheerful. As Ellen reached for the aspirin bottle and took some pills for her headache, she reflected on Proverbs 17:22: *"A merry heart doeth good like a medicine; but a broken spirit drieth the bones."* If she didn't find a job soon, she would need to quote the verse often to remind herself to think positively and look for things to laugh about.

Elkhart, Indiana

A wisp of Darla's dark hair blew in the breeze as she and Ruby stepped off the train with their satchels in hand.

Ellen let Mom, Dad, and Lenore greet the girls before she gave them big hugs. "Welcome home, Sisters. You're both so tan. How was your trip?"

"It was good. I enjoyed riding on the train more than the bus." Ruby's blue eyes twinkled. "Think I might travel the same way when I return to Sarasota this winter."

"Same here." Darla pushed a few hairs hanging loose back under her kapp. "I'm glad we'll have a few days off before we start working at the restaurant in Middlebury again. I want to spend a little time with some of my friends and get caught up on my rest."

Ruby slipped her arm around Ellen's waist. "You look *mied*. Have you been working too hard at the bed-and-breakfast?"

Ellen shook her head. "I'm not managing the place anymore. When you and Mom talked on the phone the last time, didn't she tell you the B&B sold?"

"Jah, but I figured you'd keep working there with the new owners."

"No, they have two teenage daughters who'll be helping them, so I'm currently unemployed."

"Oh Ellen, I'm sorry." Darla's sympathetic tone conveyed how much she cared.

"I'll check at the restaurant and see if they might be hiring." Ruby gave Ellen's shoulder a pat. "It would be nice if you could work there too."

Ellen shrugged. "We'll have to see how it goes." Truthfully, she didn't want to work as a waitress, but then she shouldn't be picky—especially now.

"Come on, girls, let's get your luggage," Dad said. "You can continue your conversation on the way home."

They moved over to the section of the train where their luggage had been stowed, and watched as it was removed and placed on the ground. Dad waited for some folks ahead of him to get their suitcases.

Ellen watched a mother and her young daughter grab their matching flowered bags. As they walked away, she noticed how cute the little girl's tiny case was.

Dad stepped forward and picked both girls' suitcases up at the same time. Groaning, he quickly set them back down. "Oh, boy—my hernia's bothering me again."

"Again?" Mom's eyes narrowed. "How long has this been going on, Nathan? And why haven't you mentioned anything about having a hernia before?"

Scrunching his face, he placed both hands against his abdomen. "It's been bothering me awhile but never hurt this bad before." He looked over at Ruby. "It might be better if you girls get your own luggage to the van."

"Of course, Dad. You need to take it easy."

Darla and Ruby picked up their suitcases and followed Mom and Dad across the parking lot. Ellen and Lenore walked behind.

When they got to the van, Mom followed Dad around to the door and opened it for him. "Now, take your time getting in, Nathan. I'm right here to lean on."

"Danki, Nora, but I can do this myself." It was all Dad could do to get in the passenger's seat up front. Roy Steffy, their driver, got out and put Darla and Ruby's suitcases in the back of the van, while Ellen, her three sisters, and Mom took seats in the middle of the vehicle.

"Did something happen to you, Nathan?" Roy closed the driver's door and started the van.

"It's my hernia acting up. I shouldn't have picked up both suitcases at the same time."

"Yep, a hernia can sure be a nuisance, especially if it worsens over time." Roy glanced at him, then pulled the vehicle out of the parking lot.

"I think you should see the doctor." Mom tapped Dad's shoulder.

"Don't worry. I'm sure I'll be fine once we get home."

"I hope so, but if it doesn't quit hurting, I hope you'll—"

"Okay, Nora, whatever you say."

Mom looked over at Ellen and rolled her eyes.

Reduced to an annoying dull ache, Ellen's headache was almost forgotten. She was concerned about her father, who never complained and rarely got sick. From the way Mom sat, with lips compressed and hands clasped tightly together in her lap, Ellen was certain she was still worried about Dad. No doubt she'd be calling the doctor tomorrow morning, and Dad would have no choice but to go to the appointment.

Ellen bit her lip as they drove over the Elkhart River. She hadn't seen her father in this shape before and wondered if it was serious. Perhaps the doctor would suggest surgery to repair the hernia. If so, how long would her father be out of commission?

✳

Middlebury

Ezra brought his lunch to work and decided to eat it outside in the shade, since the store was quiet. He watched the neighbor's little dog come over, wagging its tail. *If Nathan doesn't show up soon, and it gets busy in the store, I hope I'll manage okay.* He gave the pup some chips and patted its head. "Thanks for keeping me company during my break, little guy."

When a buggy came by, Ezra looked to see if it was Nathan, but the rig kept going. *I wonder what is keeping my boss. Usually you can set a pocket watch to his punctuality.*

Ezra ate his lunch and went back to the store. He'd finished washing up when he looked out the window and saw a car pull in. An elderly English man got out and headed for the store with a pair of old boots.

"Good afternoon," Ezra said when the man placed the boots on the counter.

"Hello, young man. I need these repaired. Do ya do that sort of thing here?" The man squinted through his glasses.

"Sorry, but we only sell new shoes." Ezra reached into his pocket, pulled out a hanky, and wiped his damp forehead. "But a couple of shops in Elkhart repair shoes, as well as a few in surrounding towns. Maybe one of them can help you out."

"Okay then, I'll look them up." The man turned around, and was almost out the door, when he stopped. "If I can't get these fixed, I'll probably be back to look at what you have here in this store." He gave a wave and closed the door.

Ezra glanced at the battery-operated clock, across from the counter where he stood. It was one o'clock. Nathan should have been here by now, even if he'd stayed at the house to have lunch after picking Darla and Ruby up at the train station.

Fortunately, not too many customers had stopped by during the morning hours. But even with the ones who had come to shop, Ezra kept busy—either running back and forth between the store and the shed where they kept a surplus of shoes or waiting on customers. He was glad he didn't have to work by himself at the store every day. A business like this was too much for one person to run.

Some days when lots of customers came in, Ezra wished Nathan would hire another employee. With three people working in the store, it would take some pressure off Ezra so he'd feel free to ask for a day off. As it was, he had to run all his errands in the late afternoon or every other Saturday, when the shoe store was closed. If he had to schedule a doctor or dentist appointment, that was even more difficult. None of the doctors in the area were open on Saturday, and some didn't even work on Fridays. So Ezra's only alternative was to ask for time off when he had a medical appointment.

The front door opened, and an Amish family with six children entered the store. Ezra had seen them before, but they didn't live nearby, and he didn't know their names.

Oh, boy. His cheeks felt a flush of heat. *What I could use right now is a helper.* Ezra rubbed his forehead. *If they all want shoes, I'm in big trouble.*

"May I help you?" he asked, stepping out from behind the counter.

The man nodded. "I need a new pair of work boots." He gestured to the woman standing close to his side. "And my fraa and most of our *kinner* need shoes to wear for chores and gardening."

"Okay, I'll see what I can find."

Ezra was busy helping the man's wife choose a pair of shoes, when Ellen entered the store. "When you have a minute, I need to talk to you." Her pinched expression portrayed worry as she moved closer to Ezra.

"Sure, I'll be with you in a few minutes." Ezra finished up and then excused himself, saying he'd be back to fit the woman's children for shoes.

He motioned for Ellen to join him behind the counter. "What is it?"

Tugging on the strings of her head covering, Ellen spoke quietly. "My daed hurt himself when he tried to pick up my sister's suitcases at the train station this morning. He admitted to Mom that he has a hernia, and when we got home he hurt so bad he had to lie down."

Ezra's forehead wrinkled. "Sorry to hear it."

"Needless to say, he won't be able to work this afternoon, so he wants you to be in charge." Taking a deep breath, Ellen continued. "Mom will be calling the doctor to see how soon we can get him in."

"Oh, boy. Sure hope I can manage things on my own." Ezra's head filled with fuzzy thoughts.

Ellen touched his arm briefly, before pulling her hand aside. "I can see business is heavy right now. Would you like me to stay and help out till closing time?"

He nodded, feeling a sudden release of tension. "Danki, Ellen. You showed up at just the right time."

Chapter 11

*H*ow are you feeling?" Ellen asked when her father came into the kitchen Tuesday morning.

"I'm doin' all right." Holding his hand against his stomach, he moved slowly across the room and took the coffee pot from the stove.

"Are you still in pain?" Ellen sat at the table, sipping a cup of hot tea.

"Some. But it doesn't hurt too much, as long as I don't pick up anything heavy or move the wrong way." With a groan he couldn't conceal, he lowered himself into a chair at the table.

"Where's Mom? Is she still in bed?"

He shook his head. "She got up before me, dressed, and headed outside. Said something about checking for phone messages."

"I bet she went to the phone shack to make you a doctor's appointment," Ruby spoke up from across the room, where she was thumbing through the calendar pages.

"Actually, Mom called the doctor's office yesterday to see about getting an appointment," Ellen said. Annoyance flitted across Dad's face. "Since they didn't call back yesterday, she's hoping to hear something this morning."

Dad's brows furrowed. "Don't need a doctor to tell me what's wrong. I don't have time to go either. Ezra can't run the store by himself." He lifted his gaze toward the clock. "That young man is used to me being there to run things and answer any questions he might have."

"Ezra will have to get through the day without you, because your health comes first," Ellen was quick to respond.

"Better not put the buggy before the horse, Dad." Ruby shook her head. "Maybe what you're dealing with isn't a hernia at all."

His lips compressed. "Jah, it is. I had a hernia once, before you were born, and I'm almost 100 percent sure it's happened again. But this time it involves another place on my *bauch*."

"Where on your stomach, Daadi?" Lenore asked when she came into the kitchen.

Dad touched a spot above his waist. "It not only hurts, but if I pulled up my shirt, you'd see the protrusion."

"No need for that." Ruby held up her hand and made a face. "Stuff like that makes me squeamish."

Dad snickered. "I was only kidding. Wouldn't wanna scare you girls."

Mom entered the kitchen through the back door and slipped off her shoes. "Good news! Dr. McGrath can see you at eleven o'clock this morning. The office left a message, so I called to confirm the appointment."

Dad frowned, shuffling his feet under the table. "That won't work, Nora. Did ya forget I'll be working at the store?"

"It's the only time he can see you today, and we're lucky you got an appointment so soon." Mom moved across the room and placed her hands on his shoulders. "They had a cancellation, and I told them we'd take it."

"Okay, okay." Dad looked at Ellen. "Would you mind filling in for me today? Ezra will be expecting me to show up." He released a heavy sigh. "He'll need to know what's going on."

"Well, I. . ."

"Ezra will be in charge, so you shouldn't have a lot to do."

Ellen gave a nod. "Okay, Dad. I'll head over to the store as soon as I've had breakfast."

Ezra looked at the clock on the wall near the counter. *Nathan should have been here thirty minutes ago. I wonder what's keeping him this morning.* It wasn't like his boss to be late for work. *Could Nathan still be hurting?*

Another fifteen minutes went by, and Ezra began to pace. So far no customers had shown up, which was good. Things could be hectic if several people showed up and he was the only one here.

What am I thinking? Ezra smacked his forehead with the palm of his hand. *I should be worried about my boss, not about being here by myself.*

He glanced out the front window and saw Ellen pedaling in on her bike. *Oh, boy. I bet her being here means he's not coming again today.* Ezra hoped Ellen would listen to his requests and not try to do things her own way. *She's a little stubborn but one of the prettiest young women in Middlebury. Ellen's golden blond hair and sparkling blue eyes bring out the beauty on her heart-shaped face.*

Ezra waited at the counter, tapping his boot against the wooden floor. *Maybe I have a chance to win her since we'll be working together again.*

When Ellen entered the shop, she walked up to Ezra with furrowed brows. "My daed's seeing the doctor today, so you're in charge again, and I'm here to take his place."

Ezra turned and looked at the clock again. "Then how come you're late? This is your daed's shop. Don't ya know what time it opens for business?" The thought of having Ellen here to help out again made his stomach tighten. And with her standing so close, Ezra felt like his knees might buckle.

"When I got up this morning I didn't know Dad wouldn't be working today, or that he would ask me to fill in for him again." Her forehead creased. "It took a while to get here." She reached into her purse and pulled out a slip of paper. "Here's a list Dad made out for you. Want me to read it?"

Ezra clenched his teeth. "No, thanks. I can read it myself." He stepped behind the counter and took a seat on the wooden stool. He and Ellen were off to a bad start. At this rate, he'd never get her to like him.

Ellen's face tightened. *Why is Ezra so testy with me? I'd better find something to do. If nothing else, I can sweep the floors and do some cleaning.*

Ellen started in the direction of the back room, where cleaning supplies were kept, but stopped walking and turned around when Ezra called out to her.

"Say, where ya goin'?"

"To get the broom so I can sweep the floors."

He shook his head. "That's not necessary. I'd rather you put some of the new shoes we got in last week on the shelves."

"Okay, I'll do it after I'm done sweeping."

Ezra stepped out from behind the counter, planting his feet in a wide stance. "Thought I was supposed to be in charge today. Isn't that what you said before?"

"Jah, he did, but. . ."

"Then I'd appreciate it if you do as I say."

A rush of adrenaline tingled through Ellen's body. She couldn't believe Ezra's bossy attitude. Who did he think he was, talking to her that way? After all, this was Dad's store, not his. Besides, it wasn't as if she'd never worked here before. During her early teens, Ellen had spent the summer months helping Dad in the shoe store, so she understood a thing or two about the business. By rights she should be the one in charge. But then, she wasn't a full-time employee, and Ezra had worked here for the past few years.

Ezra tapped his foot, never losing eye contact with Ellen. "If you don't want to stock the shelves, guess I'll have to do 'em myself."

Holding her hands behind her back, while gripping her wrists, Ellen said, "I'll put the shoes out."

Ellen had never seen this side of Ezra. She was sure he didn't use an overbearing, almost haughty attitude with Dad, because her father would never put up with that. In all the times she'd spoken to Ezra, he'd never acted so bullish. Maybe the power of being in charge had gone to his head.

Ellen found several shoe boxes stacked inside the storage room and bent down to gather up a few. *Should I say anything to Dad about Ezra's attitude, or just let it go? I don't want Ezra to lose his job, but he shouldn't have talked to me that way.*

Lihue

The piercing sound of his alarm going off jolted Rob Smith out of bed. He peered at the clock on the nightstand by his bed and grimaced: 6:00 a.m. It was too early to be getting out of bed. But if he wanted time to eat and take a dip in the ocean before heading out to look for some odd jobs, he had no choice but to rise at the crack of dawn.

Rubbing his short-cropped hair, Rob glanced across the room, where his buddy, Taavi Kumar, lay on a similar bunk. The young Hawaiian native hadn't moved a muscle. It was apparent the alarm hadn't woken him.

Soon after Rob arrived on Kauai, a little over a year ago, he'd met the island native when they'd been surfing on a beach in Kapaa. When Taavi heard that Rob had no job or place to stay, he'd invited him to share his tiny rental, stating that Rob could begin paying half the rent when he found a permanent job. It may have seemed strange to some people that someone would befriend, and even welcome, a total stranger into their home, but Rob had heard the people of Kauai were considered some of the friendliest folks in the Hawaiian Islands. Taavi's sunny disposition was proof that the rumor must be true, for he had the spirit of Aloha.

While the conditions weren't ideal, since the place only had one bedroom, it was a far cry from sleeping in the dense forest, or under a palm tree near a secluded beach.

Rob shuffled his way to the small kitchen and opened the refrigerator. His stomach growled as he scanned the shelves and spied a slice of pizza still in the box from their supper last night. It wasn't something most people might eat for breakfast, but Rob grabbed it anyway and took a bite. Hot pizza or cold, he didn't care, since it was one of his favorite foods.

After he finished the slice, Rob looked out the window. The dawn moved slowly as it filled the sky, and the morning tide rose and covered the beach. *Looks like it's gonna be a good day for that dip in the ocean.* He looked down at his tan chest and arms.

Rob noticed the bottle of sun protector sitting on the counter. Shaking his head, he muttered, "I'll bet Taavi put it there, but I'm not using that stuff anymore." Because his skin had turned three shades darker since arriving on the island, Rob no longer felt the need to use sun tan lotion. Even Taavi, a natural-born Hawaiian, put a barrier of lotion on his exposed skin before they went surfing.

Rob respected Taavi, but stubborn as he was, Rob wanted to prove he didn't need sunscreen anymore.

Taavi had become a good friend and recently let Rob know that a bellhop position might open up in another month or so at the hotel where he worked as a gardener. It wasn't Rob's idea of a perfect job, and he didn't want to do that for the rest of his life. But if the job panned out, it would be better than panhandling or doing odd jobs whenever he could find them. The money Rob made now, although small, helped Taavi pay the rent and put some food on the table. Since Rob didn't have a lot of other expenses, it was adequate—at least for now. But if a better job more to his liking came along, he'd take it, no questions asked.

Chapter 12

Middlebury

After putting the OPEN sign in the store window Wednesday morning, Ezra saw Ellen approaching. Unable to take his eyes off her, he stood in the open doorway, watching as she parked her bike. Ellen's golden hair, peeking out from under her head covering, looked shinier than ever in the morning sunlight.

Ezra's mouth felt so dry he could barely swallow. *Wish I had the nerve to ask her out.* He shook his head. *But what would be the point when she might say no?*

Ezra thought about yesterday and how he'd acted around Ellen. *Was I a little bit tough on her?* He rubbed his temples. *In time, I hope she'll realize I'm a nice fella. My mamm tells me that all the time.*

"How's your daed?" Ezra asked when Ellen stepped onto the porch. "What did he find out at the doctor's yesterday?"

She lifted her hands and let them fall to her sides. "Dad will be having surgery next Monday to repair both hernias."

"Both?" Ezra's eyebrows lifted.

"Turns out he has two hernias. Who knows how long he's been hurting. Until Monday when we picked Darla and Ruby up at the train station, he'd never said anything about being in pain." She shook her head slowly. "Dad wasn't happy when the doctor recommended he take it easy for several weeks following surgery."

"So he won't be able to work at the store for a while?"

"Right." Ellen stepped inside. "Which means I'll be working here until he's well enough to take over his duties."

Ezra turned and followed her into the store. The notion of working with Ellen for several weeks made his heart pound. *Sure hope I can do this without letting on to Ellen how I feel about her. If she gets any idea of it but doesn't feel the same toward me, she might leave me to deal with customers on my own.*

Kapaa

Mandy had spent a good portion of the morning helping Ken clean out dusty, smelly chicken houses—certainly not one of her favorite chores, but it needed to be done on schedule. When she looked down at her arms and saw a layer of brown dust, she grimaced. "I can't wait to take a shower and get rid of this filth and putrid odor."

"I hear you." Ken wrinkled his nose. "I'm not fond of smelling like poultry either."

Other than caring for her flowers and the organic vegetable garden, Ken's mother didn't do much outside with the chickens. She did, however, take care of the financial end of the business and kept a good record of things. They all had jobs to do, and no one took time off.

This evening, rather than cooking a meal at home, the three of them would attend their church's mid-week potluck supper, followed by Bible study. Mandy looked forward to the fellowship, as well as studying God's Word with other believers.

Middlebury

Ellen stepped into the outside storage shed and clicked on the battery-operated light. She inhaled deeply. The weather was typical of late spring—growing warmer but still less humid, making it nice to be outside. Unfortunately, it was stuffy in the shed. On top of that, as the day had worn on, her tension increased. Ezra seemed to be throwing his weight around, even more so than the previous day. *Does he think he has the right to tell me what to do?*

Unlike yesterday, they'd been busy with customers most of the day, which was good for business, but not good for Ellen. While Ezra waited on customers in the store, he kept her running back and forth to the storage shed to get shoes that weren't in the store. At least the little jaunts to the shed gave her some time away from Ezra.

Their most recent customer, John Schrock, couldn't decide what style of black shoe he wanted. Once he'd made a selection, the size wasn't in the store, which had brought her out to the storage shed. It was close to quitting time, and Ellen hoped it would be her last trip out for the day.

She gathered four boxes of the correct shoe size and started for the door. The top one almost toppled off, but she caught it in time, balancing the box with her chin.

When Ellen entered the store and discovered John wasn't there, her frustration mounted. "What happened to John?" She placed the boxes on the counter, which Ezra sat behind, looking like he owned the place. "I thought he wanted to try on more shoes."

Ezra shrugged. "He changed his mind and bought the first pair he tried on, which were close to his size."

Ellen heaved a sigh, gesturing to the boxes she'd brought in. "Guess I'd better put these on a shelf in the men's section."

"That won't work, Ellen."

She tipped her head. "How come?"

"The shelves are full with the new shoes you put out yesterday, so there isn't room for more boxes."

"But you sold several pair of shoes today."

"True, but not in the sizes you have here." Ezra nodded toward the shoe boxes.

Refusing to look at him, Ellen scooped them up and headed across the room. She almost made it to the door, when the top box slipped. In the process of trying to right it, she lost her grip, and all four boxes landed on the floor.

"Always trouble somewhere," Ellen muttered, going down on her knees to gather up all the shoes that had fallen out.

"Here, let me help you with those." Ezra knelt beside her. He reached out at the same time as Ellen. Her cheeks warmed when he grabbed her hand instead of the shoes.

"Oops! Sorry, I didn't mean to do that." Ezra's ears flamed as he quickly withdrew his hand.

Avoiding his gaze, Ellen grabbed the rest of the shoes as quickly as possible and put them in the boxes. In the shed, she would make sure each pair was in its correct box. Right now, she just wanted to get outside as quickly as possible.

Kapaa

"Looks like we may be in for some rain," Ken's mother commented from the back seat of Ken's SUV.

As huge raindrops slowly splattered on the windshield, Mandy glanced out the front window, and up at the sky. Dark, massive clouds billowed in off the ocean, while palm trees swayed in the heavy wind. Rain was typical for Kauai, but they hadn't had any moisture for the past five days, so the forthcoming storm was a good thing.

"Here we are." Ken pulled into the parking lot and turned off the ignition. "Don't know about the rest of you, but I'm hungry as a shark going after its prey."

Mandy looked over at him and rolled her eyes. "I can't believe you compared yourself to a shark."

He poked her arm playfully. "Didn't say I was a shark—just hungry enough to eat like one."

She snickered. "Okay, whatever." When Mandy opened the car door the rain fell harder. "We'd better hurry inside with our food before we're drenched."

Ken carried the box with their casserole dish and deviled eggs, while Mandy and Ken's mother hurried alongside. When they entered the fellowship hall, they were greeted by Luana and Makaio.

"Aloha!" Luana pulled Mandy into a big hug, as Ken and Makaio headed to the kitchen with their food containers. "So glad you could come tonight. I can only imagine how busy you've all been at the farm." She greeted Ken's mother with a hug too. "How are you, Vickie?"

Vickie's chin trembled. "I miss Charles so much, but thanks to my son and his sweet wife, I'm getting along okay." She slipped her arm around Mandy's waist. "I don't know what I'd do without them."

Mandy teared up. While it might seem to some that she'd made a sacrifice by moving here, she realized it was a privilege.

"Come, let's find a table," Ken called from across the room. "A little birdie told me Luana made my favorite ambrosia salad."

With hands on her hips, Luana looked over at Makaio and frowned. "Did you tell him? It was supposed to be a surprise."

Makaio winked at his wife. "What can I say? Hunger makes me do crazy things."

Mandy giggled and linked arms with Luana and Vickie. "Guess we'd better not keep our hungry men waiting."

Middlebury

Unable to sleep, Ellen crept down the stairs and into the kitchen. She'd no more than lit one of the gasoline lights when Lenore entered the room.

Ellen jumped. "For goodness' sake, Sister, you scared me. What are you doing up in the middle of the night?"

Lenore gave a sheepish grin. "Couldn't sleep, so I came down to find something to eat."

"Maybe we can share the last piece of Mom's apple pie. It would go well with a glass of cold milk."

Lenore nodded. "Sounds good. I'll get the glasses and plates while you fetch the pie and milk."

Ellen bit back a chuckle. "Aren't you the bossy one?"

Lenore dropped her gaze. "Sorry."

"It's okay. I bet you could tell Ezra Bontrager a thing or two." Ellen opened the refrigerator and took out the milk.

"What do you mean?"

"Oh, nothing. I was thinking out loud." Ellen pulled out the pie pan and placed it on the table beside the milk.

Lenore set the glasses and plates down, then opened the silverware drawer. "Don't think we can eat the pie without these." She held up two forks.

Ellen laughed. "Guess we could, but it'd be messy."

They ate their snack in silence, until Lenore posed a question. "How do you like workin' at Dad's store?"

"It's okay, I guess." *But I'd like it better if I was in charge.*

"You're lucky. I wish Dad had asked me to work there."

"Hmm. . ." An idea popped into Ellen's head. "You're out of school now, so if it's okay with our folks, why don't you go with me tomorrow and I can show you what to do."

Lenore's eyes brightened. "Sure hope they say yes. It'd be fun workin' in Dad's store."

Ellen ate a piece of pie, savoring the juicy, cinnamon-flavored apples. *If things go right, and Lenore catches on fast, maybe she can take over for me at the store, and I'll be free to look for another job. No more dealing with Ezra telling me what to do. He can deal with my feisty sister.*

Chapter 13

$\mathcal{B}$y the first Saturday of June, Ellen felt very thankful for her sister's presence at the store. Lenore's work not only lightened the load, but Ezra's bossiness toward Ellen had lessened a bit as well, since he now had two helpers to tell what to do. Ellen wished this was a job she liked more, but for Dad's sake she would work without complaint—even though dealing with Ezra at times still felt like having a burr under her saddle.

"Where shall I put this pair of *schuh*? I don't see a box for them." Lenore bumped Ellen's arm, halting her thoughts.

Ellen took the black sneakers from her sister and looked inside to check the size. "Did you look on the shelf for size nine in women's shoes? Sometimes people put the empty box on the shelf but set the shoes someplace else."

Lenore squinted her blue eyes. "You want me to go through every box on the shelf?"

"Jah." Ellen pointed in the right direction. "As soon as you find it, I'd appreciate some help opening several boxes in the back room."

"Okay." Lenore smiled. "I like workin' here in the store. Don't you?"

"It's all right, but I'm hoping to find another job after Dad comes back."

"If you quit working here, do you think Dad will let me keep helping?"

"Maybe. That's why I'm training you the best I can—so you can fill my shoes." She snickered.

"Good one, Ellen." Lenore grinned. "When I get paid I'd like to go shopping. Maybe we could go together."

"That would be nice, and we could stop for ice cream afterward." Ellen glanced out the window and saw a minivan pull into their lot. Things had been busy today, with a steady stream of customers.

Lenore headed down the women's aisle, and Ellen turned toward the front door as an English couple with three children entered the store. Since Ezra was behind the counter, waiting on a customer, Ellen greeted the couple. "May I help you?"

The woman, who wore her brown hair in a long braid, nodded. "My girls and I need new shoes." She gestured to the man and small boy. "They may want to try on a few pairs too."

Ellen smiled. "I'd be happy to assist." She directed the man to the men's and boys' section, then led the woman and her daughters to the women's department.

Ezra came out from behind the counter. "Lenore, when you get done with whatever you're doing, could you help Ellen?" he called.

Ellen looked back at Ezra. *There he goes again—telling us what to do.*

"Okay, I'll put these away and be right back to help." Lenore rushed off.

Ezra's bossiness didn't seem to bother Ellen's sister. If it did, she never let on. *Perhaps I'm just too sensitive.*

"Is this your store?" The woman looked at Ellen with a curious expression.

She shook her head. "My father owns it."

"Oh, I see. I didn't realize until we came in that it's an Amish shoe store." The woman reached into her purse and withdrew a small camera. "Mind if I take a few pictures? This is our first time visiting Amish country, and I want to take some photos to share with my friends in Chicago."

"It's okay to take pictures of the shoes, but please, no photos of those who work here."

The woman's shoulders rose as she gave a huff. "Okay, if that's what you'd prefer."

Ellen didn't have a chance to explain, for the woman grabbed her daughters' hands and hurried down the first aisle.

Lenore came back and stood by her sister. "How can I help?"

"Depending on what our customers want, I may need you to run out to the shed for more shoes." Ellen glanced over her shoulder and saw Ezra talking to the man and his boy. A few seconds later, they started down one of the aisles.

Heading down the aisle of women's shoes, she and Lenore were almost run over by the young girls, each waving a pair of shoes in their hands. Before Ellen could say anything, the girls zipped past them and raced toward the front of the store. Thinking their mother would go after her daughters, Ellen paused.

"Where's their mom?" Lenore whispered.

Glancing around, Ellen shrugged. Then, hearing some giggling in the next aisle, she hurried to see what was so funny. The girls both wore shoes several sizes too big for them and stood posed as their mother snapped a picture.

The youngest girl pointed to her feet. "I want these shoes."

"Me too." Her sister eyed Lenore, when she stepped up to her.

Ellen looked at the children's mother. "Would you like me to measure the girls' feet? Then I can check and see if we have their sizes in stock."

"Yes, please do."

"I'll get the shoes for you, once we know their sizes," Lenore said.

Ellen asked the children to take a seat on the bench at the end of the aisle. While she measured the girls' feet, their mother took a few more pictures. Ellen hoped she wasn't in any of them. Most people didn't come into the store with a camera. *Why do they feel the need to take pictures? Is our business so different from an English shoe store?*

Ezra had been talking to the English man who'd come into the store with his family, but he didn't seem interested in buying shoes. The young boy had gone outside a few minutes ago, and the father followed.

Ezra looked out the window. Father and son sat side-by-side on the bench. He felt a twinge of envy. *Sure hope I have a son someday. Of course I'll first need a fraa.*

Turning, he glanced at Ellen. He'd noticed that she seemed to be avoiding him. She spent most of her time training Lenore to restock when deliveries were made, wait on customers, run the battery-operated cash register, and sort through boxes of shoes. At this rate, he'd never get a relationship started with her. If he could only get up the nerve to ask Ellen out without fear of rejection. And it didn't help that he kept saying the wrong things whenever he talked with her.

Ezra returned to his seat behind the counter. *I wonder if Ellen is expecting her sister to take over for her when Nathan returns to the store. I haven't been very pleasant to Ellen since she started helping out while her daed had surgery and recovers. Maybe I'd better change my ways and quit telling her what to do.*

He shifted on the wooden stool. *Wish there was something I could say to make things better. Would it help if I told Ellen I was sorry?*

Nora stepped out of the kitchen and stood watching Nathan sitting in his favorite chair, staring out the window with a wistful expression. Her husband was bored, no doubt wishing he could go back to work at the shoe store. It was difficult to hold him down, and she'd be glad when the doctor said Nathan could return to work. All he'd talked about since he got out of the hospital was the store—wondering how things were going, if Ezra and Ellen were managing okay without him, and if Lenore was fitting in well.

Nora sighed. Having her husband down like this was testing their marriage. He'd become irritable and snapped at her for the littlest things. She had considered talking to their bishop or one of the other ministers about it. Instead, she'd confided in her mother when she came by earlier. Mom was in the kitchen now, fixing coffee.

Nora stepped forward and placed her hand on her husband's shoulder. "Do you need anything, Nathan?"

He shook his head, never taking his gaze off the window.

"Are you feeling all right?"

"I'm fine."

"If you're hurting, I'll bring you one of the pain pills the doctor prescribed."

"Said I'm fine. I don't like taking those pills. And if I need one, I'll get it myself."

Nora stepped back, feeling like she'd been punched. "Okay, I'll be in the kitchen with Mom if you need me." She crept down the hall, stopping in the bathroom for a tissue. She blotted her eyes and blew her nose. *Nathan doesn't appreciate anything I do. It's like he's become a different person. Doesn't he realize how much I care about him?*

Nora paused to reflect on what her mother had said earlier this morning. *"Be patient, kind, and supportive, for this too shall pass."*

Mom also explained how some people can change when pain racks their body. She'd said, "Nathan doesn't intend to be nasty. He's upset, not only because he hurts, but because his normal routine has been interrupted. Remember, the husband is the head of the household—the main breadwinner for his family. When he can't do what he normally does, it's difficult to see his family doing everything for him. I'm sure when he's feeling himself again, he will most likely apologize and say how grateful he is to have you by his side."

Looking at herself in the bathroom mirror, Nora took a deep breath. "Mom is right," she said to herself quietly. "I must show Nathan how much I love him and, at the same time, try not to overwhelm him with too much attention."

Nora pulled out a clean washcloth from storage and dampened it with cool running water. After applying the refreshing cloth to her face, she felt more relaxed.

Leaning against the bathroom counter, Nora closed her eyes. *Lord, help me be an understanding wife. Show me when to speak and when to keep quiet. Please help my husband to heal quickly so he can return to his store and things will be better between us.*

Chapter 14

Kapaa

$\mathcal{B}$y the end of June, Mandy and Ken had established a routine that allowed them to complete things well and in a timely manner.

On this beautiful Monday morning, Mandy's stress seemed to melt away as she sat on the lanai with Ken and Vickie, drinking guava juice and listening to a Hawaiian music CD.

"You should get out your ukulele and play something for us," Vickie said.

Mandy's toes curled in her flip-flops. "I haven't practiced in a while, and I'm not that good. Now, Makaio—he's mastered the art of ukulele playing."

"You're being modest, Mandy." Ken nudged her arm. "You played a lot when we lived in Indiana, and everyone who heard you enjoyed your playing."

Mandy smiled. "Guess I'll have to get it out again soon."

The doorbell rang.

"I'll see who it is." Vickie rose from her chair. A short time later she came back with Taavi and a tall, nice-looking young man with dark brown, cropped hair. Mandy didn't recognize him and wondered if Ken knew who he was.

"This is my friend Rob Smith." Taavi gestured to the young man. "He's been on the island about a year, and is staying at my place right now." Taavi introduced Mandy and Ken.

Ken got up and held out his hand. "It's nice to meet you, Rob."

"Same here." Rob shook Mandy's hand as well. He looked back at Ken.

"Taavi says you two have been friends a long time."

Ken nodded. "We struck up a friendship soon after my folks moved to the island."

"How long ago was that?"

"I was ten at the time. Of course, when I met Mandy and we fell in love, I moved to her hometown in Indiana. We lived there a little over two years." Ken dropped his gaze. "We came here a few months ago when my dad had a heart attack. After his death, Mandy and I decided to stay and help my mom run Dad's organic chicken farm."

"I see." Rob shifted his weight and looked over at Taavi. "You about ready to go?"

Taavi shook his head. "We just got here, and we haven't told Ken what we came for yet."

Ken gestured to the vacant chairs on the lanai. "Take a seat, and tell me what's up."

"If either of you would like a glass of juice, please help yourself." Vickie pointed to paper cups and a pitcher of guava juice on the glass-top table.

"Thanks, Mrs. Williams." Taavi took a cup and poured himself some juice, but Rob shook his head.

Mandy couldn't help noticing how Taavi's friend kept rubbing his hand over the top of his pale blue shorts. Was he nervous about something or just anxious to go?

After Taavi emptied his cup, he leaned closer to Ken and tapped his shoulder. "The reason we stopped by is to invite you to join us on the beach. Because of the offshore winds, the waves are just right for surfing this morning. So how 'bout? Can't be a better time for hittin' the waves."

"Sounds like fun, but I shouldn't be out on the water when there's work to be done here. In fact, I've taken a long enough break."

Taavi flapped his hand. "Aw, come on. When was the last time you got out your board and rode a few waves?"

Ken shrugged. "It's been a while."

"The last time you went surfing was before you moved to Indiana," Ken's mother interjected.

Mandy reached over and clasped Ken's hand. "We've done all our morning chores, so I think you should go. You've been working hard and deserve some down time."

Vickie's head moved up and down. "Your wife is right, Son. We can manage for a few hours without you. Please go with Taavi and Rob and have a good time."

Ken lifted both hands in defeat. "Okay, I can see I'm outnumbered here."

Mandy smiled. She was glad he'd given in and agreed to go. Maybe tomorrow, or some other day soon, she'd take time off and go looking for shells, the way she and Ellen used to do during their time together on Kauai.

Middlebury

"It's good to have you back in the store." Ellen stood behind the stool where her father sat at the counter and placed her hands on his shoulders.

He reached back and patted one of her hands. "It's good to be back, but are you sure you don't want to keep working here? We're busy enough for three workers, and I can let Lenore go."

Ellen stepped around so she could see his face. "Lenore enjoys helping in the store, and there's no need for both of us to continue working here. Besides, I heard a job might be opening at one of the hotels nearby, so I'd like to apply for that."

"No problem." Dad smiled. "You should be happy doin' whatever you want." He glanced at Ezra, as he fitted one of their church members for new shoes. "Don't know what I would have done during my recuperation if you and Ezra hadn't taken over here. That young man is a hard worker. He seems to enjoy working with shoes."

Ellen nodded. *He also enjoyed telling me what to do.* She glanced at the clock. "It's almost closing time. Would you mind if I leave a little early? I have a few errands to run and want to get to the stores before they close."

Dad shook his head. "No problem, Daughter. Go on ahead. Lenore can ride home with me."

"Danki, Dad. I'll see you both at supper."

Ezra finished helping his customer about the same time Ellen left the store. He had heard most of the conversation she'd shared with her dad about quitting the store and finding another job. *Shoulda figured it was coming,* he told himself. It didn't take a genius to see Ellen wasn't happy working here. No doubt she'd been happier at Mandy and Ken's bed-and-breakfast. He remembered Ellen saying how she enjoyed managing the B&B and that there was no other place she'd rather work.

Ezra reached around and rubbed a knot in his lower back. *It's probably my fault she's leaving. No doubt I drove her away.*

He felt like giving himself a swift kick in the pants. *Guess I have no idea how to win a young woman's heart—especially Ellen's. Maybe I'll never establish a relationship with her or any other woman. I could end up being a lonely bachelor all my life.*

Ezra glanced at Lenore as she swept past him with a broom. *She'll probably be married and starting a family before I find a woman who's interested in me.*

Ezra knew he was giving in to self-pity, but he couldn't help it. He'd botched things up with Ellen and might never get another chance.

Of course, Ezra reasoned as he headed down the men's aisle to put a pair of shoes back on the shelf, *I might see Ellen at the next young people's singing. Maybe I'll get up the nerve to offer her a ride home afterward.* Other times when the chance came, he chickened out. At the last singing a few weeks ago, he'd tried to approach Ellen, but her friend, Sadie, came along and invited Ellen to ride home with her and her brother, Saul.

"Maybe it was for the best," Ezra muttered under his breath. "She might have said no, anyways."

Kapaa

Ken enjoyed the gentle rolling of the ocean waves. It felt good to be back on his board. He'd almost forgotten the pleasure he felt when the only thing between him and the powerful ocean was the board beneath his feet. Ken lay on his stomach and paddled with his hands. *I've sure missed this. Wish I had more free days to be on the water.*

He and Taavi had taken some waves together, while Rob stuck to himself. Ken didn't ask why Taavi's friend seemed so standoffish. He figured either Rob was aloof, or took some time to warm up to someone new. Besides, for the moment Ken felt an overwhelming sense of freedom. Surfing gave him a few hours away from never-ending chores, as well as the stress of missing Dad.

Ken felt one with nature as he cut through the water, gliding with no effort on his board with each wave. With the wind and spray on his face, he had a sense of flying.

After a few practice runs on smaller waves, it didn't take Ken long to regain his balance. Feeling more confident, he watched in anticipation, hoping some bigger waves would form.

Taavi had chosen a wave to take. Ken watched as his friend stood up, then disappeared on the other side of the wave. A few seconds later, Taavi reappeared, the power of the wave surging him forward until it took him a few feet from shore. Taavi then stood in waist-deep water, holding his board and waving at Ken.

"My turn now." Ken watched as the ocean swelled. He lowered himself on the board, then paddled as the swell grew bigger. Finally, he stood to ride the wave that had formed. It was his biggest one yet today.

"This is great!" he shouted, feeling weightless as the energy beneath his board moved him forward.

Skimming along the surface, Ken felt like he was part of the ocean. After riding the wave out the whole way, he waded over to Taavi, who stood waiting for him on the beach.

"Good one, Ken! Looks like ya got your surfing legs back."

"Man that felt great." Ken couldn't help smiling. "The waves are getting bigger. Are you ready to tackle another one?"

"Naw. Think I'll sit this one out." Taavi looked toward Rob, sitting on a towel. "I need to hydrate. After I get some liquid in me, I'll join you."

"Sounds good." Ken didn't waste any time returning to the deeper depths. He paddled out past where the waves were breaking and sat on his board. It was peaceful out here where the water bobbed his board up and down. Ken shielded his eyes and looked toward the beach. Taavi sat beside Rob.

Swaying and rocking with the motion of the sea, he remained seated on his board, glancing back and waiting for the next wave to form.

It feels so right, being out here again. The one thing missing is Mandy, waving to me from the beach.

Seagulls flew overhead squawking, and farther out in the ocean, Ken saw a cruise liner slowly meandering along the horizon. *A ship is what first brought Mandy over the Pacific to this island, and then eventually to me.*

Looking over his shoulder, Ken saw the formation of another wave. As the ocean stirred, he took one more glance toward the beach. He couldn't hear them, but Rob and Taavi were waving their arms and pointing at something.

They're right! This is gonna be a big wave.

He lay down on his board and waited. *Sure wish Mandy was here to see this.*

Mandy groaned and clutched her stomach. She hadn't felt well all morning. She'd had some mint tea earlier, but it did nothing to settle her stomach. She'd gone to her room to lie down, while Vickie did some business paperwork.

Mandy lay on the bed, staring at the ceiling and listening to the zebra dove's distinctive sound through the open window. The soft breeze moved the curtains, as the gentle smell of plumeria drifted through the room. In some ways she wished she'd gone to the beach to watch Ken and the others surf. But then, feeling this nauseous, it wouldn't have been much fun.

Mandy's thoughts turned toward home. Mom had called yesterday, telling Mandy she'd be having surgery on her heel, due to plantar fasciitis that hadn't responded to more conservative treatment. She wouldn't be able to walk for a while, allowing time for healing. Mandy wished she could be there to help out, but Mom said she'd have plenty of help from other family members and friends like Ellen's mother, Nora.

Mandy thought of Ellen and wondered what she was doing right now. It would be late afternoon in Middlebury. Her friend might be helping her mother with supper or doing some chores.

Mandy remembered the first time she and Ken had been on the beach together, watching Taavi surf. It was thrilling yet frightening to observe the way Taavi kept his balance on the board and rode the high waves. Ken liked to surf too, and she'd been equally enthralled watching him. Surfing in the ocean, where danger could lurk, was not for the faint of heart. Even though Mandy had learned to swim, she'd never wanted to surf. She couldn't imagine being out where your feet didn't touch the bottom.

Another wave of nausea coursed through Mandy's stomach. She drew in a slow, deep breath and let it out, hoping to squelch the unpleasant feeling.

She placed both hands on her stomach and closed her eyes. *I wonder if I could be pregnant. Wouldn't it be something if I was carrying Ken's child?* The only problem was Ken needed her to help with the chickens, and if she were expecting a baby and continued to feel ill, she might not be up to helping. Perhaps Vickie would hire someone to assist Ken.

As the nausea settled down, Mandy relaxed. *Maybe if I sleep awhile, I'll feel better when I wake up.*

Mandy was close to drifting off when her cell phone rang. She reached over to the nightstand to pick it up. "Hello."

"Mandy, it's Taavi. Something horrible has happened."

"What's wrong, Taavi? You sound really upset."

"It. . .it's Ken—he was attacked by a shark. The ambulance came, and they're taking him to the hospital. You and Mrs. Williams had better get there right away. I hate to say this, Mandy, but it doesn't look good."

Chapter 15

Lihue

*P*acing the floor, Mandy shivered and rubbed her hands over her bare arms. *I wish Ken hadn't gone surfing with Taavi and his friend this morning.* The waiting room offered no privacy. Several others crowded the room, waiting for news about their loved ones having surgery.

Mandy crumpled the tissue she held so tight that the veins on top of her hand stood out. *If my husband dies, I'll blame myself for encouraging him to go surfing.*

Vickie sat stone faced, staring straight ahead. *Since she urged Ken to join his friends, I wonder if she's also blaming herself. Poor Vickie. She's still trying to deal with her husband's death, and now one of her sons has been critically injured. If Ken doesn't make it, his mother will be devastated, and so will I.*

Tension grew as time passed. It was hard to think clearly. Mandy wanted to be with her husband—see for herself if he was alive. But several doctors and nurses were working on him, so Mandy, Vickie, Taavi, and Rob had been ushered into this room to await the verdict.

Dear Lord, she prayed, *please don't let my husband die.* She placed both hands on her stomach as a wave of nausea hit. *What if I'm pregnant and never get the chance to tell Ken he's going to be a father?* One negative thought followed another.

As soon as they'd arrived at the hospital, Vickie had called Ken's brother in California to let him know what happened, Mandy phoned Luana and Makaio. They assured her they'd be praying and would notify their pastor, who would put it on the church prayer chain. Luana said she and Makaio would come to the hospital soon.

Mandy called her folks to tell them what had happened to Ken and left a message. She wished they could be here right now, but with Mom's foot surgery, travel was out of the question.

She'd also called Ellen and left a message, asking for prayer. *The more people praying for Ken, the better.*

She looked at Taavi, sitting with his head down and hands pressed against his forehead. "Taavi, would you please tell us with precise detail how the shark attack occurred?" When they'd first gotten to the hospital, Ken's friend had been so shook up that his account of things had been sketchy.

Vickie leaned in to listen, her eyes glistening with tears. "Yes, please explain what happened to my son."

Taavi lifted his head and looked at them with a grim twist to his mouth. He sat several seconds, before beginning to speak.

"I'd gone back to the beach after riding some waves with Ken. Rob sat on a towel by our cooler. While we enjoyed a breather, we took turns watching Ken through the binoculars. You could see it written all over his face—he was in his glory, having fun anticipating the bigger waves." Taavi paused before continuing. "Then I saw it—a large fin, cutting through the water in Ken's direction."

Vickie's tears spilled, and Mandy's vision blurred as she reached for her mother-in-law's hand. She almost felt faint visualizing the scene.

"Taavi and I were waving our arms, trying to get Ken's attention," Rob interjected. "I'm guessing he thought we were pointing at the big wave that started forming behind him."

Taavi spoke again. "Then just as he lay down on his board and started paddling, I saw the fin once more, right next to Ken's board. But before we could call out to him, the shark attacked. The water all around Ken turned red." He paused and gulped in some air. "Rob and I grabbed our boards, while Ken fought hard. When we reached him, the shark was gone."

Rob's head moved slowly up and down. "I've never seen so much blood in all my life."

Mandy felt bile rising in her throat, and she swallowed hard to push it down. She couldn't imagine what Ken must have gone through.

"By the time we got him to shore, someone had called 911, and people swarmed around, offering assistance," Rob interjected. "One man who applied a tourniquet to your husband's arm said he had survived a shark attack once himself."

"You risked your own lives to bring my husband to shore. I'm at a loss for words." Mandy shuddered. The ocean wasn't safe. Neither Ken nor his friends should have been out surfing today. What was supposed to be a fun day had turned into a tragedy.

"Mandy and I are grateful to you." Vickie dabbed her eyes with a tissue.

A doctor entered the room, bringing Mandy and Vickie to their feet. "Mrs. Williams?"

"I'm Ken's mother." Vickie motioned to Mandy. "And this is his wife."

Mandy stepped forward. "How's my husband? Is he going to be okay?"

His brows knit together. "Ken suffered severe lacerations and might lose his left arm. The shark bit his side and left leg too."

"But my son will be okay, right?" Vickie's voice sounded shaky.

"We're doing all we can, but our biggest concern is infection. We'll be taking him into surgery soon, but depending on the extent of his injuries, he may be faced with more surgeries in the days ahead." The doctor hesitated a moment, as if weighing his words. "If you're a believer, it wouldn't hurt to send up some prayers."

"We're both Christians," Vickie was quick to say. "And we believe in the power of prayer."

He nodded.

Soon after the doctor left, Luana and Makaio arrived and hurried over to hug Vickie and Mandy. As Luana gently patted her back, Mandy began to sob. "What if Ken doesn't make it? What if..."

"He's on the prayer chain, Mandy." Luana's voice was soothing. "Many prayers will be said on Ken's behalf. We must have faith and trust that God's will is done."

"Ken is young and strong," Makaio put in. "I believe he will make it. And I don't want you or Vickie to worry about anything. I'll go over to the farm and take care of things this evening."

"Don't worry about that." Taavi jumped up. "Rob and I will go. One or both of us will make sure the chickens are fed and watered for as long as you need our help."

"That means a lot to me." Vickie looked at Taavi and Rob. "Thank you for rescuing my son. Who knows what could have happened if you hadn't gone out to him."

Mandy dried her eyes on the tissue Luana gave her. She moved close to Vickie and gave her a hug. "God knows how much we both need Ken, so we have to believe He will answer our prayers."

Vickie nodded. " 'For we walk by faith, not by sight,'" she quoted from 2 Corinthians 5:7.

"Yes," Luana agreed, "And we must keep the faith."

Middlebury

"Did you or Dad check for phone messages yet?" Ellen asked her mother as they finished doing the breakfast dishes Tuesday morning.

Mom shook her head. "I haven't been out, and your daed was in a hurry when he and Lenore left for work this morning, so I doubt he took the time to check either."

"That's right. There's a sale going on at the store right now. No wonder he wanted to leave early." Ellen picked up another dish to dry. "Bet they'll be busy from the minute the store opens till closing time."

"Did you ask if your help was needed today?"

Ellen shook her head. "I didn't think about the sale until now. Guess I could drop by and see if Dad would like my help."

Mom smiled. "Good idea."

Ellen finished drying the last of the dishes and put them away. "I'm going out to the phone shack to check for messages. When I come back inside I'll get ready and head to the shoe store."

"Danki, Ellen. I hope it doesn't mess up any plans you've made for today."

"Not really. The only thing I'd wanted to do was stop by the restaurant and say hi to Darla and Ruby. Since they're both working the breakfast shift today I thought maybe I could visit with them during their break."

"Are you hoping there might be an opening at the restaurant?" Mom asked.

"No. I'm going to wait and see what happens with the hotel position that's supposed to open soon."

"You miss your job at the B&B, don't you?"

"Jah, but I miss Mandy more. It's not the same with her living so far away." Ellen moved toward the back door. "I'm heading outside now, Mom. Be back soon."

Ellen's flip-flops snapped across the graveled driveway as she made her way to the phone shack. Her nose twitched at the charred scent left over from their barbecue pit, where they'd roasted marshmallows the previous night. It was fun to spend time with her family gathered around the fire, singing and enjoying their toasted marshmallows spread between graham crackers and pieces of chocolate. Someday when Ellen had a family of her own, she hoped there would be many evenings of fun, food, and fellowship. For her and many others in their Amish community God came first and family second. Ellen's dad often said, "Put the two together and you have the key to satisfaction and happiness."

Ellen tipped her head back and looked up when a beautiful cardinal swooped past, landing in a nearby tree. It reminded her of the red-crested cardinals she'd seen in Hawaii, but only their heads were red.

Ellen's thoughts went to Mandy. She hadn't heard from her in a few days. No doubt, she and Ken were keeping busy.

Ellen reached the phone shack and stepped inside. The light on the answering machine blinked, so she pushed PLAY to hear their messages.

"Ellen, it. . .it's Mandy. Something horrible has happened." Ellen heard sniffling. "Ken was attacked by a shark while surfing." Another few seconds of silence. "Oh Ellen, he lost so much blood. I don't know anything definite yet, but it's bad, and I'm worried that Ken may lose his arm. He could even die if—" Mandy's voice broke on a sob. "Please pray, Ellen. I've left a message with my folks, and could you ask others to pray too? I'll call again, when I know more."

Ellen sat in stunned silence, barely able to take it all in. Her fingers touched her parted lips as tears pricked the back of her eyes. *Poor Mandy. I wish I could be with her to offer support. And Ken—what he went through must have been terrible.* Ellen couldn't fathom the terror he must have felt. Just the idea of being on the ocean's surface, not knowing what creature might lurk beneath, sent a tremor of fear through her body.

Why can't I be with her? I'll ask the church leaders if they will give permission for me to fly to Kauai so I can go right away.

Chapter 16

Lihue

*M*andy yawned and stretched her arms out to the sides. Her body ached from sleeping in a half-sitting position all night. She glanced over at Vickie. The poor woman hadn't slept much either. How could they get any restful sleep slouched in hospital chairs next to Ken's bed?

The doctor had said the surgery went well, but due to extensive wounds, it was too soon to predict if Ken was out of the woods. Their first goal had been to stop the bleeding and stitch and reattach what they could with Ken's arm and leg wounds. The physician added that Ken needed to rest and stay immobile to let the stitches and staples heal the torn tissue. Another surgery would happen soon.

A lump formed in Mandy's throat as she stared at her husband's motionless form. He'd drifted in and out a few times, but hadn't fully regained consciousness. She longed to speak to Ken—tell him she was here and that everything would be all right. She'd never felt as helpless as she did now.

Ken's mother needed support as much as Mandy. Losing her husband was reason enough for her not being able to cope, but now she was confronted with this situation. Mandy hoped she and her mother-in-law would get enough rest to keep up the ongoing vigil.

In addition to worrying about possible infection setting in, Mandy was concerned that Ken might not be able to use his arm as he once had.

Mandy closed her eyes. *Dear God, please bring us through this uncertain time in our life.*

Mandy's cell phone vibrated, and she pulled it out of her skirt pocket.

Realizing it was from Ellen, she rose from her chair and tiptoed out of the room to answer the call.

Middlebury

"How is Ken doing, Mandy?" Ellen twisted her head covering ties around her fingers. She'd been praying and hoping Ken would get the best care available.

"He's out of surgery and in his room, but it's too soon to tell if his arm or leg will fully heal." Mandy's voice sounded far away—as though she were talking in a box. "Oh Ellen, I'm so scared. I wish we hadn't come back to Hawaii. If we'd stayed in Middlebury, the shark attack wouldn't have happened."

Ellen could almost feel her friend's pain. She wished she could reach through the phone and hug Mandy.

"I'm going to see our ministers today and ask for permission to fly so I can come to Kauai and be with you."

"You'd really come all that way?"

"Of course. You're my best friend, Mandy. Since your mother can't make the trip, I want to be there to offer the support you need."

"It would mean so much to me if you were here."

Ellen shifted on her chair inside the phone shack. "I talked to my folks about this, and they're okay with me going. Dad said in some cases our ministers have allowed a person to fly when a friend or relative is faced with a crisis."

"Can you afford a plane ticket? I'm sure it won't be cheap—especially if you're planning to leave soon."

"Please let me worry about everything. You have enough to be concerned with right now. I'll call you back once I know for sure that I'm coming." Ellen struggled not to cry. "We're all praying here, Mandy. And if everything goes well, I'll see you soon."

"Thank you, Ellen. You have no idea how much this means to me."

"I'm certain if I were faced with a similar situation, you'd be there for me."

"Yes, I would."

"All right then. Talk to you soon."

When Ellen hung up, she remained in the phone shack. *Heavenly Father, please be with Mandy, Ken, and his mother. Give Mandy and Vickie patience and courage to deal with everything they must face. And when I approach the ministers in our church district, I ask that they would be in one accord and grant me permission to fly.*

Ellen drew a quick breath. *If the ministers give their consent, please give me the courage to get on the plane that will take me to Kauai.*

Lihue

Ken groaned, and Vickie woke up with a start. Her heart pounded as she watched her son's head thrash about. "Shark! Shark!" It was unbearable for Vickie to hear Ken's panicked words.

She jumped up and stood by his bed, speaking in a soft tone and offering reassurance that he was safe. But Ken continued to moan, and then he cried, "Help! Somebody, help me, please!"

Although he was heavily sedated, Ken seemed to be reliving the attack. Vickie picked up his hand and caressed it gently, hoping it would bring her son comfort in his restless state. The attack must have been a horrible experience, and now Ken was living through the emotional anguish of the event all over again.

With a sense of urgency, she released his hand and pushed the CALL button. A few minutes later, a middle-age nurse entered the room. Before she could say a word, Vickie stood up. "My son is in pain. Will you please give him something?"

The nurse shook her head. "It's not time yet. We don't want to overmedicate."

Vickie's nails pushed into the palms of her hands. It was all she could do to keep from screaming. "Didn't you hear what I said? Ken is in pain. He's been groaning and thrashing about."

The nurse checked Ken's vitals. For the moment, at least, he'd stopped groaning. "According to the doctor's orders, the patient will receive more pain medicine through his IV in thirty minutes." She looked at Vickie and offered a sympathetic smile. "Is there anything I can bring you—a cup of coffee or some tea?"

"No thanks." Vickie returned to her chair. The only thing she wanted was the assurance that her son would be okay. Ken loved to surf. Would he ever go in the water again?

She waited until the nurse left, then took her cell phone from her purse. Despite having told her eldest son about Ken's situation, Vickie hadn't heard whether Dan would be coming or not. *Surely he must realize how much I need him right now. If he were as concerned about his brother as he said when I told him what happened, he would have booked the first flight to Kauai.*

Although Dan didn't like hospitals, surely he'd want to be here when his brother was in need—not to mention offer his mother support. The boys were not close growing up, but Vickie had hoped they'd find some common ground as they matured. One son wanted to be inside most of the time, reading or on the computer. The other boy could have lived on the beach.

Vickie's fingers clenched around the phone. *It's too bad Ken isn't more like Dan—then he wouldn't have gone surfing.*

Vickie leaned back in the chair and closed her eyes. *Poor Mandy. Except for me, she has no one to be with her during this time. I should be more reassuring, but right now I can barely hold my head above water.*

She dialed Dan's number. He answered on the second ring. "Hi, Mom, I'm glad you called. I was about to phone you."

"Oh?" Vickie felt a ray of hope. Maybe Dan would be coming after all.

"I'd planned to catch a flight out this morning, but my wife got sick. Don't know if it's the flu or what, I wouldn't feel right about leaving her."

"What about her folks? Can't one of them stay with Rita?"

"No, it should be me."

Vickie rubbed her forehead. "Maybe once she feels better, you can come."

"We'll see." Dan paused. "How's Ken? Is he gonna be okay?"

"I hope so, but it's too soon to tell."

"Well, please keep me informed."

"Yes, of course." Vickie wondered if her son heard the regret in her tone. She understood Dan's need to be with his wife, but she needed his support right now.

A few minutes after Vickie hung up, Mandy entered the room. "I just talked to my friend, Ellen. She is going to speak to the church leaders and ask for permission to fly here."

"That's nice. I'm sure you'll appreciate her support." Vickie bit the inside of her cheek. *I wish my oldest son cared enough to come and support me.*

Chapter 17

Over the Pacific Ocean

$\mathcal{L}$eaning into her neck pillow, Ellen tried to relax. With nothing except white puffy clouds to view out the window, all she could think about was the fact that she was on an airplane, bound for Hawaii. At times she'd have a tight grip on the armrest, like now, as the plane hit some turbulence.

She remembered when the plane left Seattle, looking out the window, she could see majestic Mount Rainier. It was breathtaking. They didn't have anything like that back home in Indiana. What a beautiful view for the folks in Washington State to appreciate.

When the plane hit another bump, she shifted in her seat and looked away from the window. *It's best not to think about it. Focus on something else, like the flight attendant suggested earlier.*

She removed the airline magazine from the seat pouch in front of her. Mandy had flown a couple of times and was probably used to it by now. For Ellen, though, this was a new experience—one she wasn't going to forget.

Ellen thumbed through the magazine, then returned it to the pouch. Reaching under the seat in front of her, she lifted her tote bag and withdrew a journal. The last entry she'd posted had been yesterday when she'd flown from South Bend, Indiana, to Chicago, then on to Seattle, where she'd spent the night at a hotel near the airport. Both flights had been fairly smooth.

Another bump caused Ellen's stomach to feel queasy. She hoped she wouldn't get sick, like she had on the cruise ship to the Hawaiian Islands a couple of years ago.

Ellen opened her journal and began to write, while nibbling on a handful of pretzels. The time for this trip was about five and a half hours. She figured they were almost halfway there.

Her nerves heightened when the flight attendant announced that the pilot was going around a storm causing some of the turbulence. The passengers were instructed to keep their seat belts buckled.

Ellen glanced out the window and saw a flash of lightning in the distance. In an effort to focus on something else, she flipped back in her journal to the day she'd heard Mandy's message about Ken's shark attack. She had met with the ministers of her church district that evening and gotten permission to fly, since it was an emergency situation to help a friend. While not all Amish districts would have allowed such a thing, she was glad hers did, because another trip by train, and then on a ship, would have taken too long.

Once the decision had been made for Ellen to make the trip to Kauai, she'd hired one of their drivers to take her to a travel agency in Goshen. Mandy's parents had given Ellen the money for her ticket, since Mandy's mother was unable to travel and appreciated Ellen's willingness to go in her place.

Ellen was glad her own parents hadn't tried to dissuade her from making the trip. Mom and Dad understood her need to be with Mandy during this difficult time. Ellen's friends, Sadie and Barbara, had also been encouraging, saying they wished they could join her.

Ellen had made up her mind that she would remain on Kauai for as long as her friend needed her. Since she had no job to go back to and had purchased a one-way ticket, there was no reason to hurry home. Once Ken recuperated sufficiently, she'd purchase a ticket home.

Middlebury

"You okay, Nathan?" Ezra stepped up to the counter where his boss sat staring at a pair of men's shoes a customer had decided not to purchase.

Nathan looked up at him and blinked. "I'm fine. Just sitting here, thinking is all." He put the shoes inside the box and peered out the window as a buggy drove by.

Ezra was tempted to ask what his boss was thinking about but didn't want to appear nosey. He figured Nathan might be mulling over something related to his shoe store. Or he could be wondering how Ellen was doing. With her flying on a plane for a long distance, Ellen's parents were bound to be concerned.

Ezra gestured to the shoebox. "Want me to put that back on the shelf for you?"

Nathan shook his head. "That's okay. I'll take care of it. I need to stretch my legs anyway." He stepped out from behind the counter and pulled out his pocket watch. "I bet Ellen's almost to Oahu by now. She'll change planes there, and should arrive on Kauai sometime after three o'clock, Hawaii time."

Ezra's lips pressed together as he lowered his head. Apparently he wasn't the only one thinking about Ellen. *Why did she have to take off for Hawaii?* Ezra kept his thoughts to himself. He understood that she wanted to help, but there must be other people Mandy could call on.

Ezra shook his head. *I'm being selfish. I want Ellen here so I can see her and keep trying to work up the nerve to ask her out.*

He headed toward the storage room to see if Lenore had finished unloading the boxes of shoes that had come in earlier. Ellen's sister was young and a bit immature, but she always did as she was told.

When Ezra entered the storage room, he was surprised to see Lenore on the floor with her head bowed and eyes closed. He wondered if she might be asking God to give Ellen a safe journey.

He didn't want to interrupt, so he stood still. He couldn't get over how much Lenore resembled Ellen in appearance. But the sisters' personalities were nothing alike. Ellen seemed more serious and wanted everything to be just so. Lenore, on the other hand, tended to be carefree and a bit disorganized.

Ezra slipped out of the room. *I need to get busy and quit letting my thoughts wander all over the place.*

Lihue

Ellen's face broke into a wide smile when she approached the baggage claim area and saw Luana and Makaio waiting for her.

Luana opened her arms with a welcoming smile. "Aloha, Ellen!"

Tears welled in Ellen's eyes as she stepped into the sweet woman's embrace. "Aloha! It's so good to see you both again."

"It's good to see you as well." Makaio greeted Ellen with a warm hug. "So glad you could return to the Garden Island. Your *ohana* welcomes you back."

Ellen sniffed and swiped at her tears. Seeing Makaio and Luana again was like coming home to family. During the months she and Mandy had stayed with the Palus, Ellen had felt like part of their ohana.

"Which one is yours?" Makaio asked as people's luggage began moving along the conveyor belt.

"It's that one." Ellen pointed to a black suitcase with a green strap around the middle.

As though it weighed no more than a feather, Makaio swooped it right up. "Any more?"

Ellen shook her head. "I packed light and got everything I'll need in one suitcase." She lifted her tote bag. "My purse is in here, along with my journal and some snack food."

Luana slipped her arm around Ellen's waist and gave her a tender squeeze. "We have a room ready for you at the B&B, and it's yours, rent free, for as long as you decide to stay."

"Thank you." Ellen teared up again. "I never thought I'd be coming back to Kauai—certainly not under such unsettling circumstances. How is Ken doing?" she asked as they headed for the parking lot.

"Not well, I'm afraid." Luana's forehead wrinkled. "It's been three days since his surgery, and he's still pretty much out of it. I don't believe he's been able to talk to Mandy and give her the details of the shark attack." Luana paused. "I can hardly think about what happened to Ken. It must have been dreadful. From what Mandy told us, the doctor felt the surgery went as well as could be expected. They're keeping him sedated, but his prognosis. . . Well, it's too soon to tell."

"There's still a chance he could lose his arm," Makaio interjected.

Ellen's chest tightened. "Poor Mandy. I can only imagine how hard this must be for her. Ken's mother too. I'm anxious to see them."

"If you're not too tired, we can go by the hospital now." Makaio opened the trunk and put Ellen's luggage inside.

"I'm fine. I slept some on the plane." Despite the sleep she had, Ellen was exhausted from the long trip, not to mention the time change. But there was no way she could go to bed tonight without first seeing Mandy.

Chapter 18

$\mathcal{Y}$ou look like you're about to cave in," Vickie whispered to Mandy. "Why don't you go out for some fresh air and a snack? I will stay by Ken's bedside, and when you come back I'll take a breather."

"Okay." Mandy leaned close to the bed and kissed her husband's hot forehead. He'd been running a fever for the past three days, and it had not abated.

Clutching her purse in one hand, Mandy left the room. As she approached the nurse's station, she spotted Ellen coming down the hall with Luana. Mandy quickened her footsteps. It was all she could do to keep from running full speed ahead to greet her friend. And if she hadn't been in a hospital, that's exactly what she would have done.

"Oh Ellen, it's so good to see you." Choking back tears, Mandy enveloped her friend in a hug. "I can't thank you enough for coming." She pulled back to gaze at her friend's smiling face.

"It's good to see you too. I'm glad I was given permission to come." Ellen looked over at Luana. "I'm also thankful to Luana and Makaio for giving me a room at the B&B while I'm here."

"We're happy to do it, Ellen." Luana touched the yellow plumeria flower nestled close to her left ear.

"Where is Makaio?" Mandy asked, looking past Luana.

"He's hunting for a place to park the car." Luana shook her head. "I've never seen so many vehicles in the hospital parking lot. It's almost full."

Mandy clasped Ellen's hand. "Let's sit in the waiting room until Makaio gets here. Then we can all go to the cafeteria to visit and get something to eat." She glanced at the clock behind the nurse's station. "It is almost suppertime. I'm sure you must be hungry."

Ellen nodded. "But I'm more anxious to hear how Ken is doing."

"I'll wait for Makaio near the hospital's front door, so he knows where you are." Luana gestured to the waiting room on this floor. "You two go ahead. Makaio and I will join you when he gets here. If Ken's mother is here, maybe she'd like to have supper with us too."

Mandy nodded. "Vickie's with Ken. We've been taking turns sitting by his bedside, so she probably won't eat till I go back to the room."

Luana gave Mandy's shoulder a pat. "When Makaio was in the hospital with a broken leg a few years ago, I didn't want to leave his side either. Of course," she quickly added, "his injuries weren't nearly as serious as Ken's."

Mandy breathed slowly in and out, as a wave of nausea coursed through her stomach. If she was pregnant, why did her nausea occur at odd times of the day?

"I'm off." Luana smiled, then headed down the hall.

When they entered the waiting room, Mandy felt relief that no one else was there. It would be easier to talk.

"You look tired," Ellen commented after they'd both taken a seat. "What can I do for you, Mandy?"

Mandy clasped her hand. "Right now, just knowing you're here is enough."

"How is Ken doing?" Ellen asked.

"He's running a fever and has been in and out of consciousness, but is never coherent enough to make conversation." Mandy sniffed. "Ken mumbles a lot and sometimes yells out." She shuddered. "Oh Ellen, it must have been awful for him, being in that water and under attack. Taavi and Rob have told us what they saw from the beach and when they rescued Ken, but we won't know the whole story until he's able to talk."

Ellen squeezed Mandy's fingers. "I'm so sorry you, Ken, and Vickie are going through this. I keep asking myself why things like this happen."

"I'm trying to keep the faith and believe God will heal my husband, but my fear gets in the way, making it hard to hope for the best."

"It would be hard for anyone in a similar situation. It might help to focus on Psalm 31:24—'Be of good courage, and he shall strengthen your heart, all ye that hope in the Lord.'"

Mandy tipped her head back and closed her eyes. *Thank You, Lord, for bringing Ellen here and for the reminder of Your Word.*

Kapaa

Ellen rolled over in bed, squinting against the sun's rays peeking through the partially open plantation shutters. She felt disoriented until she became fully awake and realized she'd spent last night in a cozy room at the Palms Bed-and-Breakfast. After leaving the hospital last evening, Ellen had visited with Luana and Makaio for a while. Then, unable to keep her eyes open, she'd retired to her room and fallen into a deep sleep.

Ellen lay in the same bedroom with the twin beds she and Mandy had used the last time they'd stayed. The place looked the same, with the pretty Hawaiian quilts covering the beds. The paintings of palms, beautiful scenery, and flowers still hung on the walls.

Ellen smiled, remembering the mornings she and Mandy woke up and talked about home and their families. Then they'd clamber out of bed and hurry to the kitchen to help Luana make breakfast for the guests.

She tipped her head, hearing voices coming from the kitchen. No doubt, Luana had begun fixing breakfast.

Ellen rose from the comfortable mattress and padded across the cool tile floor to the window. Opening the shutter slats a bit more, she gazed at the beautiful flowers in Luana's garden. The rich orange-red color of the hibiscus called to her, as did the lovely off-white plumeria. While the flowers at home in Mom's garden were lovely, none took her breath away like the tropical flowers found on the Hawaiian Islands.

The tantalizing aroma of food drew Ellen's attention away from the pleasant scene. *I must hurry and get dressed so I can help Luana.*

A short time later, Ellen found Luana at the stove, frying sausage and eggs, while Makaio sat at the kitchen table, reading the newspaper.

Luana turned from the stove, and Makaio looked up from his paper. "Aloha. *Pehea 'oe?*" they asked.

"Hello. I'm doing well." Ellen was glad she still remembered some of the Hawaiian words Makaio and Luana had taught her and Mandy.

Luana pointed to the pitcher of pineapple juice on the table. "Please, help yourself. The eggs and sausage will be ready in a few minutes."

Ellen poured herself a glass of juice and took a sip, letting it roll around on her tongue before swallowing. This was no store-bought juice. Luana had obviously squeezed it from a fresh pineapple. "Is there anything I can do to help?"

Luana shook her head. "Not this morning, at least."

"There's something you can help me with." Makaio glanced at his wife, then back at Ellen.

"What would you like me to do?" she asked.

"You can have a talk with my *wahine* and convince her to fix Spam for breakfast every day." He winked at Ellen. "Luana knows it's my favorite breakfast meat, yet she fixes it so seldom."

Luana puffed out her cheeks, while wrinkling her nose. "You know that's not true, Husband. You're such a big tease."

"Just wanted to see if I could get a reaction." He chuckled and pointed at her. "And see there. . .it worked."

Luana lifted her gaze to the ceiling. "Look what I have to put up with, Ellen. When you find the man of your dreams, I hope for your sake he's not such a jokester."

Makaio held up his hand. "Ha! You like my teasing, and you know it, Luana."

Ellen laughed. "Some things certainly haven't changed around here. You two are so much fun."

" 'A merry heart doeth good like a medicine,' " Luana quoted Proverbs 17:22.

" 'But a broken spirit drieth the bones.' " Makaio finished the verse.

"It's good to laugh." Ellen sighed. "Especially when we're faced with unpleasant things."

"You mean, like Ken's shark attack?" Makaio questioned.

She nodded. "I'm eager to go back to the hospital and find out how he's doing today."

"And we shall—right after breakfast." Luana set the platter of eggs and sausage on the table.

"Do you have time to go? I could always call a taxi to take me to the hospital."

Luana took a seat and motioned for Ellen to do the same. "We don't have any B&B guests scheduled today, so I have plenty of time on my hands."

Ellen smiled. She appreciated this couple's humor, hospitality, and generosity. If anyone could make a person feel loved, it was Makaio and Luana Palu.

"Those chickens sure produce a lot of eggs," Rob commented as he and Taavi headed down the road in Taavi's Jeep with several boxes of well-packed eggs, as well as a cooler full of fresh chicken. They'd dropped a dozen eggs off at a widow's house and were now heading for a bed-and-breakfast also on the list.

Taavi and Rob had gotten up early this morning and stopped by the organic chicken farm to see what Vickie wanted done. It was Rob's first time at the farm, and he'd been curious what the place looked like. The Williamses' home was large, and so were the chicken houses.

After Vickie gave them a list of places to deliver eggs and chicken, she'd asked Rob if he wanted a full-time job, saying it could be some time before her son was able to work again. Since Rob was currently unemployed, he'd jumped at the chance. Most of the work would be done there at the farm, and he'd pretty much be on his own. It would be better than having a job where he had to deal with finicky folks, like the people he'd served when he worked at a restaurant several months ago. That wasn't the kind of work he enjoyed. Rob would much rather be outside, where he could soak up the sun and be surrounded by nature.

"Whatcha thinkin' about?" Taavi nudged Rob's arm.

"Not much. Just glad I have a full-time job."

"Yeah. I was glad when Vickie asked you to work full-time. I don't mind helping out when I can, but with my job at the hotel and the odd hours I work, I may not be available to help at the farm that much."

"No problem. I'm sure I can handle things on my own."

"Maybe, but both Mandy and Ken were working there before, so—"

"Hey, who's that?" Rob pointed to a young woman dressed in plain clothes, sitting on the front porch of a stately looking home. A sign above the door read: The Palms Bed-and-Breakfast.

Taavi leaned against the steering wheel and squinted. "Well, what do you know? I think that's Ellen Lambright, from Middlebury, Indiana. Sure never expected to see her here again."

As Taavi pulled his rig onto the driveway, Rob kept staring at the woman. Even from this distance he could see she was pretty. "Is she Amish?" he asked, turning to face Taavi.

"Yeah." Taavi turned off the engine and set the brake. "I'm surprised you knew that, though."

Rob gave an undignified huff. "Come on, Taavi. Who doesn't know about the Amish? I've seen some of those Amish reality shows."

Taavi tipped his head. "Do you think they're real? I mean, I doubt they're portraying the Amish correctly."

Rob shrugged his shoulders. "Who knows? Ya can't believe half of what you see on TV these days." He hopped out of the Jeep and went around back to grab the cooler. "Guess we'd better take the chicken and eggs inside so we can be on our way. According to the list Vickie gave us, we've still got several stops to make."

"We can't just drop them off and leave right away. At least not here; it would be rude," Taavi explained. "We won't stay long, but these folks are great people. I'll introduce you to Ellen too."

Rob remained silent. The last thing he needed was any distractions.

Chapter 19

*C*arrying a box of chicken, Rob followed Taavi up the back stairs and onto the lanai, where several lounge chairs had been placed. Too bad he didn't know these people. It would be a nice place to relax and unwind. The house had a small view of the water. Not that the cramped rental he and Taavi shared was unbearable. It just didn't offer all the pleasing comforts this place had.

Taavi shifted the box of eggs in his hands and knocked on the door. He seemed to be careful to avoid the elaborate seashell wreathe decorating the door.

A few seconds later, a tall Hawaiian man appeared. "Aloha, Taavi!" He grinned. "Bet ya brought us some eggs and chicken."

"Sure did." Taavi stepped inside, and Rob followed. After they'd set their boxes on the kitchen table, Taavi turned to Rob. "This is Makaio Palu. He and his wife, Luana, are the owners of the B&B. Makaio, this is my friend and roommate, Rob Smith."

Rob shook hands with Makaio. "It's nice to meet you." He thought this fellow seemed friendly and engaging right off the bat, in his tropical shirt with his shark tooth necklace.

Makaio's handshake was hearty. "Good to meet you too."

"Vickie Williams hired Rob to work at the farm, so you'll probably be seeing a lot of him in the days to come. At least till Ken's able to work again." Taavi's words were optimistic, but not his tone.

"We'll look forward to getting acquainted with you." Makaio glanced toward an open door, leading to a hallway. "My better half is on the phone right now, but she should be coming into the kitchen shortly to do some baking. If you have a few minutes to spare, please wait. I'm sure she'd like to meet you."

Rob glanced at Taavi. "What do you say? Do we need to go now or did you want to hang out for a while?"

"We do have a few more deliveries to make, and I have to be at work soon, so. . ."

Taavi's sentence was cut off when a dark-haired, pleasant-looking woman appeared, along with the fair-skinned Amish woman Rob had seen on the front porch.

Taavi made the introductions, pointing out that Luana was Makaio's wife, and Ellen Lambright, a friend of Mandy's, was staying with them.

The Amish woman gave Rob a shy smile, then put the eggs and chicken in the refrigerator.

"Would either of you like a glass of juice?" Luana asked. "I have fresh pineapple and orange this morning."

"Orange sounds good to me." Taavi looked at Rob. "How 'bout you?"

"No thanks, I'm good." Rob glanced at Ellen when she joined them again. "Is this your first time to the island?" From what Taavi said earlier, Rob already knew it wasn't, but he didn't want Ellen to know they'd been talking about her.

"Actually, my friend Mandy and I were here a couple of years ago." She took a seat at the table. "We didn't make it back to the cruise ship on time, and it left without us. Makaio and Luana graciously took us in. Due to unforeseen circumstances, we ended up staying here a few months."

"That must have been kinda scary."

"It was at first, seeing the ship leaving without us and not knowing what awaited Mandy and me." Ellen smiled. "Makaio and Luana were very gracious to help us out in our time of need."

Luana stepped up to Ellen and placed a hand on her shoulder. "They were both a big help to us—especially when Makaio fell from a ladder and broke his leg. We thanked God for sending them to us at exactly the right time."

These folks must be religious. Rob shifted uneasily. *Think it might be time for me to go.* He turned to Taavi. "If you're finished with your juice, I think we ought to hit the road."

"You're right. We should be on our way." Taavi put his juice glass in the sink. "Thanks for the drink. It was nice seeing all of you."

"Yeah, same here." Rob followed Taavi across the room, but when he reached the door, he looked over his shoulder at Ellen. Her vivid blue eyes matched the color of her plain blue dress. It was hard not to stare. *I bet she's spiritual too.*

With a farewell wave, Rob hurried out the door.

Lihue

The minute Ellen saw Mandy in the hallway outside Ken's room, she knew something was wrong. Mandy's face looked puffy, and her eyes were wet and dull.

Ellen clasped Mandy's hand. "Is Ken worse?"

Mandy pressed a fist against her chest. "He's fighting an infection, and when the doctor came in this morning he said Ken may end up losing his arm, despite the surgery." She blinked, pulling in a quick breath. "They are still dealing with his other wounds. The doctor said the swelling and fever need to go down before they can do more surgery."

"Oh Mandy, I'm so sorry." Ellen rubbed her friend's back. "We need to pray harder for Ken."

"I've been praying." Mandy's chin trembled as she looked upward. "I've done nothing but pray since I was notified of the shark attack. I don't understand why God isn't answering my prayers."

As her friend's shoulders began to shake, Ellen reached out and pulled Mandy into her arms. They stood like that as Mandy released heart-wrenching sobs.

Ellen waited until the tears subsided. Remembering the hospital's chapel down the hall, she guided Mandy in that direction.

When they entered the small room, Ellen was relieved that no one else was there. At the moment, she was at a loss for words. But maybe sitting with Mandy in the chapel would help her find the right words to give Mandy some encouragement and much-needed hope. *How can I explain why one person's prayer is answered and another's isn't? But then,* she reasoned, *all prayers are answered. Some, just not the way we would like.*

After they'd taken a seat on one of the benches, Ellen took Mandy's hand. "One of our church's ministers preached an inspiring sermon a few months ago. He said, 'When we pray, God will answer in one of three ways. Yes. No. Wait.' Maybe God is asking you to wait. Sometimes when a person has to wait for an answer to prayer, they grow in their faith."

Mandy slowly nodded. "Your minister was right, but I'm just struggling right now. Ken and I have only been married a couple of years, and we've never faced anything so traumatic."

"With God's help, you'll get through it."

"Thank you, Ellen. I don't know what I'd do without you right now." Mandy swiped at the tears on her cheeks. "So who brought you to the hospital today?"

"Luana dropped me off. She has some errands to run but said she'd come up when she's done."

"Vickie's in with Ken now." Mandy twisted a piece of her shoulder-length hair around one finger. "I was getting ready to go to the cafeteria for lunch when you arrived. Will you join me?"

Ellen nodded. "Of course. We can talk more while we eat."

Mandy stared at the untouched tuna salad on her plate. When she'd ordered the item for lunch, it had appealed to her, but now, as a wave of nausea hit, she could barely look at the salad.

"What's wrong?" Ellen pushed her chair in closer to the table. "Aren't you hungry?" Mandy placed both hands on her stomach. "I've been feeling queasy for several days, and I missed my monthly." Her voice lowered. "I think I might be pregnant."

"Have you seen a doctor or done a home-pregnancy test?" Ellen spoke in a tone of concern.

Mandy shook her head.

"Does Ken know what you suspect?"

"No. I wasn't going to say anything till I knew for sure." Mandy groaned. "Now, with his accident, I can't say anything until he's better."

"I understand, but. . ."

"You're the only person I've told, so please don't mention it to Vickie, or anyone else."

"Of course not. It's your place to share the news."

"If there is any news. It might be all the stress I'm under playing havoc with my hormones."

"Could be, but you won't know unless you take a pregnancy test." Ellen flicked back her narrow head covering ties.

"You're right. I'll pick one up soon." Mandy took a sip of water. After she set the glass down, she breathed deeply through her nose. It seemed to help some.

"What can I do to help out while I'm here?" Ellen asked. "Coming up to the hospital isn't enough."

Mandy took a small bite of salad. "It is enough, and I appreciate the support, but if you'd like to do more, we could use some help at the farm with the chickens."

Ellen's brows lowered a bit. "Didn't Vickie hire someone to help out? I met him at Luana and Makaio's this morning when he and Taavi delivered eggs and chicken."

"Yes, Rob is working there, but he's taking Ken's place. Before the accident, both Ken and I were caring for the chickens." Mandy dropped her gaze. "Now that I'm at the hospital most of the time and not feeling well, I can't do much at the farm."

Ellen leaned closer. "Would you like me to take over for you? Since my folks have raised chickens—although on a smaller scale—I can probably figure out what to do."

Tears welled behind Mandy's eyes. "You wouldn't mind?"

"Not at all. I can start by helping with this evening's chores. After Luana gets here and has visited with you and Vickie for a while, I'll ask her to take me back to the B&B so I can change into my everyday dress, and then I'll head over to the organic farm."

Kapaa

Rob heard the gate to the chicken enclosure open, and he turned to see who'd come in. He was surprised to see the Amish woman he'd met at the bed-and-breakfast. "Can I help you with something?"

"I'm here to help."

"Huh?" Rob rubbed one side of his temple.

"I saw Mandy earlier, and when I asked if there was something I could do to help, she mentioned taking her place out here."

Rob's eyes narrowed. "You mean working with the chickens?"

"Yes."

"In those clothes?" He pointed to her brown dress, and then the matching scarf on her head.

"These are not my good clothes. It's what I would wear if I were at home doing chores."

Rob's forehead wrinkled. "This is a dirty job. You should wear a pair of jeans and some work boots, not a dress."

"I'd never put jeans on, but I'd wear boots if I had some." Ellen pursed her lips. "I'll bet there's a pair of Mandy's in the chicken house I can borrow."

Rob lifted his hands in defeat. This woman clearly had a mind of her own.

"Come on, then—follow me and I'll show you where the chickens go during the night."

"I know where it is, because I've been here before." Ellen folded her arms. "Ken gave Mandy and me a tour of the place when we were staying with Luana and Makaio a few years ago."

Rob tapped his foot impatiently. "But have you ever worked here?"

"No, but then you haven't worked here very long, either."

"True, but I've had a little experience with chickens."

"Oh? Where did you learn about raising chickens?"

"From my grandparents."

"Oh. Do they live here on the island?"

"Nope. I've only lived here a short time myself." Rob started walking. "Now let's get busy and get the chicken house cleaned."

Coming up to the chicken house, Ellen spotted a pair of rubber boots. "Those are Mandy's work shoes. I'll use them."

Rob paused to watch Ellen switch from her shoes to Mandy's boots.

"There, that's better, don't you think?" She looked up at him and smiled.

Rob nodded and followed her into the chicken house. *Sure hope she doesn't talk my ear off while we're cleaning the place. The last thing I need is to listen to a bunch of idle chatter or be asked a bunch of questions I'd rather not answer.*

Chapter 20

*T*wo days had passed since Mandy mentioned to Ellen that she might be pregnant. As she drove home from the hospital to get some rest, she decided to find out. Mandy couldn't even think how she would be able to take care of a baby too. Her mind swirled with continuous questions, but she needed to keep her focus on the road.

Mandy slipped on her sunglasses. The stress had brought on a headache.

As she drove on, Mandy barely noticed the fresh smell of salty air reaching her nostrils. Even the fragrant flowers blooming along the way didn't faze her. Her senses were on hold. All focus was on Ken and finding out if they were in the family way.

At the light, Mandy had time to take a refreshing drink from the water she'd purchased in the vending machine on her way out of the hospital. Her heart clenched. *Will he be happy if I am pregnant? What if he can't hold the baby because of his arm? What if he doesn't get better and the Lord chooses to take him from me?*

"Please, Lord, don't take my husband. If I'm carrying our child, this baby needs his daddy," Mandy whimpered out loud.

When the light turned green, she focused on the road. *I'm giving in to negative thoughts again. Why can't I pray, believing?* So much for the pep talk Ellen had given her two days ago. Mandy's thoughts bounced like a rubber ball, and her emotions were all over the place. *I should think positive thoughts.* Mandy willed herself to seek them out—something as simple as being thankful it was Ken's left arm that was injured, and not his right. *At least my husband won't have to learn to write with his other hand. And Ken is still here. He's a fighter. He just has to make it.* Mandy swiped at tears running down her cheeks.

Except for the chapel in the hospital, Mandy hadn't been to church since Ken's accident. Could that be why she felt so disconnected from God? It took all her energy to go to the hospital each day, sometimes spending the night. Surely the Lord, as well as everyone at church, understood her reasons for not being in church these days.

Mandy was glad when the pharmacy came into view. At least now she had something else to think about. She pulled Ken's rig into a parking space, shut the engine off, and got out.

Unfamiliar with where the pregnancy tests were located, once inside, Mandy sought a clerk for directions.

In addition to the test kit, she purchased a few items they were running low on. These days Mandy spent most of her time at the hospital, so there wasn't much time for running errands.

Moving down the last aisle, she grabbed a travel-size toothpaste and brush kit. She could easily store it in her purse, which made it convenient for the overnight stays at the hospital.

Mandy paid for her items and hurried from the store. She was eager to get home and take the test. One way or the other, she needed to know.

Middlebury

Nora pulled back on her horse's reins and guided the mare up to the Freys' hitching rail. She'd come to pay a call on Mandy's mother, Miriam. *I wonder how my friend is coping with her daughter being so far away and needing support.*

Nora set the brake and sat for a moment. *It's one thing to send my daughter to help out, but at least she'll be coming home. Don't know what I'd do if Ellen ever decided to move away—or worse yet, leave the Amish faith.*

Nora got out of the buggy and secured her horse. Then she reached into the buggy to make sure things were secure in the box of food she'd brought from home. Since Miriam was still recuperating from foot surgery, friends and neighbors had been bringing in meals to help out. Today was Nora's turn. In addition to preparing supper for Miriam, Isaac, and their three boys who still lived at home, Nora was eager to find out how Mandy's husband was doing.

Walking up to the house, she noticed the pristine flowerbeds. Despite Miriam being laid up for a while, her family had been pitching in to keep things watered and weeded. Of course, most Amish helped one another when there was a need. Nora liked the ways of their church, and how their ministers fed them spiritually. She was happy to be a part of it.

When Nora stepped onto the porch, the front door opened, and fourteen-year-old Melvin greeted her. "Come in. My mamm said you'd be comin' today."

Nora smiled in response. "Are you taking good care of her?"

"Jah, she's resting inside."

"That's good. Lots of rest is good for her right now." Nora took a step, then stopped. "Oh, there's a cardboard box in my buggy. Would you mind taking it into the kitchen?"

"Sure, no problem. Mom's in the living room. If you wanna visit her, I'll put the box on the kitchen table." Melvin leaped off the porch before Nora could say thank you.

She entered the living room and found Miriam on the couch, her foot encased in a special boot-like apparatus and propped on a stool. "How are you doing?" Nora took a seat beside her friend. "Are you able to put any weight on your *fuuss*?"

"Jah, but I still have to wear this cumbersome boot and use my *gricke*." She gestured to the crutches leaning beside her against the sofa.

"I bet you'll be glad when your foot has healed and you can get back to doing everything you did before the surgery."

"I'm counting the days." Miriam frowned. "It's hard to sit in one spot and look out the window when I want to do things in the garden." She repositioned her booted foot. "I've never been one to sit around."

"Just give it some time. You'll get better before you know it."

"How are things at your place?" Miriam asked.

"I painted the bathroom yesterday but need to put things back in place later on today."

"You're a busy gal, for sure."

Nora smoothed her dress. "I brought everything to make supper for your family. But is there anything else I can do for you while I'm here?"

"I can't think of anything right now. Sadie and her mamm came by yesterday and did the laundry. They also picked produce from my garden." Miriam shifted her leg again on the stool. "The day before that, the bishop's wife and two other ladies from our district came over and did some cleaning. And lots of folks have brought in food."

"It's nice to be a part of a caring community."

"That's for sure. One of our English neighbors said she knows many people who aren't fortunate to have good friends and neighbors."

Nora's forehead wrinkled. "I can't imagine how that would be. The friendships we've established in this community are tried and true."

Miriam reached over and patted Nora's arm. "Jah, and they even reach all the way to Hawaii. I can't tell you how much I appreciate your daughter going there to be with Mandy. It's meant a lot to her and me as well. It's hard to be away from family—especially when there's a need."

Nora nodded. "I miss Ellen, but she's where she needs to be right now."

Kapaa

Ellen headed for the house. She and Rob had worked up quite a thirst, and she'd told him she would get them something cold to drink.

She looked down at Mandy's boots and noticed how dirty they were. She would clean them later, but for now she just removed the boots before going inside.

When Ellen entered the kitchen, she heard muffled sobs coming from the adjoining room.

She stepped into the dining room, where she found Mandy at the table with her head down and hands up to her face. Her sobs tore at Ellen's heart.

"What's wrong?" She placed her hands on Mandy's trembling shoulders. "Has Ken's condition worsened?"

Mandy lifted her head and took a deep breath. "I took a home-pregnancy test. It was positive."

Ellen pulled out the chair next to her friend and sat. "Congratulations! Aren't you excited?"

"I am, but with Ken still in serious condition, this news is bittersweet." Mandy pulled a tissue from her skirt pocket and blew her nose. "I can't even tell him he's going to become a father."

"Maybe not now, but when he gets better." Ellen rubbed her friend's shoulder.

Mandy's gaze lowered. "You mean, if he gets better. What if Ken loses his arm, or his leg never heals properly and he can't work again? What if—"

"There you are, Ellen. What's takin' so long with the water?" Rob marched up to her with hands on his hips. "I'm dyin' of thirst. What happened—did ya decide you've had enough work for the day and quit on me?"

Ellen ground her teeth together. *Doesn't Rob see how upset Mandy is?* She was tempted to give him a piece of her mind, but she didn't want to upset Mandy any further. *I quit working for Dad because Ezra was so bossy, and now I'm stuck dealing with Rob. Seems I may have gone from a hot kettle into the fire pit.*

Chapter 21

Seeing Ellen's face tighten, Rob realized he'd spoken too harshly. He pulled off his baseball hat and laid it on the nearby counter. *Boy, I'm sure not being careful about my tone. Think I'd better lighten up.* He glanced at Mandy and noticed her red face and tear-stained cheeks. "Are you okay? Is your husband worse?"

She sat, seeming to collect her thoughts. "He's the same as before." Mandy rose from her chair. "Excuse me. There are some things I need to do." She glanced at Ellen, then fled the room.

Ellen stood too. "I'll get your water, Rob." She headed for the kitchen and he followed.

"That's okay. I'll get it, Ellen." Rob made a beeline for the refrigerator, took out two bottles of water, and handed one to Ellen. "Sorry for speaking in a harsh tone to you when I first came in."

Ellen took a drink of water before she spoke. "I appreciate your apology."

"I shouldn't have been so demanding."

She nodded.

Rob wondered if she was still upset. Her eyes avoided his as she fiddled with the ties to her cap, looking everywhere but at him. He opened his bottle and drank all of it, then took a seat at the table. "Mind if I ask you something?"

"Not at all." Ellen looked at him.

"How long are you planning to stay on the island?"

Ellen pulled out a chair and sat across from him. "I'll be here for as long as Mandy needs me."

"Is everything okay with her today? When I saw her in the dining room, it seemed like she may have been crying."

"Mandy's going through a rough time. A lot of people are praying for her and Ken, so I'm trusting God that everything will work out."

He fingered the checkered tablecloth. "Do you believe in the power of prayer?"

"Yes. Don't you?"

No. God let me down when I needed Him the most. Rob kept his thoughts to himself. Pushing the chair aside, he stood. "I've had enough of a break. How about you? Are you ready to get back to work, or would you rather stay inside for a while where it's cooler?"

"I'm ready too."

"Okay, great." Rob raced for the door and held it open for her.

Ellen offered him the sweetest smile. "Thank you, Rob."

Mandy lay on her bed, staring at the slow-turning ceiling fan. Learning that she was expecting a baby should have been a most joyous occasion, and she felt guilty for not being more excited.

What will Ken say when I tell him he's going to be a daddy? I'm sure Vickie and my folks will be glad to hear this news.

Mandy touched her stomach. It was amazing to think a new life was growing mere inches from where her hand rested. *Ken and I will become parents in less than nine months.* She rolled onto her side. *Why did I encourage him to go surfing with his friends?* Mandy had twisted and turned that horrible day into so many different scenarios. But going over and over it didn't change what had happened.

Mandy had looked forward to the day she would surprise Ken with the news that they were expecting their first child. It would have been so special—just the two of them, alone and uninterrupted. Mandy's dream never included her husband lying in a hospital bed before learning he was going to be a father.

So many decisions fell on her now, but she didn't feel up to making any of them. All Mandy wanted to do was sleep. Despite her exhaustion, she couldn't turn off her concerns.

Mandy sat up and lifted her Bible from the nightstand. She turned to Isaiah 41, which she'd marked with a peach-colored ribbon. She read verse 13, which was underlined: *"I the Lord thy God will hold thy right hand, saying unto thee, Fear not; I will help thee."*

She clutched the Bible to her chest. *Help me, Lord, to remain calm and remember Your blessings.*

Mandy got off the bed. She needed to get back to Ken and relieve his mother. First, she would call her parents and leave a message. She wanted to give them an update on Ken and share the news of her pregnancy.

Later that evening as Ellen cleared the supper dishes at the bed-and-breakfast, she thought about Rob and how nice he'd been to her this afternoon. She couldn't get over how he'd apologized for acting bossy—and the pleasant way he'd spoken to her as they worked in the chicken house.

Nothing like Ezra. He was never pleasant to work with. Ellen didn't know why she was comparing Ezra to Rob. There was no chance of a relationship with either of them. Ezra wasn't her type, even though her mother spoke highly of him whenever the opportunity presented itself.

If Mom knew I was interested in Rob, who's English, she'd say I should nip it in the bud.

Well, Mom need not worry. There's no chance of me developing a relationship with Rob either. When I leave Kauai, Rob will go on with his life, and I'll return to mine in Middlebury. Ellen had to admit she felt drawn to Rob, even though she didn't know much about him.

Determined to concentrate on the job at hand, she grabbed a spoon and put the leftover green beans in a plastic container.

Ellen glanced at Luana, busy loading the dishwasher. *I wish I could tell her about Mandy's pregnancy. But it's not my place to say anything. Mandy will share the news when she feels ready.* Ellen put the beans in the refrigerator. Mandy hadn't even told Ken yet, which was sad, because her husband should have been the first to know. Ellen could only imagine what it felt like to be in her friend's position.

"You've been quiet this evening. Even the jokes Makaio told at the supper table didn't make you laugh," Luana mentioned when Ellen handed her a few more dirty dishes. "Are you tired from putting in a hard day at the farm?"

"Not too much. It was a pretty easy day. I'm just worried about Mandy and Ken." Ellen wet the dishrag and began wiping the kitchen table.

"We're all concerned, but worry won't change a thing." Luana folded her hands. "Remember the remedy for worry?"

Ellen nodded. "Prayer."

"Exactly."

"I've been sending up lots of prayers since Ken became injured, but sometimes worry creeps in."

"How well I know. I've had plenty of things to worry about over the years. But fretting never changed any of my circumstances. All it did was stress me out."

"I felt that way when Mandy and Ken moved to Kauai and I was left to run their B&B. At first I thought it was only temporary. But when they decided to sell, my stress level increased."

Ellen finished wiping the table and put the dishrag on the drying rack. "I enjoyed my responsibilities at the B&B and wanted to buy their business. But of course I didn't have enough money for even a small down payment."

Luana tipped her head. "Does Mandy know you wanted to buy it?"

"No. I saw no point in telling her, since I couldn't afford it. I'm just glad for Mandy and Ken's sake that it sold right away. At least they don't have to worry about mortgage payments anymore. They probably didn't get much from the equity they'd built up in the two years they owned the B&B, but whatever they made should help pay some of Ken's hospital bills."

Luana poured detergent into the proper receptacle and closed the dishwasher door. "I hope they don't have to use any of it. They're going to need money for their future. Who knows—if Vickie should decide to sell the farm, Ken and Mandy might want to buy a house of their own."

"Do you think they would move back to Middlebury?"

"Unless Vickie were willing to move to the mainland, I doubt they would leave her." Luana pursed her lips. "If that brother of Ken's had stayed here instead of running off to California because he couldn't deal with his dad's death, Vickie would have all the help and support she needs." She shook her head. "I doubt Ken will be back to work anytime soon."

When Vickie entered the house, she found Mandy on the couch, holding her cell phone. She turned to face Vickie with raised brows. "I'm surprised to see you. I assumed you wouldn't come home until I returned to the hospital."

"Ken's asleep, so I decided to get a few things done here before I go back."

"I thought we were taking turns." Mandy placed the cell phone in her lap.

"That was the plan, but the nurse gave Ken a pretty strong sedative, so there's no point in either of us being there right now." Vickie studied her daughter-in-law's pale face and red-rimmed eyes. "We both need a good night's sleep in our own beds tonight. Do you agree?"

"It would be nice, but. . ." Mandy's voice trailed off.

Vickie took a seat beside Mandy. "Is something other than Ken's situation bothering you?"

Mandy gave a slow nod. "I have some news."

"Oh? Is it about the farm?"

"It's about me. I took a home-pregnancy test earlier today. It was positive."

Vickie sat several seconds, letting her daughter-in-law's words sink in. Then she pulled Mandy into a tight hug. "That's wonderful! We needed some good news." She dabbed at the tears trickling down her cheeks. "Have you told your folks?"

"I called a few minutes ago and left them a message."

"Ken's going to be so excited about this when he wakes up and you share the good news." Vickie leaned in closer.

Mandy shook her head. "I'm not going to burden him with this right now."

"Burden him? What do you mean?" Vickie bit down on her bottom lip. "Knowing he's going to be a father will give my son a reason to get well."

"You heard the doctor say Ken has a long recovery ahead. I don't need him worrying about me." Mandy clasped Vickie's arm. "Please don't say anything to Ken about my pregnancy. I should be the one to tell him, but not till I feel he's ready."

"You're right, it is your place to give Ken the news, but I hope you won't wait too long." Vickie didn't understand Mandy's reasoning, but she would keep quiet and let Mandy do the telling.

Chapter 22

Lihue

$\mathcal{M}$andy sat beside Ken's bed, looking at the book about Hawaiian customs she'd purchased in the hospital gift shop. If Kauai was to be her permanent home, she wanted to know everything about its origin, the ways of the people, and anything that might be of interest. If her parents or any of her friends or extended family in Indiana ever came to visit, she would share her knowledge of the island with them.

Mandy longed to be with her family, although it did help to have Ellen with her.

Sighing, she set the book aside and placed both hands against her stomach. *I wonder if Mom and Dad will come when the baby is born. It would be wonderful to see them. Since it wouldn't be considered an emergency, they wouldn't fly, but maybe they'd come by boat.*

She glanced over at Vickie, dozing in her chair. *At least Ken's mother will be here to see her new grandchild when it's born.*

"Mandy. . ."

She jerked her head in Ken's direction, pleased to see his eyes were open. She leaned close to his bed and clasped his right hand.

"Wh–where am I?"

"You're in the hospital."

"What day is it?"

"July eighth. You've been here for thirteen days." Mandy squeezed his fingers. "Do you remember what happened?"

"Yeah. It was a shark that got me, but everything's kinda fuzzy." Ken moved his head from side to side. "How bad am I hurt?"

Before Mandy could respond, Vickie woke up, wide-eyed. "Oh Ken, it's so good to see you're fully awake." She left her chair and moved closer to the bed, then leaned down to kiss his forehead.

"Hi, Mom."

"How are you feeling, Son? Are you in much pain?"

Ken grimaced. "Yeah." He looked back at Mandy. "How bad are my wounds?"

"There are lacerations on the left side of your body that include your arm, side, and leg." Mandy blinked to keep from shedding tears. She needed to remain strong for Ken's sake. "You've had surgery on your arm, and your leg will be next. It's been a slow process due to an infection that set in."

"Guess I'm in a real mess. Not worth much to anyone right now."

Mandy lifted Ken's uninjured hand and kissed it. "You're worth the world to us. We're so happy you're alive."

"Taavi and Rob told us what they saw from the shore. What do you remember about the attack?" Vickie questioned.

Ken groaned and closed his eyes for a few seconds. "I'm not sure how accurate it is, but this is what I remember: I was on my board, getting ready for a big surge. Then I saw Taavi and Rob waving at me and pointing. I thought they were trying to tell me the huge wave I'd been waiting for was coming. But then I felt a bump against my board." Ken paused, sweat beading on his forehead.

"It's all right if you don't want to talk about it." It was hard for Mandy to see her husband's pained expression.

"It's okay." He took a deep breath. "After the bump, I was knocked into the water. As I swam toward my board, a fin surfaced. Then the shark came toward me." Ken looked at Mandy, his eyes wide with fear. "It was like it happened to someone else when the shark took a bite out of my arm. I felt numb—no pain, as I fought back, kicking and punching at him. Then the shark pulled me under, biting into my side, and shaking me like a rag doll. When I saw blood rising to the surface, I thought for sure I was a goner."

Mandy's throat constricted. She tried to imagine the horror of what Ken went through.

"When I kicked at the shark, its sides felt like cement," he continued.

"It had to be a miracle, because the shark gave up and let go. But in my exhaustion and with the loss of blood, I couldn't even swim. If it hadn't been for Taavi and Rob, I'd have either drowned or bled to death." Ken groaned as his eyes glazed over. "The whole time I kept thinking, 'I'll never see my family again.'"

Vickie put her finger against his lips. "That's enough talk now. You need to rest." She looked at Mandy. "Would you please call a nurse to give Ken something for pain? It's clear he's hurting."

Mandy's hand trembled as she pushed the CALL button. It scared her beyond reason, listening to the horrible ordeal her husband had gone through. How the big beautiful ocean could hold so much terror was beyond comprehension.

When the nurse came and gave Ken something for the pain, Mandy sat in silence and watched him drift off. She couldn't help wondering if he would ever go in the water again. The emotional trauma of what he'd been through would no doubt be with him for a long time.

Kapaa

"I'm glad you suggested we take a break for lunch, 'cause I'm hungry." Rob stepped into the kitchen behind Ellen.

She turned to look at him and smiled. "Some people don't work well on a full stomach, but if I don't eat regular meals, I tend to get shaky."

He lifted his hand toward her, then quickly lowered it. "Do you have diabetes?"

"No, it's nothing like that. I've noticed my blood sugar drops if I don't eat, though I don't have any other symptoms of diabetes. The last time I had blood work done, the results came back within normal limits."

"A friend from when I was in school had juvenile diabetes, and he paid close attention to his diet." Rob opened the refrigerator and took out his and Ellen's lunch sacks.

When they approached the table, Ellen spotted a note from Vickie. She picked up the paper and read it out loud: " 'Ellen and Rob, if you finish your work this afternoon and would like to cool off, feel free to use the pool.'"

Rob pulled out a chair and sat down. "A swim sounds great, but I'd have to go back to Taavi's place and get my swim trunks." He leaned forward, resting his elbows on the table. "What about you, Ellen? Do you have a swimsuit?"

"I do, but it's at the bed-and-breakfast. Guess I can walk over and get it."

"Okay!" Rob slapped his palms together. "After we eat, let's finish up what we were doing, and then we'll get our suits and meet back here."

Ellen smiled. The idea of taking a dip in the pool on this hot day sounded great. And although she would never admit it, so did swimming with Rob.

When Rob returned, wearing his swim trunks under a pair of shorts, he was surprised to see Ellen in the pool. He stood on the deck and tried not to stare. Ellen's backstrokes were graceful, but powerful. She was a strong swimmer, and looked good in her modest, but attractive blue swimsuit.

He removed his shorts and draped them over one of the lounge chairs, then stepped onto the pool ladder. *Sure hope I don't say or do something stupid. Don't know why, but I feel like a schoolboy right now, with a crush on his teacher.*

Once in the water, Rob swam toward the deep end. He'd only made it halfway, when he bumped into Ellen. "Sorry about that. Are you okay?"

"I'm fine." Her face turned pink as she treaded water in front of him. "How about you?"

"No injuries here, but I should have been watching where I was going." Rob figured his face might be red too.

She gave a small laugh and swam in the other direction.

They remained in the pool about an hour, swimming, diving, and splashing each other. Rob couldn't remember when he'd had such a good time or felt so relaxed. He was disappointed when Ellen got out of the pool.

"If you're hungry, come join me for some cookies." Ellen slipped on a terry cloth cover-up, then gestured to a tray sitting on one of the small tables.

Rob hadn't noticed it until now. Of course, her beauty kept him focused, because he hadn't taken his eyes off Ellen since he showed up at the pool. Too bad she was Amish.

He got out of the water and wrapped a towel around his waist. "Where'd the cookies come from?"

"Luana sent them when I went for my swimsuit. They're made with coconut and macadamia nuts." She pointed to a pitcher of iced tea. "I found that in Vickie's refrigerator. Since she told us this morning we should help ourselves to any beverages, I figured it would be all right if I brought out the tea." She poured two glasses and handed one to Rob.

He grinned and took a drink. "Thanks. This hits the spot."

Rob wished the day didn't have to end. He could get used to lounging around the pool—especially with such a pretty companion. Ellen might be Amish, but she was anything but plain.

"You've never said much about your family or mentioned where they live." Ellen picked up a cookie and took a bite.

"They live on the mainland, in the same old house they've lived in for years." Rob lifted his glass and took a drink. The cold tea felt good as it slid down his parched throat. He was on the verge of asking Ellen about her family, when the outside telephone rang. Ellen rose from her seat to answer it.

When she returned to the table, her wrinkled forehead let him know something was wrong. "What's up?"

"That was Mandy. Ken woke up and was able to talk."

"Well, that's good."

"Yes, but the doctor came in and gave them some bad news."

Chapter 23

*R*ob looked at Ellen. "What's the bad news? Has Ken gotten worse?"

With furrowed brows, Ellen nodded. "Even though he's awake and talking, the infection in Ken's arm has gone deeper, and if they don't get it cleared up, he could lose his arm."

"Aren't they giving him antibiotics for that?"

"Yes, but they're going to start him on a stronger one. Also, his leg needs surgery, so Ken's recuperation is a long way off."

"Sorry to hear it." Rob shuffled his bare feet under the table. "I can't imagine what their hospital bills will be like."

"It is a concern, but I believe their needs will be met." She picked up her glass and set it on the tray. "I'd like to go to the hospital to be with Mandy. Would you be able to give me a ride?"

"Sure, if you don't mind riding on the back of my motor scooter. It's not as big and intimidating as a motorcycle, but it'll get us there."

"I have no problem with that. I'll go inside, put the snacks away, and change into my dress."

"Sounds good." Rob set his glass on the tray. "I'll use the pool house to change. As soon as we're ready, we'll be off."

"I only have one helmet, but you're welcome to wear it," Rob said as they approached his motor scooter.

Ellen shook her head. "That's okay. I'll tie my scarf over my white kapp to hold it in place."

"I'm not as worried about your bonnet as I am your safety." Rob looked at Ellen as if he were sizing her up and down. "You sure you're up for this?"

"Of course."

Rob climbed on his bike and turned to Ellen. "Okay now, you need to approach the bike from the left side. Then place your foot on the foot-peg and swing your body over the seat—sorta like you're getting on a horse. You can put your hands on my shoulders for balance if you need it."

Feeling more than a bit awkward, Ellen followed his instructions.

"Now place your other foot on the second foot-peg and sit up straight. Now put your hands around my waist and hang on tight."

Ellen's insides quivered as she placed her hands around Rob's middle. Was the nervousness she felt from anticipation of riding the scooter, or could it be the nearness of him?

Rob looked over his shoulder. "Make sure when I lean that you lean with me. And when I stop for a light, keep your feet on the foot-pegs."

"Okay."

"One more thing. Don't put your head too close to mine or we'll bump heads when the bike slows down."

"I'll do what you said." Ellen never imagined herself on the back of a motor scooter, and with an English fellow, no less.

Lihue

When they arrived at their destination, Rob told Ellen he'd wait for her in the waiting room, while she went to look for Mandy. "I'll just hang around in case you need a ride home. I mean, back to the bed-and-breakfast." He didn't understand why he felt so rattled all of a sudden. All that time with Ellen in the pool this afternoon, and now he struggled to manage a sensible sentence. *Must be the exhilaration of the ride over here.* He had to admit, having her arms wrapped around his waist felt pretty nice.

Ellen smiled. "Okay, I'll be back soon."

When she headed toward the nurses' station, Rob picked up a magazine and took a seat. He couldn't concentrate on the magazine, however. All Rob could think about was Ellen and how much fun he'd had with her today. He hadn't enjoyed the company of a woman that much since... He closed the magazine and slapped it on the table. *I can't let my mind go there again. I'm glad Ellen won't be staying on the island indefinitely, so there's no chance of us developing a permanent relationship.*

He moved over to the window and looked out at the cars in the parking lot. *Coming to this island has been good for me. It's helped me feel calm and relaxed—at least till Ellen showed up and messed with my head. Bet anything she doesn't have a clue I've been thinking about her.* Rob tapped his foot. *I wonder what she thinks about me.*

Someone tapped Rob's shoulder, and he whirled around, surprised to see Ellen looking up at him. "You're back already?"

She nodded. "I spoke to Mandy, and she wants me to stay for a while. So either she or Vickie will take me back to the B&B when one of them is ready to go home."

He pulled his fingers through the ends of his thick hair. "Okay, then. Guess I'll see you tomorrow at the farm."

"Tomorrow's Sunday, and I'll be going to church with Luana and Makaio. You're welcome to join us if you like."

"No thanks. Those squawking chickens still need to be fed, so I'll be over at the farm at least part of the day.

"I'll see you Monday morning then."

Was that a look of disappointment I saw on her face? Rob wondered as Ellen walked away. *Did Ellen invite me to church because she thinks I need religion, or could she want to spend time with me?*

Middlebury

"That was one good supper, Nora." Ezra leaned back in his chair and gave his belly a thump. "Stuffed peppers and mashed potatoes are my favorite meal. Danki for inviting me to join your family tonight."

Nora smiled from across the table. "It was nice you could come, and I'm glad you enjoyed the meal." She began collecting the plates. "We could have our desserts outside on the front porch."

"Maybe in a while, after my supper settles." Nathan patted his midsection.

"All right, we can hold off for a while." Nora picked up a few glasses.

"Can I help with the dishes?" Ezra rose from his chair.

She shook her head. "My daughters will take care of that, but it was nice of you to ask."

"Why don't the two of us head out to the living room for a friendly game of checkers?" Nathan suggested. "Unless you're not up to the challenge."

"Dad's a hard one to beat," Lenore spoke up as she cleared a stack of plates from the table.

"I'm pretty good at checkers, so jah, I'll take you on, Nathan." Ezra grinned at Lenore and winked. She was a cute girl—full of spunk.

"When you're done playing, and my daed's food settles, we'll have dessert." Lenore grinned. "We're having peanut butter cream pie."

"Well, I'll be. That's another one of my favorites."

"I know." Lenore's gaze dropped.

Ezra found the blush of pink that spread across the girl's cheeks to be kind of cute, but his thoughts went straight to Ellen, since Lenore resembled her.

Ezra rubbed the back of his neck. He'd wanted to ask about Ellen all evening but was too embarrassed to say anything in front of everyone. If he could get Lenore alone for a few minutes, he might have a chance to make an inquiry.

I could ask Nathan about Ellen, Ezra thought as he took a seat at the card table in the living room. *Maybe if I mention her in a nonchalant way, he won't catch on.*

"Have you done much fishing this month?" Nathan asked as he got the checker game from the bookcase and set it between them.

Ezra took a seat and began helping Nathan set up the game pieces. "Nah. I'd sure like to, but I don't seem to have the time."

"Maybe if we have a slow day at the shoe store, I'll close up early, and we can go fishing together." Ellen's dad placed the empty checker box on the coffee table and took a seat at the card table.

"Sounds good to me." Ezra enjoyed spending time with Ellen's family. He wished she could be here too. "Say Nathan, I've wondered what you've heard from Ellen these days. Is Mandy's husband doing any better?"

"The last we heard, Ken was still struggling with his injuries."

"That's too bad." Ezra pulled out his hanky to blow his nose. *Something in the room must be bothering my allergies.* "Guess Ellen won't be back for a while."

"She plans to stay in Hawaii for as long as Mandy needs her. Could end up to be several more months." Nathan pushed Ezra's checker pieces toward him. "Ready to play?"

"Jah, sure." Ezra's hope of seeing Ellen soon had gone out the window. He wondered if he'd ever get the chance to tell her what was in his heart. And when he got the chance, would she be receptive?

Chapter 24

Lihue

*M*andy was almost sick with worry. It had been two weeks since Ken's doctor put him on a stronger antibiotic, and today he was scheduled for another surgery. This time it involved his arm and leg.

She glanced out the window, watching the clouds billowing in the blue sky. Oh, how she wished her husband felt better.

Mandy turned away from the window and began to pace the floor of his hospital room. Was there no end in sight for Ken? *Maybe I'm not praying hard enough, or in the right way. There must be some reason God's allowing us to go through this right now.*

In addition to her husband being faced with a long recovery, the hospital bills were mounting. She'd called her folks an hour ago and left a message, asking them to return her call. *If only they could be here with me right now.*

Vickie had stepped out of the room a few minutes ago to call Dan and give him the latest on Ken. Mandy didn't understand why Ken's brother hadn't come back to Kauai, at least to see Ken and offer his mother support. It wasn't her place to judge, but she thought Dan seemed selfish. Could he have taken his father's death so hard that he couldn't deal with coming home?

Mandy looked outside the window again. A few vehicles whizzed by, with colorful surf boards tied to the roof. *I wonder if the authorities put signs on the beach, warning people of the recent shark attack.* Mandy hated to think of anyone else getting hurt if there were no warning signs posted.

She jumped when her cell phone vibrated. Seeing it was her folk's number, she stepped outside in the hall to take the call. Ken slept, and she didn't want to disturb him.

"Hello."

"Mandy, it's Dad. I heard your message and wanted to call right away."

She swallowed hard and choked back tears. "Oh Dad, it's so good to hear your voice. Ken will be going in for another surgery soon, so he could use some extra prayer."

"You've got it. I'll spread the word and get those in our church district praying."

"Thank you."

"How are you doing, Mandy? You sound like you're about to cave in."

"I–I'll be all right. I have to be, for my husband's sake." Mandy took a deep breath. She needed to get herself together and stay strong. "How's Mom doing? Is her foot healing okay?"

"Yes, she's staying off it as much as possible and wearing the boot the doctor ordered."

"That's good." Mandy blew her nose on a tissue she'd pulled from her pocket.

"Have the hospital bills started coming in yet?" Dad asked.

"Some. But there will be more in the days ahead."

"Well, try not to fret about it. I've talked to a few people in our area, and everyone wants to help. There's going to be an auction to help raise money for Ken's medical expenses."

"That will help so much. Ken and I have some money in the bank from the sale of our bed-and-breakfast in Middlebury, but with his extended hospital stay that money will be gone in no time."

"Mandy, there's no reason for you to use all your savings when others can help. With a baby on the way you're gonna need money for future expenses."

Mandy's vision blurred. She wished she could reach through the phone and give her dad a hug. His words were a great comfort to her.

Kapaa

"Sure hope I don't have to feed and water chickens the rest of my life." Rob grunted as he filled another container with fresh water. He glanced at Ellen. "Don't get me wrong—I'm grateful for this job. But it's not something I want to do forever."

She set the bag of chicken feed aside and looked up at him. "What would you like to do?"

He shrugged. "I'm not sure. Guess I won't know till I find the perfect job."

"I had what I thought was a perfect job once, but I lost it when new owners took over the bed-and-breakfast Mandy and Ken used to own."

"Did you look for a job at another B&B?" Rob continued to fill the feeders.

"I did, but there weren't any." Ellen sighed. "If I'd had the money I would have bought my friends' business and run the place myself."

He tipped his head. "You liked it that much, huh?"

"Yes."

"Sounds like a lot of work to me." He rinsed off the waterers.

"It is work, but enjoyable—at least it was for me. When I took over for Mandy and Ken after they moved here, I learned firsthand how much responsibility goes with running that type of business." Ellen's forehead wrinkled as she swatted a place on her arm.

"What's wrong? Did you get a mosquito bite?"

"Yes, and they're quite pesky today."

"There are a lot more mosquitoes during the summer months here on Kauai."

She glanced around. "In some ways, being here reminds me of home."

He quirked an eyebrow. "How could Hawaii remind you of your home?"

"It doesn't. I just meant being here and taking care of the chickens. My family has laying hens, although not this many. I'm used to caring for them."

"I see. So, do you like it here on Kauai?"

"Oh, yes. It's a beautiful place."

"Think you could ever live her full-time?"

"No, my family means too much to me." Ellen held a hand against her chest. "My home is in Indiana, and I'm a member of the Amish church, so there's no way I'd ever move to Hawaii for good."

"Oh, I see." Rob finished up with his chore, then leaned against the door frame and folded his arms. "What's it like, being Amish in Middlebury, Indiana? I mean, you dress different than the English, but does your church have special rules?"

"Yes, of course. Our regulations are taken from the *Ordnung*, passed on from our ancestors. But of course, each church district is led by a bishop, two ministers, and a deacon. They guide the congregation in making wise decisions regarding any changes to the rules."

"Hmm. . . Interesting."

Their conversation was interrupted when Taavi showed up. "I just got off the phone with Mandy," he announced. "I called to check on Ken, and she let me know that he's having more surgery today."

Ellen's eyes widened. "Really, I didn't know."

"No one did—not even Mandy till she went to see him this morning." Taavi moved closer to Ellen. "Came by here to see if you wanted a ride to the hospital."

"Yes. Yes, I do. I'll have to change out of my work clothes first." Ellen looked at Rob. "I hope you don't mind me leaving you with all the work here today, but I need to be with my friend."

"Sure, no problem. Go ahead with Taavi. I understand."

She gave him a brief smile, then hurried out the door.

Rob looked after her, slowly shaking his head. *I wonder if Mandy knows what a great friend she has. Wish I had a friend like that—someone who'd do just about anything for me. But the one person who would have. . . Well she's. . .* Rob grabbed the chicken feed and hauled it across the room, bringing a halt to his disconcerting thoughts.

Lihue

Ellen sat quietly beside Mandy in the waiting room. She'd spent lots of hours here since her arrival on Kauai. She could see out the door to the waiting room, as nurses and doctors walked past in a flurry of activity. A few patients came by, pushing their IV poles. Others were in wheelchairs that family members maneuvered down the hall.

Ellen couldn't get over how many people were sick or recovering from some sort of injury. She closed her eyes. *Dear Lord: Too often I take my good health for granted. Thank You for allowing me to get out of bed each morning and for the good health I have. Please keep me strong and healthy, so I can continue to help where I'm needed.*

And most of all, Dear Jesus, please guide the doctors' hands as they perform surgery on Ken. Bring healing to Ken's body, and strength to his wife and mother. Amen.

"I wonder how long Ken will be in surgery."

Ellen opened her eyes and saw Taavi looking over at her, as if expecting an answer. Vickie answered instead.

"It could take several more hours."

Mandy groaned. "It's hard to sit and wait when I don't know how my husband is doing."

"Waiting is always the hard part." Vickie's chin quivered. "I remember how anxious I felt when Charles had his heart attack and I could do nothing but wait and pray while he was in surgery."

Ellen wished something she could say would ease the tension everyone felt. Maybe it would help if they talked about something else. She turned to Vickie and said, "Rob and I got the chickens watered and fed before I came here. This afternoon he will do the other chores on the list you left him."

"Things would be a lot easier if I didn't own that silly farm." Vickie twisted her gold wedding band around her finger. "But it's all I have left to remind me of Charles and the memories we made there together." Her face tightened as she turned toward Mandy. "If you and Ken hadn't stayed to help me after Charles died, my son would not be in surgery right now."

"But you're family, and we wanted to help." Mandy's voice choked.

"We all have a tendency to blame ourselves when tragedy occurs," Ellen spoke up. "But often the people blaming themselves are not the ones responsible." She clasped both women's hands. "While we can't change the past, we can pray about the future. Why don't we do that now?"

They all bowed their heads, and Taavi volunteered to pray out loud.

"Heavenly Father, You know how hard it is for us to wait for news about Ken. He's in Your hands and those of the skilled doctors and nurses. We ask that You heal Ken's injuries and restore his health. In Jesus' name we pray, amen."

Hearing Taavi's heartfelt prayer caused Ellen's throat to clog. Opening her eyes, she saw moisture in Mandy and Vickie's eyes as well.

A few minutes later, a doctor entered the room. "Mrs. Williams?"

Both Mandy and Vickie stood up.

"I'm Ken's wife." Mandy's voice trembled. "And this is his mother."

The doctor nodded. "I wanted you to know that Ken is out of surgery and in the recovery room."

Mandy stepped forward. "How is he? Can his arm be saved?"

"We believe the arm will heal, but it's too soon to know about his leg. It could be six months or longer before the muscle will attach itself and establish blood flow, and with any luck, regenerate a nerve."

Ellen stood and slipped her arm around Mandy's waist. "He will be fine—you'll see. And it won't be luck. It'll be all the prayers going up on Ken's behalf."

"Yes." Vickie nodded. "We are so thankful for the prayers."

Mandy leaned her head on Ellen's shoulder. "I don't know what I would do without your friendship. Thank you for being here with me."

Ellen hugged Mandy and Vickie. "I want to help in any way I can. If there's something specific either of you want done, all you need to do is ask."

Chapter 25

The first Tuesday of August, Ellen went with Mandy to see an ob-gyn. While Mandy saw the doctor, Ellen sat in the waiting room. After almost an hour had passed, she wondered what could be taking so long.

I hope everything's all right. Ellen picked up a magazine, then set it down. *Too bad Ken can't be with Mandy this morning instead of me. What a shame he doesn't know about the baby.*

Ellen didn't feel it was fair of Mandy to keep her pregnancy from Ken. He had a right to know he was going to be a father. It would give him something to look forward to. But it was Mandy's decision to make, and she would honor it.

She picked up the magazine again, flipping through the pages of prenatal information and advertising. Ellen scanned an article about different birthing methods, as well as classes expecting parents should consider.

Instinctively, she rested one hand on her stomach. *I wonder what it would feel like to have a tiny life growing within me. If I never get married, I won't experience the joy of being a parent.*

Ellen set the publication aside, and browsed through a few more magazines. Finally Mandy came out. "How'd it go?" Ellen whispered as they headed for the door.

"I'll tell you about it when we stop for lunch on our way to the farm."

"I'm anxious to get to the hospital and see how Ken is doing," Mandy said as they headed toward the farm in his SUV. "I hope you don't mind if we eat at a fast-food restaurant. There's a place up ahead that makes some tasty fish tacos."

"It's fine with me, but if you'd rather not stop for lunch, we can eat when we get to the farm."

"Maybe that would be better. We can talk in private about everything that's going on." Mandy looked over at Ellen and smiled. "My mother-in-law always has plenty of food in the fridge, so I'm sure we can find something we like."

"Okay. Sounds good."

Kapaa

When they reached the Williamses' place, Ellen went to see how Rob was doing, then met Mandy in the kitchen.

"There's a three-bean salad, and you could use some ham slices for a sandwich." Mandy pointed to the refrigerator. "Of course we have plenty of bottled water or juice."

Ellen stepped over to retrieve the food. "Aren't you going to join me?"

"I'm not hungry right now. Maybe I'll grab a bite at the hospital later on."

Ellen closed the refrigerator and placed the bread, ham, and all the fixings on the table. "You need to keep up your strength, Mandy. Remember, you're eating for two now. And you want the baby to be healthy, right?"

"Of course, but the doctor said I'm doing fine. My pregnancy is going well, and I have another appointment set up, so you needn't worry."

"I don't mean to sound bossy. I'm concerned about you."

"I appreciate that, but my biggest concern is for Ken right now." Mandy's forehead wrinkled as she leaned against the counter. "Even though he's been doing okay since his last surgery, Ken's getting antsy waiting for them to make a cast, and then a brace, for his left leg. My poor husband wants to get out of that hospital."

"I don't blame him." Ellen took out a paper plate and a napkin. "Have the doctors said how much longer he will have to remain there?"

"It depends on how much time it takes for him to be fitted and make sure the brace is functional and supporting his leg in order to help with the attachment of the muscle." Mandy clasped her hands together. "I've decided to wait until Ken comes home from the hospital to tell him about the baby. He has enough on his mind right now." She opened the refrigerator and took out two bottles of water, handing one to Ellen. "If you don't mind, I'm going to head for the hospital right away. I'm sure by now Vickie needs a break, and I am eager to see Ken."

"No problem. I'll eat lunch and then see what Rob needs me to do outside." Ellen gave her friend a big hug. "Everything will be easier once Ken comes home. And don't forget. I'll stay for as long as you need me."

Mandy squeezed Ellen's arm. "Thank you so much. You're a good friend. Oh, and one more thing."

"What's that?"

"You've been working hard since you got here, so why don't you take some time off for yourself?"

"No, that's okay. I don't need to."

"You should see a few sights while you're on the island. Your time on Kauai shouldn't be all work." Mandy stood with her arms crossed.

Ellen dished some of the three-bean salad onto her paper plate. "I didn't come here for a vacation. I came to help out and be a support to you."

"Even so, it could be a long time before you return to Hawaii, so you should have a little fun while you're here." Mandy moved toward the door. "Just think about it, okay?"

"All right. Tell Ken I said hello. Now that he can have other visitors besides his family, I'll come see him soon. Maybe if Luana and Makaio are free, they'll want to join me."

Rob entered the kitchen and found Ellen at the table with her back to him. He had to fight the sudden urge to step up behind her chair and kiss the back of her neck. *What a dumb idea. Ellen would wonder what made me do such a thing. And how could I explain my behavior to her when I can't even justify it myself?*

Rob cleared his throat to announce his presence and was surprised when Ellen didn't turn around. He tried again, a little louder this time.

She jerked her head. "Oh Rob, I was deep in thought and didn't hear you come in. Would you like me to fix you something to eat?"

"Thanks anyway, but I brought a sack lunch with me today." He opened the refrigerator and returned to the table with a paper sack.

"As soon as you finish eating I'll help you outside with the chickens."

Rob shook his head. "No need. I've been busy all morning, got a lot done, and there's nothing left to do till the chickens are put away this evening."

"Okay. Guess I'll go back to the B&B."

"Say, I have a better idea. Why don't you and I go somewhere for a few hours and do something fun for a change?"

"Where do you want to go?"

"Well, there's Spouting Horn. Have you ever been there?" Rob pulled out his sandwich and chips.

"Just once. It was the day Mandy and I missed the ship. We didn't stay long, so it would be nice to see it again and not be hard-pressed for time." Ellen smiled.

Rob was pleased that she wanted to go. "As soon as I'm done eating, let's grab some bottles of water and head out." He had to admit he too was eager to go.

Ellen picked up her tote bag. "I have some trail mix in here. Should I bring that too?"

"Sure, why not?"

Spouting Horn

When they arrived at their destination, Ellen went to the restroom to check her appearance. Although the ride on Rob's motor scooter exhilarated her, it left her feeling windblown. After removing the scarf she'd tied around her traditional head covering and tucking in a few stray hairs, Ellen returned to the grassy area where Rob waited for her.

She smiled, pointing to the hens and chicks roaming around. It still amazed her how many chickens ran wild on the island. It was one more thing that made Kauai unique. She'd even seen some in the parking lot by the airport the day Makaio and Luana had picked her up.

"Before we go to the overlook, why don't we check out some of the trinkets and souvenirs being sold along the walkway?" Rob suggested.

"Who knows, you might find something you like."

She shrugged. "We'll see."

Many of the vendors sold jewelry, which Ellen had no interest in buying. When they came to a booth selling potholders made by a local woman, she stopped to look at them. "These remind me of the potholders some Amish women make back home," she told Rob. "Only most of ours aren't this colorful."

"Would you like one?" He pushed his sunglasses on top of his head.

"I probably shouldn't spend the money on something I don't really need."

"No problem." Rob reached into his pocket and pulled out his wallet. "I'll get it for you."

"Oh, no, you don't have to do that, Rob."

"I want to."

"Thank you, Rob." She picked up the purchase and placed it in her tote.

"*A'ole pilikia*—You're welcome, no problem." He grinned and took hold of her other hand. "Ready to see the water spout?"

"Oh, yes." Her fingers tingled beneath his grasp. *Does Rob feel it too?*

As they approached the lookout, Ellen's thoughts went to her friend. *This is the spot where Mandy met Ken.* Ellen had often wondered if Ken and Mandy's meeting was a coincidence or God ordained. They seemed to be meant for each other. Mandy had once said that she believed Ken was her soul mate.

Staring out at the ocean, Ellen clasped the handrail in front of her. *Do I have a soul mate somewhere? I hope I discover him before I'm too old for marriage.* Ellen thought about her aunt, Dianna, who hadn't gotten married until she was forty-five. *I certainly wouldn't want to wait that long.*

Unexpectedly, a plume of water shot up from one of the blowholes, causing Ellen to gasp. "Oh, what a magnificent sight! And look over there, Rob." She pointed. "Did you see the rainbow that formed?"

"It is pretty awesome, isn't it?" Rob reached into his pocket and pulled out his cell phone. "I'll wait for the next one to spout and get a picture. But first, let's take a selfie."

Before Ellen could offer a response, Rob pulled her close, held up his phone, and snapped a picture. Then he showed her the photo. "Turned out pretty good, don'tcha think?"

"We Amish don't normally pose for pictures, Rob."

"Sorry about that. If the photo offends you, I'll delete it."

Ellen studied the picture. "Oh, look, the water spouted behind us, and you even captured the rainbow."

"That makes it even more special." He smiled. "If you don't mind, I'd like to keep the photo. It'll help me remember this day after you leave Kauai."

Ellen swallowed hard. She didn't need a photo to remember this day, but how could she say no when he looked at her so sweetly?

Chapter 26

Kapaa

$\mathcal{M}$andy glanced at her cell phone to check the time. It was hard to believe it was the middle of August already. She and Ellen had arrived moments ago at the church for supper and Wednesday night Bible study. It was the first one she'd been to since Ken's shark attack. It would be good to fellowship with other believers at their church again, and she was thankful Ellen could join her this evening. It would have been nice if Vickie could have been here too, but she said she had some important paperwork to do.

Since Mandy's nausea had lessened, she had an appetite this evening and anticipated trying out some of the different foods offered at the potluck. She spotted Luana and waved.

"Mandy and Ellen, it's so good to see you." Luana moved across the fellowship hall and gave them both a hug. "Ellen said you might be coming to Bible study tonight." She patted Mandy's back. "How is Ken doing?"

"A little better. There's no more sign of infection, at least." Mandy explained.

"I'm so glad. Will there be any more surgeries ahead for him?" Luana asked.

"The doctors don't know for sure, but we're hoping it won't be necessary." Mandy sighed. "Ken wants to go home."

"That's understandable. This has been quite an ordeal for both of you." Luana stroked Mandy's cheek. "You look tired. I suspect you're not getting enough rest. Are you still spending nights at the hospital?"

"Sometimes, but now that Ken's out of danger, we've been sleeping at home."

Luana glanced across the room. "Let's join up with Makaio. Then we can sit together to eat our meal."

Mandy smiled. "That would be nice. I'd like to hear how things have been going at the B&B."

"I feel bad that I haven't been able to help out at the bed-and-breakfast more," Ellen told Makaio as the four of them found seats at a table.

He shook his head. "We're getting things done, and your help is needed at the Williamses' farm more than at our place."

"That's right," Luana agreed. "You came to Kauai to help Mandy, not us."

"But you're giving me free room and board."

"It's our way of helping out." Luana's expression sobered. "We got some disappointing news yesterday."

"What was it?" Mandy asked.

"Our son-in-law got a job offer on the Big Island, so he and Ailani will most likely be moving. This means we won't get to see little Primrose as often as we like, not to mention their new baby after it's born." Luana's brows furrowed. "If they should decide to move, I'll miss seeing their *keiki*."

Makaio placed his hand on her shoulder. "We'll manage. A flight to the Big Island is less than an hour away."

"True, but it's never easy for us to leave the B&B when it's our busiest season."

"Don't worry. We'll work it out somehow."

Their conversation was interrupted when Pastor Jim came over to their table. Ellen had seen him at the hospital a few times, visiting Ken.

He stood next to Mandy's chair. "I wanted to let you know that a fund has been started to help with Ken's hospital expenses. Please let me or one of the elders know when you receive a bill. Then our church treasurer will write you a check. Although we can't pay for everything, we still want to help."

"Thank you, Pastor." Mandy's gratitude showed by her wide smile.

Ellen felt pleased that both the Amish church back home and Mandy and Ken's church here had offered to help. This kind of giving was Christianity in action.

Middlebury

Nora rolled over in bed, turned on her small flashlight, and looked at the clock near the bed. It was one in the morning, and she couldn't sleep. Ellen had been on her mind most of the day, and even after going to bed. She wasn't used to having her daughter gone so long. The fact that Ellen was so far away bothered Nora. Some Amish families were separated by several miles or lived a few states away, but having a family member living clear across the ocean was not the norm. Of course, Ellen wouldn't be staying there permanently, so it helped to know that much at least.

Nora glanced at Nathan—sleeping like a baby. Not wanting to disturb him, she got up, put on her robe, and slipped out of the room.

When she entered the living room, Nora turned on a battery-operated light, picked up her Bible, and took a seat in the rocker. Some time spent alone with God might help relieve her tension.

She prayed first, then opened her Bible to Isaiah 54. Verse 13 in particular caught her attention: "All thy children shall be taught of the Lord; and great shall be the peace of thy children."

Nora reflected on the words. She and Nathan had taught their daughters to love God and obey His commandments. They'd committed the girls to the Lord at a young age. Nora hoped each of them felt God's peace and would always seek His will.

Nora thought back to over a month ago, when they'd invited Ezra to dinner. Before he'd left to go home, Ezra had asked her for Ellen's address in Hawaii.

I've often wondered if Ezra is interested in our eldest daughter. Nora would keep her thoughts to herself, but maybe the next time she talked with Ellen, she might ask if Ezra had written to her.

Hearing footsteps approach, Nora looked up. She was surprised to see Darla shuffle into the room, the hem of her long robe, brushing the floor.

"Mom, what are you doing up in the middle of the night?" Darla released a noisy yawn.

Nora grinned. "I could ask you the same."

"I heard the squeak of the rocker."

Nora tipped her head. "The sound of this old chair moving woke you, all the way up to your room?"

"Well, at first I got up to get a drink of water. Then when I heard the squeaking noise, I came down to see who was out of bed." Darla took a seat on the couch. "So how come you're up, Mom?"

"Ellen was on my mind, and I couldn't sleep. She's been on Kauai almost two months, and the last time we talked it sounded like she could be staying several more months." Nora's hands fell to her lap as she heaved a heavy sigh. "I miss her and wish she were home."

"Maybe it would help if you called her more often."

"I would if I could catch her. Hawaii time is six hours behind us, so that makes it difficult. Besides, she's often busy at the organic farm or at the hospital offering encouragement to Mandy."

"Any recent word on how Mandy's husband is doing these days?"

"Ken came through his last surgery, but he's still in the hospital. Once he goes home, he won't be able to do any chores around the farm, so Ellen's help there is still needed."

"I thought Ken's mother hired a young man to take care of the chickens."

"She did, but there's too much work for one person. That's why Ellen volunteered to help out." Nora's hands rested on the Bible as she rocked.

Darla brushed some long stray hairs away from her face. "My sister is a good friend. I hope Mandy appreciates the sacrifice Ellen is making for her and Ken."

"I'm sure she does." Nora laid her Bible aside and stood. "I don't know about you, but I'm going back to bed. Before you know it, the old rooster will be crowing, letting us know it's time to get up."

"Okay. *Gut nacht*, Mom. I hope you sleep well." Darla stood and hugged

Nora. "I'll say a prayer for Mandy and Ken. And remember—Ellen's in God's hands. I'm certain my sister will return home as soon as she can."

Thursday morning, Ezra woke up earlier than normal. While he could have gone back to sleep for another hour, he decided to get up and do something he'd been thinking about for several weeks. He couldn't get Ellen off his mind. Last month when he went to dinner at the Lambrights', Ellen's mother had given him her address in Hawaii at his request. It was past time to write her a letter.

It wasn't like Ezra to be so bold, but the longer Ellen had been gone, the more determined he had become to win her heart. He was convinced she was the girl for him, but he was concerned that she might do something foolish and stay in Hawaii.

Ezra went to the open window and lifted it higher. He breathed in the predawn air and looked up at the stars, wondering if they were this bright in Hawaii. In the distance, he heard a dog barking, and the faint hooting of an owl. He enjoyed the peacefulness of a new morning.

Shaking his head, he went to his desk, got out some paper and a pen, and began to write:

> *Dear Ellen,*
>   *I think about you almost every day, and I miss seeing*
> *your pretty face at your daed's shoe store. Whenever I see your*
> *sister, Lenore, I think of you.*

Ezra dropped the pen and slapped his cheek. *What am I doing? I can't tell Ellen any of that.* He wadded up the paper and tossed it in the trash can. *Guess I'd better start over and be a little more subtle this time:*

> *Dear Ellen,*
>   *I'd like to first offer you an apology for my behavior when*
> *I was in charge at your daed's store. I was wrong for acting so*
> *bossy, and I hope you'll forgive me. Maybe when you're back*

here, we can start over fresh.

So, how are you doing? Is Mandy's husband getting better? Your daed mentioned that you've been working at an organic chicken farm. Do you have any idea when you might be coming home?

Everything here is going okay. We've been busy at the store the last few weeks. Maybe when you return to Middlebury, you can start working there again.

Take care, and I hope to hear from you soon.

Sincerely,
Ezra Bontrager

Ezra sat back in his chair, locked his fingers together, and held them behind his head. *Looks like a good letter to me. I hope Ellen responds.*

Chapter 27

Kapaa

J'm going to step out front to check the mail," Luana told Ellen after they'd finished breakfast.

Ellen smiled. "That's fine. I'll put the dishes in the dishwasher while you're doing that."

Luana brushed the idea away. "Don't bother with those. You need to get ready to work at the farm. I'll take care of the dishes after you're gone."

Ellen knew better than to argue with Luana. She hadn't won a disagreement yet and couldn't change Luana's mind. Even so, whenever Ellen had an opportunity, she did whatever chores she could in Makaio and Luana's home.

As Ellen headed to her room to get her purse, she stopped in the living room to see if anything needed to be straightened. Nothing seemed out of place, so she paused to say good morning to one of their guests and moved on to her room.

When Ellen returned to the kitchen, Luana held a stack of mail. "There's a letter for you on the table, Ellen."

Eager to see who it was from, Ellen picked it up. She was surprised to see the return address was Ezra's. According to the postmark, the letter had been mailed a week ago.

I wonder why Ezra would write to me. And how did he get Luana and Makaio's address?

Ellen took a seat at the table and read the letter.

"What's wrong, Ellen?" Luana asked. "Did you receive bad news?"

"No. It's a letter from the young man who works for my dad."

"Ah, I see. So you have a boyfriend back home you haven't told us about?"

Ellen shook her head. "It's nothing like that. Ezra and I are just friends. I've known him a long time."

"Then why would he write to you?" Luana peered over the top of her reading glasses as she placed the rest of the mail on the table.

"I don't know." Ellen stared at the letter, still in disbelief. "This was a surprise to me."

Luana chuckled. "In my younger days, when a young man wrote a letter to a woman, quite often it meant he had a romantic interest in her."

"Well, it's not that way with Ezra." Ellen reflected on the way he'd acted toward her during the time she'd worked at the shoe store. Never once had Ezra showed any romantic interest in her. It fact, it seemed quite the opposite.

Ellen thought about how she'd gone out to lunch with Rob two days ago. The more time they spent together, the more she enjoyed being with him. He was a lot kinder to her than Ezra had ever been.

"Have you ever done anything like this before?" Rob asked as he and Ellen painted the wooden fence surrounding the Williamses' yard.

"Why do you ask?"

"Just wondered, 'cause from the way you're holding that brush and moving your hand back and forth, it seems like you've had some experience painting."

"I have helped paint some things around my parents' place. How about you, Rob? Have you done much painting before?" Ellen stopped painting and reached up to her face and scratched at a fresh mosquito bite.

"A bit." Rob stared at a smudge of paint near the bite on Ellen's cheek. Pulling a hankie out of his back pocket, he poured liquid from his water bottle onto the cloth. As he reached toward Ellen to wipe the paint off, she pulled her head back.

"Wh—what are you doing?" She gave him a quizzical look, then glanced around, as though worried someone might be watching.

"When you scratched your cheek, you smeared paint on your face." Rob held the dampened hankie up. "May I?"

Ellen didn't resist this time and nodded.

Rob bit back a chuckle as she closed her eyes until he was done.

"Did you get it?" Ellen peeked up at him.

"Yep, it's gone. Good thing the paint washes off with water." Rob's brows furrowed when a movement caught his attention. He looked to the left and spotted a gray-and-black pigeon lying near the fence. "I wonder what's wrong with that grounded bird."

Ellen saw it too. "Is the poor thing hurt, or just scared?" She clambered to her feet, went over to the bird, and then went down on her knees. The pigeon lay still in the grass, as though dazed.

Rob knelt beside her and held the pigeon in his hands. He looked the bird over. Neither of its wings had been broken. "Think it may have plowed into something and is stunned."

Ellen reached over. "Is it okay if I hold it?"

The pigeon didn't struggle when he handed her the bird. Rob wouldn't have struggled either, being held with such tenderness by Ellen. He almost envied the bird.

"Look, it's not afraid and seems like it's used to being handled." She smiled in Rob's direction.

While Ellen talked in a soft tone to the pigeon, Rob noticed a plastic tag around the bird's leg. "This pigeon is banded." He pointed, then touched the bird's foot with the band around it. "I wonder if the pigeon belongs to someone. On occasion, I've seen homing pigeons flying together in a group." Rob ran his hand down the bird's back. "I've heard of people using them around here like a hobby of sorts."

"Is there a way we can find out who the owner is?"

"I'll have to do some checking and see what I can find out." Rob pointed to the band. "I'll write the number and letters down. Maybe that's a clue."

Ellen stroked the pigeon's head just as Rob's hand moved up the bird's back. When their fingers touched, he felt a warm tingle travel all the way up his arm. It was a familiar feeling—one he used to feel whenever he and his girlfriend from back home used to touch. But that was behind him now. He needed to move on. There was no point in dwelling on the past.

Rob concentrated on the pigeon. If there was one thing he didn't need right now, it was a romantic complication—especially with someone like Ellen. It was good she wouldn't be staying on the island indefinitely. *But that shouldn't keep me from enjoying her company while she's here*, Rob told himself.

Mandy arrived home, feeling more lighthearted than usual. She was eager to find Ellen and share some good news.

Mandy put the keys in her purse and set it on the counter. Assuming Ellen must be out back with Rob, she headed in that direction. At least there was a light at the end of the tunnel for Ken.

When Mandy went outside, she spotted Ellen and Rob on their knees with their heads so close, they were almost touching. It appeared as if Rob held Ellen's hand.

Mandy stopped walking and stood, staring. *Has Ellen fallen for Rob? Is the feeling mutual? Should I be concerned?*

Mandy remembered how things had been between her and Ken when they'd first met. It hadn't taken them long to realize they wanted to be together, but there'd been a problem. Ken was English, and she'd been raised Amish.

But that was different, she told herself. *I was not a member of the Amish church, and Ellen is. I hope she's not getting serious about Rob. The last thing Ellen's Mom and Dad need is for her to leave the church and marry an English man or move to Hawaii, so far from home.*

Mandy was reminded once again, that her own parents lived thousands of miles away. She couldn't help wondering if she would ever see her home in Indiana again.

"Hey, Mandy, come see what we found," Rob called. When he and Ellen stood up at the same time, Mandy realized her friend held a pigeon.

"What's going on?" she asked, joining them by the fence.

"We found an injured pigeon," Ellen responded. "Its wings don't appear to be broken, so we're thinking it may have hit a window and is only stunned."

"This bird is banded, so I'm going to try to find out who it belongs to," Rob explained.

Ellen lifted the bird so Mandy could see its leg. "We think this is a homing pigeon."

Mandy smiled, relieved that Ellen and Rob hadn't been holding hands after all. Even when they were children, Ellen had had a soft spot for injured animals, so it was no surprise that she was concerned and wanted to find the pigeon's owner.

"I'm going to put the bird someplace where it's safe from any predators and see if it stays there or flies off." Rob took the fowl from Ellen and headed toward the chicken house.

Mandy stepped up to Ellen. "I have some good news about Ken."

"Oh? What is it?"

"Today the doctor said that if things go well with the cast for Ken's leg, he might be able to come home within the next few days.

Ellen gave Mandy a hug. "That is good news—jah, an answer to prayer."

Mandy nodded. "But once he comes home, it'll take many weeks for him to recover, and he might never be able to walk without a limp or certain restrictions."

"You'll need to take one day at a time. And remember, I'm here for as long as you need me."

"Thank you. It's a comfort to know that."

Ellen pointed to the chickens running around in their fenced-in yard. "It will be some time before either you or Ken can work here again, and I'm more than willing to help out for as long as necessary."

Mandy appreciated her friend's offer, but she couldn't help wondering if at least part of Ellen's willingness to remain here longer had something to do with Rob.

Chapter 28

Wailua, Hawaii

As Ellen hung on to Rob's waist, she felt his muscles through the T-shirt he wore. A sense of exhilaration came over her as they sped down the road on his motor scooter toward their destination. She was ready for some casual fun with Rob, away from the repetitive organic chicken farm and all the hard work.

Ellen thought about the letter she'd received from Ezra. She'd sent him a response the next day. It still surprised her that he'd sent the letter. Could Luana have been right when she'd said when a guy sent a letter to a girl, it meant he was interested in her? Ellen didn't get that impression from anything Ezra wrote.

As they sat at the stoplight, Ellen tightened her scarf. "Are we almost there, Rob?"

"Our turn is at the next light, and it's coming up in a couple of miles." Rob glanced back to look at her.

Before long, he sped down a hill and into a dirt parking lot. Rob found a spot to park the scooter near some other vehicles. Then they headed toward a thatched hut to inquire about the kayak rentals. After Rob paid, he suggested they watch a few people go out ahead of them. "It'll give you a better understanding of what to expect."

"That's a good idea." Ellen stood next to Rob, watching as a man and woman came down from the hut to pick out lifejackets. They each found a vest, adjusted the dangling straps, and clipped them on.

"The water looks inviting," Ellen commented.

Rob nodded. "It's a nice way to cool off on a warm day like this."

The couple walked onto the dock. The man climbed in first. When he was settled in his seat, the attendant and his helper held the kayak with a firm grasp against the dock, while the woman stepped in.

"That looks easy enough." Ellen smiled at Rob. "I don't think I'll have a problem getting in when it's our turn."

Soon the other couple left the dock. Ellen enjoyed watching them use their paddles at the same time. They took a few tries to get in sync and moved with smooth strokes along the water. In no time they were heading out to the main part of the river and had started on their trip.

"Are you ready to see some nice scenery?" Rob asked.

"Sure, and it will be good to get some exercise like those people ahead of us are doing."

Ellen and Rob put on their life vests and waited for the attendant to bring the kayak around. Once it was close enough, Rob climbed in. Then Ellen did the same.

"The Fern Grotto tour boats have the right of way on the river," the young man who'd brought the kayak to them stated. "So stay close to the edge of the river when you encounter them."

"No problem. We'll be sure to watch out," Rob replied.

Ellen sat still, eager to start the trip.

When the attendant asked if they were ready for a push off from the dock, Rob and Ellen responded with nods.

Once they were free and floating along, Rob suggested Ellen paddle on the right, and he'd take over the left. They moved along at a nice pace. It seemed a bit intimidating at first, but once Ellen got the hang of things, she found it fun to paddle the kayak.

"There are quite a few people out here today." Ellen pointed to the boats ahead of them.

"I bet a lot of them are tourists." Rob turned his head to look at her. "I'll try to take some pictures of whatever you'd like on my cell phone—just let me know. I'm sure Vickie wouldn't mind if I download the photos to her computer and print them for you."

"Thanks. It would be nice to have a few pictures to show my friends and family back home." Ellen slowed her paddling.

Despite the warmth of the day, the tree branches hanging over the water in places created some nice places to get a reprieve from the heat.

Rob looked over the side of the kayak. "Look how crystal clear the water is, Ellen."

She couldn't agree more. "The scenery is beautiful from this view on the river."

Rob rested the paddle he held. "Yep. We couldn't experience this kind of view on my scooter, that's for sure."

Ellen nodded. She almost felt guilty for having such a good time, when poor Mandy had been going through so much with Ken. But when she'd told her friend about this trip Rob had planned for them, Mandy had encouraged Ellen to go, saying she deserved to have some fun.

Ellen's thoughts turned to the injured bird they'd found the other day. "I'm glad you were able to track down the owner of the pigeon."

"Yeah, it was pretty easy after I found the website of a local pigeon club. When I emailed the man in charge, he was able to tell me who the bird belonged to by the identification number on the tag. After I called the owner, he came right away to get his bird. He was grateful and explained that he lived three miles away. So the pigeon almost made it home by itself."

As they paddled along, Ellen smelled a wonderful fragrance. "Where is that nice aroma coming from?"

Rob pointed to a group of light yellow flowers growing above the river bank. "I'm almost sure those are from the plumeria plants. They have a pleasant odor."

Traveling farther up the river, Ellen noticed some fish jumping. They reached a place where they could beach their kayak and walk along a path. Rob said the trail led to a waterfall, but they'd have to wade through waist-high river water first, in order to get to the falls. Deciding against that option, they walked farther up the river before turning around.

As they paddled toward the Fern Grotto, Ellen saw the tour boat come up behind them.

"Here comes the big boat; we'd better get out of their way." Rob helped Ellen direct the kayak closer to the water's edge.

"There's a large group of people on that boat." Ellen paddled more to keep them from drifting outward.

The tour boat moved fast through the water and passed them by. Ripples of small waves reached their kayak, causing them to bob up and down in the water.

As they traveled on, the river got narrower and shallower. For a few seconds, Ellen imagined being back home on their pond, floating in an inner tube, like she and her sisters had done when they were young girls. She was glad she was here, though, and wished the day never had to end. It was fun spending time with Rob.

"Would you like to pull over along here and drink some of the water we brought?" he asked.

"I could use a break, and rehydrating is a good idea." Ellen followed his lead, paddling their way to the bank.

Once close enough, Rob grabbed a root and held on to it to keep them snubbed close.

They got out their waters and drank, while resting along the bank. Ellen watched another couple from the other direction and waved.

"This was a good idea. I'm glad we could come here today." Rob took a long drink and wiped his mouth on his shirtsleeve.

"I'm enjoying the view, and I've been putting my hand in the water sometimes to cool off," Ellen admitted.

"I've taken some scenic pictures for you along our route, and even one of the tour boat that went by us earlier." Rob kept a hold on the root holding them close to the bank.

"I can't wait to see the pictures you've taken." Ellen put her water bottle away.

"Shall we continue our boat ride?" he asked.

"I'm ready to head on when you are," Ellen replied.

They rowed until they reached a shallow bend in the river, making it difficult to go on. So they turned and headed back to the dock where they'd started almost two hours before.

Ellen sighed. She didn't want this outing to end.

Middlebury

Ezra glanced at the clock on the store wall. It was four o'clock—almost quitting time. *Let me think. . . What time would it be in Hawaii right now? As I recall, Nathan mentioned Hawaii is six hours behind us, so that would make it around ten in the morning. I wonder what Ellen's doing right now.*

Ezra stood with his back to the counter, continuing to stare at the clock. He hoped she had received his letter and would send him a response soon.

Ezra closed his eyes, visualizing Ellen's pretty face. He could almost hear her calling his name. "Ezra. . .where are you? Ezra, can you hear me?"

Ezra was jolted out of his musings when Nathan thumped his arm. "Hey, what's the matter with you? Didn't you hear Lenore calling for you from the back room?"

"Oh, sorry. I'll go see what she wants." With his face feeling as warm as bread fresh from the oven, Ezra hurried off.

When he entered the back room, Lenore stood with her arms folded, frowning at him. "How come you didn't answer when I called? Couldn't ya hear me shouting your name?"

"No, not at first. I mean. . . Well, I was deep in thought." He gave Lenore his full attention. "What'd ya need?"

She pointed to some shoe boxes on a shelf overhead. "I can't reach those and wondered if you'd get them down for me."

"Oh, sure thing." Ezra reached up and pulled down one box after another. "There you go, Lenore."

She looked up at him with a sweet, dimpled smile. "Danki, Ezra. It must be nice to be so tall."

"It does have some benefits. Is that all you needed?"

"Jah."

"Okay. I'll be heading for home soon. See you tomorrow, Lenore." When Ezra glanced at his reflection in the mirror on the back wall, he noticed his hair needed a trim. *Think I'd better see if my mamm will give me a haircut soon.*

As he headed back to the front of the store, Ezra found himself wishing yet again that Lenore was Ellen. It was probably no more than wishful thinking, but in truth, he hoped Ellen would end up working here again.

Wailua

"We should head back to the farm soon, but before we go, it might be fun to take the self-guided tour of the reconstructed old Hawaiian village," Rob said as he and Ellen left their kayaks.

Ellen smiled up at him. "From what I read on the brochure I picked up, it sounds quite interesting."

"Great! Let's go." Rob grabbed Ellen's hand and was pleased when she didn't pull it away. *I'm glad she likes being in my company because I sure enjoy having her close to me.*

As they walked through the thatched-roof structures, including a canoe house, birthing house, the chief's assembly house, and doctor's house, Rob enjoyed seeing Ellen's reaction. Based on the almost continuous smile on her face, he felt sure she was having a good time. Artifacts and storyboards explained each structure's purpose, and lush green gardens grew in and around the village, yielding traditional Hawaiian fruits and flowers.

Rob looked up as some heavy gray clouds moved in overhead, shadowing the sun.

He bent down to pick up a deep coral-colored Hibiscus that had dropped on the ground. Then, without so much as a thought, he tucked it behind Ellen's right ear, in front of her white head covering. "You look beautiful," he murmured. "Pretty as the flower behind your ear."

Ellen's cheeks colored, and she gave a slight dip of her head. "Thank you, Rob."

It began to rain, but they continued on. Rob wouldn't allow anything to interfere with their wonderful day.

As they finished their tour, he found himself thinking: *This day has been wonderful. I'll remember it long after Ellen is gone.*

Chapter 29

Kapaa

On the last Monday of August, Ken finally came home. As he sat on the couch, he remembered how nice it had been to roll out of the hospital into the sunshine after being cooped up for weeks. Even though he had emerged from the hospital in a wheelchair, he didn't care. Mandy and Mom were attentive, getting him into the car and making sure he was comfortable as could be.

Now as Ken reclined on the couch with his injured leg propped on a pillow, frustrations piled up. He'd been lying here, feeling useless for the past hour, watching his wife and mother scurry about trying to make everything just right for him. Well, nothing was right, and if he didn't gain full use of his left arm and leg, things might never be.

From what the doctor had said, Ken might always have a limp and be forced to use a cane. He couldn't believe how much his life had changed. Adjusting to it was grueling. Ken wondered how long it would take him to be somewhat normal again, and he couldn't stop thinking about all the problems he faced.

His jaw clenched as he looked at the twirling ceiling fan. *Mandy and I agreed to remain on Kauai to help Mom run the farm. If I'm not able to do the things I used to, then what good am I?*

Ken pulled himself to a sitting position and stared at his cast. *Sure can't sit back and watch Mom and Mandy do all the work. And watching Rob do everything will make me feel like even less of a man. It's my job to provide for my family, not some stranger I don't know well. Should have never gone surfing with Taavi and Rob that day. My place was here, taking care of things on the farm.*

Ken wasn't one to give in to self-pity, but he couldn't seem to help himself. The shark attack had changed everything—including Ken's outlook on life. He kept asking himself why God had allowed this to happen. Was it punishment for being selfish and running off to do something fun when he should have stayed home to help Mandy that day?

Grimacing, Ken ran his fingers through his hair. To make matters worse, he still dealt with pain and had to take medication to keep it under control. Ken didn't like taking pills, and except for an occasional ibuprofen for a rare headache, he had never been on any medications. But the shark attack had altered that. Now he had no choice but to do everything the doctor instructed—including taking pills for the pain. *I could use some good news about now.* Ken drummed his fingers on the sofa cushion.

Mandy came over and knelt on the floor in front of the couch. Smiling, she reached up and took hold of his hand. "There's something I need to tell you, Ken."

"Oh?" He hoped it wasn't anything negative. They'd already dealt with enough bad news.

She sat up and leaned close to his ear. "We're going to be parents."

Ken blinked several times, wondering if he'd heard her right. "Would you please repeat that?"

"I'm expecting a baby. It'll be born in late January or early February."

"Now doesn't that lift your spirits, Son?" Mom asked when she entered the room.

"How long have you known about this?" Ken directed his question to Mandy.

"Several weeks." She continued holding his hand.

"Why are you just now telling me this? Didn't you think I had the right to know I was going to be a father?"

"Of course you have the right, but I didn't want you to worry about me when you were going through so much yourself."

He let go of her hand and stroked her cheek with his thumb. "You're my wife. I'm always going to worry about you."

Mandy smiled. "Well, you needn't worry. I'm doing fine."

Ken's jaw clenched. "I'm also concerned because I don't know if I'll be capable of providing for my family now. It's obvious I'm not going to be able to do all the things I used to do around here."

"It's okay, Son." Mom moved across the room. "Rob is working here full-time, and Ellen has also been helping out."

"That's fine for now. But what's going to happen when Ellen goes back to Indiana? Rob can't manage things on his own, and Mandy sure won't be able to help."

"When Ellen leaves, I'll look for another person to assist Rob with his chores on the farm." Mom placed her hand on Ken's uninjured shoulder. "Let's not worry about all of that right now. You need to rest and concentrate on getting well. We have to trust God to work out the details for everyone involved."

Ellen came into the house to get something cold to drink for her and Rob, when a knock sounded on the back door. Makaio and Luana stood at the door.

"Aloha!" Grinning, Makaio gave a nod. "We heard Ken came home today, so we wanted to come by and say hello."

"He's in the living room with Mandy and Vickie. I am sure he'll be glad to see you." Ellen led the way.

When they entered the room, Ellen held back, while Luana and Makaio greeted Ken.

"It's good to see you're back where you belong." Makaio gave Ken's good shoulder a squeeze. "And I'll bet you're tired of eating hospital food and lookin' forward to some of your mom's home cooking."

Ken nodded.

"How are you feeling?" Luana stood in front of the couch.

"About as good as can be expected, I guess." Ken looked over at Mandy. "Have you told them the news?"

She shook her head. "Not yet."

"What news?" Luana and Makaio asked at the same time.

"We're expecting our first baby." Mandy smiled, looking over at Ellen. "And my best friend has promised to stay until after the little one is born."

"Oh, my. . . Now, that is good news." Luana clapped her hands, before giving Mandy a hug.

Makaio also hugged Mandy. "Yes, it sure is good news. Congratulations, you two."

"Thank you." Mandy gestured for Luana and Makaio to take seats, and Ellen offered to get them something to drink.

"No, thanks. We just had lunch." Luana fingered her lei. "We have some news of our own to share."

"What is it?" Vickie asked.

"Our daughter and son-in-law are for sure moving to the Big Island, so. . ." Luana paused and looked over at Makaio. "Why don't you tell them?"

"Okay. After much prayer and consideration, Luana and I have made plans to sell our bed-and-breakfast and move to the Big Island too."

"We want to be near our ohana," Luana put in.

Ellen stood near Mandy, too stunned to say a word. She never expected Makaio and Luana would sell their B&B, much less leave Kauai. She couldn't imagine the possibility of visiting this island again and not seeing the Palus.

Vickie sat in her room that evening, staring at the pile of bills that had accumulated this past month. While sipping on warm hibiscus tea, she wondered what her next move should be. In addition to debts of her own that had to do with the organic farm, Ken's hospital bills kept coming in. Even though he was out of the hospital, he'd still have to go to therapy sessions, and those wouldn't be cheap. Even with the help they'd gotten from their church, as well as the Amish community in Middlebury, Mandy and Ken were financially overextended. Truth be told, so was she. With a baby on the way, her son and daughter-in-law would need all the help they could get.

"So many memories," Vickie murmured. Looking around the bedroom, her gaze fell upon the picture hanging above her husband's dresser. *Oh, how I remember the day Charles gave me that painting.* It was an anniversary gift he had surprised her with many years ago—one he'd seen her admiring when they'd visited an art store. Charles told Vickie the beautiful colors of the Hawaiian sunset were a reminder of all the times they had walked hand-in-hand along the beach, watching the sun descend into the horizon as if the ocean had swallowed it whole. The painter had captured the sky's vivid colors, which reflected on calm ocean waves. Over the water, big beautiful clouds, darkened by impending dusk, hung in the sky. A palm tree stood in the foreground, and Vickie could almost see it swaying.

"One day he was here, and the next he was gone." Vickie reached up and touched the heart-shaped locket she wore around her neck, another gift from her husband. This one held a black-and-white picture of them on their wedding day. *I miss you, Charles.* Vickie's husband had been her strength, her rock. Charles would know what to do with this situation, but he wasn't here to ask.

She tapped her fingers on the desk, thinking things through. *Should I sell the farm and downsize?* The thought had crossed her mind several times since Ken's shark attack. The profit Vickie could make by selling the farm would help pay Mandy and Ken's expenses. From the looks of things, it would be a long time, if ever, before Ken could return to his duties on the farm. The sensible thing to do would be to sell it. *But will I be able to give up all these memories?* she wondered.

Vickie set the bills aside and sat on the edge of her bed. The responsibilities once shared with Charles fell on her shoulders now. *What would Charles want me to do if he were here? Is there a way out for all of us?* Vickie had to be the strong one and make some decisions on her own. She hoped she could make the right one and that if her husband was here, he'd be pleased.

Chapter 30

*E*zra's heart beat a little faster as he sat on the front porch of his parents' home, holding an envelope. He'd picked up the mail for his mother and found a letter to him from Ellen. Of course, with mail coming from such a long distance, he figured it would take a longer time to get a response from her, but he'd almost given up.

Eager to know what Ellen said, he tore the envelope open and read:

> *Dear Ezra,*
>
> *I was surprised when I got your letter. It was nice of you to write. I miss my family and friends, but it's good I came to Kauai, because I'm needed here.*
>
> *Ken is out of the hospital now, but he has a long ways to go in his recovery.*
>
> *I've been working on the chicken farm with a young man named Rob. He seems to know a lot about chickens and many other things too. Several days ago we took a break from our work and rented some kayaks. It was hard to get the hang of it at first, but once I did, I had a lot of fun. Another time, Rob and I visited Spouting Horn, an amazing sight to see.*
>
> *Take care, and please tell my family I said hello.*
>
> > *Sincerely,*
> > *Ellen*

Ezra crumpled the letter in his hands. He'd hoped Ellen might say she missed him. But no, she'd mentioned some fellow named Rob.

His fingers tightened around the wad of paper. *Is Ellen interested in this man? All this hope of us being a couple may be for nothing. I wish she'd never gone to Kauai. If I could, I'd go there right now and bring her home.*

Kapaa

Mandy sat in the rocking chair next to the couch where Ken reclined. It was hard to believe it was the first day of September. Ken had been home from the hospital five days, and with each passing day, his short-fused nature, along with depression, increased. He wouldn't take the pain medicine unless she forced the issue. Ken seemed to be holding in all his problems, along with the discomfort he had to deal with every day. Sometimes he acted worse than a cantankerous old grizzly bear.

She'd hoped the news of her pregnancy would help, but as Ken grumbled on about the future, he focused on his inability to do all the things he'd done before. It seemed that her being pregnant made things even worse, because Ken dwelled on what he wouldn't be able to do once their child grew older.

She glanced at him, lying there with his eyes closed. Was he sleeping or trying to tune her out as he sank deeper into his own little world of misery?

Mandy swallowed hard, struggling to keep from crying. Nothing seemed right in their lives anymore. What had happened to all their hopes and dreams for the future? She missed running the bed-and-breakfast and struggled with the desire to see her family back home. With the exception of their baby's arrival, there wasn't much to look forward to in the days ahead. There was no doubt about it—her faith was being put to the test. The question was, could she rise above her worries and remain firm in her beliefs?

"Are you two hungry?" Vickie asked when she entered the room. "It's almost time for lunch." She stopped and looked at Ken. "Is he sleeping?" she whispered to Mandy.

"I'm not sure. His eyes have been closed for half an hour or so."

"Maybe we should go into the kitchen so we can talk without disturbing him." Vickie took a step back.

Mandy was about to respond, when Ken's eyes snapped open. "I wasn't sleeping, and I wish you two would stop talking about me." He pulled himself to a sitting position.

Mandy flinched at her husband's sharp tone. The old Ken would never have responded like that. *I need to be more understanding*, she told herself. *I don't know how I would act if I were in Ken's position.*

"I need to talk to both of you about something." Vickie took a seat on the end of the couch by Ken's feet. "I've done some serious thinking and praying and have made a decision about the farm."

"What about it?" Ken's face was almost expressionless.

"I'm going to sell it and buy Makaio and Luana's bed-and-breakfast." Ken's eyebrows shot up, and Mandy's lips parted a bit.

"Why would you do that, Mom?" he asked.

"For one thing, by selling the farm it'll take care of the rest of your hospital bills." Vickie smoothed her hair back away from her face. "The B&B will also give us a nice place to live, while providing a decent income."

"Have you spoken to the Palus about this?" Mandy questioned.

Vickie nodded. "They are willing to sell it to me on the contingency that our place here sells within sixty days. And since you and Mandy have had experience running a bed-and-breakfast, I believe it will be a good thing for all of us."

"Humph! You really believe that's gonna happen?" Ken placed his scarred arm awkwardly across his chest. "Not many people can afford to buy a place as big as this, not to mention all the work involved in raising the chickens." He glanced down at the cast on his leg. "Besides, how much help do you think a cripple like me is going to be running any kind of business?"

Mandy wished her husband wouldn't be so negative. The idea of living in Luana and Makaio's B&B and helping run it appealed to her. Even though she wouldn't be living near her family, she would enjoy the prospect of having a place of business similar to what they had in Middlebury.

"I am sure there will be many things you can do, Son." Vickie touched his good leg. If nothing else, you can take care of the books and be in charge of all reservations."

Ken grimaced. "Yeah, right—that's just what I've always wanted to do. And what about all the indoor and outside maintenance? Someone will have to do that, you know."

"Yes, I'm well aware. If necessary, I'll hire someone for that." Vickie rose to her feet. "It's all settled, and I'm trusting God to work everything out. In the meantime, I'm going back to the kitchen to fix us all something to eat." She smiled at Mandy and hurried from the room.

"We need to give this a chance," Mandy said, looking at Ken. "If it's meant for us to move to the B&B, then the farm will sell in two months or less."

Ken's only response was a soft grunt, then he closed his eyes again.

Mandy left the rocking chair and leaned over to kiss his forehead. If the farm sold, and they bought the B&B, Ellen would be there to help out—at least until after the baby was born. That was a comfort in itself.

Middlebury

Nora got down on her hands and knees to plant iris bulbs. She'd wanted to purchase some at the local market but hadn't gotten around to it yet. Then out of the blue, Birdie Mitchell had stopped by the other day, with a whole box of bulbs. Birdie said she needed to separate her bulbs and Nora was happy to accept the gift from her English friend.

Funny how things work out sometimes, Nora thought as she used the small hand rake to pull more dirt out of the depressions she'd made. *Now I'll have something to look forward to next year, when these flowers come up and bloom.* Nora sat back on her heels and looked at the area where she'd be planting the bulbs. The irises, Birdie told her, were a bluish, purple variety and would add even more color to this flowerbed. The irises would fit right in because Nora had planted perennials, bulbs and self-seeding annuals so that she didn't have to replant every year.

"I wonder how Ellen is doing." Nora sighed and continued talking to herself. "I miss her and can't wait until she comes home. I'll bet she's getting homesick and is anxious to get back to her family."

Nora's thoughts went to Ezra. *Once Ellen comes back, it sure would be nice if she became interested in Ezra. He's a hard-working, reliable man and would make a good husband for her.*

As she covered each bulb with dirt, Nora smiled. Although Ezra hadn't come right out and said it, she had an inkling his interest in Ellen was growing. Sometimes a person just knew these things.

Kapaa

Shortly before noon, Ellen was surprised when Mandy came outside and said she wanted to speak with her. "Vickie has lunch on the table, and she wondered if you and Rob would like to join us."

Ellen smiled. "I'd be happy to, but Rob had an errand to run, so he's not here right now. He'll be ready to grab a bite to eat before he comes back this afternoon."

"Oh, I see." Mandy joined Ellen by the flowerbed she'd been weeding. While the chore had nothing to do with the chickens, it was something Vickie didn't have time for, so she'd asked Ellen to do it. Working in the flowerbeds was something Ellen enjoyed, especially back home when she'd helped her mother plant different flowers around their house. "Did Rob let Vickie know he'd be taking some time off?"

Ellen shrugged. "I'm not sure, but I assume he did. If not, then I'll let her know when I go inside for lunch."

"Okay, but before we go in, I wanted to make you aware of something Vickie shared with Ken and me a little while ago." Mandy slipped both hands into her skirt pockets. "My mother-in-law is putting the farm up for sale and hopes to buy Luana and Makaio's bed-and-breakfast."

Ellen's fingers touched her parted lips. "Well, now, that's a surprise."

"I know. She's doing it in order to pay Ken's hospital bills and also to provide us with a home and a job." Mandy placed her hands on her growing belly. "I never expected she would part with the farm, and I feel humbled by her generosity. Her husband's organic business is important to Vickie, and she is making a real sacrifice on our behalf."

"She wouldn't do it if she didn't want to." Ellen placed her hand on Mandy's shoulder. "How do you feel about this decision? Is helping run the B&B something you would like to do?"

Mandy rolled her neck from side to side, then reached up to rub a spot on the left. "I've given it some thought and believe it would be a good thing for us. But Ken is concerned he won't be able to do much to help out. And until the baby is born, and I'm back on my feet, my help will also be limited."

"Not to worry, my friend. As I've said before, I'll stay and help out for as long as you need me." Ellen was excited about the news Mandy had told her. She loved working at the B&B back home, and now she'd have the opportunity to work at the bed-and-breakfast she'd become familiar with here in Hawaii. *I should give my parents a call and give them an update on everything. I'm sure they'll understand my reasons for not coming home real soon.*

Chapter 31

*H*olding a glass of strawberry-guava juice, Ellen entered her room at the Palms Bed-and-Breakfast and sat on the bed. It was hard to believe this was the first Thursday of November. She couldn't understand how the last two months had gone by in such a blur. The farm sold the first week it was on the market; the sale of the B&B went through soon after; and Makaio and Luana moved to the Big Island to be with Aliana and her family.

The move from the farm to the bed-and-breakfast went well, with Vickie, Ken, and Mandy adjusting to their new positions. Vickie hired Rob to do the yard work and maintenance. Since Ken was still recuperating and Mandy wasn't up to doing much, most of the indoor work fell on Ellen's shoulders. She didn't mind, though. Helping at the B&B was more enjoyable than working around chickens all day and cleaning smelly poultry buildings. Besides, this home was familiar and reminded Ellen of the days she and Mandy stayed with Luana and Makaio. It seemed empty without the Hawaiian couple, though. It had been a tearful goodbye when they'd left for the Big Island, knowing she might never see them again.

Ellen's thoughts scattered when someone knocked on her bedroom door. "Come in," she called.

The door opened, and Vickie poked her head inside. "If you're not busy, I wondered if you'd like to help me decorate for Thanksgiving."

Ellen smiled. "I'd be happy to." Even though they had no guests scheduled to stay over the holiday, three couples were coming the week before Thanksgiving.

Vickie stepped into the room and shut the door. "I've said this before, but I want you to know how much I appreciate your willingness to stay and help out. I'm sure you'd rather be home with your family during Thanksgiving and Christmas."

"This is the second time I've been in Hawaii during the holidays," Ellen stated. "Mandy and I helped Luana decorate the B&B for Christmas while we were staying here."

"How do your parents feel about you being here now?"

"Mom and Dad miss me, of course, but they understand. And I enjoy being here to spend time with Mandy." Ellen almost added that she liked spending time with Rob too, but kept those thoughts to herself.

Since Ellen and Rob both worked here, they saw each other every day. When things had been slow at the B&B, they'd gone on a few more excursions—one that included a trip to the lighthouse on the north end of the island. It had been fun, climbing to the top of the structure and looking out over the water. The Pacific Ocean looked enormous, making the Island of Kauai seem like a mere speck in the middle of it.

Pushing her musings aside, Ellen smiled at Vickie. "Would you like me to look through the boxes of decorations Luana left, to see what we can use, or do you have some of your own?"

"Mine are still in boxes we haven't gone through yet, so if you're able to find the ones Luana left, we'll use those. But before you begin, can you tell me how much you know about Rob?"

"Not a lot," Ellen replied. "Why do you ask?"

"Rob's a hard worker, but he doesn't say much, and whenever I try to engage him in conversation about something not work related, he clams up." Vickie took a seat on the end of Ellen's bed. "I don't know much about him, other than that he's Taavi's friend and shares expenses while living at Taavi's house. Rob seems honest and upright, but one can never be too careful."

Ellen tipped her head. "What are you saying? Has Rob done something to make you not trust him?"

"Nothing specific. However, his personal life is a mystery."

"Rob is a little private, even with me. But aside from that, he's been living with Taavi awhile, and Taavi seems to think highly of him."

"You're right, but it seems like he might be hiding something." Vickie smoothed the Hawaiian quilt on Ellen's bed. "I didn't have much chance to observe him when he worked at the farm. Now that Ken's out of the hospital, and since Rob's working here, I've had more opportunity to deal with him, and. . ." Vickie lifted her hand. "Oh, never mind. I'm probably being too cautious." She rose from the bed. "Let's get those decorations out now, shall we?"

"Of course." As Ellen followed Ken's mother from the room, she couldn't help wondering if Vickie's suspicions about Rob were legitimate. Could his unwillingness to talk about his past indicate that he was hiding something? If so, Ellen couldn't imagine what it might be.

Ken sat on the lanai, watching Rob in the yard, hauling off a stack of limbs he'd cut from an overgrown tree. Ken could see their hired help had made good progress on the landscaping. Ken's mother had mentioned the other day that keeping things neat as a pin would help bring in new guests.

Ken wished it could be him out there doing the chores. He felt useless, and wondered if he'd ever be able to work again.

Ken heard his wife indoors, humming a church song. She seemed happier since he came home from the hospital and they'd moved to the B&B. Ken had certainly put her through enough heartache, yet she always bounced back and kept a cheerful attitude—at least in his presence and probably for his sake.

Ken stared down at his hands—one good—one badly scarred. The attack could have been far worse, but it didn't seem to help his situation right now.

What's my purpose in life these days? Ken's cast was off his leg, and the incision had healed, but he walked with a limp and relied on a cane. He could use his left arm for some things, but there was no strength in it. Even with therapy, he doubted he'd ever be whole again. How was he supposed to take care of his wife and baby? Would he spend the rest of his life watching Mandy work, while he gimped around, struggling to do the simplest things? And he'd never be able to surf again. Even if he could get up on a board, the thought of encountering another shark terrorized him.

"Oh, there you are, Ken. I've been looking for you." Mandy placed her hands on his shoulders.

He looked up at her from the cushioned wicker couch and forced a smile. "Did you want something? Because if you did, I probably can't do it."

Ken couldn't keep the sarcasm out of his tone, but felt bad the minute he said it. "Sorry, Mandy. I shouldn't have spoken to you like that."

"Apology accepted." She took a seat in the chair beside him, then reached over and took hold of his hand. "Feel this, Ken. Our baby is quite active this morning." She placed his hand on her stomach.

Ken drew in a sharp breath, and tears stung the back of his eyes as he felt movement beneath the surface of his wife's belly. His son or daughter was inside Mandy's womb and would make an appearance soon. Ken could either sit around feeling sorry for himself or figure out a way to take care of his wife and child and become the best dad he could be. He needed to count his blessings and be thankful God spared his life.

The sun beat down on Rob's head. Even through his ball cap he felt the intensity of this warm afternoon. *Fall weather in Hawaii is sure different from what I dealt with on the mainland. I wouldn't go back there for anything, though.*

He glanced at the lanai, where Ken sat. He appeared to be watching him. Rob felt bad Mandy's husband was laid up and couldn't do certain things around the place. It had to be hard for Ken to sit and watch while others did most of the work. Rob gave Ken a brief wave, then bent to pick up another pile of branches he'd trimmed this morning. He was about to haul them across the yard, when Ellen came out of the house. His breath caught in his throat at the sight of her in a plain, but pretty lavender dress. *I wonder how she'd look in a Hawaiian mu-mu.*

"I brought some lemonade," she called, placing a tray on the picnic table.

"Sounds good. I could use a break." Rob put the branches on a pile and joined Ellen at the table.

"The yard looks nice," she commented as they took seats on the same bench.

"Thanks. What have you been up to today?"

She handed him a glass of lemonade. "I spent most of the morning helping Vickie decorate the B&B for Thanksgiving."

Rob reached under his cap and rubbed his forehead. "Oh, yeah. Guess that's coming up in a few weeks."

"Will you spend Thanksgiving or Christmas with your family?" Ellen drank from her glass.

He shook his head. "I told you before—they live on the mainland."

"I remember, but I thought some of your relatives might fly to Kauai to spend the holidays with you, or that you might go home for a few weeks."

"Nope." Rob drank the rest of his lemonade and set the glass back on the tray. "I have no desire to go home."

Rob figured from Ellen's slight grimace that she probably wondered why he didn't want to be with his family—especially during the holidays. Well, she wouldn't understand how things were, and he wasn't about to tell her.

"How long has it been since you've seen your family?" Ellen asked.

"A couple of years."

"How come?"

"It's complicated, and I'd rather not talk about it." Rob poured himself more lemonade and glanced over at her. "Why don't you tell me more about your family?"

"I've told you a little bit. What else would you like to know?" Ellen shifted on the bench.

"How many siblings do you have?

"Three younger sisters."

"No brothers, huh?"

She shook her head. "What about you? How many siblings do you have?"

"Two brothers and two sisters." Rob was quick to change the subject. "What does your family normally do for Thanksgiving?"

Ellen smiled. "We always have a big get-together with some of my aunts and uncles. This year, though, I'll be celebrating the holiday with Mandy, Ken, and Vickie." She scooted a little closer and offered him a cookie from the plate she'd also brought out. "I made chocolate-chip cookies last evening."

Rob reached for one. "They look good. Thanks, Ellen."

"You're welcome." She picked up a cookie and took a bite.

His heart beat a little faster as he gazed into her beautiful blue eyes. *Oh, boy, I'd better watch it. I'm falling for this girl.*

Chapter 32

When Rob entered the B&B to see if any inside work needed to be done, he discovered Ellen knelt beside a cardboard box in the living room, pulling off the tape that held the flaps together.

"Hey, is there anything I can do to help?" He went down on his knees beside her.

She looked up at him and smiled. "I found this box of fall decorations that I missed five days ago, and I discovered there are some Christmas things in here too. So, if you're not busy with something else, maybe you could help me separate things."

"Sure, I can do that." Rob pushed his bangs back off his forehead. "You have my undivided attention."

"All right then. Why don't we take everything out of the box and put them in two piles? The Christmas items over there, and the fall decorations over here."

"Sounds easy enough." Rob reached into the box at the same time as Ellen. When their hands touched, he clasped her fingers and gave them a squeeze. "This is a lot more fun than takin' care of squawking chickens, huh?"

Her cheeks colored slightly as she nodded. "Working here brings me such pleasure, like it did at the B&B Mandy and Ken used to own in Middlebury. I enjoy seeing to the needs of others."

"It shows, and you do it well. Mandy's lucky to have a good friend like you."

The pink that had erupted on Ellen's cheeks deepened. "I feel fortunate too. Mandy's a good friend. We've known each other since we were children."

Wish I'd known you when you were a girl. Things might be different for me now. Rob bit the inside of his cheek to keep from voicing his thoughts. He delighted in the sound of her voice.

They took turns pulling items from the box and placing them in piles on the throw rug. Ellen seemed to be fixated on the shiny globes she pulled out and held up to the light.

"Look at all these pretty tree ornaments." Ellen showed Rob one with a beautiful snow scene painted on the front. "I'd hate to see any get broken."

"Don't worry. I'll be careful with them." Digging deeper into the box, Rob felt something bristle against his fingers. "Well, look what I found." He lifted a bundle of synthetic mistletoe. "You know what this means?" Before Ellen could respond, he held it over her head, leaned close and gave her a kiss. He would have kissed Ellen longer, but when Mandy came in, he quickly pulled away.

Wide-eyed, she stopped in front of them and cleared her throat. "Am I interrupting something?" Mandy's tone was cautious.

"Umm. . .no. I was just helping Ellen sort through some decorations." Rob clambered to his feet. "Guess I'll go find Vickie and see what else she has for me to do before I head back to Taavi's place."

"Vickie's not here right now," Mandy said. "She went to the grocery store."

"Oh, okay. Guess I'll head out now then." Rob turned to go, but when Ellen called out to him, he turned back around.

"When you see Taavi, would you let him know that you're both invited here for Thanksgiving dinner? This morning, Vickie mentioned asking you to join us."

"Sounds good. I have no other plans, so I'll be here for the meal. I'm not sure about Taavi, but I'll extend the invitation." Rob gave a wave and headed for the door. The thought of a home-cooked Thanksgiving meal made his mouth water. Of course, spending the day with Ellen made it even more enticing.

After Rob closed the door behind him, Ellen looked up at Mandy, who stood staring down at her with a disapproving expression. "What's wrong? You look *umgerennt.*"

"I am upset. You seem to be acting careless around Rob, and why did you let him kiss you?"

Ellen's face tightened. "I am not being careless, and I didn't *let* Rob kiss me. It sort of happened when he held a piece of mistletoe over my head."

"I didn't see you pull away from him. It looked to me like you enjoyed the kiss."

Ellen couldn't deny her feelings, but she wasn't about to admit how she felt when Rob's lips touched hers. It was difficult to admit that her attraction to him grew. She might even be falling in love with Rob. But this didn't change the fact that she'd be going home in a few months, or that he was English and she was Amish. They were obviously not meant to be together, so she needed to set her feelings aside—however hard that would be as long as she remained on Kauai. But she'd already agreed to stay and help. Plus, she wanted to hold Mandy and Ken's precious baby. So while she was here, she would try not to let her feelings for Rob get in the way of good sense.

Mandy took a seat in the rocking chair and placed her hands across her stomach. "I'm sure the last thing you want from me is a lecture, but I'm concerned about you, Ellen."

"What are you concerned about?" Ellen took a seat on the couch.

"I've seen the way you and Rob look at each other whenever you're together, and it spells trouble." Mandy leaned back in the rocker. "It's obvious that you're falling for Rob, and you know the old saying: 'If you play with fire, you're bound to get burned.'"

Ellen's knuckles turned white when she clasped her hands together. "What is that supposed to mean?"

"You're Amish and have joined the church. If you and Rob were to pursue a relationship, and you left the church, your parents would be hurt."

"Yes, I know. I don't need the reminder." Ellen rolled her shoulders to release some of the tension she felt. "You fell in love with and married an English man. And now, you're living in Hawaii."

"My situation is different. I was not a church member when I married Ken."

"You're right, but Rob and I have made no commitment to each other, so you have nothing to worry about."

Mandy got the rocking chair moving. "I hope you can keep it that way. As much as I would love having you stay here permanently, if you gave up the Amish way of life to marry an outsider, you'd most likely have regrets."

"Do you have regrets?" Ellen blinked rapidly.

"I'm not sorry I married Ken, but I wish we could live near both of our families. It was hard on my folks when I chose not to join the Amish church." Mandy stopped rocking and came over to sit on the couch beside Ellen. "Please promise you'll give what I've said some serious thought before you make any decisions that could affect the rest of your life."

Ellen slowly nodded. "Danki for caring enough to express your thoughts."

"You're welcome." Mandy stood. "Now I'd better see if my husband needs anything." She offered Ellen a brief smile and left to find Ken.

Ellen leaned against the sofa cushions and rubbed a finger over her lips where Rob had kissed her moments ago. Could she give up the Amish life she'd always known to become English if her relationship with Rob became serious? She couldn't expect him to become Amish. While she'd heard of a few people who had given up their modern, English world to join the Plain faith, it had been a difficult transition. Some gave up and went back to their old way of life.

Ellen touched her hot cheeks and drew in a deep breath. *I am being silly for thinking about this. Rob has not said anything about loving me or suggested I leave the Amish church.* Mandy's lecture had confused Ellen. The only way she could put these thoughts out of her head was to get busy working again.

She knelt beside the box and began sorting things again. When her gaze came to rest on the mistletoe Rob had dropped back into the box, a shiver ran down her spine. She couldn't deny that she'd enjoyed his kiss. But since it was the first real kiss she'd received from a man, she had nothing to compare it with.

Chapter 33

Middlebury

*T*hanksgiving was always a busy time in the Lambrights' home, and this year was no exception. Visiting relatives were in the living room sitting by the toasty fire and talking to Nathan. Nora and her three daughters had been bustling around the kitchen all morning. Soon the turkey would be done, and it would be time to gather around the table. At least the house was filled with people, which would help take Nora's mind off Ellen's absence.

"Do you know what Ellen's doing today?" Lenore asked as she picked up a stack of plates to take them out to the dining-room table.

Nora grabbed some utensils from the counter, then turned to face her daughter. "I spoke with her yesterday, and she said they'd be having dinner at the B&B, and had invited Rob, the young man who works for them, as well as Ken's friend Taavi." She opened the oven to check on the turkey. The delicious aroma permeated the kitchen. "Ellen also mentioned that they don't have any guests at the bed-and-breakfast right now."

"Sounds like my granddaughter will have a nice Thanksgiving there in Hawaii." Nora's mother said as she entered the kitchen.

Nora smiled. "I hope so, Mama."

Darla took some glasses down from the cupboard, while Ruby got out the silverware. "Did Ellen say how Mandy and Ken are doing?" Ruby asked.

"Jah. Ken's injuries are healing, and Mandy's due to have her *boppli* on January tenth. Originally, they thought it would be February, but Mandy miscalculated."

"Will Ellen be staying on Kauai until after the baby arrives?" Darla questioned.

Nora nodded. "And did you hear that Mandy's folks are planning to go there?"

"Oh, really?" Grandma's silver-gray brows lifted. "To Kauai?"

"Jah. They've made arrangements to go to California on the train, and then they'll get on a cruise ship that will take them to Kauai. Once Mandy's folks arrive, Ellen plans to fly home." Nora could hardly wait for that.

Kapaa

Mandy sat on the couch beside Ken, strumming her ukulele and enjoying the tantalizing aromas floating in from the kitchen. Even though she couldn't be with her family in Middlebury today, she felt content. It would be a few hours before their company arrived for the meal, so this was a good time to sit and relax. Beforehand, she'd helped Vickie prep the potatoes and make a tropical fruit salad. Ellen made the stuffing for the bird, along with her favorite dinner rolls.

Ken seemed at peace today, as he placed his hand on Mandy's stomach. "Our little fella—if it is a boy—is sure active today."

She smiled. "Yes, and I'll bet he will take after his father—strong and brave."

Ken's brows drew together. "I may have been those things once, but not anymore. Since the shark attack, I've felt like a weakling and a coward."

"You're not a coward. And you'll regain your strength. It's just gonna take time. Even if your physical abilities are limited, you can still do things to help around here." She placed her hand over his. "When Luana called last week to see how things were going here, she said how pleased she and Makaio are that we are the ones who took this place over for them. They worked hard establishing their business, and we don't want to let them down."

Ken moved his head slowly up and down. "You're right, Mandy, and despite my limitations, I'll do my best to help you and Mom in any way I can."

"Everything tastes great." Taavi's gaze went from Vickie, to Mandy, and then Ellen. "Mahalo, ladies. You did a terrific job with this meal."

"Ellen did most of it," Vickie said. "She's an excellent cook and will make some lucky man a fine wife."

Ellen's face warmed. "I appreciate the compliment, but you and Mandy were a big help preparing this delicious Thanksgiving meal."

"I didn't do as much as you and Vickie." Mandy gave her stomach a few taps. "This little one has been sapping my energy, and I'm not up to doing much."

"It's not a problem." Vickie smiled at Mandy. "You need to rest whenever you can."

"Your mother-in-law is right," Ellen put in. "Even after the baby comes you'll need to take it easy."

"Since my folks are coming in January, and plan to stay several weeks, I'll have plenty of help."

Ellen wished she could stay longer, but her family missed her, and she needed to return home after Mandy's parents arrived. She glanced across the table at Rob and swallowed the piece of turkey she'd put in her mouth. He looked at her too, and her heart skipped a beat. Did Rob realize their time was running out? *He must never know the way I've come to feel about him. Once I leave this island, whatever may have been between us, will be a thing of the past.*

Ellen blotted her lips with a napkin and focused on finishing her food. Wishing for the impossible only saddened her. Once she was back home and found a new job, she could put Rob and all the fun times they'd had together out of her mind.

When the meal was over, everyone helped clear the table. Then the women went to the kitchen to do the dishes and put the leftovers away. Rob joined Taavi and Ken in the living room to watch TV and visit. Rob's mind wasn't on the conversation, however. All he could think about was Ellen and wishing he could spend some time alone with her today. Since she'd be going back to Indiana sometime in January, they didn't have much time left to be together. *I wonder what she would say if I asked her to stay. Could I put the past behind me and begin a relationship with Ellen? Would she turn me away if I told her about my past?*

Taavi bumped Rob's arm. "Hey, wake up. Did you hear the question Ken asked you?"

Rob jerked his head. "Uh. . .no, sorry, I did not." He looked at Ken. "What was it you asked?"

"I wondered if you play any musical instruments."

"Not really. I've fooled around with a harmonica a bit, but never got the hang of it. Someone told me once that playing a mouth harp isn't hard. All you need to do is blow and suck." He slapped his hand against his knee. "So I gave it a try, but it didn't help. Guess I'm not cut out to play an instrument."

Ken chuckled. "Makaio taught Mandy to play the ukulele. I bet she could teach you. Would ya like me to ask?"

"No, that's okay. I'll stick to outdoor sports like kayaking and leave the musical stuff to those who have talent."

Taavi looked at Ken and rolled his eyes. Rob figured his roommate thought he was ridiculous. But truthfully, he had a good reason for not wanting to learn to play an instrument—a reason that had left a scar on his heart. But he'd never talk about it—not to Ellen or even Taavi. The past was in the past, and it needed to stay buried. It was the only way he could deal with the unpleasant memories.

Rob stood up and moved across the room. What he needed right now was some fresh air, but he'd enjoy it more if Ellen went outside with him. He popped into the kitchen to see what she was doing, and found her putting a stack of clean dishes in the cupboard. "I need some air. Are you free to take a walk with me?" he asked.

"That sounds nice. I have a few more dishes to dry, and then I'll be ready."

Rob stood back and watched as she completed her task.

"When you two come back inside we'll have some pie and coffee," Mandy said as she put the clean silverware in a drawer.

Rob gave his stomach a thump. "Oh, boy. I'd better take a long walk if I'm gonna make room for any pie. I ate way too much turkey and dressing."

"I think we all did." Vickie put the last pot away. "Maybe in another hour or so we'll all have room for pie."

"I'm ready to go now." Ellen smiled up at Rob.

When they stepped outside, Rob reached for Ellen's hand and led her across the yard and down the street. It was a beautiful evening, with a light breeze to cool the warmth of the day. Several people sat on their lanais, and others were out walking.

Rob glanced at Ellen. He'd miss her when she left Kauai and wished he could ask her to stay. They paused to look at some colorful flowers growing in someone's yard. Except for the meal they'd eaten and the fall decorations placed throughout the B&B, it didn't seem much like Thanksgiving.

Ellen had a faraway look in her eyes. "It's funny to see flowers blooming this time of year. Back home the weather on Thanksgiving tends to be cold, and sometimes it snows. But inside, it's always warm and toasty, and the smell of turkey roasting goes all through the house. Dad usually has a fire going, and we all gravitate to the living room after the meal is eaten." Ellen snickered. "Dad and my uncles end up snoozing, while we women visit. In the background, the firewood would be popping and cracking. I can almost hear it."

Rob tried to visualize what she'd told him. He could only guess how much Ellen must miss her family today.

"About an hour or so after we eat, the desserts are brought out," she continued. "Along with what Mom bakes, my aunts bring a few desserts." Ellen sighed. "After indulging in the desserts, we're all stuffed—and then some. But oh, everything is always so good."

"What kind of desserts do you have?" Rob couldn't help it. Memories from past Thanksgivings flooded back to his mind.

"Mom usually makes a pumpkin pie and also mincemeat. My aunts will often bring home-made cookies or cake. A few days before the holiday, Dad freezes home-made vanilla ice cream." Ellen slowed her pace. "So on top of everything else, we end up having that too. You can only imagine how full we are by the end of the day."

Oh, I think I can. Rob's fingers itched to stroke Ellen's soft check. *You're beautiful, Ellen. I wish I'd met you a few years ago.*

Middlebury

When Ezra pedaled his bicycle into the shoe store parking lot the day after Thanksgiving, he saw Nathan putting his buggy horse away in the corral. This was the busiest shopping day in the English world, and shoppers flocked to the shoe store as well.

The front door of the store was ajar, so Ezra figured Lenore must be inside. He parked the bike near the building and hurried into the store, where he found her sitting on a stool behind the counter. "How'd your Thanksgiving go?" Ezra asked.

"It was good. My aunts and uncles came, and all our family was together except for Ellen. It didn't seem the same without her." Lenore frowned. "Christmas won't be the same without her either. But she's doing a good thing by staying in Hawaii to help Mandy and Ken."

Ezra leaned on the counter. "Your sister's been there a long time. Any idea when she might be coming home?"

Lenore's face brightened. "She'll be back sometime in January, after Mandy has her boppli and Mandy's folks arrive to help out."

Ezra smiled. "That's good to hear." *I wonder if I should write her another letter, and express my feelings for her. Or I could just wait till she gets home.* Ezra's mind worked overtime as he thought about what he ought to do once Ellen returned home. One thing was for sure: he wouldn't waste any time. He'd already missed too many opportunities to let her know his feelings. *This time I'm going to be more direct.*

Chapter 34

Kapaa

Christmas Day was overcast, with the promise of rain. Ellen stood on the lanai, looking out at the yard, and wondering if her parents had snow at home. More often than not they were blessed with a beautiful dusting of snow on Christmas Day. Sometimes it occurred as soon as Thanksgiving, and by Christmas there would be enough snow for a sleigh ride.

Today, more than ever, Ellen struggled to keep her feeling of homesickness under control. It might be Christmas, but the temperatures on Kauai seemed more like early summer.

Ellen longed to be back in Indiana. She would miss the evening hours, with a glowing fire in the living room and family members gathering around together to sing Christmas carols.

There were so many things she missed about home—starting with her family and friends.

Mom had called Ellen this morning to wish her a Merry Christmas, and she'd been able to talk to Dad, as well as her sisters. Hearing their voices brought tears to her eyes. *But I'm needed here right now,* she reminded herself.

Taavi planned to spend the day with his parents, so he had dropped by last night to wish them all a Merry Christmas. But Rob would be joining them for Christmas dinner. Ellen looked forward to spending the day with Rob. But each time they were together, her heart longed for more. She hoped someday Rob might come to Middlebury to visit. But seeing him there would only make it more difficult to say goodbye again. Sometimes she wished she'd never met Rob. Other times, Ellen found herself hoping he'd proclaim his love for her, and they could figure out some way to be together.

Ellen stepped into the kitchen to check the time. Rob should be here soon, and since there was nothing else to do at the moment, she decided to wait for him on the lanai.

She'd no more than taken a seat on the swing when Rob pulled his motor scooter into the yard. He looked handsome in his green shirt and dressy dark trousers. Ellen smiled when he got off and walked toward the house, carrying a small paper sack in his hands.

Grinning, Rob joined Ellen on the lanai and handed her the bag. "Merry Christmas! Here's a little something from me to you."

A tingling sensation swept up the back of Ellen's neck and across her face. "Oh Rob, I appreciate the gift, but I'm sorry to say, I have nothing for you."

He took a seat beside her on the swing. "I didn't buy you a gift because I wanted something in return. Besides, being here with you is gift enough for me."

The homesickness Ellen had felt previously was replaced with goosebumps stretching from her head down to her toes.

Ellen struggled to find the right words. "Thank you, Rob. I'm glad you could join us today."

"Me too." Rob pointed to the paper sack. "Go ahead and open it."

Ellen reached inside and pulled out a bar of pineapple-fragranced soap, some coconut lip gloss, and a tube of Plumeria-fragranced hand lotion. "These are so nice. Thanks."

He clasped her hand. "Glad you like them."

"You look nice today. Is your shirt new?" The nearness of him caused Ellen to shiver.

"Yeah." Rob smoothed his shirt collar. "It's not what you're used to seeing me in, but I'm glad you like it."

"Shall we go inside now?" Even though she'd rather stay here with Rob the rest of the day, Ellen rose from the swing. "Dinner should be ready soon."

As Rob sat at the table, enjoying a tasty meal and pleasant conversation, a sense of homesickness washed over him. *I wonder what Mom, Dad, and*

the rest of my family are doing today. Should I give them a call to say Merry Christmas? Would they be glad to hear from me, or would I be in for a lecture about being gone so long without contacting them?

He shifted on his chair, while glancing at Ellen. Could she sense his unrest? Did she know he struggled with deep emotions today?

From her seat across the table, Ellen gave Rob a smile. *Sure wish she wasn't so sweet.*

He looked away, concentrating on finishing what was left on his plate. If Mandy had her baby within the next few weeks, this might be the last meal he'd share with Ellen.

When everyone finished eating, the women cleared the table. Ken said he was tired and wanted to lie down for a while, so Rob decided this would be a good time to call home. He excused himself and went out to sit on the lanai. If he was going to do this, he didn't want anyone to hear his conversation.

"Rob left his cup of coffee sitting on the table," Mandy mentioned as she put some of the leftovers in the refrigerator. "I wonder if he wants it."

"I'll go see." Ellen went to the dining room and picked up Rob's cup. It was still warm, so she opened the door to the lanai, and was about to step out, when she saw Rob sitting in a chair with his cell phone up to his ear.

A rush of adrenaline shot through her body when she heard his spoken words.

"En hallicher Grischtdaag."

Ellen gasped. Rob had just wished someone a Merry Christmas in Pennsylvania Dutch. But how could it be? Rob wasn't Amish. He was English.

She stood quietly behind him and listened as he continued to speak in the Amish dialect. By now she could tell he was talking to his family since she heard him say *mamm* and *daed*. When Rob put his cell phone away, she cleared her throat.

He whirled around. "Ellen! How long have you been standing there?"

"Long enough to hear you speaking Pennsylvania Dutch." Ellen set Rob's coffee down on the table by his chair. "What's going on, Rob? Who were you talking to?"

"No one." His face flamed. "I mean, I left a message for my folks."

"Are—are you Amish?"

He nodded slowly. "I was raised Amish but never joined the church."

Ellen blinked rapidly, her body heat rising. "Why have you been lying to me about this?"

"I didn't lie—just didn't give you any details of my previous life. No one else on the island knows either."

Barely able to stand, she lowered herself into the chair beside him. "What are the details, Rob? Why did you keep the truth of your heritage from me? And what is the reason you are here on Kauai?"

He drew in some air and released it with a huff. "First of all, my name's not Rob Smith. I took that name on after I left my parents' home."

"What is your real name?"

"Rueben Zook. I was raised in an Amish home in Ronks, Pennsylvania." His face sagged. "Up until now, I've never told anyone about my Amish heritage, or that I changed my name after I ran away and came here with a new identity."

Ellen's fingers tightened around the band of her apron. "Why were you running from your past? Are you ashamed of the Amish way of life?"

Shoulders hunched, Rueben shook his head. "It's not that. I left because I killed my girlfriend, Arie Stoltzfus."

"What are you saying?" Ellen felt as if all the color had drained from her face.

"Arie and I were in the car I'd bought during my running-around years." He paused and rubbed his eyes. "As we approached the train crossing, I heard a whistle blow. She pleaded with me not to cross over, but I was sure I could make it." Rueben's hand shook. "The car stalled on the tracks. I got out and hollered at Arie to slide across the seat, but before she could make a move, the train slammed into my vehicle. I saw the whole thing happen, and I will never forget the sound of the crash. Somehow, I made myself walk toward the mangled car." Rueben's voice lowered to a whisper, and his breathing seemed erratic. "Arie would never laugh, sing, or play the guitar again. She was killed outright, and it was my fault."

Ellen sat in stunned silence as Rueben rocked back and forth, as though reliving the tragic event. "I've been angry at God ever since and vowed never to fall in love again." His eyes watered as he looked at Ellen and shook his head. "I'm sorry for letting you believe something might be happening between us. I can never return to my Amish heritage, and I can't commit to a relationship with you because you're committed to the Amish faith."

A sob rose in Ellen's throat and she leaped out of her chair. His confession only added to her confusion. She couldn't wait to go home and put this nightmare behind, but she had an impulse to take Reuben in her arms and comfort him for what he'd been through.

Ronks, Pennsylvania

Elsie Zook sat in the phone shack, shaking her head tearfully as she replayed Rueben's message. After his sudden disappearance, nearly two years ago, this was the first time she'd heard from her son. He'd made no contact with anyone else in the family either. The joy of hearing his message was almost her undoing. Rueben had called to wish them a Merry Christmas, but said nothing about where he was or if he might be coming home.

She reached under her glasses and wiped away tears as they trickled down her cheeks. *I wish Rueben had left a phone number so I could return his call, but thank You, Lord, for nudging my boy to call home. I praise You, Jesus, for keeping my son safe and for letting me hear his greatly missed voice.*

She rested her forehead on the bench in front of her. *Oh Rueben, why did you have to run off? Why couldn't you have stayed and let us help you deal with your grief over losing Arie? Don't you know how much we miss you? Doesn't it bother you that Arie's parents are grieving too?*

Elsie stood. *I must get in and share this with the rest of the family, who have gathered at home for the holiday.* She took a step toward the door of the phone shack, then paused to send up a silent prayer. *Dear Lord, please bring our son back where he belongs.*

Chapter 35

Lihue

*B*etween my job and yours, we haven't seen much of each other lately."
Taavi reached for the loaf of bread Rueben set on the counter. "Christmas
has come and gone, and I still haven't heard how your day went. Did you
have a good one?"

Rueben's jaw clenched. This wasn't a conversation he wanted to have.
Christmas was ten days ago, and he figured by now Taavi wouldn't bring
the subject up.

He undid the top button on his Hawaiian-print shirt and rubbed the
lower part of his neck. "It did not go well."

"How come? Didn't Ellen like the gift you got her?" Taavi popped a
piece of bread into the toaster.

"She said she liked it. What she didn't like was finding out that I'm not
who she thought I was."

"Huh?" Taavi tipped his head. "What are you talking about?"

Rueben recounted the whole thing—beginning with when Ellen
overheard him speaking Pennsylvania Dutch while leaving a message on
his folks' answering machine and ending with how upset she was because
he hadn't told her the truth about his heritage right away.

Taavi's head jerked back, and he gave Rueben an incredulous stare. "All
this time you've let all of us believe you were just some guy who'd come to
the island to get a little sun and have some fun, when you were running
from your past?"

Rueben nodded.

Taavi broke eye contact with Rueben. "I'm disappointed in you, man.

It hurts to know you've been feeding me a line and all the people close to you here. That's not cool."

"I'm sorry I deceived you. It was wrong, but I was ashamed to admit who I was and that I'm responsible for the death of the woman I loved."

"Carrying a burden like that is unhealthy. You've gotta forgive yourself and have faith that the Lord will help you through all this." Taavi looked at Rueben again and shook his head. "Without the Lord's help, you'll never put this behind."

"That's easy for you to say. You're not the one it happened to."

"Oh my dear *hoapili*." Taavi placed his hand on Rueben's shoulder. "I wish there was something I could do for you."

"Well, there isn't, and I guess I'm not much of a friend." Rueben tossed a cluster of grapes in his lunch pail, along with the sandwich he'd made. The last thing he wanted was pity. "I've gotta go. I can't be late for work." Before Taavi could respond, Rueben grabbed his lunch and dashed out the door.

Kapaa

Ellen fumbled with the fruit she'd finished cutting for their B&B guests. Ever since she'd learned the truth about the man she thought was English, she'd been a ball of nerves. Her emotions were so mixed, she could hardly think straight. And today, with Mandy going into labor, she was even more apprehensive. Mandy, Ken, and Vickie went to the hospital around three in the morning, but so far Ellen hadn't heard a word. Ellen wanted to be at the hospital when the baby was born, but someone had to be here to take care of their B&B guests.

She placed the kiwi, papaya, and pineapple slices on a platter and went to the refrigerator to get a carton of eggs supplied by the new owners of the organic farm. Ellen was about to crack the first egg into a bowl, when Rueben entered the kitchen. He moved past her to get a bottle of water, but didn't say a word. He didn't even look at her.

Ellen flinched. *If only he'd been honest with me from the beginning.* "Mer sedde immer ehrlich sei," she mumbled.

Rueben stepped in front of her and tilted his head. "We should always be honest, huh? Have you forgotten that I speak Pennsylvania Dutch and knew exactly what you were saying?"

"Rob... I mean Rueben. It's not easy getting used to you being Amish when all along you led me to believe you were English."

He lowered his gaze. "I couldn't get up the nerve to tell you because I was afraid of your reaction."

"I would have reacted better if you'd been truthful from the beginning. Aren't you aware of what the book of Proverbs says about dishonesty? 'Lying lips are abomination to the Lord: but they that deal truly are his delight,'" Ellen quoted.

Rueben glared at her. "I don't need a reminder. I've been lying to myself for years."

"It's not your fault Arie didn't get out of the car when you warned her."

"No, but I am to blame for trying to beat the train. I am a *glotzkopp*, and because of my stubbornness, Arie is dead. She was too young to have her life end that way."

"So what are you going to do—stay here on Kauai the rest of your life and try to bury your past?"

He nodded. "The farther I am from home, the less likely I'll think about what happened."

"Do you truly believe miles or even an ocean will change all that?" Ellen tried to be sympathetic, but her nerves were on edge. "I've never mentioned this to you before, but ever since I met you, I felt there was something sad behind your eyes. This weight you carry will eventually beat you down, if it hasn't already." Ellen paused, then added, "Rueben, you deserve to be happy."

"I can't go back and look my family in the eyes, or Arie's folks either." He scuffed the toe of his sneaker against the tile. "And happiness—well, that's the last thing I deserve."

"Don't you care how much they must miss you?"

He shrugged. "They're better off without me."

"Rueben, you can't mean that."

"I do."

Ellen looked away. She wanted to say more, but heard their guests coming into the dining room, awaiting their breakfast. "We can discuss this some other time if you like. Right now I have guests to feed." She moved over to the stove.

Rueben grabbed a second bottle of water and went out the back door.

Lihue

Ken sat beside Mandy's hospital bed, fretting. It seemed like she'd been in labor a long time. He wondered if something was wrong. The nurse who'd checked on her recently assured them everything was fine, and that many women experienced a long labor with their first child. Still, it was hard not to be concerned. He and Mandy had been through a lot since coming to Kauai, and he hated to see her suffer during labor. Ken was glad that for the moment at least, she'd dozed off.

He looked over at his mother reading a magazine in the chair across the room. *I wonder if Mom suffered much when she gave birth to me or my brother.* His fingers clenched. *I can't believe Dan didn't bother to come see me after the shark attack. What kind of brother is he? For that matter, he's been no support to Mom since Dad died.*

Ken felt thankful Ellen had come to help out and that his mom had hired Rob. Although, from what Ellen had told him and Mandy the day after Christmas, Rob wasn't even the young man's name. It was hard to understand how Rob, a.k.a. Rueben Zook, could lie about his Amish heritage and run away from home. His situation seemed similar to Ken's brother, only they'd left home for different reasons. And at least Dan wasn't trying to hide his identity.

People can make all kinds of excuses for the things they do, Ken thought, *but it all boils down to one thing: everyone is responsible for the way they deal with what life throws at them, and I'm certainly no exception.*

It had taken a while, but Ken had finally accepted the fact that he had to learn to live with his disability and stop feeling sorry for himself. It wasn't like he was completely incapable of doing things. He just couldn't do all the physical chores he used to do. But he would do what he could and leave the rest to Rueben, or whomever Mom chose to hire in the future at the bed-and-breakfast.

Ken's cell phone rang, and Mandy's eyes opened. "Sorry for waking you, honey. I forgot to silence my phone. Is there anything I can get you?"

"No. Go ahead and see who's calling."

Ken answered the call and was surprised to hear Mandy's mother on the other end.

"Hello, Ken. Isaac and I are at the port where the ship came in, and we need a ride to the B&B," Miriam said.

Ken slapped the side of his head. He knew Mandy's folks were supposed to arrive today. He just hadn't expected it to happen this early. He looked at his mother. "Mandy's folks are here already, and they a need a ride. Would you mind going to pick them up? I know they'll want to come here."

"Not a problem." She rose from the chair and picked up her purse. "I'll be back soon."

Ken got back on the phone with Miriam and told her his mother would come to get them.

Mandy looked over at Ken with a wide-eyed expression. "The pains are coming harder now. Oh, I hope my folks get here before the baby is born."

Chapter 36

Kapaa

I can't believe you're leaving in the morning. The time you've been here has gone too fast." Mandy slipped her arm around Ellen's waist as the two of them stood looking down at the baby, asleep in his crib. "I appreciate all the help you've given, as well as the emotional support I needed. I'm going to miss you so much."

Ellen swallowed hard, hoping she wouldn't break down. "I'll miss you too. Maybe when little Isaac Charles is older you can come to Middlebury to visit. I'm sure everyone in your family would like to meet him."

"I know they would, and we will do that whenever Ken is up to traveling." Mandy smiled. "Maybe you can come back to Kauai to visit us sometime."

"That would be nice." Truth was, Ellen didn't think she would ever return to Kauai or any of the other Hawaiian Islands. Unless it was another emergency, she wouldn't be able to fly, and coming by cruise ship didn't seem possible anytime in the near future either.

Ellen thought about Mandy's parents and how difficult it would be when the time came for them to return to Indiana. Miriam and Isaac had been a big help since they arrived. But they'd stayed with their new grandson and his parents only ten days, and would be going home in a few weeks.

Ellen wondered if Isaac or Miriam resented Mandy marrying Ken. If they did, they'd never shown it. They had always been kind and loving toward him. When a son or daughter married outside the Amish faith, it was difficult enough. But being separated by so many miles made it worse.

I could never marry outside the faith or move thousands of miles away, Ellen told herself. *I would miss my family, and they would miss me.*

Her thoughts went to Rueben. It was hard to believe he hadn't seen his family since he'd left home almost two years ago. Ellen understood the guilt he must feel over his girlfriend's death, but staying away from family and friends was selfish and hurtful. If Rueben had remained in Pennsylvania, his parents or church ministers could have helped him deal with the grief and guilt.

Ellen dreaded going to the airport tomorrow—not just saying goodbye to her friends, but having Rueben drive her there in Ken's SUV. When Rueben heard Vickie would be taking Ken to a doctor's appointment in the morning and had guests checking in during the afternoon hours, he'd volunteered to see that Ellen got to the airport.

Since Christmas, Rueben seemed to be avoiding Ellen, so it seemed strange he wanted to see her off. The thought of being alone with him, even for the short drive to the airport, sent shivers of apprehension through her body. Ellen hoped she wouldn't break down when she said goodbye to Rueben. She cared for him and was angry with herself for allowing it to happen.

Ellen turned her focus on the baby again. His little eyes were open, and he seemed to be smiling at her. She looked at Mandy. "Would you mind if I hold him for a while?"

"Of course not." Mandy gestured to the rocking chair in her bedroom. "Why don't you sit there and rock him? I have one little request from you first, though."

"What do you want me to do?"

"I would like to take a photo of you holding him, so I'll have this memory to look back on." Mandy's eyes misted.

"Okay. I'm all right with that." Ellen picked up the baby and took a seat in the rocking chair.

Mandy got her camera and took a couple of pictures. "Okay, Ellen, you can keep rocking the baby while I go visit with Mom and Vickie. Ken and Dad are both dozing in the living room, so they're not good company right now." Without a sound, Mandy slipped out of the room.

As Ellen rocked baby Isaac and stroked his silky dark hair, she closed her eyes and imagined what it would be like to have her own precious child.

Lihue

When Rueben drove Ellen to the airport the following morning, he tried to think of something to say. What was there to talk about? He'd messed things up with his deception. He'd ruined any chance of a relationship with her, and now she was going home.

I can only imagine what Ellen is thinking. She's committed to her church and Amish family, so I can't ask her to stay. Rueben blew out a breath. *Besides, even if she were willing to give up her Amish life, I'm not ready for a commitment to another woman.*

Rueben had left a trail of bad decisions—at home and here on Kauai. He didn't trust himself not to make more.

Rueben's thought went to his friend Taavi. *He said I need to have faith that the Lord will help me deal with all this, but I'm not sure I can. My faith in God faltered after Arie died, and I began blaming myself.*

He glanced over at Ellen. Her posture was rigid as she stared out the passenger window. *She's probably as uncomfortable as I am right now. Is there anything I can say to make things better before we part ways?*

As they drew closer to the airport, Ellen looked over at him and said, "I appreciate the ride, but you can just drop me off at the terminal. That way you won't have to pay for parking or trouble yourself any further."

"It's no trouble." Rueben shook his head. "I want to take your luggage in for you."

"I can manage."

"Your suitcase is heavy, and you'd have to lift it onto the conveyor belt where they check for items that can't be taken off the island." Rueben drove Ken's car into the parking lot and turned off the ignition. Then he got out and took Ellen's suitcase and carry-on tote from the back of the vehicle.

When Ellen exited the car, she carried her tote, while Rueben pulled the suitcase. He kept his steps slow, trying to delay the inevitable. If only he could make time stand still. *Why can't I remember what I wanted to say to Ellen?* Last night in bed, he'd rehearsed what he wanted to tell her, but now all he could do was grope for the right words to say.

Rueben had made sure Ellen was here in plenty of time, so she wouldn't miss her flight. They walked side by side, but no words were uttered between them. When they approached the conveyor belt, Rueben lifted the suitcase for her and picked it up on the other side. Then he waited as Ellen went to the counter and got her boarding pass. Once that was done and the luggage had been sent through, he began walking with her again.

As they came closer to the security line, Rueben began to panic. He still hadn't said what was on his mind, and he was almost out of time. "Wait, Ellen." He touched her arm. "There's something I need to say."

She stopped walking and turned to face him.

"Listen, I want to apologize again. I was wrong to deceive you."

She nodded.

A quick look around, and his eyes honed in on a couple who were saying goodbye with a hug and lingering kiss. He looked back at Ellen, wanting nothing more than to kiss and hold her the same way. His throat felt so dry he struggled to swallow. For this one moment, it felt as if they were the only two people in the terminal. No sounds could be heard, except for the beating of his own heart drumming in his ears. It was only he and Ellen, and as she looked up at him, Rueben felt as if he were drowning in her beautiful blue eyes.

He reached for her hand, and was pleased when she didn't resist. "I care for you, Ellen, and if things had been different, I think we could have begun a serious relationship." He paused and moistened his lips. "But I'm sure you realize under the circumstances a future for us is not possible."

"I know." Ellen's eyes glistened with tears. Her thumbs rubbed against his fingers, and her touch nearly drove him insane. "I hope someday you'll go back home and make things right with your family."

Rueben shook his head forcefully. "That's not possible. I can never return to Pennsylvania." He pulled Ellen closer and gave her a hug. *I can't believe I'm letting her go.* His mind thought one thing, but his heart said the opposite. "Goodbye, Ellen. I wish you all the best."

"I wish the same for you." Ellen turned and hurried toward the ever-growing security line.

As Rueben watched her go, the lump that had formed in his throat thickened. Then, as the line started moving, she was out of sight, swallowed up by those passengers who had followed. *If things were different, I'd go with her.*

Over the Pacific Ocean

Tears streamed down Ellen's face as she looked at the pictures Rueben had printed for her from several of their outings, including the one he'd taken of them at Spouting Horn. Saying goodbye to Mandy and her family had been difficult, but leaving Rueben had been heart wrenching. Her head told her there was no chance of a relationship with him, no matter how much she longed for it. Her heart ached, thinking about Rueben's estrangement from his family. Surely they had to miss him, and no doubt he wanted to be with them. If he could get past the guilt, Rueben might be able to go back to Pennsylvania and reestablish a relationship with his family, even if he chose not to stay there permanently.

Unable to drink the water a flight attendant had given her, Ellen watched the huge thick clouds hanging weightless in the sky like giants. *Rueben is wrong.* She squeezed her fists until her fingers ached. *Things could be different if he wanted them to be. Why won't Rueben release his guilt and give his burdens to God?*

Ellen never expected her trip to Hawaii would turn out the way it had. She'd gone there to help Mandy but had fallen in love with a man she could not have a future with. Even as the distance between them grew longer, how could her feelings be reversed?

Maybe once I get home and into a routine again, it will be easier to forget I had feelings for Rueben. Ellen closed her eyes. *I will pray for him. And also for his deceased girlfriend's family. They all have to be in pain.*

When her plane landed in Seattle, Ellen would spend the night at a hotel near the airport. Tomorrow morning, she would board another plane and should arrive in South Bend, Indiana, that evening. She looked forward to being reunited with her parents and sisters, although this homecoming would be bittersweet. *I hope the old saying "absence makes the heart grow fonder" won't hold true for me.*

Chapter 37

*O*n January sixteenth, Ellen stepped off the plane that had brought her back to her home state. The problem was, it didn't feel like home. After being in the Aloha State almost seven months, sometimes she had begun to feel it was where she belonged. Already, she missed Mandy and everyone else who'd become like family to her.

Pulling her cape tighter around her neck, Ellen had almost forgotten how cold January could be here in the Midwest. A shiver went through her body, making those warm temperatures she'd become so accustomed to that much harder to leave behind. Her cape felt heavy and bogged her down. The gray and dismal sky had no life to it.

As her feet walked on Indiana soil, Ellen's heart remained in Hawaii with Rueben. She'd thought of little else the whole trip home. Would she be able to shed the feelings that had grown within her for him?

Ellen made her way to baggage claim. The best antidote for thinking too much was work, and she hoped to remedy that by finding a job right away.

As Ellen approached the carousel to wait for her luggage, she spotted her mother and sister Ruby. Tears sprang to her eyes. It was so good to see them.

Mom enveloped Ellen in her arms with a hug so tight it nearly left her breathless. "Oh Daughter, we've missed you something awful. It's *wunderbaar* to have you home."

Ellen could barely get the words out. "I've missed you too."

When she pulled away from her mother's embrace, Ruby gave her a hug. "*Ach*, you're so tan. And here it is the middle of winter."

Chuckling, Ellen shook her head. "Not in Hawaii. Well," she corrected herself, "technically it is winter there, but you'd never know it by the beautiful warm weather they have."

"Bet you're going to miss it." Ruby pointed to the luggage, circling on the carousel. "Look, there's your suitcase coming off now. I'll go fetch it for you."

While her sister raced off to get the luggage, Ellen grinned at Mom. "You'd think she was *eiferich* to get me home."

Mom's face broke into a wide smile. "We've all been eager for that, Ellen. You've been gone much too long. And since Ruby and Darla decided not to go to Florida this winter, it'll be nice to have all of my daughters at home."

"Jah, it will be nice, but I wouldn't have felt right coming home sooner, when Mandy needed me so badly." Gripping her tote with one hand, Ellen placed the other hand on her chest. "She and Ken have been through so much these past several months. They were ever so thankful for all the support they received—not just from me, but from everyone who helped with Ken's hospital, doctor, and therapy expenses."

Mom squeezed Ellen's arm. "You did a good thing by going there."

Ruby returned with the suitcase. "Are we ready to go?"

"Jah." Mom slipped her arm around Ellen's waist. "Our driver's waiting outside the terminal, so we'd best not keep her waiting."

"I assume Dad and Lenore must be working in the store this afternoon," Ellen said as they all began walking.

Mom nodded. "You'll see them at supper in a few hours."

"What about Darla? Will she be there too, or is she scheduled to work at the restaurant this evening?"

"She's there right now," Ruby spoke up. "Darla was able to work the breakfast and lunch shift, so all our family will be together for supper."

"I'm glad." Ellen swung her tote bag as she stepped lightly. Despite missing her friends in Hawaii, it felt good to be home.

Middlebury

"How come you're panting for breath?" Ezra asked when he saw Lenore coming in the back door of the shoe store.

"I was out in the storage shed putting some boxes of shoes away that a customer didn't buy." Lenore blew on her hands and hung up her shawl. "It's cold out there, and I ran all the way back to the store."

He gave a nod. "Guess that's why your *gsicht* is red too."

Lenore touched her nose and snickered. "Bet my *naas* is as red as my face." She glanced at the clock on the far wall. "Oh, good. It's almost quitting time. I can't wait to go home."

"Are ya doing anything special tonight?" he asked, grabbing a pen.

"Jah. Mom hired a driver so she and Ruby could go to South Bend to pick Ellen up at the airport. We're gonna have a celebration supper tonight, and Mom's cookin' Ellen's favorite meal."

"That's great news." Ezra's cheekbones almost hurt from smiling so hard. "Say, what is Ellen's favorite *iems*?"

"Noodles over mashed potatoes." Lenore took a seat on a nearby stool. "Why do you care about my sister's favorite meal?"

Ezra couldn't help noticing how Lenore eyed him with suspicion, but it didn't stop him from blurting out what he wanted to do. "Think I may drop by later on to say hello."

Lenore's eyebrows squished together. "Are you sweet on my sister? Is that why you asked me about her so many times when she was gone?"

A warm flush crept across Ezra's cheeks. After working with Lenore all these months, he'd learned that she wasn't a bit shy about coming to the point. To his relief, some customers came into the store just then. Nathan began talking to one of the men, and Ezra quickly headed for the other Amish man.

He wasn't about to answer Lenore's question. The last thing he needed was Ellen's little sister blabbing to Ellen about his intentions or spreading gossip around the community. If anyone did the telling, it had to be him. Now he needed to find the right time to do it.

"It's sure nice to have you back home with us." Ellen's dad smiled at her from his seat at the head of the table. "Didn't seem right with one of my *dochder* missing."

Ellen returned his smile. It was nice to be missed, and it felt good to be home, sitting around the table with her dear family. From what she could tell, nothing had changed since she left.

Ellen took a bite of mashed potatoes. *Rueben should be with his family as well, but he chooses an unyielding life.*

"Tell us all about your time on Kauai." Darla leaned forward as she gazed at Ellen from across the table. "Did you get to do anything fun while you were there?"

Ellen nodded, thinking about all the things she and Rueben had done. "But of course, most of my time was spent helping at the organic farm, and later, the B&B Ken's mother bought from Luana and Makaio."

"I imagine you enjoyed working at the bed-and-breakfast more than taking care of smelly *hinkel*." Lenore wrinkled her nose.

Ellen laughed. "I didn't mind helping care for the chickens, but you're right—working at the bed-and-breakfast was more enjoyable."

"What kind of fun things did you do when you weren't working?" Darla asked.

Ellen blotted her mouth with a napkin. Could she tell them without letting on that she cared for Rueben? "Well, I got to see Spouting Horn again." She paused for a sip of water. "Another time, I was able to tour a replica of an ancient Hawaiian village."

"Did you go alone?" Lenore questioned.

Ellen swallowed hard. "No, I went with—"

A knock sounded on the front door, bringing their discussion to an end.

Mom went to see who it was, and returned to the dining room with Ezra. Holding a cardboard box in his hands, he moved toward the table. "My mamm made two apple pies today, and I brought one over to share with all of you." His gaze moved to Ellen, and he offered her a wide smile. "Welcome back. I bet you're glad to be home."

She nodded.

Mom took the box from Ezra. "Tell your mamm we said danki. It was a nice gesture."

With hands in his jacket pockets, Ezra rocked back and forth on his heels. "Well, um. . .guess I'd better head for home."

"Oh, don't rush off," Mom was quick to say. "Have a seat at the table and join us."

He glanced at Ellen again, then back at Mom. "It's nice of you to offer, but I already ate supper."

"That's okay," Mom said. "You can visit with us while we eat, and then we'll have some of that pie your mamm made, along with hot coffee." Grinning, she hurried from the room.

Ellen pursed her lips. *It seems odd that Mom would be excited about a pie, when she made my favorite banana whoopie pies for dessert.*

Ezra went over to one of the empty chairs at the table and sat down.

"How's the weather out there?" Dad asked. "When Lenore and I came home from the store earlier it looked like it might snow."

"No snow yet." Ezra looked at Ellen again. "Think ya might come back to work at the store?"

She shook her head. "Dad has plenty of help with you and Lenore working there. I'll start looking for a job elsewhere soon."

Ezra cleared his throat louder than Ellen thought necessary. "There's to be a young people's gathering, with a bonfire, at your friend, Sadie's soon. Think ya might go?"

Before Ellen could respond, Ruby blurted, "Darla and I will be there, and I'm sure our sister will go too. Right, Ellen?"

Ellen nodded. What else could she do? There was nothing like being put on the spot. She would most likely go because it would be nice to see all her friends again.

She rose from her seat. "Think I'll see if Mom needs any help in the kitchen."

Ellen had no more than entered the adjoining room, when Lenore showed up. "Know what I think?" she whispered to Ellen.

"What?"

"I think Ezra likes you. I'll bet he's gonna ask if he can take you home after the get-together."

Mom gave a curious look their way, but didn't say anything. Ellen noticed a faint smile on her mother's face as she continued to cut the pie.

Hoping Ezra hadn't heard their conversation, Ellen leaned closer to

Lenore and whispered, "Why would you say something like that?"

"'Cause the whole time you were in Hawaii he kept asking questions about you." Lenore rolled her eyes. "And didn't you see the way he looked at you when he sat at the table? I'm certain that poor fellow's in love with you."

Ellen's face warmed. *Could it be true? Is Ezra interested in me? If so, what should I do?*

Chapter 38

$\mathcal{T}$he day after Ellen returned home, she decided to pay Sadie a visit. Since it was Wednesday, Sadie would be working at the hardware store. She looked forward to visiting her friend and hoped she and Sadie could go out to lunch during her noon break.

As Ellen headed down the road toward Shipshewana, it felt a bit strange to be traveling by horse and buggy again. During her time in Hawaii, she'd gotten used to either riding in a car or on the back of Rueben's motor scooter. She'd enjoyed all those times spent with Rueben and hadn't even minded getting windblown on the back of his scooter. Truthfully, Ellen had found pleasure in everything she'd done with Rueben.

"There I go, thinking about him again." Ellen clamped her mouth shut. How long would it take her to get past the feelings she had for him? Perhaps the longer she was home, the more distant her memory of Rueben would become. She hoped so, because it did no good to pine for something she couldn't have.

Soon another buggy came from the opposite direction. As it drew closer, Ellen realized it was Ezra's mother. They greeted each other with a hearty wave, and their horses trotted on.

Ellen reflected on Lenore saying the other night that she believed Ezra might be in love with her. "What nonsense." She snapped her horse's reins. "Let's go, Flame. It'll be lunchtime soon, and we need to get to Shipshewana."

Shipshewana

When Ellen entered the hardware store, she found Sadie behind the counter, but there were no customers at the moment.

As soon as Ellen stepped up to the counter, Sadie put down her notepad and leaped off the stool. "Ellen! What a joy it is to see you. When did you get home?"

"Yesterday, late afternoon." Ellen hugged her friend. "If you haven't taken your lunch break yet, I thought we could go to the little café in this building and visit while we eat."

Sadie nodded. "I haven't eaten yet. It'll be great getting caught up and hearing all about your trip."

Ellen smiled and slipped off her outer bonnet. Even though she'd written Sadie several letters, she hadn't told her everything—especially about Rueben.

Sadie informed her boss she was going to lunch, and the two of them headed down the hall to the restaurant. After placing their orders at the counter and finding a place near the back, they took a seat.

Sadie leaned forward, with her elbows on the table. "I'm eager to hear how Mandy and Ken are doing, and also their boppli."

"That baby is adorable. Little Isaac has Mandy's brown hair and Ken's blue eyes, but that could change as he grows older." Ellen took napkins from the holder for her and Sadie. "Mandy's doing well and getting her strength back."

"How about Ken? Is he getting along better now?" Sadie asked.

Ellen nodded. "He uses a cane and has some limitations, but Rueben's there to help out, so they're getting along as well as can be expected."

Sadie tipped her head. "Who's Rueben? I thought you said Ken's mother hired a young man named Rob to do the yard work and maintenance at the bed-and-breakfast."

Ellen's shoulders hunched. "Rueben Zook is Rob Smith's real name. He was raised in Pennsylvania, and his parents and siblings are Amish."

"What?" Sadie's brows lifted high on her forehead. "Tell me more."

"It's complicated. That's why I wanted to share this with you in person and not in a letter or phone call."

Sadie leaned closer. "You have my undivided attention."

Ellen explained everything about Rueben's situation: his girlfriend, the accident, and why he'd hidden out in Hawaii.

"It hurt me deep inside when he admitted this to me." She lowered her head. "If Rueben cared for me, like he said, then he should have been honest from the beginning."

"Is he ashamed of his Amish heritage?"

"I don't believe so. It has more to do with Rueben blaming himself for his girlfriend's death and being unable to face her family or his."

Sadie rubbed the bridge of her nose. "It's a good thing you didn't show your romantic side and get involved with him. He's not an honest person."

"To be frank, I do have strong feelings for Rueben." Ellen fingered her napkin. "But I'll get over it. It's just going to take some time."

"You should get a job so you'll be too busy to think about Rob—I mean, Rueben." Sadie shifted against the back of her seat. "And if someone asks you out on a date, you should go."

Ellen shrugged. "I'll consider it."

Kapaa

Mandy smiled, watching her father sitting in the recliner, holding his precious namesake. Mom sat near him, watching little Isaac. "He's such a good boppli."

"Jah," Dad agreed.

What a precious sight to see her parents' joy as they interacted with their newest grandchild. Mandy wished Mom and Dad could stay here permanently, but they needed to return to their family and Dad's job back home. They would board a ship next week that would take them to California. Then it would be a train ride to Indiana.

Mandy moved closer to Ken on the couch and reached for his hand. It comforted her to see his strength returning and know that he had accepted his limitations with a more positive attitude. For a while, she'd been worried about his emotional state, but since the baby came, Ken seemed much calmer and upbeat. Their lives seemed to be back on track, although it did seem strange to be living in the home that used to belong to Luana and Makaio. She missed their smiling faces and gentle spirits. Maybe someday she, Ken, and little Isaac could fly to the Big Island for a visit. It would be fun to meet Makaio and Luana's newest granddaughter too.

Mandy thought about Ellen, and how much she missed her. It was selfish, but she wished things could have worked out between Ellen and Rueben and that they could live in Indiana. It was strange how her thinking had changed, because Mandy hadn't wanted Ellen and Rueben to develop a relationship at first—not until she learned that Rueben had been raised Amish. If only he'd get right with God and go back to his family, there could be a possibility of him and Ellen getting together. But Rueben seemed determined to wallow in self-pity, letting the guilt of his girlfriend's death swallow him up like a bottomless pit. All Mandy and Ken could do was continue to pray for Rueben.

Mandy sighed, shifting positions. *Guess some things just aren't meant to be. I'm sure someday Ellen will find the right man and get married.*

Needing a break from his work in the yard, Rueben entered the kitchen and got a piece of fruit from the refrigerator. As he ate the papaya, he watched the middle-aged Hawaiian woman who'd been hired to take Ellen's place. She moved about the kitchen, helping Vickie get a midday snack ready for the two couples currently staying at the B&B. Every time he saw the native woman, he thought about Ellen and how much he missed her.

Well, I can't stand around here all day, feeling sorry for myself. Rueben wiped his hands on a paper towel and headed back outside.

He'd begun watering some of the plants, when Ken came out of the house. Using his cane, Ken limped over to Rueben and stopped in front of him. "How long are you gonna let this go on?"

"What?"

Ken gestured to the picnic table. "Let's take a seat. I'm more comfortable sitting down."

"Okay." Rueben turned off the spray nozzle and put the hose on the ground. As he followed Ken across the yard, he could almost predict what this conversation would be about.

Rueben took a seat on one side of the table, and Ken seated himself on the other.

"I've been watching you mope around here ever since Ellen left, and I think you were foolish for letting her go." Ken stared right at Rueben, as though daring him to say otherwise.

Rueben lifted his shoulders. "She needed to go home. Her place is with her family, not here on Kauai."

"I'm well aware, but you should have gone with her."

Rueben shook his head with force. "No way! I can't go back to the mainland and face my demons."

Ken groaned. "Thanks to the shark attack that nearly took my arm and crippled my left leg, I've had to face my own share of uncertainties."

"Yeah, I know."

"I also lived near the Amish the first two years of my marriage, and I've come to know Amish values, as well as their ways."

Rueben massaged his forehead. "What are you getting at?"

"If you return to Pennsylvania and talk to your deceased girlfriend's family, I'm bettin' they'll offer their forgiveness right away." Ken leaned forward. "As I'm sure you must be aware, the Amish realize that without forgiveness there can be no healing."

With both hands clutching his stomach, Rueben rocked back and forth. It was difficult to speak, or even think. Before he could ask anyone else's forgiveness, he needed to forgive himself. The agony he felt over Arie's death screamed for release.

Rueben's shoulders shook as he rested his head in the palms of his hands. *Dear Lord, forgive me for what I did. Give me the courage to go home and face my deepest fears.*

Chapter 39

Now buck up and stop feeling sorry for yourself, Mandy thought as she changed her little one's diapers. *Living here isn't so bad, and you have much to be grateful for.*

Baby Isaac gurgled and kicked his tiny feet. "Look at you, my little sweetie. You just wanna go, don't you?" Mandy chuckled, in spite of her melancholy mood. Her bundle of joy overwhelmed her heart with happiness. She loved watching everything about her tiny son: his smiles, when he slept, and even his healthy cries, letting her know he was hungry. Isaac was two weeks old, and other than when he was hungry, he hardly ever cried.

Mandy, Ken, and Vickie were good about taking pictures of the newest family member. Mandy planned to mail pictures to her parents, so they could share in the things they'd be missing as this little one grew.

Vickie had sold her car a week ago and bought a minivan so she could carry more passengers. This morning, Vickie had driven Mom and Dad to the port in Lihue so they could begin their return trip to the mainland. Of course, Mandy, Ken, and the baby went along. It had been difficult saying goodbye to her parents, especially because Mandy didn't know when she might see them again. Their future was uncertain, but at least she and Ken had been blessed with a healthy child.

Mandy was grateful for Vickie. In addition to paying off the remainder of Ken's hospital bills with the money she'd earned from the sale of the farm, Ken's mother had provided an income for them by buying the B&B. She was a good grandma, loving mother, and the best mother-in-law a girl could ask for. It was a shame Vickie's other son didn't care enough to come see her or his brother, not to mention his first nephew.

Mandy lifted Isaac into her arms and kissed his soft cheek. *If my folks could come here all the way from Indiana, surely Dan could fly to Kauai from California.* She'd been praying since the time Dan and his wife left Kauai that things would work out for the best for all of them. She just never expected Dan would stay away so long.

As Mandy headed down the hall toward the living room, she spotted Rueben's baseball hat on the entry table. In addition to taking Mandy's folks to the ship, Vickie had dropped Rueben off at the airport.

Ken had told Mandy about his conversation with Rueben last week, and how Rueben had asked God to forgive him. She wondered if Rueben might end up staying in Pennsylvania. Either way, she hoped things worked out well when he met with Arie's family.

"Where would you like me to put this vase after I throw out the wilted flowers?" Kamilla, the woman who'd taken Ellen's place, asked Vickie as they worked together to clean one of the guest rooms.

"I keep all my vases in the lower cupboard on the right side of the kitchen sink," Vickie responded. Since Kamilla had only been working here a few weeks, she hadn't learned where everything should go.

"Okay, I'll take care of that now." Kamilla sent a smile in Vickie's direction and hurried from the bedroom.

Vickie hummed to herself as she opened a window to air out the room. She inhaled deeply, watching the sheer curtains blow inward as the breezes filtered through. It had rained yesterday, and the fresh air felt cleansing.

Things were running smoothly at the B&B, with the new people she'd hired to replace Ellen and fill in for Rueben while he was gone. Even, so, it didn't feel right without them. Ellen was always so cheerful and didn't have to be asked to do the chores. Kamilla, on the other hand, sometimes seemed unable to make a decision on her own. Perhaps, being new, she was overly cautious, not wanting to overstep her bounds.

In some ways, Vickie wished Ellen could have stayed on, but it was unrealistic to expect her to remain when her family was on the mainland. Besides, to stay would have meant Ellen would have to give up her Amish way of life, as Mandy had done. Only Mandy had never joined the church, so that made it easier.

Pilipo, the man taking Rueben's place, was a hard worker, but he rarely said anything unless spoken to. The only time she heard him talking was when he had his cell phone up to his ear.

Rueben, who'd once seemed like an introvert, had become outgoing and made conversation with the B&B guests when they were in the yard.

Pulling her thoughts in another direction, Vickie picked up the feather duster. She was about to tidy up the top of the dresser, when Kamilla called her from the kitchen. "You're wanted on the phone, Mrs. Williams."

Vickie stuck her head out the open doorway. "Can you take a message?"

"It's your son."

Vickie pushed an errant piece of hair away from her face. "Did you say someone needs to speak to my son? If so, Ken's on the lanai with Mandy and the baby."

Kamilla stepped into the hall. "The call's not for Ken. The man on the phone said he's your son, Dan, and he wants to speak to you."

Vickie's heart raced as she dropped the duster and rushed down the hall. Her hand trembled when she picked up the phone. "Aloha, Dan."

"Hi, Mom. How's it going? Are you, Ken, Mandy, and the new baby doing okay?"

"We're fine." Vickie took a seat at the table. It was good to hear Dan's voice. "Ken's getting by with the use of his cane. Mandy and little Isaac are doing well too. How about you and Rita?"

"We're both good." Dan cleared his throat. "Uh, the reason I'm calling is because I owe you a long-overdue apology."

"Oh?"

"I let you down by leaving Kauai soon after Dad died, and I'm sorry. I've been afraid to come back and face the loss I felt when he died." Dan paused, and Vickie heard him blow his nose. "Rita's settled in here with her family, so it wouldn't be fair to uproot her. But we'd like to come to Kauai for a visit soon, if that's okay with you."

Joy bubbled in Vickie's soul. She'd almost given up on her son returning home, even for a visit. His apology moved her to tears. "I forgive you, Son. You and Rita will always be welcome to come and stay for as long as you like. We have a room we don't rent to our guests. It's for family and close friends when they visit. Please let us know whenever you're free to come, and we'll roll out our Hawaiian welcome mat."

Dan chuckled. "Since we have that settled, I'd like to talk to Ken now, if he's available."

"He's on the lanai with Mandy and the baby. I'll take the phone out to him."

"Okay. Mahalo, Mom."

Vickie stepped onto the lanai and smiled when she saw Ken stretched out on the hammock with the baby across his chest. Mandy sat on the porch swing, reading a book.

"Your brother's on the phone. He wants to talk to you, Ken." Vickie went to the hammock.

Ken's eyes widened. "Okay, Mom. Would you mind taking Isaac so I can sit up?"

She leaned over and swept her precious grandson into her arms. The warmth and sweet scent of the little guy's baby lotion brought back pleasant memories of when her boys were babies. Oh, how she missed those days when she and Charles raised their children together. But now she had something else to look forward to.

Ken sat up and swung his legs over the side of the hammock, while Vickie took a seat on the swing next to Mandy. She patted the baby's back and was rewarded with a burp.

"Hi, Dan." Ken held the phone close to his ear. "How are things in California?"

"Everything's fine here, but I didn't call to talk about me. I called to tell you how sorry I am for running out on you and Mom after Dad died. I was selfish and should have had the courage to stay and help out—not leave you stuck with all the responsibility." Dan paused a few seconds. "I should have been there for you after the shark attack too. Will you forgive me, Brother?"

Ken swallowed, in an attempt to push down the lump in his throat.

" 'Course I forgive you. I just wish you didn't live so far from us now."

"I know, but Rita's family is here, and. . ."

"No need to explain. I understand where you're comin' from." Ken smiled when Mandy came over to stand by his side. He appreciated it even more when she put her hand on his shoulder and gave it a squeeze.

"We hope to visit Kauai soon," Dan said. "I'm looking forward to holding that new nephew of mine. Is it him I hear gurgling in the background?"

"Yeah, that's my son. I can't wait for you to meet him."

"I'm anxious too. As soon as we get reservations made I'll let you know."

"We'll look forward to that."

"I'll call again soon. It was great talking to you and Mom."

"Same here. Oh, and be sure to say hello to Rita for us."

"Will do. Please tell Mandy I said the same."

When Ken hung up he took Mandy's hand. "I think things are gonna be okay with me and Dan. That's one burden lifted from my shoulders."

She bent down and gave him a kiss. "I'm so glad."

Over the Pacific Ocean

Rueben fidgeted in his seat, trying to find a comfortable position. He'd booked his airline ticket in coach, and there wasn't much leg room for a man of his stature. Looking beyond the extended seats and into first class ahead of that, he wished he'd spent the extra money for a better seat. He'd only have to put up with the cramped quarters a few more hours. Then he could get off the plane in Seattle and stretch his legs.

Rueben glanced at his Hawaiian-print shirt. Then he got to thinking about the hat he'd left behind. *No problem. I'll get it when I go back to Kauai.* Unless things went better than he hoped, Rueben probably wouldn't stay in Pennsylvania.

He had mixed feelings about seeing his family again. While it would be great to visit and catch up on their lives, they might criticize him for running off to Hawaii instead of staying home and dealing with Arie's death.

Rueben dreaded more than anything seeing Arie's folks and not knowing what their reaction would be. He hoped they'd forgive, but his nerves were on edge. *Oh man.* Rueben glanced at his cell phone to check the time. *After punishing myself since the accident, getting criticized by Arie's folks can't make me feel any worse. But thanks to Ken, I decided to go home, and I plan to see it through.*

The man sitting next to Rueben began to snore, so Rueben slipped on his earphones to drown out the aggravating noise. He could have paid to watch a movie, but right now all he wanted to do was close his eyes and try to relax. Rueben had made a mess of things in his young life, and if nothing else, he needed to make things right with Arie's parents. Unfortunately, it may be too late for him and Ellen.

Chapter 40

Ronks

*R*ueben sat on the edge of the bed in his old room, staring out the window at the dismal winter weather. The backyard, covered with snow, sat in sharp contrast to the murky gray sky. He heard someone downstairs stoking the wood stove, but the heat hadn't made it to his chilly room.

As soon as Rueben woke up, he felt an ache above his eyes. Using his fingers to massage the area, Rueben moaned. "I don't need a *koppweh* today."

Rueben had arrived at his parents' home late Thursday evening. He'd rented a car after his plane landed in Philadelphia and gone straight to Ronks. He wasn't surprised that Mom, Dad, and his siblings had greeted him with warm embraces. What had surprised Rueben was they thought he'd come to stay. When he explained his reason for returning home was to make things right with Arie's folks, Dad had given him a stern look and said, "So you're not going to take classes and join the Amish church?"

Rueben said he hadn't made up his mind, and Mom started to cry.

"Don't know why they're trying to push me to join the Amish church," Rueben mumbled as he slipped on a pair of jeans. "I just got back and don't know yet if I'm staying." He bent to tie his shoes.

He realized how hurt his family must feel; especially when he'd told them this trip was mainly to see Arie's parents. He'd need to apologize for that.

Rueben put on a shirt and made his way downstairs, where he found Mom in the kitchen, fixing breakfast.

"*Guder mariye.*" She offered him a pleasant smile. "Did you sleep well, Son?"

He nodded, choosing not to mention his headache. "Good morning. It felt strange to wake up to a cold room, though. I'm used to the warm, balmy weather in Hawaii and being able to open windows most of the time."

Mom pursed her lips, looking at Rueben over the top of her metal-framed glasses. "Why Hawaii, Rueben? If you had to leave home, what made you go so far away?"

"I've always wondered what the Hawaiian Islands were like." He took a glass down from the cupboard and poured orange juice from the container on the kitchen table. "I was sure nobody would know me there and figured it was a chance to start my life over and leave the past behind. Thought it would be easier to be around strangers." He laid a hand against his chest. "'Course, the past has a way of catching up to a person, and when it does, there's no place one can hide. Miles—and certainly not an ocean—didn't help me forget."

Mom clucked her tongue while shaking her head. "You should have stayed here, Rueben, and let us help you deal with Arie's death."

"I didn't want anyone's help. I needed to deal with it my own way." He sank into a chair at the table. "Thought I was doing a good job of it too. That is, until Ellen came along."

Mom quit stirring the pancake ingredients and came to join him at the table. "Who's Ellen?"

Rueben drank his juice, and then told his mother all about Ellen.

Mom pushed her glasses higher on her nose. "Are you in love with her, Son?"

"Yeah, but I can't even think about pursuing a relationship with Ellen till I talk with Arie's parents and seek their forgiveness."

Mom gave Rueben's arm a loving pat. "You need to go talk to Marcus and Susan soon."

"You're right, Mom." Rueben rose from his seat. "And I'm goin' over to see them now before I lose my nerve."

"What about breakfast?" she called as he grabbed his jacket and headed for the back door.

"The juice was enough. I'll see you when I get back. Maybe I'll be hungry by then."

After leaving Arie's parents' home, Rueben sat in his car, staring at the dreary landscape before him. He couldn't believe Susan and Marcus had forgiven him for being the cause of their daughter's death. Rueben would always remember the way Susan touched his arm and said, "Of course we forgive you. After all, it was not your fault Arie didn't get out of the car when you warned her that the train was coming."

"Maybe she didn't realize how close it was and thought she had plenty of time," Marcus had added. "I'm sure Arie wouldn't have stayed in the car if she'd known what would happen."

Rueben rubbed his forehead, where the headache had been earlier. *But it was my fault for trying to beat the train.* He had told Arie's parents that, but they'd said they didn't hold him responsible for their daughter's death.

He closed his eyes. *They've forgiven me, Lord. Now I need to forgive myself and try to get my life back on track. But where do I begin? How do I start over?*

Pulling his cell phone from his pocket, Rueben opened his eyes. It was ten o'clock, which meant in Kauai, it was the wee hours of the morning, so he couldn't call Mandy. He would go back to his parents' house and wait till everyone at the B&B would likely be up before calling to ask for Ellen's address. Tomorrow after breakfast, Rueben would tell his folks goodbye and head for Indiana. According to his GPS, Middlebury was an eight- or nine-hour drive from here. But if the weather didn't cause a delay, he should make it by Saturday evening.

Middlebury

"I don't know about you, but I'm sure looking forward to the young people's gathering at Sadie's." Holding the horse's reins with one hand, Darla reached across the buggy seat and tapped Ellen's arm. "Did you hear what I said?"

"Jah, I'm sure it will be fun." Truthfully, Ellen would prefer to stay home this chilly Saturday evening, but Sadie had mentioned her dad planned to build a bonfire in their yard. As long as she stayed close to its warmth, she probably wouldn't be cold.

This was Ellen's first young people's outing since she'd gotten home, and she looked forward to a time of singing, eating, and socializing. Hopefully, it would help take her mind off Rueben and wondering what he was doing in Hawaii. She'd also been thinking about Mandy, hoping things were going okay at the bed-and-breakfast now that she and Mandy's parents weren't there to help out. Vickie had hired a native woman to take over her position. No doubt, things were working out.

"Too bad Ruby has to work at the restaurant until eight." Darla broke into Ellen's musings. "Yesterday she thought she'd be able to join us tonight, but then the manager asked if Ruby could work someone else's shift who'd called in sick."

"There will be other gatherings." Ellen pulled her cape a little tighter around her neck. During the holidays on Kauai, she'd missed seeing snow. Now, as a chilly breeze blew in through the cracks around the buggy door, she longed for warmer weather.

Ellen saw the glow from the bonfire and smelled the scent of wood smoke as they approached the large white farmhouse where Sadie lived.

"Here we are." Darla led their horse and buggy down the lane and up to the barn, where several other buggies were parked. They both got out, and Ellen helped her sister unhitch the horse.

While Darla led him to the barn, Ellen took the container of brownies she'd brought along into the house. She found Sadie in the kitchen, getting paper cups, plates, and plastic utensils from the cupboard.

Sadie smiled when Ellen set the brownies on the table. "*Willkumm!* I'm so glad you came." She placed the items she held on the counter and gave Ellen a hug.

"I'm glad I did too. The big bonfire looks inviting."

"Dad was having fun getting it built." Sadie glanced past Ellen. "Did Darla and Ruby come with you?"

"Just Darla. Ruby had to work." Ellen looked out the window, where the yard was aglow from the fire. "Who all is here?"

"Let's see. . . .Mary Ruth Zimmerman and her boyfriend, Andrew; the Lehman sisters, Sharon and Debra. Ezra Bontrager is here too, and so is. . ."

Ellen's thoughts drew inward. It was a silly notion, but she wished Rueben could be with her tonight. How nice it would be to sit around the bonfire with him and roast marshmallows.

As Ezra sat close to the fire, roasting a hot dog, he watched Ellen sitting between Darla and Sadie.

Ellen's sure pretty. I'm glad she's back from Hawaii and came here tonight. I wonder what she'd say if I asked if I could take her home? Think I might muster the courage to ask.

Ezra let go of his roasting stick with one hand to scratch an itch on his nose. In the process, he almost lost his hot dog. He grabbed the meat in time, and finished roasting it just the way he liked—not too blackened, but heated all the way through.

After placing the meat in a bun, Ezra got up from his folding chair and walked over to the picnic table where the condiments, chips, and baked beans had been set. His stomach growled, thinking how good this meal would taste. He was glad everyone had prayed silently before the food was set out. That meant he could dive right in.

While Ezra squirted ketchup on his hot dog, he overheard Ellen talking to Sadie.

"Have you heard anything from Rueben since you left Kauai?" Sadie leaned close to her friend.

Ellen shook her head. "I've thought about sending him a letter, or even calling the B&B. But I'm not sure if. . ."

Ezra's jaw clenched as Ellen moved to the back of the line, where others waited to get their food. His frustration mounted, unable to hear the rest of her sentence. He wanted to know what else she'd said to Sadie about this fellow Rueben. Who was he anyway, and why would Ellen want to call or write to him?

Ezra remembered Ellen mentioning in the one letter she'd written him that she'd done some fun things while on Kauai with someone named

Rob. But she hadn't said anything about anyone named Rueben.

He finished dishing up, and walked toward the end of the line on the way back to his chair by the fire. As he strode past the young women, he heard Sadie say, "You shouldn't have let yourself fall for him, Ellen. You should keep your focus here, not on someone you met on Kauai."

Ezra hurried past, barely able to hang on to his plate. It wasn't the cold causing his hands to tremble. Unless he was mistaken, Ellen was in love with this Rueben.

He took his seat and stared at the food on his paper plate, no longer hungry. Ezra picked up his soda can to take a drink and ended up sloshing it on his sleeve. *How can Ellen be in love with Rueben? Why, the guy isn't Amish, so how could it work?*

Ezra wiped his sleeve with a napkin. *Maybe I've been fooling myself, thinking I had a chance with Ellen. Truth is, she's never given any indication that she has feelings for me. Could be it's time to move on.*

Ezra glanced in Ellen's direction. *Or maybe I ought to let Ellen know how I feel about her and see how she responds. After all, I'm here, and this fellow from Kauai is not.*

Chapter 41

*W*hen Rueben's vehicle drew closer to the address Mandy had given him for Ellen, his palms grew sweaty. He remembered during his phone conversation with Mandy, she had said she and Ken would pray for a good outcome. The Lord had been working in his life each day since he'd had the talk with Ken, and Rueben's faith was growing.

Holding the steering wheel with one hand and wiping the other on his pant legs, Rueben began to fret. *What if Ellen doesn't want to see me? I hope I didn't make a mistake coming here.*

He drew a quick breath. *But I'm here now, so I may as well see it through.*

Rueben drove up the snow-covered driveway and parked his car near the barn. He got out quickly, before he lost his nerve, and sprinted for the house, unmindful of the slushy snow.

He stepped onto the porch and hesitated at the door before he knocked. A striped feline sauntered up to Rueben, meowing and pawing at his leg. Rueben looked down and chuckled. "Are you as cold as I am, kitty?"

When the door opened, a young Amish girl, who looked a lot like Ellen, greeted him. "Can I help you?"

"Umm. . .is this where Ellen Lambright lives?" Rueben's mouth felt numb. He struggled to get his words out.

"Jah, but my sister's not here right now."

Rueben blew on his cold hands. "Would you mind telling me where she is? I need to speak with her."

She tipped her head. "About what? Who are you anyway?"

"Oh, sorry. My name is Rueben Zook. I met Ellen in Hawaii." He leaned against the door frame. "And who are you?"

"I'm Lenore."

Rueben smiled. "Ah yes, she told me about you."

Lenore stared up at him with a placid expression. "You must be from Hawaii all right, 'cause your face is so tan."

"Yes I am." He glanced at the snowflakes drifting down, as though in slow motion. "Would you please tell me where your sister is?"

"She went to her friend Sadie's place. There's a young people's gathering there tonight." Lenore crossed her arms over her chest. "I wasn't invited, 'cause I'm only fifteen. The others who'll be there are all courting age."

"Can I have the address? I need to talk to Ellen right away."

The girl's jaw jutted out. "Guess it's okay. I'll be right back." She stepped inside, leaving Rueben on the porch to shiver and wait. Through the slightly open door, he watched the contented tiger cat take a bath near the entrance table. *At least the feline is allowed inside. But I'm a stranger to Ellen's sister, so what can I expect?*

Rueben blew on his hands again. He wished he'd thought to buy a heavier coat before he left Pennsylvania. And he didn't have warm gloves either. The lightweight jacket Rueben wore did little to keep out the chill.

A few minutes later, Lenore returned and handed Rueben a slip of paper. "Here's Sadie Kuhn's address."

"Thanks." Rueben stepped off the porch and hurried back to his car. His stomach fluttered at the thought of seeing Ellen. He hoped this wasn't a mistake.

By the time Rueben reached the address Lenore gave him, the snow was coming down harder. He pulled onto the driveway and parked his car near several black-topped buggies. Thanks to the glow of the bonfire on one side of the yard, he had no trouble seeing where the carriages were parked. The Indiana buggies were different from those in Lancaster County, where the tops and sides were gray.

Rueben got out of the car, and was about to head toward the group of people sitting around the fire, when he spotted Ellen. She stood next to one of the buggies, talking to a young Amish fellow. The man stood close to Ellen. His head was mere inches from hers.

Heart pounding, Rueben stepped into the shadows and watched. He wasn't close enough to understand what they said, but his throat tightened when the man put his hand on Ellen's shoulder.

I'm too late. Ellen already has a suitor. Who knows—maybe they'd been courting before Ellen went to Kauai. She had never mentioned having a steady boyfriend, but that didn't mean she wasn't being courted.

Rueben rubbed his arms as he made his way back to the car. The icy chill he felt had nothing to do with the wintry snow drifting down from the sky. He should have made things right with Ellen before she left Kauai, and now it was too late. Rueben would find a place to stay the night and then leave for Pennsylvania in the morning. He'd spend a week or so with his family before returning to Kauai. Without Ellen in his life, there was nothing here for him.

As a car backed down the Kuhns' driveway, with its headlights shining in her face, Ellen shielded her eyes and stepped away from Ezra's buggy. She couldn't make out the driver but wondered if he or she was an English neighbor or perhaps someone who was lost and had used this driveway to turn around. Of course, the vehicle hadn't actually turned around—it had backed down the driveway, going faster than it should, especially in the snow.

"I wonder who that was," Ezra commented.

Ellen shook her head. "I don't know."

"Well, whoever it was, they nearly blinded us with their bright lights." Ezra spoke in a high-pitched tone.

Ellen glanced at her friends by the bonfire. "We should get back. Sadie's probably wondering where I went."

"Okay, but there's one more thing I want to say." Ezra shuffled his feet, making a horseshoe design in the snow. "I'm glad you came out to your sister's buggy to get your gloves. It gave me a chance to speak with you alone, but I didn't get everything said."

Ellen stirred restlessly, shivering as she shifted her weight from one foot to the other. She could hardly feel her toes, as the cold seeped into her shoes. Ezra had already asked if he could court her, and Ellen had told him that she was sorry, but she didn't see him as anything more than a friend. She hoped he didn't think he could change her mind. "What else did you want to say, Ezra?"

He reached out his hand, like he might touch her arm, but then let it drop to his side. "Earlier, I heard you tell Sadie about some other fellow."

All Ellen could do was nod.

"Well, after thinking it over, I realized you and I are not meant to be together. So I wanted you to know that there are no hard feelings. I want you to be happy, and if it's not with me, then I hope you find someone else."

Ellen smiled. "Danki, Ezra. I wish the same for you as well."

"Okay, then. Now that we have that settled, let's go roast some marshmallows."

Hobbling on near-frozen feet, Ellen followed Ezra back to the bonfire. She was glad they'd had this opportunity to chat. The one thing that puzzled her, though, was why, if he was interested in her, he'd been so bossy when they'd worked at Dad's store together.

It was nice of Ezra to say he hoped I would find someone else, but the man I love lives in Hawaii. I wish now I'd never met Rueben or discovered his past.

When Ellen and Darla arrived home from Sadie's that evening, Ellen said she was tired and headed for her room. She was almost to the door, when Lenore stepped into the hall from her bedroom. "How'd the gathering go this evening?"

"It was nice." Ellen smoothed her sister's long hair away from her face. "I'm surprised you're still up. The house was dark when Darla and I came in, so I figured everyone had gone to bed."

"I waited up for you."

"How come?"

"Wanted to find out what the tan fellow from Hawaii said when he saw you."

Ellen's brows drew inward. "What are you talking about?"

Lenore motioned for Ellen to come to her room and shut the door. "He said his name was Rueben, and that he'd met you in Hawaii. When I said you weren't here, he asked where you'd gone." Lenore took a seat on the edge of her bed. "Wasn't sure if I should tell him, but I ended up giving him Sadie's address, 'cause he said he needed to talk to you."

Ellen collapsed on the bed beside her sister. She never expected Rueben would show up here. But there was no reason Lenore would make up such a story.

"So did he get to Sadie's? And did he tell you what he wanted?" Lenore tugged on Ellen's dress sleeve.

"No, I never saw Rueben." Ellen brought her hands up to her face. *Could Rueben have been driving the car that came into the Kuhns' yard? But if it was him, why'd he leave without looking for me?* Ellen jumped up and raced for the door.

"Where ya goin'?"

Ellen looked back at her sister. "Out to the phone shack to make a call."

"At this hour?" Lenore yawned and stretched her arms out to the sides. "Nobody we know will be in their phone shack to check for messages this late at night. Don't you think you ought to wait till morning?"

"The phone call I'll make is to Mandy. It'll be early evening on Kauai—not close to midnight, like it is here."

"How come you're callin' her?"

"To ask for Rueben's cell number. I'm sure either she, Ken, or Vickie must have it." Ellen didn't wait for her sister's response. She grabbed the flashlight from Lenore's dresser and hurried from the room. If Rueben had shown up at Sadie's house, she needed to find out what he wanted.

Chapter 42

*W*hen Rueben woke up the following morning, he felt as though his head had been stuffed with cotton. He didn't know if it was from jetlag or not getting enough sleep the night before. After returning to the Pleasant View Bed-and-Breakfast, where he'd booked a room in Middlebury, he'd lain awake for several hours.

As he lay there, looking around his room, Rueben compared the B&B to the one on Kauai. This place had a country vibe, with its rustic furniture and dried flowers, unlike the Palms Bed-and-Breakfast, which featured tropical décor and wicker furniture. There was a brightness to the Hawaiian B&B and a scent of flowers when the windows were open, allowing the warm breezes to come in.

Rueben sat up in bed, stretching his arms over his head, then plopped back down in the warm sheets. He had asked God's forgiveness, as well as Arie's parents', and was certain he'd been forgiven. One would think that should be enough, but it wasn't. Rueben had prayed about things last night and come to the conclusion that he needed to speak to Ellen before returning to Kauai. If there was even a chance she might choose him over the man he'd seen her with, he had to take it. He was determined to let her know how he felt, and it was worth the risk of rejection just to see her one more time. If Ellen sent him away, he'd have to come to grips with it, because more than anything, Rueben wanted her to be happy.

Since it was nine o'clock, Rueben figured Ellen would be in church with her family. So he'd hang around the B&B all morning and go back to Ellen's house this afternoon when she would likely be home. He had paid for one more night here and didn't have to check out until Monday morning, at which time he would head for Pennsylvania.

Rueben arrived at the Lambrights' home shortly before four that afternoon.
Sure hope Ellen's here this time and I can speak with her face to face.

His steps were solid as he made his way through the snow and up to the porch. After two knocks, the front door opened.

"Oh, it's you again." Ellen's youngest sister, Lenore, looked up at him with a curious expression. "If you came to see Ellen, she's not here."

"Again?" He frowned. "Where is she this time?"

"Ellen went to visit some of her friends, and I'm not sure where she is right now or when she'll get home."

"Can I speak to one of your parents? I'd like to leave a message for Ellen." Rueben didn't trust the girl to give her sister a message.

Lenore shook her head. "My folks aren't here either. They're also out visiting."

Rueben groaned inwardly. This conversation wasn't taking him anywhere.

"If you have a piece of paper I can write on, I'll leave my number for Ellen."

"Okay, I'll go to the kitchen and get a notepad."

Lenore disappeared, and Rueben stepped into the entryway. He wasn't going to remain in the cold this time.

As he waited for Lenore to return, Rueben peeked into the living room. He saw a fireplace with two chairs on either side. At the other end of the room sat a large couch, recliner, and a rocking chair. The room had a warm, inviting feel. He fought the temptation to take a seat by the fire to warm his gloveless hands. *This must be where Ellen's family gathers after their holiday meals*, he thought, remembering what Ellen had described.

A few minutes later, Lenore came back with a pen and tablet. "Here ya go." She handed them to Rueben.

Holding the tablet steady in one hand, he wrote the number where Ellen could reach him and handed the tablet back to Lenore. "Would you please give this to her when she comes home?"

"I'll let her know." Lenore nodded and closed the door.

Rueben hoped the young girl would follow through. At the rate things were going, he wondered if he'd ever connect with Ellen.

By the time Ellen returned home, it was late and the house was dark. She figured her parents and sisters were all in bed. It has been a long day, but she'd enjoyed her time with Sadie and their friend Barbara.

Ellen smiled, thinking about Gideon and what a good husband he was for Barbara. He had volunteered to watch their daughter, Mary Jane, so his wife could spend time with Ellen and Sadie.

The time Ellen spent today with two good friends was enjoyable, but she wished Mandy could have joined them, like she used to before moving to Kauai.

As Ellen stood in the hallway with her flashlight, she noticed a familiar aroma. It smelled like the musky aftershave Rueben wore. *Could he have been here again? If he did stop by, surely someone would have left me a note.*

She hurried to the kitchen, and looked on the table. No note there. Nothing on the counter or roll-top desk either.

Ellen tucked in her upper lip. *This is silly. If Rueben came by, someone would have told me. What I need now is a good night's sleep. Tomorrow morning I'll do some shopping and continue my search for a job.*

Ellen's mind shifted gears, remembering how she'd called Mandy to get Rueben's cell phone number. After their short but meaningful talk, Ellen had tried calling Rueben. All she got was his voice mail. Before coming into the house, she'd stopped by the phone shack to check for messages. There were none. If Rueben had come by to talk to her, why hadn't he answered her call? Should she try calling him again in the morning?

Chapter 43

𝓡ueben took a seat at the dining-room table, where several plates had been set out. Apparently, he wasn't the only one staying at this bed-and-breakfast.

Glancing at the clock on the far wall, he thought about the cell phone he'd accidentally left at his folks' in Pennsylvania. In addition to using it for calls, he relied on the phone to check the time.

"Hi, I'm Tom. Where you from?" A tall, bald man entered the room and reached out to shake Rueben's hand.

"My name's Rueben. I'm originally from Pennsylvania, but my current home is the Island of Kauai."

The man's brows lifted as he took a seat across the table. "What brings you to Indiana?"

"Umm. . . Guess you might call it business."

"What kind of business?" Tom leaned against the chair, cupping his chin with one hand.

"It's of a personal nature." Rueben felt as if he were being interrogated. He wished their B&B hostess would bring on the food so he could eat and be on his way. He'd learned earlier that he hadn't received any phone calls, so he assumed Ellen either didn't want to talk to him or hadn't received his message.

I'll give it one more try before I head out of town, Rueben told himself.

When Rueben arrived at the Lambrights' place, he spotted a young Amish woman coming out of the barn. It wasn't Lenore this time, but she had the same hair color. He figured she was one of Ellen's other sisters.

"Hello. My name is Rueben Zook." He approached the girl. "Ellen and I worked together in Hawaii. Is she at home?"

She looked at him strangely and tilted her head. "Ellen went to the shoe store to give Ezra Bontrager something he left when he was at our house last week.

Rueben reached under the baseball cap he'd bought the other day, and scratched his head. "Who's Ezra?"

"He works for our dad. He and Ellen went to school together, and a few days ago he asked if he could court her, but. . . Achoo!" She pulled a tissue from her jacket pocket and wiped her nose. "I don't mean to be rude, but I need to get back in the house. Do you have a message for Ellen? I'll give it to her when she gets home."

"No that's okay. She doesn't need to know I was here." Feeling as though he'd been kicked by a horse, Rueben headed back to his car. Ellen had a suitor, and he would do nothing to come between them.

Shipshewana

After filling his tank at a gas station, Rueben stopped in Shipshewana. He'd heard it was an interesting town with lots of gift shops and restaurants. Since his mother's birthday was coming up, he would look for a gift in one of the stores.

Coming to Indiana had been a waste of time as far as connecting with Ellen. Now that he knew she was being courted by someone, there was nothing to do but go home and try to forget he'd fallen in love with her.

Rueben pulled into a parking spot and went into one of the buildings. He browsed around in the hardware store and then the store across the hall, hoping to find the right gift for Mom.

When he headed down the nearest aisle, a gray-haired English woman stepped in front of him with her cart. As Rueben tried to skirt around her, he spotted a young Amish woman at the end of the aisle and realized it was Ellen. His heart skipped. *What should I do? Should I make myself known or get out of the store before she sees me?*

Rueben didn't want to draw attention to himself by shouting Ellen's name, so he backed away from the English woman's cart and went down the next aisle, thinking he'd start up the previous aisle. But by the time he'd gone the rest of the way down the first aisle and headed up the next one, there was no sign of Ellen.

Rueben was on the verge of calling her name when someone from behind tapped his shoulder. He whirled around. It was the same woman who'd blocked his way in the previous aisle.

"Excuse me, sir, but do you know where I might find women's shoes?"

"Sorry, Ma'am, but I don't work here. It's my first time in this store. Maybe there's a clerk around who can point you in the right direction."

"Okay, thank you." The elderly lady pushed her cart toward the front of the store.

I hope Ellen is still in here. A sense of urgency welled in Rueben's soul. He didn't want to miss an opportunity to talk with her before she left the store, if for no other reason than to tell her that he'd returned to Pennsylvania to talk with Arie's folks.

Rueben was about to head down another aisle, when a young woman came up to him.

"I can't reach that hat. Would you mind getting it for me?" she asked.

Rueben couldn't ignore her request. "Sure. Which hat did you want?"

"That one." She pointed to a wide-brimmed straw hat. "It's my dad's birthday, and he needs a new hat."

Rueben got it down for her. "Here you go."

"Thanks." With a sweet smile, the woman moved on.

"At this rate, I'll never get to see Ellen," Rueben muttered. In an act bolder than anything he'd ever done, he cupped his hands around his mouth and shouted, "Ellen Lambright, if you're still in this store, I need to talk to you. I'm in the aisle where the men's hats are sold."

Rueben remained where he was and waited. The people around him stared, but he didn't care. Several seconds went by, and Ellen appeared at the end of the aisle. "Rueben?"

Nodding, he moved toward her.

With eyes as blue as the ocean, Ellen stared at him, motionless. She was the prettiest thing he'd ever seen. More beautiful than the islands he'd left behind.

As Rueben approached, two redheaded girls showed up out of nowhere. Laughing and poking each other, they ran in front of him.

Rueben looked at Ellen and lifted both hands, while she stood with one hand over her mouth. He saw her dimples, and knew she was stifling a chuckle.

"There you two are." A frazzled, pregnant woman entered their aisle, pushing an overflowing cart of items. She shook her finger at the girls. "You kids come with me right now. If you don't behave, there'll be no ice cream after lunch."

That seemed to quiet the rambunctious children. Rueben watched as the pouting girls went to stand beside their mother's cart. She looked up at him. "I hope these rascals didn't bother you too much."

"It's okay. No harm done. I was a kid once too."

As the woman and her children walked away, one of the little girls turned to look at Rueben. He winked before she disappeared around the corner.

Rueben started walking toward Ellen again. She did the same. He would not let her out of his sight now. As they approached each other, Ellen spoke first. "Rueben, I'm surprised to see you here. I've tried to call you several times, but you haven't responded to any of my messages."

"That's odd. The owner of the bed-and-breakfast where I stayed said I had no messages." Rueben scratched his head. "Didn't your sister give you the piece of paper I wrote the phone number on?"

"No. When Lenore said you had stopped by, I called Mandy to ask for your cell number." A touch of pink erupted on Ellen's cheeks.

"I came by your house a second time," Rueben explained. "Only I talked to one of your sisters that day. The reason you got my voice mail is because I accidently left my cell phone at my folk's house."

Her eyes widened. "You went to Pennsylvania?"

"Yeah. I stopped to see my folks first, and then I went to speak with Arie's parents."

Ellen offered Rueben a hopeful smile. "How did it go?"

"It went well, but I'd rather not talk to you about it here." He gestured to the store entrance. "How about we sit in my rental car, so we can talk privately?"

She nodded.

Rueben took a couple deep breaths and headed for the door. Seeing Ellen again made him wish even more that they could establish a permanent relationship. But if all she could offer was friendship, he'd take it.

As Ellen slipped into the passenger's seat, her stomach fluttered. She'd never been this nervous with Rueben before. By the way his knees bounced, she figured he was apprehensive too.

He opened his mouth, then shut it.

"What did you want to say?" she asked.

He clenched the steering wheel and looked straight ahead. "I know you're being courted by some fellow name Ezra, but I—"

"Now where did you hear that?"

"When I stopped by your house Saturday night, your sister Lenore gave me the address of the place you'd gone." He let go of the wheel and swiped a hand across his damp forehead. "So I went there, and when I drove up the driveway, I saw you talking to a young Amish man near a buggy."

She nodded. "That was Ezra Bontrager. He works at my dad's shoe store."

"Yeah, I know. One of your other sisters told me that when I stopped by your house again this morning and found out you weren't home." Rueben paused. "Between seeing you two together, and a comment your sister made, I got the impression you and Ezra were courting."

Ellen shook her head so hard her head covering ties whipped across her cheeks. "Ezra and I are not courting. He's just a fellow I've known since we went to school."

Rueben released an audible sigh. "That's a relief."

She watched as his expression softened. When Rueben lifted his hand and stroked Ellen's cheek, her throat constricted.

"After completing my mission in Pennsylvania," he continued, "I came here to tell you that for the first time since Arie's death I feel free of the guilt. I asked God's forgiveness, her parents forgave me, and I forgave myself." He continued to caress Ellen's face. "I feel like a new person inside, and I'm ready to move on with my life."

"Oh?" The one word was all Ellen could manage. Her throat felt swollen, and her eyes stung with tears.

"I want you to be part of my life, Ellen. I know it's too soon to speak of marriage, but I love you, and I'd like to stay in Indiana so we can court. That is, if you're willing."

Ellen's body felt weightless. She could hardly believe Rueben was here and had confessed his love for her. "I love you too, and I'd be honored to have you court me."

As Rueben gazed at Ellen, she took in his brown eyes and the darkness of his hair. His skin, still tan, was smooth beneath her fingers as she reached up to touch his face.

Gently, Rueben pulled Ellen into his arms and kissed her lips.

Ellen melted into his embrace and sighed. What a wonderful discovery she'd made when she met this young man in Hawaii. She closed her eyes and offered a short prayer. *Thank You, Lord, for answered prayer.*

Epilogue

One year later, Middlebury

$\mathcal{E}$llen stood in the living room, with arms folded, watching delicate snowflakes swirling outside the window.

She released a contented sigh. It was hard to believe all that had happened in the last year. In addition to Rueben joining the church in her district and them getting married in the fall, they were now the happy owners of a bed-and-breakfast—the same one Mandy and Ken used to own. The couple who'd bought the business from Ellen's friends decided it was too much for them to handle, even with the help of their daughters. Their main complaints were not wanting to be tied down, and having to deal with sometimes picky clientele.

Ellen didn't mind staying close to home or dealing with a variety of people. She found running the B&B to be fun and rewarding. Her dream of owning a bed-and-breakfast had finally come true.

Rueben enjoyed running their new business too. They'd changed a few things back to the way the B&B had been before the previous owners made some modifications. Now, it almost felt as if she'd never left. Someday when children came along, Rueben might add on to the house.

Ellen's life seemed perfect, and daily she counted her blessings.

She shivered and put more wood on the fire. *I'll bet it's warm in Hawaii.*

Ellen had heard from Mandy the other day and was pleased to learn they were planning a trip to Middlebury in the spring. They would stay a few days at the B&B and spend the rest of their time with Mandy's parents.

Ellen couldn't wait to see her friends again, as well as their precious little boy. From the pictures Mandy had sent, it wasn't hard to see how much the little guy had grown. Ken had improved, although he still used a cane, and their bed-and-breakfast in Kapaa was thriving. Ken's mother was happy, and they'd enjoyed a recent visit with Dan and his wife.

Rueben stepped up behind Ellen, disrupting her thoughts as he wrapped his arms around her waist.

She leaned against his muscular chest and closed her eyes. "Mandy, Barbara, and I are all happily married," she whispered. "I hope that someday my dear friend Sadie will find someone who will make her as happy as I am."

Rueben turned her around to face him. "And you, my pretty fraa, make me happy too."

Hawaiian Lemon Chicken

Ingredients

1½ pounds boneless chicken
    breast cut into small pieces
1½ teaspoons soy sauce

1 cup cornstarch
½ cup milk
2 cups olive oil or coconut oil

Lemon Sauce

¾ cup water
¼ cup white vinegar
½ cup sugar or sugar substitute
2 tablespoons cornstarch

1 tablespoon lemon juice
½ teaspoon salt
5 lemon slices cut thin

Marinate chicken in soy sauce for 10 minutes. Dip in cornstarch, then milk, then cornstarch again. Fry in hot oil for three minutes or until golden brown. Drain on paper towel. Mix all sauce ingredients, except lemon slices. Cook in saucepan on medium-high heat, stirring constantly until mixture comes to a boil. Add lemon slices and cook another minute. Pour over chicken and arrange lemon slices for garnish.

Discussion Questions

1. Ellen left her home in Indiana to be with her friend Mandy in Hawaii because of an emergency. Have you ever been in a situation where you had to leave all that was familiar to help someone who lived far away? How did you deal with the feelings of homesickness?

2. How difficult do you think it was for Mandy and her husband, Ken, to sell their bed-and-breakfast in Indiana and move to Kauai to help Ken's mother? Have you ever had to make a sacrifice such as moving in order to help a relative?

3. Change was difficult for Ellen, and when the bed-and-breakfast where she worked was sold, she had to find another position that wasn't to her liking. Have you ever lost a job you really liked and had to take something you didn't enjoy? If so, how did you deal with the situation?

4. When Ezra took over for Ellen's father during his hernia surgery, he became an overbearing boss. What could Ezra have done to make things more workable between him and Ellen? Have you ever had to deal with an overbearing employer? How did you handle the situation?

5. Taavi reached out to Rob/Rueben when he didn't know him well and gave him a place to live. Have you ever helped someone you barely knew? What does the Bible say about helping strangers?

6. When Ken's accident occurred, Mandy's faith was put to the test. She was not only concerned for her husband's welfare, but worried that they would not have enough money to pay the bills. Between Ellen coming to help out and others donating money, Mandy and Ken's needs were met. Mandy accepted it with gratitude, but some people in similar circumstances are too proud to ask for or accept help. Have you or someone you know been in a comparable position? If you were on the receiving end, how did you respond? If you were on the giving end, how did it make you feel to help someone in need?

7. When Ken realized some of his injuries would hamper his ability to function in the manner he'd been accustomed to, he became depressed and withdrawn. How can we help someone whose life has been altered by sickness or an accident to rise above their circumstances and have a sense of self-worth?

8. Ezra thought he was in love with Ellen. If he had expressed those feelings and been kinder to her, what do you think the outcome would have been?

9. Rob/Rueben hid from his past and had become bitter and angry at God. He blamed himself for an accident that took someone's life and chose to deal with it by moving away and pretending to be someone else. What should he have done in order to deal with his guilt? And should he have been honest about his situation?

10. When Ellen found out about Rob/Rueben's deception, she felt betrayed. Have you ever been deceived by a friend? How did you respond to their deception?

11. Ken's mother, Vickie, suffered a devastating blow when her husband died. A short time later, her oldest son, Dan, unable to cope with his father's death, left Kauai and moved with his wife to California. This left Vickie with only Ken and Mandy's help in running her husband's business. She needed both sons, not only for their physical help, but for emotional support as well. How would you feel if an adult child or close family member moved away from you during a difficult time?

12. Did you learn anything new about the Amish by reading this story? If so, what was it?

13. Did you learn anything in particular about the Hawaiian culture you felt was similar to the way the Amish live?

14. Were there any verses of scripture in this story that spoke to your heart or bolstered your faith?

About the Authors

New York Times bestselling and award-winning author **Wanda E. Brunstetter** is one of the founders of the Amish fiction genre. She has written close to 100 books translated in four languages. With over 11 million copies sold, Wanda's stories consistently earn spots on the nation's most prestigious bestseller lists and have received numerous awards.

Wanda's ancestors were part of the Anabaptist faith, and her novels are based on personal research intended to accurately portray the Amish way of life. Her books are well-read and trusted by many Amish, who credit her for giving readers a deeper understanding of the people and their customs.

When Wanda visits her Amish friends, she finds herself drawn to their peaceful lifestyle, sincerity, and close family ties. Wanda enjoys photography, ventriloquism, gardening, bird-watching, beachcombing, and spending time with her family. She and her husband, Richard, have been blessed with two grown children, six grandchildren, and two great-grandchildren.

To learn more about Wanda, visit her website at www.wandabrunstetter.com.

Jean Brunstetter became fascinated with the Amish when she first went to Pennsylvania to visit her father-in-law's family. Since that time, Jean has become friends with several Amish families and enjoys writing about their way of life. She also likes to put some of the simple practices followed by the Amish into her daily routine. Jean lives in Washington State with her husband, Richard Jr. and their three children, but takes every opportunity to visit Amish communities in several states. In addition to writing, Jean enjoys boating, gardening, and spending time on the beach. To learn more about Jean, visit her website at www.jeanbrunstetter.com.

OTHER BOOKS BY WANDA E. BRUNSTETTER:

PRAIRIE STATE FRIENDS
The Decision
The Gift
The Restoration

KENTUCKY BROTHERS SERIES
The Journey
The Healing
The Struggle

INDIANA COUSINS SERIES
A Cousin's Promise
A Cousin's Prayer
A Cousin's Challenge

BRIDES OF LEHIGH CANAL SERIES
Kelly's Chance
Betsy's Return
Sarah's Choice

THE DISCOVERY–A LANCASTER COUNTY SAGA
Goodbye to Yesterday
The Silence of Winter
The Hope of Spring
The Pieces of Summer
A Revelation in Autumn
A Vow for Always

DAUGHTERS OF LANCASTER COUNTY SERIES
The Storekeeper's Daughter
The Quilter's Daughter
The Bishop's Daughter

BRIDES OF LANCASTER COUNTY SERIES
A Merry Heart
Looking for a Miracle
Plain and Fancy
The Hope Chest